THE LAST ILLUSION

RHYS BOWEN

WHEELER
CHIVERS

This Large Print edition is published by Wheeler Publishing, Waterville, Maine, USA and by AudioGO Ltd, Bath, England.
Wheeler Publishing, a part of Gale, Cengage Learning.
Copyright © 2010 by Rhys Bowen.
A Molly Murphy Mystery.
The moral right of the author has been asserted.

LIBRARY OF CONGRESS CATALOGING-IN-PUBLICATION DATA

Bowen, Rhys.
    The last illusion / by Rhys Bowen.
      p. cm.
    ISBN-13: 978-1-4104-2658-1
    ISBN-10: 1-4104-2658-0
    1. Murphy, Molly (Fictitious character)—Fiction. 2. Women private investigators—New York (State)—New York—Fiction. 3. Houdini, Harry, 1874–1926—Fiction. 4. City and town life—New York (State)—New York—Fiction. 5. Large type books. I. Title.
    PR6052.O848L37 2010b
    823'.914—dc22   2010006165

BRITISH LIBRARY CATALOGUING-IN-PUBLICATION DATA AVAILABLE
Published in 2010 in the U.S. by arrangement with St. Martin's Press, LLC.
Published in 2010 in the U.K. by arrangement with the author.

U.K. Hardcover: 978 1 408 49132 4 (Chivers Large Print)
U.K. Softcover: 978 1 408 49133 1 (Camden Large Print)

Printed and bound in Great Britain by
CPI Antony Rowe, Chippenham, Wiltshire.
1 2 3 4 5 6 7 14 13 12 11 10

*This book is dedicated to the memory of
my dear friend and fellow mystery author,
Lyn Hamilton,
who died after a long, gallant battle with
cancer
on September 10, 2009.*

ONE

New York City, July 1903

"Ladies and gentlemen. For my final illusion I will perform a feat that will amaze and astound you — a feat never before attempted in the history of magic, a feat fraught with danger and horror." The showman, presented to the audience as the stupendous, sensational Signor Scarpelli, paused for dramatic effect. The atmosphere in the theater was electric. A lovely young woman stepped from the shadows at the side of the stage. She was dressed in a white spangled costume that revealed shapely legs right up to mid thigh, and she was wearing white fishnet stockings and knee-high white boots. The illusionist, a dapper little man with an impressive handlebar mustache, extended his hand to her and she took it, moving gracefully into the spotlight. "Ladies and gentlemen, I present to you the lovely Lily. Tonight I shall attempt to saw this ex-

7

quisite young lady in half."

There was a gasp of horror from the auditorium. I think I must have given a small gasp myself. I glanced at Daniel, seated beside me, and was annoyed to see that he was grinning. As a policeman who had seen everything, he was not likely to be alarmed by a mere spectacle onstage. I, still very much the unsophisticated Irish country girl, had been baffled and impressed by the simplest tricks that had started this evening of illusion at Miner's Theatre on the Bowery — doves that appeared out of nowhere, then were placed in cages, only to vanish again, hats that produced great bunches of flowers, and even clever card tricks. Frankly I'd never seen anything like it and was enjoying myself immensely. As much as anything I was relishing an evening spent with my intended for once. It wasn't often that a New York police captain like Daniel Sullivan found himself with free time to take his lady love to a theater.

A large contraption was being wheeled onto the stage. It was covered in a red velvet cloth, which Scarpelli whipped away dramatically to reveal a table on legs on which reposed a large, oblong box, garishly painted with flames and shooting stars. He then spun it around to show that it had small openings at either end. Scarpelli then opened the box lid and let down a front panel to reveal a white-satin padded interior, as one might see in a superior type of coffin. Then he extended his hand to the girl.

"I'll now ask my lovely assistant, Lily, to step inside this contraption of horror," he said.

Lily smiled and waved to the crowd as she allowed the Great Scarpelli to assist her into the box, where she lay while the lid was closed, leaving her head exposed at one end and her feet sticking out of the other. The box was then latched with two large locks. From the orchestra pit came a low, ominous drumroll. Signor Scarpelli then produced an impressive-looking saw, bent it, and waved it around.

"Ladies and gentlemen, a common ordinary saw, with which I'm sure the gentlemen among you are familiar. This particular specimen has been sharpened to perfection, in fact I'm sure any one of you would covet it for your own woodpile. Allow me to demonstrate."

A male assistant now pushed out a small table on which lay a log of wood. Scarpelli removed his jacket, rolled up his sleeves, and proceeded to saw most efficiently through the log until the two halves fell onto

9

the stage floor.

"So you'll agree that I should have little problem slicing through such a delicate specimen as sweet Lily," he said, giving the audience a wicked grin. "Right then. To work. Drumroll if you please, Maestro."

The drumroll started again, louder and louder until it filled the theater with sound. I could almost feel those around me holding their breath. I knew I was holding mine. Carefully he placed the saw on the middle of the box and started to move it back and forth. It went through the top layer of wood like butter. We could see it protruding with each thrust, lower and lower. It must have reached the girl's body by now. Suddenly, over the noise of the saw and the drum, there came a bloodcurdling scream. Screams echoed back from the audience. Some people had risen to their feet. Some ladies were already swooning. It was clear that something had gone wrong.

"Holy Mother of God," I heard myself muttering.

Signor Scarpelli extracted the saw with difficulty, threw it down, then rushed around the table, and began clawing frantically at the locks. The screaming had now stopped and the theater was ominously silent.

"A nice touch," Daniel muttered into my ear. "Get everybody good and scared."

Then we saw something dripping from the bottom of the box onto the floor. Great drips of red.

"It's blood. See, it's blood," someone gasped from the row behind us.

"No! It can't be!" Scarpelli shouted. "Somebody help me get her out."

Stagehands rushed to his aid.

"Don't worry," Daniel whispered to me. "It's all for effect, you mark my words."

At that moment Scarpelli wrenched open the lid of the box.

"Oh, God in Heaven, no, no!" he yelled. "What fiend has done this? Help her, somebody help her."

At that moment the theater manager came onto the stage. "Ladies and gentlemen," he said holding up his hands for silence, even though most of the crowd was standing still, staring in horror, "I'm afraid there has been a slight mishap. It appears that something has gone horribly wrong. Is there a doctor in the house?"

"Yes, I'm a doctor," came a deep, booming voice from somewhere in the darkness and a distinguished-looking man with impressive gray side-whiskers came up the steps to the stage with sprightly agility for someone of his age and build. "Stand back, please," he commanded, waving everybody out of the way. He took one look at the girl lying there, then addressed the manager. "This looks extremely serious," he barked. "Send for an ambulance immediately and bring down the curtain." He turned back to minister to the girl as the manager came to the front of the stage.

"Ladies and gentlemen, I'm going to ask you to leave the theater and go home. The rest of tonight's show is canceled."

At those words there were mutterings of annoyance and disappointment from the audience but they began to leave their seats.

The curtains began to close. Daniel had reached the aisle, ahead of me. He was pushing his way through the departing crowd, like a salmon swimming upstream, making for the stage. I followed in his wake. I didn't stop to think that I might not want to witness what had happened up there. Up the steps I went after Daniel. He pulled aside the curtain that had now fallen on the stage. It was almost as if a tableau was taking place before our eyes — the men clustered around the open box, the doctor bending over it. They looked up as they saw us come onto the stage.

"Are you also a physician, sir?" The doc-

12

tor demanded, looking up from his patient, "because if not, I'll ask you to leave instantly. . . ."

"No, I'm a police detective," Daniel said, "Captain Sullivan." He fished in his pocket and produced his badge. "And before any of you go around touching everything, I assume we now have to treat this as a crime scene."

"We do indeed, Captain." Scarpelli moved toward Daniel. "Someone must have tampered with my equipment. There was no way the saw should have come anywhere near her. I had perfected the illusion."

"How bad is it?" Daniel moved closer to the box. I followed, unnoticed. Lily was lying still and pale in the white-padded box and there was a great slash of red across her middle. She really had been almost sawn in half. Her white spangled costume was now ripped open and stained bloodred. Blood was still welling up from that horrible gash and dripping steadily onto the floor. I swallowed down the bile that rose in my throat.

The doctor had been taking Lily's pulse and looked up to meet Daniel's gaze. "She's still alive but barely," he said. "I doubt that anything can be done for her, poor thing. The blade has undoubtedly sliced into her intestines and they will be beyond repair.

And to lose so much blood . . . it won't be long before the body goes into profound shock."

Scarpelli reached into the box and picked up Lily's limp, white hand. She had elegant, long fingers and her hand was now so pale that it could have been made of porcelain. "Lily, my poor darling Lily. What have I done to you? Forgive me, Lily. Forgive me, God." He kissed her hand tenderly before replacing it at her side.

"Has anyone gone for an ambulance?" Daniel said.

"Ernest went," one of the stagehands muttered.

"Then one of you men go and find the nearest constable," Daniel ordered. "Tell him Captain Sullivan says there's been an attempted murder and he's to report to the duty officer at HQ. I need men out here right away."

"Attempted murder?" The theater manager looked aghast. "An accident, surely. A horrible accident."

"The illusionist claims his equipment was tampered with. I have to therefore treat this as an attempted murder. Now, someone, go and find the nearest policeman." He pointed at a pimply-faced youth standing staring in

14

horror-struck fascination nearby. "You, boy."

"Very good, Captain, sir," the youth said. "I know where to find the nearest constable." He ran off the stage, his footsteps clattering on the wooden floor and echoing through the backstage area.

"Someone get blankets and cover her," the doctor commanded. "She's going cold. We're going to lose her before she makes it to the nearest hospital."

"Here, she can have my wrap," I said.

They looked up at me as if they had noticed me for the first time.

"Young lady, you shouldn't be here," the manager said. "This is no place for a delicate, young woman like yourself."

"I'm with Captain Sullivan," I said, "and I've seen worse than this before."

I saw Daniel give me a look of annoyance. "I think the man is right, Molly. You should go on home. I'll have one of these lads find you a cab. I may be quite a while yet."

"I don't mind. I'll stay," I said. "There may be something useful for me to do."

"I really don't think —" Daniel said, now giving me a clear look that said, "I want you to obey me for once, without a fuss."

"Young woman, there is nothing you can do. Go home," the doctor snapped at me.

15

"The less people around her the better."

I decided that there was no point in causing a scene or annoying Daniel at this stage. There really was nothing I could do here and why would I want to stay around watching some poor girl bleed to death? In truth I was feeling a little queasy.

"All right," I said. "I don't want to be in the way here."

"That's my girl." Daniel gave me a relieved smile. "Would one of you go and hail Miss Murphy a cab? I see some of my men." He went down the steps to meet several police constables who had just entered the theater.

Another stagehand departed. I was about to follow him when I heard fast-approaching feet coming toward the stage and a small, muscular, dark-haired man appeared, followed by a pretty, petite girl, dressed in a page-boy costume with tights.

"What's this all about?" the man demanded. "I've just been told that the show's been canceled." He approached the manager, his dark eyes flashing in dramatic manner, as he was in full makeup.

I recognized him at once as Harry Houdini, the handcuff king, the man we had come to see. Daniel had been following his career with fascination ever since he presented himself at police headquarters several

16

years ago and challenged the police to produce handcuffs from which he could not escape. They had not succeeded.

"That's right, Mr. Houdini," the manager said. "I'm afraid there's been a nasty accident and I had no choice but to send the audience home."

"You had no right to do that," the small man stormed. I noticed that he spoke with a slight foreign accent. "They came to see me, you know. You have deprived them of their one chance to see the greatest illusionist in the business. These others are merely amateurs."

"Who are you calling an amateur?" Scarpelli demanded, turning to face Houdini. "I've been in this business more years than you've had hot dinners. Just because you headlined once on the Orpheum Circuit, and just because you've had a bit of success over on the Continent, don't think you've come back here to act the big star."

"But I am the big star," Houdini said, spreading his arms dramatically. "All over Europe I have entertained kings and emperors. Tsar Nicholas of Russia tried to persuade me to stay on at court as his personal adviser. I'm only home for a couple of weeks and now my debut in New York has been ruined by a little accident."

"Little accident?" the theater manager began, staring at Houdini with distaste. "My dear sir, we are talking about a great tragedy here. . . ."

The pretty girl put a hand on his shoulder. "Don't upset yourself so, Harry. There will be other nights. The audience will come back tomorrow, and . . ." She had now apparently noticed the box with Lily in it for the first time and let out a shriek of horror. "Oh, my God, Harry. She's really been cut in half!" She put a hand to her mouth and swayed as if she was about to faint. Houdini caught her.

"It's okay, Bess, babykins. You're going to be okay." He helped her to a nearby chair onto which she collapsed, gasping and gagging. Then he too caught sight of the bloodstained figure in the box.

"Oh, geez," he muttered, putting his hand up to his mouth. "I'm sorry. I had no idea it was this bad. What happened? What went wrong?"

"Someone must have tampered with it," Scarpelli snapped. "The trick was foolproof. I had perfected it. There was no way. . . . Someone is out to do me harm. To destroy my reputation. Maybe someone who thinks of himself as the new king of illusionists?" He advanced on Harry Houdini, staring at him, eyeball to eyeball.

"Don't be ridiculous," Houdini said. "I would never tamper with a fellow illusionist's act. I would never stoop so low. And I would never —" His gaze moved to Lily. "Is she dead?"

"I still detect a faint pulse," the doctor said.

"Then what are we waiting for?" Houdini demanded. "Thing's on wheels, isn't it? Then let's get it down to the nearest entrance where she can be taken to the hospital." He motioned the remaining men to join him, then looked back at Bess, who was hunched on the chair, her body still wracked with great sobs. "Someone should take my wife back to our dressing room."

"I will," I said.

"That would be very kind. Most obliged to you, miss," Houdini said before she could answer. "She's a delicate little thing at the best of times and a sight like this would upset even the strongest of constitutions."

The men were already getting in place to wheel out the box with Lily in it. I remembered what I had planned to do and laid my wrap over her. It was only a silky wrap, as befits an outing on a July evening, but it was better than nothing and at least it covered that horrible wound. I gave her one

19

last pitying look, then I went over to the hunched figure of Bess and put a hand on her shoulder. "Come on, Mrs. Houdini. Let me take you where you can lie down."

"Thank you," she managed in a whisper between sobs. "Get me out of here, please, before I throw up." I noticed that the accent belied her delicate, china-doll appearance. It was pure Brooklyn.

I left the stage, supporting Mrs. Houdini as I steered her through the backstage area, avoiding the usual pitfalls of a backstage: the ropes, the curtain weights, the scenery flats. Luckily I had worked as a chorus girl once while on a case involving the theater so I felt right at home there. It was good that I did because Bess Houdini was in no state to walk alone. She staggered like a drunken person, clutching my arm so tightly that her nails dug into me. "He cut her in half," she kept on gasping. "All that blood!"

"I know. It was truly awful, but there's nothing you or I can do for her, and you're going to be just fine when you lie down."

We found the Houdinis' dressing room at last at the end of a long hallway. It had a star on the door but inside it was nothing fancy. Clearly this Houdini fellow was not going to be treated like someone who entertained kings and emperors in his own country. There was a plain horsehair couch in one corner and I helped Bess onto this. "There," I said, and covered her with a knitted afghan.

"My smelling salts," she gasped. "On the dressing table."

I found them among the usual paraphernalia of the theater — sticks of greasepaint, cotton wool, cold cream, and various patent medicines designed to calm the nerves and restore vitality. She held the little bottle up to her nose, coughed, and then handed it back to me. "That's better," she said in a more ordinary voice.

Really I've never seen what women want with smelling salts. Horrible stuff. But then I've never worn a corset so I've not been in the habit of swooning that often.

"I'll be all right now. Thanks again, Miss — ?"

"Murphy," I said. "Molly Murphy."

She looked up at me and smiled. She really was a sweet, delicate little thing. Fragile as a china doll. "Thank you for your help. You're most kind. Do you work here in the theater?"

"No, I was in the audience with my intended who is a policeman, so naturally he rushed straight to the stage when he saw what had happened."

She shuddered and wrapped the blanket more tightly around her. "It's too terrible to think about, isn't it? That could have been me. And my Harry risks his life every night onstage. Every single night.

"I know they are only illusions," she continued, "but they have to have that touch of danger or the public wouldn't come. When we do the stunt we call the Metamorphosis, I'm always secretly afraid that I'll suffocate in that trunk if I can't get out one night."

"It's not a life I'd want for myself," I said. "I spent a short time in the theater and I can't say that I saw the attraction."

"You were an actress?" She looked at me incredulously, noting I'm sure the healthy bones and the distinct lack of makeup and froufrou.

"A chorus girl." I laughed. "Yes, I know I'm a little too big and healthy-looking for the average chorus girl, but I'm really a private investigator and I was on a case."

"A lady detective? No — are there such things?"

"There are and I'm one of them," I said. I reached into my purse. "Here, this is my card if you want proof."

She examined it carefully, then looked up into my face as if she was still trying to make sense of the facts she had just read. "A lady detective," she repeated. "Geez, that sounds exciting."

"Sometimes a little too exciting," I said. "My intended wants me to give it up when we marry."

"Well, he would, wouldn't he? I'm lucky that I'm in one of the few professions where I can work alongside my husband. And a good thing too. Too many flighty girls in the theater who would just love to get their claws into my poor Harry."

"I'm sure he only has eyes for you," I said diplomatically.

"I hope that's true," she said. "In spite of all his bluster and swagger, he's still easily impressed. He's a simple, small-town boy at heart. A real rags-to-riches story. His dad was a rabbi, you know. He was born in Hungary and when they came over here, the family was real poor — almost starving."

I thought I'd better make my escape before she told me that story in detail. "I really should be getting back," I said. "There's a cab waiting for me, and my intended will wonder where I've got to."

She reached out a dainty, white hand this time. "Thank you again. You've been very kind."

"Take care of yourself," I said.

"Oh, I will. It's not me I worry about. It's Harry. I worry about him every single day."

I went out, closing the door quietly behind me. I was also about to marry someone in a profession fraught with danger. Would I be worrying about Daniel every single day?

TWO

I came back to the stage to find Daniel, Signor Scarpelli, and the theater manager in conversation. No sign of the box containing Lily, nor of Houdini.

"Molly, you're still here." Daniel looked up in surprise. "I thought the cab came for you ages ago."

"I took Mrs. Houdini to her dressing room and she was in such a distressed state that I couldn't leave her until she calmed down," I said.

"Good of you, miss," the theater manager said. "It was a most distressing sight. Awful. I've never seen a thing like it happen in my theaters and I've had fire-eaters, lion tamers, you name it."

Daniel cleared his throat, obviously wanting to get down to business. "Now, Mr. Scarpelli — is that your correct name?"

"My stage name," the man said. "In real life I'm Alfred Rosen."

"And the girl's name?"

"Lily Kaufman."

"A relative of yours?"

Scarpelli looked almost coy. "No, just a professional associate."

"I see." Daniel nodded. "I'll need the name and address of her next of kin. They'll have to be notified."

"If you don't mind, I'd rather do it myself," Scarpelli said. "I feel responsible. It's only right that I should go and see them. Lily thought the world of her parents. Sent money home to them every month regular."

"Very well, but I'll still need their names and address for our records."

"I can come down to your police station and bring you all that in the morning, if you don't mind," Scarpelli said. "I don't know the address off the top of my head and I'm all at sixes and sevens at the moment. My heart still hasn't stopped thumping. I still can't believe it, if you want to know the truth. I keep thinking it's a horrible nightmare and I'll wake up any second."

"You stated that someone must have tampered with your equipment," Daniel said, showing no sign of sympathy. "Why are you so sure of that? Why couldn't it simply be a malfunction of your trick?"

"Because the trick should have been foolproof," Scarpelli said.

"Explain it to me."

Scarpelli raised his hands in horror. "My dear sir. An illusionist never reveals his secrets to anybody."

"As you wish," Daniel said, "but you have to realize that the only evidence I have so far of a crime being committed is yourself wielding a saw and almost certainly killing a young woman. A most convenient way of dispatching someone you might have wanted dead."

Scarpelli's face flushed. "You think that I — Captain, I assure you that I was exceedingly fond of Lily. I would never have done anything to harm her."

"So what makes you think anyone else would have wanted to harm her?"

Scarpelli paused, looked around, then lowered his voice. "There have been little things," he said. "Small glitches in the act. Locks that wouldn't open, props that mysteriously disappeared right before showtime. I put them down to Lily's lack of organization. She was something of a scatterbrain, you know. But now I'm wondering if someone was trying to disrupt my act all along. It wasn't someone who wished harm to Lily, it was someone who wished to destroy my

27

reputation as an illusionist."

"So tell me why I should believe the accident was not a mere malfunction of your equipment," Daniel insisted. "Your secret will have to come out anyway in a court of law if you're tried with negligence or even worse, homicide."

Scarpelli glanced at first the theater manager then me. "They are not to know," he said.

"Molly, I think it's about time you went home," Daniel said. "The cab has been waiting for hours and you've no place in a police inquiry."

As if on cue several more policemen burst in through the front doors.

"Up here, men," Daniel called. Then he put a hand on my shoulder and gave me a quick peck on the cheek. "Off you go, then," he said.

I had no choice but to leave just when things were getting interesting.

The cab took me safely back to my little house on Patchin Place. I made myself a cup of tea, then went up to bed. The window was open, letting in the summer breeze, scented with the roses growing over my garden wall. I stood at the window and took deep breaths, trying to shake the horrifying image from my mind. Suddenly I felt horribly alone and vulnerable. I had always considered myself to be a strong and independent woman until now. I had been in no hurry to get married and give up my independence. But at this moment I longed for strong arms around me and thought how reassuring it would be to fall asleep in his arms feeling safe and protected. Then, of course I reminded myself that I would be marrying someone whose own life would be forever tinged with danger. Like Bess Houdini, I'd be constantly worrying about my husband every time he came home late.

I slept at last and woke to a glorious summer morn with the sun streaming in through my window and the net curtain flapping idly in the breeze. The terrors of the night were dispelled. I got up, dressed, and was ready to start the day when there was a knock at my front door. I rather hoped it might be Daniel, stopping by on his way to work to give me the details of what transpired at the theater after I went home. Instead it was my neighbor Augusta Walcott, of the Boston Walcotts, usually known by the irreverent nickname of Gus. She had a basket over one arm.

"Good morning," she said. "I've just been to the bakery on Greenwich Avenue and

I've returned with croissants hot from the oven. Come and have breakfast with us. We are dying to hear your impression of this man Houdini."

"As to that, I didn't have a chance to see him perform," I said. "I take it you haven't read this morning's *Times* yet."

"No, I haven't. It's lurking at this moment in the basket with the rolls. Besides, Sid always likes to read it first. Houdini didn't perform after all then?"

"There was a horrible accident in the act preceding his," I said. "The illusion was supposed to be sawing a girl in half. But something went wrong and she really was sliced with the saw."

"Good God," Gus said. "Seriously hurt?"

I found it hard to force out the words. "She was not expected to live, I'm afraid. The manager stopped the show and sent everyone home."

"How awful for you. You need a dose of Sid's coffee to restore you to sorts."

In truth I didn't need a dose of Sid's coffee. She made it in the Turkish fashion, abominably strong and more like drinking thick sludge. But my friends' cheerful company more than made up for the coffee. I followed Gus across the street to her house on the other side of our little backwater. It was a charming haven of twenty brownstone houses set in a cobbled alleyway and gave the feeling of being miles away from the traffic and bustle of Greenwich Avenue and the Jefferson Market opposite.

Gus flung open her front door. "Sid, dearest. Here she is, and with such a dramatic tale to tell."

We went down the long hallway and through to the kitchen at the back of the house. They had built a conservatory onto it and Sid was sitting in a white wicker rocking chair, the picture of country elegance. I should probably explain that Sid's real name was Elena Goldfarb. She and Gus led the most delightfully bohemian existence, with Gus's inheritance to keep them in that lifestyle. Their house was always full of artists, writers, actors — and extremely heady for a girl who until recently had lived in a primitive Irish cottage and whose entertainment had been the occasional dance at the church hall.

Sid jumped up as we arrived. She was wearing a red silk kimono with a large golden dragon curling over it and the effect with her black bobbed hair was stunningly oriental.

"Molly!" she cried, opening her arms to me. "We see you too seldom these days and

31

now you've come to cheer up our drab little lives with a dramatic tale."

I had to laugh at this statement. "Drab little lives? I don't know of any lives less drab. Who else would convert their living room into a Mongolian yurt?"

Sid looked surprised. "Well, we decided we didn't really want to go to Mongolia after all. Too cold and windy and bleak, you know. So we decided to have the Mongolian experience at home. Of course we've had to do without the horses galloping over the plain, but there are riding stables nearby . . ."

A vision of Gus and Sid, dressed Mongolian fashion and galloping astride through Central Park flashed into my mind before Sid said, "So tell us your dramatic tale."

"A horrible tale, actually," I said and repeated what I had told Gus.

When I'd finished there was stunned silence.

"How utterly awful," Sid said at last.

"She needs coffee, Sid," Gus said and started to put the French rolls into a wicker basket.

"She most certainly does. You must have been most upset last night. Why didn't you come over to us when you got home? You know what late hours we keep and we could have given you a stiff brandy."

"Perhaps her intended was there to offer her more comfort than we could give," Gus said, giving us a knowing look.

"No, I came home all alone. Daniel sent me home in a cab," I said. "He had to stay on to conduct an investigation into the incident."

"A nasty accident, surely?" Sid looked up from putting a small cup of thick black coffee in front of me.

"The illusionist himself didn't seem to think so," I said. "He thought his act had been tampered with."

"Who would do such a fiendish thing?"

"I have no idea. I had to take Mrs. Houdini to her dressing room so I missed a lot."

"There is a Mrs. Houdini?"

"Indeed yes. A delicate little thing like a china doll. She was in hysterics when she saw the poor girl."

"Most women would be," Sid said, giving Gus an amused glance. "I am afraid you have doomed yourself to not being socially acceptable by not being able to produce an attack of the vapors, Molly. A most useful accomplishment for a woman."

Sid sat beside me at the table and opened the newspaper. She scanned the first pages while Gus and I sampled the French rolls.

"Ah, here we are. 'Tragedy at Miner's Bowery Theatre.' Here's the whole thing in grim detail, written by someone who was an observer on the spot. They are certainly on the ball at *The New York Times,* aren't they? All the news that's fit to print indeed." She read us the piece out loud. "Oh, and you'll be pleased to hear this, Molly. The management has agreed to provide free tickets to a subsequent performance for those who were not able to see Houdini last night. Well, I call that big of them."

"The show must go on. That's what they say, don't they?" Gus commented as she slathered more apricot jam onto her croissant. "We should go and see for ourselves, Sid. Will you and Daniel be going back tonight, Molly?"

"I have no idea. It all depends when he can get away. I know Daniel will want to catch Houdini's act before he sails back to Europe. In truth I don't know if I'm so keen, after what I witnessed last night. I'd keep expecting something else to go horribly wrong."

"I'm sure these things are usually perfectly safe. Why don't you come with us tonight, if Daniel isn't free to escort you. Then we can go to a coffeehouse afterward for a heated discussion on how the illusions were done."

"I watched many of them last night and I was completely baffled," I said. "Even simple tricks like making a card rise from the pack. But then I'm Irish and easily impressed by anything that appears to be supernatural, I suppose."

"So what are your plans for today, Molly?" Gus asked. "Ever since your engagement you have been so caught up with that policeman of yours that we've hardly seen you."

I nodded. "Daniel keeps wanting me to look at houses and flats," I said. "When all I want is to stay here and have him move into my house. I promised he could furnish it to suit his taste and it is a perfectly acceptable address, is it not? So close to Fifth Avenue, and to his police headquarters, but for some reason he is not keen on the idea."

Sid and Gus burst out laughing. "For some reason?" Sid said. "My dear Molly, the reason is sitting before you. He doesn't approve of your associating with us. He's afraid we are filling your heads with wild, radical thoughts."

"If he stopped to think for a moment he'd know that I am not easily led by anyone," I said. "And you are my dearest friends. Why would I not want to live so close to you, especially when his career entails working to all hours? It would be most reassuring to me to have friends I could call upon in need."

"Then stick to your guns," Gus said. "We don't want you to move away. So tell him it's the new Ansonia building or you're not moving."

I smiled. "I'd rather live here than one of those fancy new buildings. And of course Daniel couldn't live so far uptown. He has to be within reach of police headquarters."

"Then this spot seems ideal to me," Gus said.

"Me too," I said.

"You haven't yet revealed the secret of your latest cases." Sid pulled her chair up closer to me. "What dastardly crime or sordid divorce are you working on? Come on, spill all. We won't let you go until you confess."

"I wish I had something to confess," I said. "In truth I'm currently unemployed. Not a case on the horizon. I suppose people go out of town in the summer months."

"The sort of people who want divorces do," Gus said. "I know among my family and their set it is the done thing to divorce these days. It used to be such a scandal. Now, it's fashionable."

"I hate divorce cases," I said. "I find them

so underhanded and unpleasant — lurking outside bedroom windows is not my cup of tea."

"So will you give up your career when you marry?" Sid asked.

"Obviously Daniel wants me to, and I have to confess that it is sometimes a little too dangerous, but I do so enjoy being my own woman and having my own money. Let's just say it's a small detail we still need to work out before we marry."

I finished my coffee and got up. "I shouldn't detain you any longer. I'm sure you have a busy day ahead."

"I suppose we do," Gus said. "Sid has to plan the agenda for the next suffragist meeting that we are going to host at our house and I have promised to paint something with a Mongolian theme for our yurt."

I chuckled as I left them. Such a delightful existence, I thought. Then I reminded myself that their lifestyle was frowned upon by most respectable households. They had essentially cut themselves off from the majority of polite society where they belonged.

THREE

I walked to the post office to see if any requests had come into P. Riley and Associates, which was the name of the small detective agency I had inherited when my mentor, Paddy Riley, was murdered. There were none. And no prospects of a job on the horizon. I had never been good at soliciting business. Now I might have to swallow my pride and visit my friends like the playwright Ryan O'Hare who was up on all the theater gossip, to see who might be in need of my services — and could afford to pay me.

I returned home and immediately went through my file of people who had hired me previously. I composed a letter suggesting I'd be delighted to assist any friends they might refer to me, then I tore it up again. Somehow it sounded like groveling and I've never been good at that. So I got up, swept the kitchen, picked some flowers from my tiny square of back garden, then paced with annoyance. Idleness did not sit easily with me. I couldn't picture myself as a lady of leisure. What on earth did they do all day? There was no way I'd be happy discussing my dressmaker or the best place to buy feathers.

Around lunchtime I was about to go in search of Ryan at his rooms at the Hotel Lafayette on Washington Square when there was a fierce rap on my front door and Daniel stormed in without waiting for me to answer it.

"That damned woman," he blustered.

"Such language, Daniel. Really your speech has deteriorated since you became betrothed to me," I said with mock severity. "I hope you aren't already starting to disregard my delicate sensibilities."

"I apologize," he said, then seemed to realize what I had said to him. "Since when did you have delicate sensibilities?"

"I may yet learn to acquire them," I said. "I understand they are deemed a useful attribute. So which woman has annoyed you so much that you resort to swearing in a lady's presence?"

He pulled up a chair and stretched out his long legs. "Why — the girl who was cut in half last night."

"She didn't seem to be in a state to offend anyone," I said. "Don't tell me that she survived after all."

"I couldn't tell you that. It's hardly likely but this morning she's nowhere to be found. My men tried all the hospitals and none of them seems to have admitted her or even treated her."

"She was probably dead before she could be admitted," I pointed out. "She'd lost so much blood and was on the verge of death when I saw her."

"I also tried the morgue," he snapped. "And what's more that Scarpelli fellow himself has vanished."

"Vanished? A good illusionist indeed."

"Well, he did leave a note for the theater proprietor saying that he couldn't face anyone after what he had done and needed time to be alone with his grief."

"There you are then," I said. "That explains it all. I remember his saying that he wanted to break the news to Lily's parents in person. What's the betting he's taken her body home to them so that she can be buried in the family plot."

"A possibility, I suppose," he said grudgingly because obviously he hadn't thought of it. "But now we have no idea where her home is and no chance of finding him. My personal opinion is that he's just pulled off a nice little murder and has skipped town before we have a chance to find out whether he had a motive."

"What motive could he have?" I asked.

"Several I can think of. She was becoming a burden to him. She was blackmailing him. Maybe he was living with her and had left a respectable wife at home somewhere. Or maybe she was in the family way and was insisting that he marry her."

"Do you always think the worst of people and come up with dark motives?" I asked.

He smiled. "Experience has taught me to expect the worst and take nothing for granted."

"I expect you'll manage to track him down and find a perfectly simple explanation for all this," I said.

"If I had the manpower to spare I'd send men out hunting for him," he grunted. "As it is, we have bigger fish to fry. We have the Secret Service breathing down our necks over a huge influx of forged money. Such large amounts that it could even bring down the U.S. currency if it's not stopped."

"Goodness," I said.

"So as you can imagine I've got the commissioner and my boss wanting to make sure we look good to the Secret Service and they've put every available man onto it."

"I could help, if you like," I said breezily.

"You?" He looked up sharply.

"Why not? You've said yourself that I'm a good detective. I could go back to the theater, ask a few questions, find out where Scarpelli was lodging . . . all that kind of stuff. People are more willing to gossip to a woman, you know."

"Molly, you know very well that I can't possibly involve you in police work," he said testily.

"Nobody needs to know."

"Oh, and how would it look if it was discovered that I'd used my future wife to help me solve a case. I'd be the laughing-stock of the force."

"Oh, I see," I said. "So it's not that it wouldn't be allowed, it's that you don't want to look like a fool, is it? May I remind you that if I hadn't taken on one very serious case myself, you'd still be in jail?"

He got to his feet again. "I do realize that, and I'm forever grateful. Of course, if you hadn't proved my innocence, you'd not be looking forward to an upcoming marriage."

"Oh, I'm supposed to be looking forward to that, am I?" I teased.

He came around the table and took me in his arms, holding me so tightly that I was almost crushed. "Are you telling me that you're not looking forward to the day we can be together?"

"I suppose I might be," I said, holding him at a distance from me so that I was looking into his eyes. "I can't wait to be a lady of leisure and take up embroidery and breeding Pekinese."

He laughed and brushed my hair with a kiss. "I am looking forward to a time when I can start kissing you like this" — he kissed me full and hard on the mouth this time — "and not be rebuffed for fear that we get carried away."

I didn't admit that I was also looking forward to that part of it. Daniel's lovemaking always left me breathless, so I had to put a stop to it while I was still in control. "So did you just come round to vent your frustration to somebody?" I asked, turning my face from his kiss.

"No, I came to tell you that I wouldn't be free tonight to take you back to the theater, and to apologize for depriving you of your chance to see Houdini. I don't see myself having any free time before he sails back to Europe."

"Don't worry about me. I'm sure there will be plenty more chances," I said. "Everybody's talking about him. His star is definitely rising in the firmament and I'm sure he'll be invited back to New York before long. And having seen one act go horribly wrong, I don't know if I'm all that keen to watch someone risking his life in a death-defying stunt."

"Ah, but this man's different," he said. "It's not so much illusion as skill and physical strength. There isn't a handcuff that can hold him or a lock he can't undo," he said. "I saw with my own eyes when he came to Mulberry Street. He challenged us to produce a handcuff from which he couldn't escape. We locked his arms behind his back with four or five of our best cuffs and he was out in no time at all. Simply amazing."

"Then I will come with you next time we have a chance, I promise," I said, "and in the meantime my offer still stands to pay a visit to the theater and look around for you."

"And my decision is still absolutely no. Under no circumstances are you to get involved in a criminal case or are you to give any impression that you help me in my job."

"Very good, sir," I said. "I hear and obey."

"That's my girl," he said, giving me a peck on the cheek and not detecting the sarcasm in my reply. "Now if you really wanted to do something to help me —"

"Yes?" I looked up expectantly.

"You could make me a nice sandwich to take with me. I'll have no time to stop for a bite to eat today."

"Oh, I see." My good humor had now definitely faded. "All I'm good for is cold beef sandwiches."

"I can think of other things," he said, trying to flirt with his eyes and being met with my cold stare. Then he reached out and stroked my cheek. "Molly, all criminal cases involve danger and it is my job to protect you at all costs. Surely you understand that. I want to take care of you. I don't want to have to worry about you."

I was about to say that I could take care of myself pretty well, then I remembered certain times when my life actually had been in danger and it hadn't been very pleasant.

"I suppose so," I admitted grudgingly. "I'd better make those sandwiches then."

FOUR

Sid and Gus finally persuaded me to go to the theater with them that night. I protested that Daniel would probably rather that I waited until I could see Houdini with him, but they thought this was bosh. "You don't have to tell him everything you do," Sid said. "A good wife learns when to speak up and when to keep wisely silent."

"A lot you know about being a good wife." I laughed.

"I'm a good observer of humanity," she pointed out.

So I went along with them, only to find a huge crowd milling around outside the front doors of the theater and the manager himself standing just inside the doors and trying to drive them away.

"It's no use standing there, we're completely sold out, I tell you. There's not a seat to be had in the house. Go home like good folks."

"But you promised us last night that we could come back," an angry male voice said.

"How was I to know the news in today's paper would sell out the entire engagement in New York? And it's not as if Scarpelli will be on the bill tonight."

There were more angry murmurs, plus some expressions of sympathy.

"Of course he is in no state to go on with his act at this point," the manager said.

"We came to see Houdini," someone yelled from the crowd. "He's the one we want."

"He's only here for a week."

The manager held up his hand to quell the rising mutters. "I tell you what — I'll try and see if we can arrange a performance on Sunday, even though the theater is normally dark then. And those who missed seeing Houdini perform last night will be given first pick of seats. I can't do fairer than that, can I?"

We came away with the rest of the crowd.

"It's amazing how great horror will draw more people than great sweetness," Gus said. "They came to see if another girl might be sawn in half tonight."

"They'd be out of luck," I said. "Signc Scarpelli has done a bunk, much to the a noyance of Daniel and the police department."

"Well, wouldn't you want to get away if you'd been responsible for someone's death?" Gus asked. "Come on, the night is still young. Have you seen *The Wizard of Oz* yet, Molly?"

"*The Wizard of Oz*. Isn't that a children's show?"

"They've made it into a delightful musical extravaganza. We've seen it twice but I'm game to see it again. How about you, Sid?"

"Game for any form of entertainment at any time, as you very well know," Sid replied. "Come on, Molly. Our treat. Let's find a cab, Gus."

So I was whisked off to the Majestic, in a rather more salubrious part of town. It was a children's story about good and wicked witches and a useless wizard, but I have to say that I enjoyed it. Of course the spectacle in itself was breathtaking. Characters flew around the stage and the wizard had all kinds of machinery to make himself seem terrifying. As I watched, I realized that to a certain extent everything on the stage is a matter of illusion. A good performer can make the audience believe anything he wishes.

■ ■ ■ ■

The next morning, when I was going through my closet, preparing to do a load of clothes washing, I realized something I had overlooked until now. I had covered that poor girl with my wrap. And of course I realized I now had a good excuse to go back to the theater if ever there was one. And I wouldn't be going against Daniel's orders if I just happened to look around a little and ask some questions while I was there, would I?

I wasted no time and went back to Miner's Bowery Theatre. In daylight it looked rather seedy. The front doors were shut this early in the day. I picked my way down a side alley that was piled with garbage and smelled of cats, and worse, and found the stage door. I had learned from my brief experience in the theater that the stage doorkeeper is the one who knows exactly what is going on. I pushed open the door and stepped into complete darkness.

"And where do you think you're going?" came a gruff voice from one side.

My eyes accustomed themselves to the gloom and I saw his bald head floating eerily white over the bottom half of a donkey door. It was amazing how all stage door-keepers looked the same. I smiled at him in what I hoped was charming innocence.

"Hello," I said brightly. "I was here two nights ago when the accident happened to poor Lily."

"If you're one of those reporters you can turn right around and get out before I call some of our stagehands and have you thrown out," he said in surly fashion. I should add that most stage doorkeepers are surly too, at least until they know you.

"Nothing of the sort," I said. "You see I went up onstage with my young man when he tried to help, and the doctor was asking for blankets to cover the poor dying girl. So I covered her with my wrap until they could come up with something warmer. I came back just on the off chance that it had been discarded here in the theater. I know it's probably covered in blood and beyond us-ing again, but I was particularly fond of it."

He stared at me for a while, trying to size me up.

"I didn't see it personally," he said.

"I don't know if the girl was carried out of the front door or she came through this way."

"Out the front. I certainly didn't see her leave. They'd have never got a stretcher out

50

through here. Too many steps and the alley's too darned narrow."

I put my head prettily on one side, in the way that children always think is endearing. "Would you mind if I took a look for my lost wrap? I know it's probably been thrown out by now, but I'd kick myself if it was still lying in a rubbish bin. I was rather fond of it, you know."

Another long pause, then he said, "You're probably going to cost me my job, but go on with you. There's nobody around at this hour anyway, so you can't do no harm. But don't go doing any snooping into dressing rooms or the like. Not that you can get at the illusionists' props. Always locked up good and proper, they are."

"Really? So does each illusionist lock his props away separately or are they all in one locked room?"

This made him laugh. "Listen, girlie, that lot wouldn't trust their own grandmothers. They live in constant mortal fear that a rival illusionist is going to steal their tricks. You hear of the brotherhood of magicians. Don't you believe it. Rivals, that's what they are. They'd cut each other's throats if they had a chance." Then he realized what he had said. "Didn't really mean that," he stammered.

"I'm sure you didn't," I said soothingly. "But from what they are saying, I understand there was little love lost between the one who calls himself Scarpelli and Houdini."

"They all hate Houdini's guts," the old man said confidentially. "Just because he can get himself publicity like nobody else — and he gets paid for it too. But none of them can do what he does — challenging police departments all over the country, defying anyone to come up with a lock or a jail cell that can hold him. And I've watched him, young lady. If they're illusions I'll eat my hat. If you ask me, I reckon the man's not quite natural. One of the stagehands said he had to be in league with the devil and I'm half inclined to believe him."

"How about Scarpelli. Did he get along just fine with the others?"

"Scarpelli? I don't think he antagonized anyone in particular. Jealously guarded his props, of course, but they all do."

"So you don't think anyone could have tinkered with his props that night? Because that's what he claimed — that someone was out to ruin his reputation and do him harm."

"That's rubbish," the old man said. "Do him harm? Between you and me, young lady, he wasn't much of a threat, until he came up with this latest stunt, that is. If his sawing the lady in half hadn't gone wrong, he'd have made his reputation. Nobody else in the world does that illusion on the stage these days, although I understand a Frenchy used to do it, long ago."

I made a mental note of this. A new trick that nobody else could do. Of course it would put Scarpelli on another level. And a fellow magician might well want to make sure the trick didn't succeed.

I decided to push my luck just a little further. "That poor girl seemed so sweet and nice," I said. "I can't imagine a girl like that having an enemy in the world."

"She didn't. And I tell you what — he thought the world of her too. Scarpelli, I mean. Nothing was too much trouble for her. You should have heard him and Houdini fussing over their womenfolk when they were rehearsing. Both of them had to run out because their 'honeylamb' or their 'babykins' wanted a soda or some candy. If ever you've seen two men on strings it was those two."

"It's amazing, isn't it?" I laughed with him. "And have you noticed it's always the small delicate women who can lead their men a dance. If I tried that with my young man, he'd tell me to go and get my own soda or candy!"

He chuckled at this. "You're right. It doesn't pay to be too independent for a woman."

I decided I had probably pushed my luck for long enough. "I'd better go and look for that wrap," I said. "I've enjoyed chatting with you, Mr. — ?"

"Likewise, miss. And I go by Ted. Old Ted, they call me." He nodded in a most civil fashion. "Watch your step back there. Things lying around all over the place that can trip you up if you're not careful."

I thanked him again and off I went, down the dark passageway until I found myself in the backstage area. The whole place was lit by a couple of anemic electric bulbs, which were not strong enough to cast more than small pools of light and the stage was bathed in gloom, the various props and scenery flats looming over me like menacing shadows. Even though I told myself I had no reason to be afraid, I found I was holding my breath. After all, if Scarpelli's mishap had not been a malfunction or miscalculation, then someone had wanted a person dead badly enough to have taken a frightful risk in this very theater, at this very spot. And it seemed as if that person had to be

Scarpelli himself, if the props were really locked up like the stage doorkeeper had told me. Of course I couldn't forget that the headliner on the bill was the self-proclaimed King of Handcuffs who could open any lock. But he had appeared shocked and surprised when he saw what had happened. He had also, I reminded myself, been the one to suggest that Lily should be carted away in an ambulance before the police arrived to uncover any clues from the scene.

I tiptoed carefully across the stage, my feet sounding unnaturally loud in the vast empty area. This was about the spot where the tragedy had taken place. I got down on my knees and searched the floor, looking for bloodstains, but it had been well scrubbed. Then I prowled around the rest of the backstage area. I came across some big wooden crates, padlocked, plus a couple of tarpaulins, wrapped around with chains and likewise locked with massive padlocks. I assumed these to be the magicians' props that they guarded so carefully. I wondered if Scarpelli had also kept his sawing-the-lady trick under a similar tarpaulin. If so it would probably have been easy enough to break into, especially for a fellow magician — especially one who made his living from picking locks.

In truth I had little hope of finding my wrap. There was no reason anyone would have removed it from Lily's body before transporting her to the hospital. And since no hospital had apparently admitted her, then the wrap was lost with the girl and the illusionist. Not that I really fancied having it back, all covered in blood. Then another thought struck me — Scarpelli made it quite clear that he wasn't about to divulge his illusion to anybody. If he had fled, wouldn't he have made sure that he left nothing behind but took that contraption with him? It would be covered in blood and probably beyond use now, but it would hold the secret to the illusion. That's why he made sure she was wheeled out still lying in the box.

I hadn't seen what happened when she reached the ambulance and whether she was lifted out of the box and onto a stretcher at that point. In which case, what happened to the contraption itself? I stared longingly at those tarpaulins. If I could just peek under them, maybe I'd recognize the leg of that table. Maybe there would still be evidence of bloodstains on the leg. And if it was still here, then maybe Scarpelli hadn't run off after all. Maybe the murderer had made sure that he finished off both Scarpelli and his assistant. I knelt on the floor and attempted to lift up the bottom of the tarpaulin.

"Hey, what do you think you're doing?" called a voice from across the stage.

I jumped up guiltily and was relieved to find it was only one of the stagehands and not one of the illusionists. He was a big, burly man in his shirtsleeves and braces, so I decided to act the helpless female.

"Oh, my goodness, you startled me," I said, putting my hand to my chest in a dramatic gesture. "It's so dark back here, isn't it?"

"The public's not allowed backstage," he said, still glowering. "Who let you in?"

"Your doorkeeper said I could come and look for my lost wrap. I hope that's all right."

"Your wrap?"

I nodded. "I was here the other night when there was the terrible accident, and I used my wrap to cover that poor girl until they found blankets for her. I came back on the off chance that it might still be here, although it probably won't be much use to me, all covered in blood like that. However I'd like to retrieve it if I could. It came from Paris, you know. Cost me more than a month's wages." I hoped I was babbling on like a scatterbrained female. I even attempted a pretty smile.

"You wouldn't find it under there," the stagehand said, giving me a frosty stare. "Those belong to the illusionists and they're most particular about them."

"Oh, dear. Of course, they would be. I'm sorry." I backed away hastily. "You didn't find a wrap, did you? A pretty lilac color with a silky fringe, but it would have had blood on it, of course. You probably wouldn't have noticed the color."

He shook his head. "Can't say that I've seen such a thing, and the boss had us cleaning up the stage after the tragedy. I can tell you it's not easy cleaning up that much blood. Scrubbing until all hours, we were."

"How awful for you. I'm sure it was a most horrid task," I said.

"Not your favorite either, was it Ernest?" the stagehand called to another fellow who was apparently watching us from the shadows. The first stagehand turned back to me with a smirk on his face. "Gives himself airs and graces that one. Thinks he's too good for the menial tasks. I told him why doesn't he go back to the old country if it doesn't suit him here?"

Ernest gave us a look of contempt. "I just didn't like touching blood," he said. "It's bad luck where I come from if someone dies in the theater."

He spoke with a slight accent, not unlike Houdini's. "What does the young lady want?" he asked.

"She's looking for a stole she left here," the first stagehand said.

"Something was stolen?" Ernest asked, frowning.

The first stagehand and I exchanged a laugh and I saw his demeanor change toward me. "A stole," he said. "You know a wrap, a shawl."

"Ah. This I have not seen."

I gave a shy, sideways glance toward the one who wasn't Ernest. "Well, if you don't mind, I'll just take one last look around, just in case it's been discarded in a corner, then I'll be off."

"All right, miss." The first one was now looking at me as if he'd just noticed I was a woman. "Just don't go near that stuff belonging to the illusionists. It would be more than my job's worth if they caught anyone poking around it."

"Don't worry. I won't go near it, I promise," I said.

He nodded and went back to work putting a coat of paint on a pillar. Ernest gave me a long questioning stare and disappeared into the shadows again.

I started peering into corners, then I turned back to my friend. "That contraption for sawing the lady in half," I said. "Did Scarpelli keep it locked up under one of those tarpaulins?"

"He did."

I gave a dramatic shudder. "I saw the whole thing. It was horrible, wasn't it? I still feel faint when I think about it. It's not still there, is it?"

He shook his head. "I don't see how it could be. It went in the ambulance with the girl on it. I helped carry her out."

"Did you? And if it was all locked up with chains like that, then I don't see how anyone could have tampered with it ahead of time, do you?"

"Beats me," he said in disinterested fashion. "Unless you were Houdini. Those locks would be a piece of cake to him. But I can't see Houdini tampering with another fellow's act. He's the big star, isn't he?"

"And if anyone came in from the outside?" I suggested. "What chance would they have?"

"At tampering with the illusionists' equipment?" He put down his paintbrush and looked up at me, as if he was really taking in what I had said for the first time. "Here, what are you getting at? You're one of those newspaper reporters, aren't you? Slipping in here on some flimsy pretext and then asking questions."

He got to his feet, towering over me.

"Oh, no." I backed away. "I promise you I'm not a reporter. I suppose it's just morbid curiosity. I was up onstage, you see, covering up that girl with my wrap, and I heard Mr. Scarpelli say that someone must have tampered with his equipment, so I just wondered how anyone could have done that."

"Curiosity killed the cat," he said bluntly.

"I know. My mother was always telling me that I ask too many questions. It's a failing of mine, and I'm taking up your time. I should be going. Thank you again."

I turned away.

"I don't see how anyone could have tampered with Scarpelli's table," he said. "How are they going to get in, to start with? They'd have to get past Ted at the stage door."

"Can't you get to the stage from the front of the theater?"

"Nah. We only open the doors an hour before the performance and then there's always something going on backstage. We're all here, aren't we? The illusionists are getting ready. We'd spot an outsider in a second."

"Of course you would. You spotted me right away, didn't you?"

"And if any stage door Johnny slips in, well, he'd be tossed out on his ear."

"I really have taken enough of your time," I said hastily. "I should be going. Nice talking to you, Mr. . . ."

"Reg," he said. "Just plain Reg."

"Nice talking to you, Reg."

"And you too, miss." I saw that he was now eyeing me with interest. Perhaps he thought I'd been flirting with him. "So you're not in the theater yourself then?"

"I have been," I said, stretching the truth only a little. "At this moment I'm not working."

"Happens to the best of performers," he said. "Say, if you'd like to go for a malt sometime?"

"That's kind of you, but I have a very jealous boyfriend," I said.

I beat a hasty retreat then and made my way back to Ted at the stage door.

"No luck then, miss?" he asked.

"I didn't really expect to find it," I said, "but at least I can say that I tried now."

He nodded with sympathy.

"Ted, you're here all the time, aren't you?

62

You'd know if anyone tried to sneak into the theater?"

"I've been stage doorkeeper for twenty years now," he said proudly. "I can keep out unwanted intruders better than anybody."

"So you didn't find anyone trying to get into the theater earlier this week?"

He shook his head, then he frowned. "Exactly what are you suggesting?"

"I was wondering if somebody wished Scarpelli harm and deliberately tried to ruin his act."

His eyes narrowed. "You seem remarkably interested in this. Are you sure you're not a reporter? Old Ted don't take kindly to being tricked, you know."

"I swear I'm not a reporter," I said. "I guess I was just being too curious. You know, when something like that happens, you can't help wondering why. And I was wondering whether it really was an accident or someone had a grudge against Lily or Scarpelli himself."

"I wouldn't know," Ted said. "I just stand here at my post and mind my own business, and you should do the same, young lady. It don't pay to meddle, or to ask too many questions."

I came out into the alleyway. Was that just

a general word of advice or was I being
warned off?

FIVE

As I picked my way back down the alley I noticed the dustbins. On impulse I took the top off the nearest one and started rummaging through it. It was just possible that my wrap had wound up here. It was disgusting work and I had just told myself that I didn't want to reclaim the wrap that badly, and that almost certainly it would be beyond redemption, when I came upon a blood-soaked piece of fabric. It was so stiff and caked with dried blood that it was impossible to see what it had once been, but definitely not my wrap. It had no fringe. I was about to drop it back when it occurred to me that this was valuable evidence. If the girl and Scarpelli had vanished, then this blood-soaked rag was the only proof that a crime had taken place. I wrapped it in a piece of newspaper that was lying nearby and tucked it into my handbag.

I looked up to see a disreputable-looking

man staring at me. He was unshaven, unwashed, and dressed in tatters. "If you're that hungry, girlie, there's the Salvation Army mission a block away," he said in a gravelly voice. "They hand out free soup."

I tried not to smile as I thanked him and walked away. I had never been mistaken for a tramp before!

When I got home I took the rag, still wrapped in newspaper, and wondered if I should bring it directly to Daniel. Then, of course, I realized this would show that I went to the theater against his wishes. No sense in rocking that boat unnecessarily. I'd keep it here unless and until it was needed, then I could produce it triumphantly. I wrapped it well in tissue and shoved it into a drawer out in the scullery. I had just washed my hands and was about to make myself some lunch when there was a knock on my front door. Not Daniel, because it was a timid little tap. I opened it and at first didn't recognize the young woman who stood there. She was dressed demurely in a simple muslin, with a pretty bonnet-style hat, and at first I took her for a schoolgirl, but then she said, "Miss Murphy. I hope you'll forgive me for calling on you like this but I wanted to thank you for your kindness to me the other night You did give me your card."

Then I realized that it was Bess Houdini. The other night she had been in full stage makeup. Without it she looked pale, innocent, and frail — but not quite as young as I had thought. She was definitely older than me. In her thirties, maybe.

"Please, come inside, Mrs. Houdini," I said. "It was nice of you to stop by, but it certainly wasn't necessary to come and thank me in person."

I ushered her inside and offered her a seat in my one halfway decent armchair.

"I have to confess, Miss Murphy, that I do have another reason for seeking you out," she said. "You said you were a lady detective."

"That's right. I am."

"Well, I'd like to engage your services."

Of course my brain went straight to divorce. As I'd mentioned, I didn't like handling divorce cases in the first place, and I had no wish to cross swords with a man like Houdini — reputed to be in league with the devil.

"Really?" I tried to sound only mildly interested. "May I offer you a cup of tea or a glass of water?"

"A glass of water would be swell, if you

don't mind. It's hot and muggy out there today, isn't it?"

I went and got her the glass of water, then sat across from her, waiting patiently while she drank it.

"So what sort of assignment did you have in mind, Mrs. Houdini?" I asked when I thought she'd had long enough to compose herself. My sainted mother would be impressed at the way I'd learned patience at last.

"I want to hire you to protect my husband," she said.

I couldn't have been more surprised. I started to say, "Jesus, Mary, and Joseph," but I swallowed it back. "You want me to protect your husband?" I repeated.

"I think that someone's trying to kill him," she said.

My mind went immediately to the horrifying scene I had witnessed. "Is this because of what happened to Scarpelli's assistant the other night?"

"That did make me think that it wasn't just my nerves and I hadn't just been imagining it," she said.

"If someone's trying to kill him, then surely it's a matter for the police," I said.

She shook her head vehemently. "No, that wouldn't do at all. Harry would never countenance it. He's a very proud man, Miss Murphy. You might even say a very vain man. He'd hate the thought that he couldn't take care of himself. And he'd hate the thought even more that someone wanted him dead. That's why I came to you."

"What exactly do you think I can do?" I asked.

"Two things, I hope. Keep an eye on him and find out who wants him dead."

I tried to compose my racing thoughts. One part of my brain was saying this was a plum assignment and I could forever after advertise that I'd been hired by none other than the premier magician of our time, the great Houdini. But the more sensible part of my brain was asking me how I could ever protect a man who risked his life on a daily basis and how I could ever hope to discover who might want him dead. But I've always loved a good challenge, and I had no other case on the books.

"Very well, Mrs. Houdini," I said. "So tell me how your husband may be linked to what happened to Lily the other night. Do you suspect that Lily's death was a murder and that the same person is trying to kill your husband?"

She shuddered as she remembered. "I'm not sure. But I tell you that's the first thing

69

that came into my head when I saw her lying there."

"So you're suggesting that a murderer is loose in the theater — someone who is trying to kill illusionists or at least ruin their reputations?"

She shook her head. "I don't know who that could be. The other acts on the bill, they're real nice. They seem like gentlemen and it's not as if they're Harry's particular rivals. None of them tries to do what Harry does. Of course he does have his rivals, but not on this bill. And it would be hard for an outsider to get backstage, particularly when a show's going on."

She paused, looking at me expectantly.

"So maybe you'd better start by telling me why you suspect someone wants to kill your husband."

She leaned closer to me. "Ever since he got back to this country last week I've had this feeling of danger," she said. "I can't explain it, but I'm sort of looking over my shoulder all the time. Do you know what I mean?"

"I do," I said. "We Celts are supposed to have that sixth sense and it has served me well in the past. So is there anything more concrete than a feeling of danger?"

"I think that we're being watched," she

70

said. "And I'm pretty sure that someone tried to break into our house the other night. I heard someone outside. I woke Harry and when he turned on the light the fellow ran off."

"Surely someone with your husband's notoriety would be watched all the time," I said. "He's a recognizable figure. I imagine that gentlemen of the press would follow him, hoping for a sensational story. And if you really think someone tried to break into your house, then maybe that was also an unscrupulous newspaper reporter, trying to find out how his tricks are done. Or maybe a rival illusionist. That's what Scarpelli claimed, you know."

"Did he? Maybe he's right, but I don't know who that would be."

I looked at her sitting there, staring at me with big timid eyes. If the person who wrecked Scarpelli's act and killed Lily was also out to ruin Houdini, he had already proved that he'd stop at nothing and Mrs. Houdini was right to believe her husband in danger. "But being watched and even a break-in don't amount to death threats, do they?"

"But there have been other things," she said. "While Harry was out, a man came to the front door — two days ago, I think it was. I don't know what there was about him, but he made me afraid. Just the way he asked the questions, they came across as threats. And he said to tell Harry that he'd be back." She paused and plucked at her muslin skirt nervously. "And when I asked his name, he said that Harry would know who he was."

"I see," I said. "Then maybe we are looking in quite another direction. Houdini is an Italian name, isn't it? Could this be somehow tied to a Sicilian gang to whom your husband might owe money?"

She looked at me and laughed. "Oh, that's real funny," she said. "Harry isn't Italian in any way. He's Jewish, and he was born in Hungary. His real name is Ehrich Weiss. And I'm German Catholic from Brooklyn. So it's not likely we'd have dealings with any of these new Italian gangsters."

"Not all gangsters are Italian," I pointed out. "I've had to deal with a brutal gang on the Lower East Side and they were not at all Italian. Are you sure your husband doesn't owe money, or hasn't run foul of the criminal classes?"

She thought about this, then shook her head. "No, Harry's not like that. The only times he's borrowed money have been from friends and family. And he's always good about repaying it. We don't live beyond our means, Miss Murphy. We still stay at cheap boardinghouses and travel third class, even though Harry's making good money now. Of course he sends a big chunk home to support his mother, like he promised his father he would. He plans to buy her a house pretty soon."

I didn't know whether gang members demanded protection money from stage performers. Since these performers were not confined to one area but were constantly on the move, I thought this was unlikely.

"So not a gang member then. What did this man look like?"

"Nothing special. The type of guy you'd pass in the street and not look at twice."

"Well dressed?"

She frowned as if trying to remember. "Respectable. Like a clerk maybe. Wore a derby. Nothing flashy."

"So probably not a gang member nor an entertainer," I said.

She thought about this. "Probably not."

"Did he actually say anything that you could possibly think was a death threat?"

She thought again, then shook her head. "I can't say that he did."

"Then maybe you're reading more into this than you need to. Maybe your nerves

73

are still upset from what happened the other night after all the travel you've been doing recently and the voyage home from Germany."

"No, I don't think so," she said. "Oh, sure, seeing that poor girl all sliced open like that did upset my nerves. I mean who wouldn't be upset when they saw something like that? It's enough to turn the strongest stomach. But the voyage home was as smooth as anything and Harry was in good spirits, and all."

"And what about when you were on the Continent? Did you get any feeling of danger over there?"

She thought about it, then shook her head. "Not in the same way. Of course I'm always nervous when we're away from home — especially on the Continent, you know. The people don't speak our language and I don't like the food, and those types over there give Harry the most impossible challenges he should never accept. But he won't turn them down. He won't be defeated, no matter what." And she continued to toy with her skirt, plucking at it, smoothing it. I thought of her hysterics the other night and the way Houdini had babied her. So it was possible that these death threats were all in her overactive imagination. And it was also possible that if that proved to be the case, Houdini, who controlled the purse strings, wouldn't want to pay me.

"Mrs. Houdini," I said. "I have heard nothing yet that convinces me that anybody wants to kill your husband. Are you sure you're not imagining things?"

"Harry's jumpy too," she said. "Oh, he'd deny it if you asked him, but something's not right. He was looking forward to coming home so much, but then I've woken at night to see him pacing the room, or sitting at the table scribbling away. And when I ask him what he's doing, he says working on a new illusion."

"Well, there you are then. He's concentrating hard on working it out in his own mind and he won't be satisfied until he's got it down on paper."

"I suppose so," she said, "but we were out walking once and he looked across the street and grabbed my arm and changed direction. Then he hailed a cab and off we went. And when I asked him what it was about he said he'd seen someone he'd rather not have to talk to."

This enforced my suspicion about a gang connection. And something of this nature was out of my league.

But at that moment she leaned forward

and grasped my hands. "He means everything in the world to me, Miss Murphy. I don't know what I'd do without him. Please say you'll help us."

My sensible side wanted to say no, but a voice in my head was shouting, "This is Houdini, you dolt. Crack this case and you'll be famous." Who knows, maybe in solving this, I'd be able to solve the Scarpelli incident as well. I could legitimately be at the theater, snooping around, without having to tell Daniel. All in all an exciting challenge for a detective. Better than divorce cases, anyway. And certainly better than no cases at all.

"All right, Mrs. Houdini," I said. "I'll take the assignment. I should tell you that I charge a hundred dollars for a successfully concluded case."

"The money is no problem," she said. "Harry did well for himself in Europe and he's getting four hundred dollars a week now."

"Four hundred dollars!" I blurted out thus wrecking the impression I might have given of the sophisticated urbanite detective. But I had no idea entertainers could earn that kind of money when twenty dollars was a good wage for the average employee. Then my mind turned back to more practical matters. Those who make good money often are unwilling to part with it. I had seen this demonstrated before when I had been hired by another famous stage personality, the actress Oona Sheehan. She had done everything in her power to wriggle out of paying me.

"But do you think he'll be willing to pay me if he has such an aversion to my kind of service?" I asked.

She smiled prettily now. "He'd do anything to make his babykins happy," she said. "He worships the ground I tread on."

"Exactly how long are you in New York?" I asked.

"Only three weeks, then we're booked on the *Deutschland* to sail back to Europe at the end of the month."

I still wasn't sure whether to talk myself out of a job or not. "If it's only three weeks, then surely it's hardly worth hiring me, is it? You'll be safely far away again before you know it."

"And Harry could be dead," she said bluntly. "If someone wants him dead, then three weeks is plenty of time to kill him."

This, of course was true. "All right, Mrs. Houdini. Let's get started and you can tell me what you want me to do," I said. I went to the desk and took out a sheet of paper.

"Well," she said. "After what happened to that poor girl the other night, I'm especially worried that someone is going to try and get at him during his act. It wouldn't be that hard, you know. One little thing that doesn't work and you're a goner. And it looks like an accident. So I want you to be there with him all the time onstage."

"What?" This came as a bombshell. "You want me onstage?"

She nodded. "Yes, I thought that maybe you could take over my part in the act. Oh, I know you won't be able to do everything. You'd never be able to learn the famous Metamorphosis that we do — you're not small enough to fit into the trunk, for one thing. But I can teach you the other things. We open with the mind reading, you know. That always goes down well with the crowd. We've done spiritualism in the past too, but Harry's so against it now that we don't do it anymore."

"You really communicated with spirits?"

She laughed. "No, it's all bunkum. All illusions. My Harry loves to go to these spiritualists' meetings, then show everyone what frauds they are. They're really just illusionists like us, Miss Murphy. We've never come across a genuine one yet."

I nodded agreement. "I can believe that. I

once had to investigate the Sorensen Sisters. Have you come across them?"

"They're good," she said. "Even Harry had to admit they're convincing. But he's had great fun exposing some of the others."

"I don't suppose they took that well."

She chuckled. "No, he's made them mad all right."

"I was going to ask you if you had any idea as to who might want to wish your husband harm. Certain spiritualists he has exposed should go on my list then. Who else?"

"Everyone worships him," she said.

"You just said he has his rival illusionists."

"No one can rival Harry," she said. "He's in a class by himself. Oh, he has his imitators right enough — men who call themselves 'Boudini,' or 'Houdani,' or 'the Real Handcuff King.' Harry's taken on quite a few of them. He loves a good scrap."

"Fought them, you mean?"

"No, set up a public challenge to do what he does. And on every single occasion they've been humiliated. Totally humiliated. He's made a laughingstock of them."

"I see. So one of them might well want to get even, don't you think?"

"I suppose," she said.

"But none of them has actually threatened

your husband that you know of?"

"Not that I know of. Of course Harry doesn't tell me everything. He doesn't like to worry me."

This was not going to be easy. If she was delicate and he babied her, there might be quite a lot he didn't tell her, and was not likely to tell me either. And my first and biggest challenge would be persuading him to take a tall, healthy-looking Irish woman who had never been either dancer or contortionist as his assistant.

"Mrs. Houdini," I said. "Are you sure you really want me onstage as Houdini's assistant? Couldn't I just watch as well from the wings?"

"Of course you could, but people would get suspicious, wouldn't they? Most theater folk think it's bad luck to have someone watching backstage."

"But I could never learn the sort of things you do in such a short time."

"Let's face it, the crowd really comes to see Harry. What the assistant does is to distract the audience at the crucial moment. You could do that. And I'm sure we could teach you some of the mind reading too."

"But I thought the show only ran for the rest of this week. That's hardly enough time to train me to do anything."

"Next week we're in Brooklyn," she said. "Twelve shows in all. That's a lot of opportunity for someone who's up to no good."

"And how are you going to persuade your husband to go along with this?"

"I tend to have — nervous turns — from time to time. I could easily claim that the sight of that poor girl all sliced up has made my nerves play up again and I simply can't face going onstage with him. Then I'll present you as my friend who's a quick learner."

"Wait a minute," I said. "Your husband saw me the other night."

"Yes, but he didn't know who you were, did he? You were just someone on the stage. So that works in our favor. He'll already associate you with the theater. I'll tell him I invited you to see the show the other night and you were watching from backstage when the accident happened."

I examined myself critically. "I don't look much like a magician's assistant," I said. "I'm not petite and delicate enough and I'm certainly not glamorous. And as for a costume . . ." I held up my plain broadcloth skirt.

She frowned, thinking. "That might be a problem," she said, giggling girlishly. "You certainly wouldn't fit into mine. I only weigh ninety pounds. And you're bigger than most. I'll have to see what I can do. But you said you'd been onstage once. So you know about makeup and that kind of thing."

"Yes, I do still have my theater makeup, and I know how to apply it," I said. "And I do have friends in the theater who might be able to help me."

"That would be swell. I tell you what. Why don't you come and see the show tonight — as my guest. Come and watch from the wings."

"I thought you said that was bad luck."

"We'll chance it for once. I'll tell them I'm not feeling well and you're holding my smelling salts." She glanced up and smiled. "Then after the show I'll introduce you to Harry and we'll take it from there."

"All right," I said.

She got to her feet. "I can't tell you how grateful I am, Miss Murphy. It was a godsend meeting you the other night. I've been so worried about my poor Harry. This is such a relief."

"I'll do what I can, Mrs. Houdini," I said as I escorted her to the door. But as I closed it behind her I stood in the cool stillness of the front hall, my head buzzing with thoughts and actually feeling sick.

"Molly, my girl, what have you done now?" I said out loud.

Six

The first thing I did was what most women would do in a similar situation: decide that I had nothing to wear. If I was to meet the famous Harry Houdini at the theater tonight and be presented as a future assistant I had to look the part of a theater artiste. And as to finding something I could wear onstage — something like Lily's glittering white ensemble — well, I had no idea where I might rustle up one of those.

I went upstairs and examined the few items of clothing hanging in my wardrobe. My own clothing was plain and practical in the extreme. I had, after all, arrived in this country with literally the clothes on my back and my earnings since had just about kept body and soul together. But at the far back of the wardrobe I found something that encouraged me. It was the outfit Oona Sheehan had lent me when she had hired me to impersonate her. It was a smart black-

and-white striped grosgrain two-piece. I took it out and examined it in the light. It was unfortunately rather the worse for wear, having been through a lot while I was in Ireland, but it would do at a pinch for tonight's meeting with Houdini.

But as to what I could wear as a magician's assistant . . . I did the next thing I always did in moments of crisis like this: I went across the street to Sid and Gus.

Gus opened the door, a riding crop in one hand and wearing an elegant riding habit. Her cheeks were flushed. "Molly!" she exclaimed. "We've just returned from Central Park. We've been out riding."

"Pretending to be Mongolian warriors?" I asked cautiously.

"Not quite. We thought that we ought to brush up our riding skills before we undertook an expedition somewhere wild like the Jersey shore and tried a flat-out gallop along the sands. I'm afraid those poor, tired horses will never be the same, especially after Sid's little episode."

"What did she do?" I asked.

"You know Sid. Always pushes everything to the limit. First she was most annoyed because they insisted on giving her a side-saddle. Then she asked if she could ride bareback instead and of course they refused.

85

So no sooner were we out of the stable than she urged the poor animal into a gallop, throwing up the dust along the drive and terrifying children. Then she decided she wanted to see if she could leap into the saddle while the beast was moving, the way they do it in Mongolia."

"Jesus, Mary, and —" I started to say before I caught myself. These Irish expressions tended to come out in moments of crisis. I was trying to eliminate them if I was ever to become the sophisticated New Yorker. "So what happened?" I asked.

"I talked her out of it, of course. She's come home quite miffed. And the outcome is that we are *personae non gratae* at that particular stable in the future after we returned her horse exhausted."

As she was saying this Sid appeared, dressed in men's riding breeches and tall boots, a crimson scarf tied over her black hair. She gave a marvelous impression of a bandit, if not a Mongolian.

"Gus has told you, I suppose," she said, frowning. "I was forced to ride sidesaddle on a tired old nag. I kept telling them I was a superb horsewoman and I'd rather go bareback, but they simply wouldn't listen. I don't know where we're going to get in our Mongolian practice."

"Go and have a lie down, dearest," Gus said, "and I'll make us some iced tea. My, but it's warm today, isn't it."

She opened the door of what used to be the drawing room and was now draped, from the central chandelier downward, with fabric to resemble a Mongolian tent. "It's cooler in here," she said. "Do sit, Molly, and I'll be back with the tea."

I sat, on a leather cushion on the floor. I don't know what they had done with the sofas. Perhaps they were still behind all that drapery. Gus reappeared with a tray with glasses of iced tea and some chocolate biscuits. "So is this just a friendly call or was there something particular you wanted?" she asked.

"I know you two love your playacting, so I wondered if you had any sort of costume that would make me look as if I was a theater performer," I said.

"Oh, what fun. Is it for a costume party?"

"No, an assignment. I have to meet some people at a theater tonight and convince them that I am one of their fraternity. Then I'm rather afraid I may have to appear onstage, so I just wondered . . ."

"Appear onstage? As what?"

"I can't really tell you too much," I said.

"What a hoot," Gus said. "Molly onstage

again. We can't wait to see you."

"I'd rather you didn't," I said. "It's bound to be highly embarrassing. In fact I am not at all sure about this whole assignment. But on the off chance that I'm expected to play a part, I will need a costume."

"Let's go upstairs and see, shall we?" Gus led the way up two flights of stairs and opened a large trunk. It was full of what we at home would have called "dress up" clothing.

"What kind of role are you expected to play?"

"Glamorous," I said. "Spangles."

"This we have to see." Gus was chuckling now. "You'll not keep us away, Molly."

She produced one piece after another, carrying on a constant commentary. "Lion tamer? Harem dancer? French maid? Japanese geisha? Oh, how about this — French cancan dancer?"

She held up what amounted to a black corset with fishnet stockings attached by large suspenders.

"Gus, I could never wear that. It's not burlesque and anyway I wouldn't have the nerve," I said. "I'd be arrested!"

"I believe Sid was, when she wore it." Gus laughed. "Then it appears I don't have anything suitable in here for your costume.

And as to your outfit for tonight — you're welcome to check out our wardrobe, but you know that we don't dress to appease fashionable society any longer. Sid has some divine silk trousers and mens' smoking jackets, but I suppose they might give the wrong impression."

"Yes, they might," I agreed.

So I left empty-handed. Whom did I know in the theater who might have something suitable for me? Oona Sheehan came to mind, of course, because she did still owe me a favor and she was my size. So I caught the Sixth Avenue El up to Madison Square and went to the Hoffman House, where Oona had rooms.

"I'm afraid Miss Sheehan is not in residence," the hall porter said. "She has left the city for the summer. I have not been informed when she will return. If you care to leave a message?"

"Drat it," I muttered, coming out into the warm sunshine again. So whom did I try now? Of course, how thick of me. Anyone who could afford to do so left town to escape the summer heat. My only hope was to see if Ryan O'Hare was still in the city. He knew everybody in the profession and besides, seeing him was always a pick-me-up. It also occurred to me that Ryan might prove to be useful in my current assignment. He loved to gossip and probably knew every piece of juicy scandal in the theater world. I returned posthaste to Washington Square and to the Hotel Lafayette, where Ryan had rooms.

I tapped on the door to Ryan's suite and was greeted by a doleful voice saying, "Go away and leave me to die quietly and alone."

I bent down and tried to see through the keyhole, but the key was in it. "Ryan," I called through the crack in the door, "Ryan, it's Molly. Is something wrong? Please let me in."

After a moment I heard shuffling feet and the door was opened. A fearsome apparition greeted me and I took a step backward. Ryan was still in his nightshirt. His long dark hair stood out wildly. His eyes were bloodshot and stared me at blearily.

"Holy Mother, Ryan. What in God's name's the matter with you. Are you sick?"

"Dying," he said dramatically. "Probably won't last the day."

"My dear man, have you seen a doctor?"

"No doctor. No hope," he said.

I led him back into his room and closed the door. "Lie down and let me go for one."

"No use," he said, sinking dramatically onto the bed.

That was when I noticed an empty bottle of Jameson Irish Whiskey on his bedside table.

"Did you drink all this?"

"How else was I going to drown my sorrows?" he exclaimed.

"Then I suspect that all you've got is an almighty hangover," I said. "Lie there, I'll have them send up some black coffee."

"Don't bother. I just want to die anyway," he said. "There is no point in continuing to live."

I ignored him and phoned down to the front desk.

"What on earth is wrong?" I asked.

He turned his face away, staring bleakly out of his window, where a large sycamore tree shimmered in the breeze. "Everything," he said. "Life has no meaning."

I waited and at last he said, "You remember the divine young man with the yacht? We went on a cruise up the Hudson?"

"I do remember," I said.

"He's left me," Ryan said bleakly. "His father told him to shape up and marry a suitable girl or he was going to cut him off without a penny, so money won out over my broken heart."

"Ryan, why did you decide to be a playwright," I said, chuckling, "when you could have been such a marvelous tragic actor?"

"How heartless you are, Molly Murphy. I bet if that great brute of a policeman abandoned you, you'd be a little down in the dumps yourself."

"I'm sure I would," I said, "but I don't fall in and out of love with someone new every few weeks like you."

"But this time was different," he said. "I had such high hopes. We were going to sail his yacht to the Med for the summer. He was going to back my new play."

"Ah, I see. So maybe money did play a small part for you as well."

"A very small part," he agreed. "One does like to dine well and a summer on the Med sounded so delightful. Better than being stuck in this sweltering cesspool for the summer. And now what will happen to my new play?"

"I didn't know you'd written a new play," I said.

"Only the most brilliant thing so far this century," he said. "It will make that oaf George Bernard Shaw look like an illiterate schoolboy."

"What's it called?" I asked, since he was clearly perking up.

"I don't have a title yet. And I have to confess that most of it is still in my head, but the smattering that is on paper — sheer, unadulterated brilliance."

"Modesty, thy name is Ryan," I said.

"One knows one's worth," he said.

"Then it seems to me that you have a lot to live for right now. You need to get that play on paper before it all vanishes from your head. And I tell you what, if it's as brilliant as you say, then we'll take it to the impresario Tommy Byrne. He's a fellow Irishman, isn't he?"

Ryan sat up, clutched at his head in dramatic gesture for a moment, then reached out and grabbed my hand. "Molly, you are a true lifesaver. You've given me hope. If things were different, I'd fight off that horrible policeman and marry you myself. You always know how to lift my spirits."

A knock at the door heralded the arrival of black coffee. He drank it, protesting with each sip, then lay back down again.

"Now you can do something for me," I said. "First of all, I need a costume to be a magician's assistant."

The bloodshot eyes opened in surprise and he laughed. "Molly, my sweet. You do not look the part of a magician's assistant. They are tiny and weigh no more than a feather. How else can they fit themselves into those terrible contraptions for the tricks?"

"I don't intend to be put inside any kind of contraption," I said. "I'm just going to stand there and be helpful."

"Have you abandoned your current profession for the stage then? Daniel won't approve."

"Daniel won't know and this is for an assignment."

His eyes lit up. "An assignment? Do tell?"

"To the most notorious gossip in New York? Ryan, you know I can't discuss my cases. But you may be able to help me."

"You only have to ask, you know that."

"What do you know about illusionists?"

"Not very much. We move in different circles. They are vaudeville, I, my dear, am legitimate theater."

"So you don't know much about Houdini?"

"Only that I'd adore his fame and money. My dear, he is the darling of Europe at the moment. He was feted by the Kaiser, the Tsar of Russia. He has them eating out of his hand."

"He's back here for a few weeks this summer and part of an evening of illusion at Miner's."

"Is he? I must go and see it. I understand

he has muscles like iron. They positively ripple."

"I understand the whole show is sold out," I said.

"My dear, I can get my way into anything. The theater owners all adore me."

"So you would have no way of knowing if there were any current feuds going on between Houdini and other magicians?"

"No, but I expect I can come up with someone to ask, if I put my mind to it."

"And I did just save you from imminent death," I reminded him.

"You know I'd do anything for you," he said. "So let me think who I know in the sordid world of vaudeville. And who loves to gossip." A wicked smile came over his face. "Yes, I can think of one or two people, although whether they'll be in town at this time of year, I can't tell you. But I'll do my best."

"Thank you. I really appreciate it, Ryan. So about the costume. Where do you think I could find one in a hurry that would fit someone as large and healthy-looking as me?"

"You wouldn't find one anywhere, darling, but I do know a divine little dressmaker," he said.

"That may be the answer," I said. "How

do I find her?"

"It's a he," he said. "I've no doubt he could make you one in a hurry, but he's not cheap. I'll take you to him if you like."

"This afternoon?"

"Darling, I am not venturing forth looking like this. I do have my public to think of. Tomorrow, if all is well. Come round but not before ten. I am not at my best in the early morning."

I was obviously not going to get any more out of him, so I took my leave.

SEVEN

I arrived home to find Daniel standing outside my house and hammering on my door. He had just turned away with a disgruntled expression when he caught sight of me entering Patchin Place.

"Ah, there you are." His face lit up. "I really must get you set up with a telephone, Molly. I never know whether I'll find you at home or not."

"I do have a business to conduct," I said. "I'm not yet the obedient little wife sitting home and waiting expectantly for her husband's return."

"I can't see you ever being the obedient little wife." Daniel looked at me fondly. "In fact sometimes I wonder what I've gotten myself into. But no time for chitchat, Molly. I've arranged to get off early this evening and I want us to go and see a house."

"What sort of house?" I asked cautiously.

"It's a simple brownstone on West Twenty-first," he said, "but I think it might do very well for us."

"Oh," I said, finally realizing what he was talking about. "For when we get married, you mean."

"Exactly."

"But Daniel, we haven't even set a date yet."

"I know, but it's not often that the right property becomes available, so one has to strike while the iron is hot."

I looked fondly around Patchin Place. "I'm sorry, but I have to meet a client this evening," I said.

"Send a message and cancel it."

"I can't, Daniel. This is an important case for me with a new client. Besides," I added, probably unwisely, "I really like my current address. Why can you not consider it for both of us? It's close to headquarters, it's quiet, and it's big enough for the two of us."

"For the two of us, yes," he said. "But we'll need room for a servant, and then when the children start arriving . . ." He paused. "And I am the youngest police captain on the force. I need an address with some prestige."

"Then why not the new Ansonia building?" I said flippantly. "Or I gather that the Dakota is still very much in fashion. Or a

98

mansion on Fifth Avenue would do at a pinch."

He frowned. "Not that much prestige," he said. "I still only have a policeman's salary."

I reached out and put my hand on his lapel. "Daniel, please let's not rush into things."

"Are you getting cold feet?"

"About marrying you? No, of course not. But you keep talking about children and servants and I'm not sure that I'm ready to give up my own life yet."

He scowled. "Molly, we've been through this a hundred times before. A man in my position can't have a wife who works, especially not as a private detective. It simply isn't done. It would go against our whole code of ethics. And I'd be a laughing-stock — nasty little jokes about getting my wife to solve my cases for me." He took my hands in his. "I make enough money, Molly. I can support you. We will live a good life together."

I stood there, looking up at him, not knowing what to say next. Because in truth I didn't know what I wanted myself. I wanted to marry Daniel, but I didn't want to become a wife — not in the way that was accepted for wives to behave — a submissive adornment only good for dinner parties and having children. I wanted to be Molly Murphy, free to come and go as she pleased, free to make her own friends.

"You don't want to live here because you don't approve of my friendship with Sid and Gus," I said.

Daniel flushed. "I must admit that — that their views and behavior could be detrimental to my career," he said. "But of course I'm not going to forbid you to see them."

"That's big of you."

"But neither do I want you under their constant influence."

"I'm not under anybody's influence," I said hotly. "You should know that better than anyone, Daniel Sullivan."

"Molly," he said calmly, "I just want our marriage to get off to a good start. I don't want to live where you can run across the street to your friends every time we have an argument."

"You must think little of me if you imagine that I'd do that," I said, breaking free of his grip. "Anyway, this conversation is going nowhere, Daniel. I am not ready to look at houses yet and I have an appointment with a client for which I must get ready soon."

"Then I guess that's that," he said grumpily. "Very well, Molly, perhaps you'll be good enough to tell me when you are ready to set a date for our wedding and to start making concrete plans for our future. I'm over thirty, Molly. I want a home and a family. I love you but I'm not going to wait forever."

He started to walk away.

"Daniel!" I called after him. "Don't be like that. I do want to marry you. And we will set a date, just as soon as we get our current cases settled. I promise."

He turned back. "Really? That's a promise? This will be your last case?"

"I didn't exactly say that."

"Then think about it Molly. Think which is more important to you, a life with me, or this constant striving to prove your independence." He pulled out his pocket watch. "I must go. I'm already late."

Then he stalked off without kissing me. I let myself into the house feeling sober and a little scared. I didn't want to lose Daniel, did I? But I didn't want to lose Sid and Gus and my independence either. Why did women have to settle for one or the other? It just didn't seem fair.

An hour or so later I was on my way to Miner's Theatre, dressed in the black-and-white two-piece, which still managed to look smart, in spite of a few stains and rips. My hair was more or less tamed into a bun with the jaunty black hat perched on top. I was also wearing rouge and lipstick, which felt strange. But I had to look the part. As I rode the trolley southward I had time to reflect upon what I had undertaken. I had seen a girl killed onstage in what appeared to be no more than a horrible accident. I had witnessed Bess Houdini's attack of hysteria on seeing that girl, and her nervous disposition. And there was really nothing she had told me that fully convinced me that someone was out to kill her husband. But I had a well-developed sixth sense myself. If she sensed danger, then I couldn't completely dismiss it. Besides, it was a challenging case and if nothing else, I dearly wanted to get to the bottom of the Scarpelli accident before the police did. If I was going to leave my profession, then I was going out with a bang!

I went around to the stage door of the theater. The doorkeeper recognized me instantly. "You back again? Lost another shawl?" he asked.

I gave a nonchalant laugh. "No, tonight I'm here to see the show as guest of Mrs. Houdini," I said. "I helped her the other day when she became upset after seeing Scarpelli's assistant lying there with blood all over her. She was grateful and when she heard that the show was sold out for the rest of its run, she invited me to come and watch it from backstage."

"I see." He was staring at me hard. He started to say something, then he shrugged his shoulders. "Well, if you've been invited by one of the performers, then I guess there's nothing more for me to say. I'll have the callboy send up a message to them that you're here."

"I'm sure I can find my way," I said.

"I'm sure you can but it's more than my job's worth to have an outsider wandering around backstage when illusionists are setting up their acts. They are so cagey about their secrets that they wouldn't even allow their own mothers anywhere near them."

At that moment a reporter showed up. "So what's the news on Scarpelli, then?" he asked. "Has he been found? Has the girl's body been found?"

"No good asking me anything, son," the doorkeeper said calmly. "I'm just the guy who guards the door. Nobody tells me anything. If you want to know that, you'd better ask the police. All I can tell you is that his name's not on the bill tonight. Now beat it."

While they were talking I had moved down the little passageway that led to the backstage area. I wasn't intending to make a run for it, but I thought I might just be able to see what was going on back there. As I came near the end of the hall I heard voices. Two men talking. One of them said, "I don't know what you're doing here. I told your boss I'd get it to him and I will."

"He just wanted to make sure that it reached him safely," the other voice said. "If what you've hinted is true, then this is serious stuff."

"It sure is. Very serious."

"Then we'll be watching your back," the second voice said. "You can't be too careful. I'd hurry up and hand it over, if I were you."

"Not until I can deliver it to your boss personally," said the other voice. "This is too important to take any risk."

Before I could move back to the doorkeeper's booth a man came past me. He was slim, well dressed with neatly parted blond hair, and carrying a silver-tipped cane. He pushed past me arrogantly, not pausing to apologize when he knocked my arm.

"Who was that gentleman?" I asked the doorkeeper as he disappeared into the night. "He didn't look like a theater type."

"Never seen him before in my life," the doorkeeper said. "I don't know how he got

104

in here either. Must have come from front of house."

"So you can get backstage from the front of the theater, can you?" I asked.

"There's the pass door, isn't there? Every theater has a pass door."

Of course, I realized that I knew that. I'd used one myself before now. So all those theories about the backstage area being carefully guarded were wrong. Anyone could have gotten through the pass door if they were willing to take that risk. And it might have taken only a second or two to tamper with Scarpelli's equipment.

The callboy appeared then and was instructed to tell Mrs. Houdini that I was waiting down by the stage door. A few minutes later he returned, breathless.

"Mrs. Houdini says she'll meet you in the wings, on the dressing room side," he said. "Come with me."

He set off again at another lively trot. I tried to keep up, while avoiding the normal hazards of the backstage. It was still poorly lit back there, although chinks of light shone through the closed curtains and the excited murmur of the audience could be clearly heard. I noticed that the locks and tarpaulins had been removed from those mysterious heaps and boxes beside the stage. A tall man in a long black cape, lined with scarlet, was standing beside one of the big crates, extracting glass trolleys, birdcages, velvet drapes. I remembered him as the opening act on the bill: Marvo the Magnificent. He looked up in annoyance as he heard our footsteps approaching.

"What's she doing here?" he demanded.

"Guest of the Houdinis," the callboy said.

"Then keep her away from me," Marvo snapped, waving me away as if I was an annoying fly.

"I saw your act the other night," I said, giving him my winning smile. "I was most impressed. I still can't imagine how you make those birds appear and disappear."

"Magic, my dear," he said smoothly. "Now keep out of my way, like a good girl. I have to prepare in peace."

"I was here the other night when that awful accident happened to Scarpelli's assistant," I said. "I bet that has upset all of your magicians."

"Illusionists, if you don't mind. We are all illusionists. And if you want my opinion, Scarpelli was asking for trouble."

"He was? How?"

"Sawing a girl in half? I mean, really! The act has never been tried, at least not in living memory although they claim an illusionist in France had performed it long ago. They will keep taking greater and greater risks to impress the public. And the horrid thing is that the public has come to expect greater and greater risk. It's Houdini, you know. He's setting the bar too high — putting his life in jeopardy every night. They all try to compete, but they can't, can they? I, with my doves and my gentle sleight of hand, am no longer anything more than a warm-up act, however good I am. Now please be a good girl and buzz off."

I retreated as instructed and found a chair tucked between two of the side curtains that gave me an excellent view of the stage, also the occasional sneaking glance at Marvo the Magnificent. I was especially interested to see how and where he managed to secrete his doves, but no birds were in evidence as he wheeled out his props table and placed it in the center of the stage.

I heard sounds of the orchestra warming up beyond the curtains and picked up the tension that is always evident just before a show is due to start. Stagehands scurried around, steering well clear of the magician's props, I noticed. I was just wondering whether Bess would put in an appearance before the show started when she came toward me, arms open.

"Molly!" she exclaimed. I remembered that it had been "Miss Murphy" when we were discussing business at my house, but then it came to me that she was giving the impression of dear friends meeting.

I stood up and extended my own arms. "Bess. How good of you to invite me. I'm so thrilled."

We embraced and while our heads were together she whispered, "I haven't said a word to Harry. He's not in a good mood, tonight. Something's upset him particularly. So we'll have to tread carefully. Somehow I'll have to convince him that you need to take my place for a while."

"Could I not be your dresser or something?" I asked. "I really can't picture myself onstage in tights and spangles like you. I'm not graceful, for one thing, and I'm not decorative. And it must take years to be able to do all the things you do."

"But my dresser would stay up in our room," she said. "I need you beside him, onstage."

"Beginners, please. Five minutes to curtain," the callboy announced, crossing the stage. Marvo the Magnificent ran a comb through his hair, patted it into place, then strode out onto the stage. Bess vanished and I was left alone, surrounded by curtains in my own little world. The orchestra struck up a lively tune and I felt that thrill of excitement that one always gets when the curtain goes up on a show.

The theater manager came out onto the stage and the music became softer. "Ladies and gentlemen," he said. "Welcome to Miner's Theatre and an evening of illusion starring an assembly of the greatest illusionists the world has ever known. We begin with a performance of prestidigitation that will take your breath away. Direct from his triumphant tour of the West Coast, it's Marvo the Magnificent!"

Marvo strode out, his hands outstretched to the audience. He produced a handkerchief from his pocket, crumpled it up, threw it into the air, and it turned into a dove that fluttered and wheeled before coming to rest on his shoulder. Even sitting a few feet away and watching him in side view I couldn't see how it was done. The audience clapped. More feats of sleight of hand followed, culminating in the disappearance of a cage full of doves from under a velvet drape. The audience clapped, without much enthusiasm. Marvo took as many bows as the applause would allow, then made his exit right past me.

"Good audience tonight," he said. I

couldn't tell if it was to me or someone I couldn't see standing in the wings.

His act was followed by the magician with the card tricks. Unlike the others with their fancy names he was introduced as Billy Robinson and his only distinguishing feature seemed to be a drooping mustache, which gave his face a lugubrious appearance. His card tricks received only lukewarm applause even though I thought they were pretty clever myself. Then followed Abdullah, the Fakir from Egypt, who was a last-minute replacement for Scarpelli. Apparently he had come straight from his success at the Cairo Pavilion on Coney Island. He was a fire-eater and sword swallower — in fact I remembered seeing him there. He got a better reception, especially when a whole long cavalry sword that had previously sliced an apple in half disappeared down his gullet. But the audience was clearly waiting for the high point. I could hear the murmur of anticipation.

"And now, ladies and gentlemen, I give you the act you've all been waiting for," the theater manager announced. I didn't think this was particularly diplomatic to those acts that had preceded. "Straight from his amazing successes in Germany and Russia, where he played to kings and emperors, Miner's

Theatre is proud to present Houdini, King of Handcuffs!"

There was a tremendous roar from the crowd and Houdini swept onto the stage, resplendent in white tie and tails. His smile lit up the whole stage and I saw instantly that this man had presence. Bess stood out of the spotlight to one side while he accepted the applause. At last he held up his hands. "Please. You are too kind. We have magic to please you all tonight. Tricks of the mind and feats of strength and endurance that will take your breath away. And, as always, my hundred-dollar challenge. Anyone who presents me with a pair of handcuffs from which I can't escape will earn one hundred dollars."

An excited buzz ran through the audience.

"Any takers tonight?" Houdini paced the front of the stage.

"Any legitimate pair of handcuffs," he went on. "Several times while I was in Germany some guy too smart for his own good brought me handcuffs that had been tampered with. Locks that were plugged so that they wouldn't open. But in America we play fair, don't we? We like a good fair fight and a good challenge. So remember, if you come up here with your cuffs, I may want to try them out on you first."

A laugh went around the audience at this. "What, no takers tonight?"

"Down here!" A shout went up from the audience. One man was making his way toward the stage. Houdini greeted him like an old friend. "Oh, it's you again, Cunning. Still haven't given up, have you? Still trying to catch me out." He turned back to the audience. "Ladies and gentlemen. This man is a fellow illusionist and he's determined to get the better of me. Well, let's see what you've come up with this time."

A pair of monstrous-looking handcuffs were passed across to Houdini. He examined them, then handed them back and nodded. "Seem fair enough. Where did you dig these up?"

"The new regulation handcuffs of the Chicago Police Department. State-of-the-art, these are."

Houdini looked amused. "Okay, let's give it a shot, shall we? Let's see what the Chicago police department can do."

"Behind your back," the man insisted. "And in full view of the audience. No funny business."

"No funny business, he states." Houdini gave the audience an amused look.

"And I get to search you first."

"I'm not stripping naked as I've done at

quite a few police stations," Houdini said. "There are ladies present."

"Take off your jacket and shirt at least."

"Very well." Houdini was still in good humor. Bess came forward and he removed his jacket and then his shirt. Underneath he was wearing what looked like a shiny red singlet. I saw what Ryan had meant about Houdini's torso. He was as well muscled as any bodybuilder.

"Right, turn around," the man commanded.

Houdini turned. The man put on the handcuffs, high on his forearms so that his arms were jammed together at a strange angle. It looked very cruel to me. I could see them digging into Houdini's flesh, but he didn't complain or even make any comment.

"Right, let's see you get out of that," the man said with satisfaction.

Houdini wriggled and jiggled and shook his shoulders a bit. He turned away from the audience, then back again. Suddenly there was a clatter and the handcuffs fell to the floor. Houdini picked them up and handed them to the visibly shaken man.

"Really, Cunning, I'm surprised at you. I thought you could come up with something better than that. Even my dear Bess could escape from those." He turned to her and she came back with his shirt and coat, helping him to dress.

The man left the stage to catcalls. "There you go, fellows," Houdini said to the audience. "If you plan to commit a crime, then I suggest Chicago. You'd be out of their handcuffs in no time at all."

As the fellow magician departed one fact clicked into place in my head — something that had been bothering me while I had watched the act. The other voice I had heard speaking in low tones in that hallway had been Houdini's.

EIGHT

Houdini's act continued. Bess was presented as the incredible mind reader.

"I'm the brawn, she's the brain," Houdini told the audience.

He went down into the audience with a pack of cards. He stopped by an elderly woman and asked her to pick a card, memorize it, then place it into a little black box.

"Bess will now read your mind and tell you what card lies inside the box," he said.

Bess appeared to go into a trance.

"When you are ready, Bess. We don't want to rush you."

"I see the card," she said in a high, tense voice. "It's — it's the nine of spades."

"The nine of spades. Was she right?"

"Yes, she was," the woman replied.

"Then please open the box and show us your card."

The woman opened the box. "It's empty!" she exclaimed.

"How unfortunate. Something must have gone wrong," Houdini said. "Wait a minute."

He ran nimbly back onto the stage. "Bess, would you please stand up? I believe you are sitting on something."

She stood. A card was on her chair. It was the nine of spades.

The audience cheered. Then a black hood was placed over Bess's head after audience members were given a chance to examine it and declare that nothing could be seen through it. Harry went down into the audience again and asked people to hand him articles. Bess identified, without hesitation, a lady's handkerchief, a pocket watch, even a photograph of a child.

"This child is no longer with us," she said. "Am I right? She wants you to know that she is safe and happy where she is."

There were murmurs through the audience. "Can she contact the spirits?" someone asked. "Can she talk to my dead husband?"

"Ladies and gentlemen, we don't profess to be spiritualists," Houdini said. "Bess is — well, let's just say she has a gift in that direction. But now let's move on to the part of the show you have all come to see. We now present for you the Metamorphosis, as

116

performed before the great houses of Europe. The Kaiser offered me a thousand marks if I would tell him how it is done. Others have claimed that I can dematerialize my body or that I am in league with the devil. I assure you I am not in league with him."

A trunk was pushed onto the stage. It was bound with metal straps and held with two large locks. Houdini removed his jacket and his tie. Then he removed his shirt and trousers, so that he wore nothing more than a one-piece, form-fitting costume rather like a pair of combinations that have shrunk in the wash.

"I now invite two strong men from the audience to come up on-stage to examine me and this trunk," he said.

There was a stampede to get to the stage and the first two were allowed up the steps. They were burly young men, both of them, the kind you'd expect to see hanging around some less reputable type of tavern.

"Perfect for the task," Houdini said. "Now if you would be good enough to search me to see that I carry no tools on my person that might enable me to free myself from any lock or key."

They duly patted his body and pronounced him clear. Then he opened the

117

trunk. They felt around inside, tried the locks, and nodded.

"Now," Houdini said. "Here on the table you will find an assortment of handcuffs and leg irons. I invite you gentlemen to examine them, then apply them to my arms and legs any way you see fit."

The two men went to town, clamping the cuffs and irons on him with his arms tightly behind his back and his legs bound together.

"Thank you, you have been most helpful," Houdini said. "Don't go away. I have more work in store for you. Now I ask Madame Houdini to wheel onstage my special cabinet."

I felt the curtains brush at me as a contraption was wheeled out. It was nothing more than a three-sided frame with velvet drapes, about shoulder-high.

"The bag, if you please, Bess," Houdini said. He turned to the audience. "Ladies and gentlemen, I shall now place this bag inside the trunk, and ask these gentlemen to help me into it, then tie the drawstring tight. Then when I am in the trunk, they will secure the locks." He turned back to his volunteers. "Is that clear to you, gentlemen?"

The men nodded again. A drumroll started in the orchestra pit. Bess held open the velvet bag and the men helped Houdini into it. They drew it tight and tied it shut, then they forced the bag, with Houdini in it, into the trunk. The lid was closed, the locks snapped shut. The men returned to their seats.

Now the drumroll increased in tempo. Bess rotated the cabinet so that it concealed the trunk from the audience.

"Ladies and gentlemen," the theater manager announced. "This trunk has about enough air to keep a person alive for about seven minutes. Of course inside a thick velvet bag, that's another matter altogether. A couple of minutes at the most. We have men standing by offstage with axes, just in case."

As he finished speaking Houdini sprang up from the cabinet, his hands above his head to reveal he was free of his bonds. The audience broke into thunderous applause. Then Houdini wheeled aside the cabinet. The trunk was still locked, the great fetters quite undisturbed.

"Let's open it, shall we?" he said, a mischievous smile on his face. "Who knows what it may contain."

He bent to open one of the locks. Then he frowned, tried again, rattled it.

"The lock is stuck!" he called out. "It's

jammed. Quick — where's the key? My jacket, quickly."

Someone handed him his frock coat and he felt desperately inside. "Where's the key?" he demanded. "It's gone. Someone run up to my dressing room and get the spare key. Go!"

At this point a muffled voice shouted, "Harry, get me out of here!"

Bess was now inside the trunk.

Houdini summoned stagehands to help him. Bess was now pounding from inside the trunk.

"Get me out! I can't breathe!"

"She's already been in there nearly five minutes, Mr. Houdini." The stage manager came to join them. "We can't wait for the key. Bring the ax."

One of the stagehands reappeared with an ax.

"Go carefully, that's my wife in there." Harry said.

The stagehand swung the ax and cracked the lid of the trunk. Houdini himself tore apart the trunk lid and finally managed to open it. He and the stagehands dragged out the velvet bag, containing what seemed to be a lifeless figure. As the neck of the bag was untied, Bess lay unconscious on the stage.

120

"My God, I've killed her. Bess, baby, honey, don't die!" Harry shouted, slapping at her cheeks.

Bess gasped, coughed, and tried to sit up. "What were you doing?" she demanded. "Trying to kill me?"

For the second time in a week the theater manager dismissed the audience before the end of the show. A doctor was summoned. I had stood up the moment the ax was brought onstage. Now I dragged out my chair and assisted Bess to it. She sank onto it, still white-faced and gasping. Someone produced a glass of water. Harry was on his knees beside her.

"Sweetie pie, baby, I don't know what went wrong. I swear I don't. As if I would want anything bad to happen to you. Are you okay? My God, if they hadn't had that ax nearby . . ."

"I can't do this no more, Harry," Bess said. She was crying now, her body jerking with great sobs. "I can't live with us risking our lives every night. I want out. I want you to find another profession."

"Are you crazy?" Harry rose to his feet now. "Just when we're hitting the big time? Bess, baby, we're going to be big stars. I mean really big. You want me to buy you a fancy house in New York City? A nice home

121

in the country? Just a little longer, then you can have it. Anything you want, baby. Then I swear I'll quit. We'll raise chickens, okay?"

At this Bess laughed through her tears and pushed him away. "You know I hate chickens," she said.

"Come on, I'll take you up to the dressing room and you can have some of your calming mixture and lie down," he said. He swept her up into his arms as if she weighed nothing and started to walk away with her. I stood watching, undecided as to whether I dared follow or not. This option was taken from me by the theater manager who fell into step at Harry's shoulder.

"So what went wrong, Mr. Houdini?" he demanded.

"The lock jammed. Accidents happen," Harry said, not turning back to him.

"Two accidents in a week? Are you trying to shut me down?" I heard the manager's voice echoing in that vast backstage area.

I was left alone onstage, not sure what to do next. Clearly Bess was in no state to see me. Did this now mean I was out of a job before it started? I started to make my way from the stage, unnoticed by everyone. Just my luck that a lock would jam on the night I was supposed to be introduced as her replacement. Then I froze, standing beside a mock pillar in the backstage darkness. Had Bess had some kind of premonition that this was going to happen to her, so had she sought me out to replace her and to be suffocated instead? In which case it was indeed just my luck that the accident had happened too early.

I tiptoed out of the theater, feeling like an invisible ghost. I should make a rule for myself: never deal with hysterical women, I told myself. I remembered the last time I had been employed in the theater by an actress who had lied to me and was using me for her own ends. Was no one in the theater to be trusted? I had been misled and used on two occasions now. Which then brought another train of thought into my mind. Was what I had witnessed just another illusion? Had Bess arranged for the lock to jam so that she could have an attack of hysterics onstage and thus claim to her husband that she was afraid to perform anymore?

I realized I was dealing with a world in which nothing was what it seemed. The smartest thing I could do was walk out of this theater and not look back.

NINE

I was feeling both angry and relieved as I rode the trolley back home. I hated being used, and I was relieved that I was not the one almost suffocating in that trunk. Had Bess really had a premonition or was there information about a threat that she had kept from me? I had heard that theater folk were superstitious — so had Lily had a similar premonition when she climbed into that box to be sawn in half, I wondered. Then naturally I had to connect the two incidents. Bess had come to see me because she feared that someone was about to kill her husband. She had seemed genuinely worried. So was it possible that this was an attempt not on her life but on Harry's? Perhaps the person who had rigged the lock on the trunk had expected it to be Harry's coffin, not Bess's. Any way you looked at it, someone had tried to kill two people in one week at the same theater and that was too much of a coincidence. I couldn't walk away from this case until I knew more. My curiosity just wouldn't let me.

Of course my mother often told me that my curiosity would bring me to a bad end. She probably wasn't wrong, but one of my faults is not knowing when to back down. I resolved to go and see the Houdinis in the morning. It would be only natural that I paid a call on my poor, dear friend Bess to see how she was faring. And I should also pay a visit to Daniel. For one thing I should probably try to patch things up with him. I could understand his frustration with my refusal to act like a normal young bride-to-be. And the best way I knew to do this — at least the best way that wouldn't lead to complications before we were married — was to cook him a nice meal. Whoever said that the way to a man's heart was through his stomach was perfectly right. I'd also like to add that a good meal is also the best way to soften up a man if you want information out of him — and I was dying to find out if Daniel had made any progress on the disappearance of Lily and Scarpelli. All in all a busy day ahead tomorrow.

I arrived home and got ready for bed, but it was too warm in my bedroom, my brain was now racing, and sleep was impossible.

So I got out a piece of paper and sat at my window, savoring the gentle night breeze on my face and arms as I jotted down my thoughts.

There were several explanations for what I had witnessed tonight:

a. The trunk locks jamming had been a nasty accident, which Bess, being psychic, had foreseen.
b. Bess planned the whole thing to look like an accident so that she'd have an excuse to drop out of the act and let me take her place.
c. Someone in that theater was trying to kill illusionists or at least ruin their acts.

If the last, then the best possibility was one of the other illusionists, those two men who opened the bill with their doves and their card tricks. Marvo had actually stated to me that Houdini had raised the bar too high for all the illusionists and that the audience was no longer satisfied with just a clever act. They wanted danger. They wanted excitement. And he had been prowling around backstage, clearly annoyed that I was hanging around and might be in a position to watch him.

Then there was the quiet Mr. Robinson. I

should check into him also. I decided I could dismiss Abdullah the sword swallower as he had come straight from Coney Island and this show was clearly a step up for his career, so he wouldn't want anything to happen that might ruin it for him.

So far I had left out the rest of the backstage crew. Any one of those stagehands could be a failed illusionist or merely an antisocial person with a grudge. And as I had found out, it wasn't that hard to sneak into the backstage area. The young man whose confrontation with Houdini I had overheard had somehow gained entrance without passing the stage doorkeeper. I thought about that confrontation. Houdini had definitely sounded rattled, or at the very least annoyed, and as for the other man — well what he said had sounded very much like the sort of threat that might come from a gang. Houdini was supposed to have delivered something and hadn't done so. He had stated he'd only deliver it to the boss in person. Money of some kind, then. Blackmail, protection money . . .

I stopped at this thought. Houdini hadn't delivered and his act had gone wrong. Was that a warning from a gang as to what could happen to him if the money wasn't forthcoming? Were any of the powerful gangs now demanding protection money of theatrical performers? That would be another thing to ask Daniel in the morning.

The sound of a distant police whistle and the clatter of feet on cobbles made me pause and look up from my thoughts. In a backwater like Patchin Place it was easy to forget that I was in the heart of a big city. But every now and then something happened to remind me that crimes were happening every minute. Someone was having a pocket picked or jewelry stolen or their head bashed in at this very moment, and I was never completely safe. I stood up, half resolved to close my open window, then told myself that my nerves were on edge and I was being silly. But it did make me pause to wonder if perhaps Daniel was right. Had I really had my fill of this kind of work and the danger it brought me and wouldn't it be wonderful to know I was safe, loved, and protected, and would never have to jump from a rooftop or take a fearful risk again? I had half promised Daniel that this would be my last case. Did I really mean it?

The morning dawned with the sun shining in fiercely through my window at six o'clock and the day promising to be a scorcher. Not ideal weather to be running around on a case. If I were married, I told myself, I'd go to stay with Daniel's mother out in Westchester during this kind of weather. I'd sit on a shady porch, sip lemonade, and play croquet. Maybe one day my husband would be able to afford to build me a house on Long Island, or on the Hudson, where I could escape from the heat in the summer while he toiled on in the city. The idea of being a wife was beginning to show some benefits after all!

I got up, washed, and dressed. There was no way I could wear Oona Sheehan's theatrical two-piece on a day like this. I'd expire with heat. The Houdinis would just have to put up with me in my usual muslin, however untheatrical it looked. There was no point in my going to visit them too early: theatrical folk are notoriously late risers. So now I was all ready, champing at the bit, with nowhere to go.

Ryan had offered to take me to his dressmaker, of course, but not before ten o'clock. And I wasn't going to order a costume at this stage, not until I knew a lot more about what had happened and what would be involved. I decided I could always pay a call on Daniel at his rooms, just in case he had not gone into work early. I'd bring supplies and promise to come by later to cook him dinner. If that wasn't extending the olive branch, then I don't know what was. I went across to the market and bought lettuce and cucumber for a salad. I even threw caution to the winds and purchased a tomato. Then I went to the delicatessen and came away with some lovely slices of cold boneless leg of pork, stuffed with sage and onion. Some small potatoes and we were ready for a delicious summer meal.

I took the Sixth Avenue El up to Twenty-third Street and walked toward Daniel's apartment on the corner of Ninth Avenue with great anticipation. Our time spent together recently had been tense and uneasy. I suppose it's always that way before a marriage. I realized I was possibly being the difficult one, unwilling to let go to one ounce of independence. If I hadn't known people like Sid and Gus and Nellie Bly, that newspaper reporter whose risky exploits are legend, I suppose I should just have succumbed to the notion that wives were supposed to be submissive. But I had never been submissive to anybody, even when I lived in a cottage in Ireland and we were as poor as church mice.

TEN

I reached Daniel's building, already feeling the heat of the day at this hour, and made my way up the stairs. If he wasn't at home, then I'd get the key from Mrs. O'Shea, who lived on the ground floor, and have the meal all ready for him in his meat safe when he returned. I had just tapped on his door when I thought I heard voices. The voices stopped and footsteps came to the door.

Daniel opened the door. "Yes?" he demanded impatiently, then he saw me. "Molly! Is something wrong?"

"Not at all," I said. "I've come to make amends for my behavior last night. I come bearing gifts — or rather the ingredients to make you a nice meal."

He gave a rather embarrassed smile. "Why, that's good of you. Much appreciated. Unfortunately I've got company at the moment or I'd ask you in." He held out his hands to take the basket from me.

131

"Don't leave the little lady standing outside, Sullivan. Invite her in, for God's sake. I'm anxious to know what kind of young woman comes to cook for you."

Daniel's face flushed red. "This is actually my intended, Mr. Wilkie. Come on in, Molly, and let me introduce you."

I stepped into the room. A pleasant-looking man with light brown hair and neat mustache was seated in Daniel's leather armchair. He was probably in his forties and had a distinguished air about him, but he rose to his feet as I came in and gave me an encouraging smile.

"So you are the young woman who has finally managed to rein in the wayward Captain Sullivan, are you?" He held out his hand. "John Wilkie. A pleasure to meet you."

"Mr. Wilkie, this is Molly Murphy, my future bride," Daniel said.

Wilkie chuckled. "So you're marrying an Irish lass. That should make for a lively household."

Daniel smiled. He was normally the sort of man who was supremely self-confident. There was a swagger about him as if he knew he held an important position and expected respect. To see him so deferential and embarrassed reinforced my own feelings that this was indeed an important man.

I was curious to find out who he was and what he was doing in Daniel's rooms at breakfast time.

"Do you live in New York, Mr. Wilkie, or are you just visiting?" I asked.

"I'm up from our nation's capital," he said. "Captain Sullivan is aiding me in a little matter of forged banknotes. You've heard about it, maybe?"

I wasn't sure whether I was supposed to have heard about it or not. "I believe I read about it in the papers," I said cautiously.

Wilkie threw back his head and laughed. "She'll make you an ideal mate, Sullivan. Not going to divulge a thing. Well done, my dear."

"In truth Daniel really doesn't mention many details of his work to me," I said. "Just as I don't confide details of my work to him."

I saw a flash of annoyance or warning cross Daniel's face.

"You are a working woman then?" Wilkie asked.

"Yes, I run a small detective agency," I said.

The smile faded. "Good God — pardon the profanity — but you have to admit that yours is not a usual occupation for a young woman."

133

"Nor one I fully approve of," Daniel said before I could answer. "She has put herself in harm's way too many times. I, for one, shall be glad when we are married and she can settle to more normal female pursuits."

"Please take a seat, Miss Murphy." Mr. Wilkie offered me the armchair and perched on an upright chair himself. "I find this most intriguing. Sullivan, I wouldn't say no to another cup of your good coffee."

"With pleasure, sir." Daniel shot me another warning glance as he retreated to the kitchen. "Don't say anything that might prove embarrassing to me." I heard the words as clearly as if he'd spoken them out loud.

"So what kind of cases do you handle, Miss Murphy? Or do you just do the paperwork and have men out on the streets doing the actual detection?"

"No, I'm actually an agency of one at the moment," I said. "And I handle all kinds of cases. Nothing criminal, of course," I added hastily, even though this wasn't quite true. "Anything from locating missing persons to proving a claim to an inheritance. And sometimes divorces, of course; although I find the whole idea rather repugnant."

"Fascinating." He nodded. "And how do people react to a female detective?"

"Not very well, on the whole," I said. "Men are loath to confide in me. Women are always suspicious of one of their gender who does a man's job. And there are many places to which I can't gain entry — saloons, gentlemens' clubs. On the other hand, a woman is better suited to detective work in some ways."

"Such as?"

"Women are more observant. They pick up on tiny, insignificant details — why a woman is wearing a particular pair of gloves that don't really go with her dress. That kind of thing. And they also are better at sensing interaction between people. They can sense tension better than men. And they can blend into a crowd more easily. The only thing we can't do is fight or make a hasty retreat. Skirts and petticoats are a confounded nuisance, especially when being chased or trying to climb a wall."

At this Wilkie threw back his head and laughed again. "You are a rum one, Miss Murphy. I can see what Sullivan finds attractive in you. Never a dull moment, huh, Sullivan?"

"No, sir," Daniel replied as he came back into the room with a cup of coffee.

"Pity you're about to be married, Miss Murphy," Mr. Wilkie said. "I rather think my service could use someone like you." He took the coffee cup from Daniel and drank with relish.

"Oh, no, sir," Daniel said hastily. "I have enough trouble protecting my own back without worrying about hers."

Again a quick glance from Daniel told me I had outstayed my welcome. I rose to my feet. "You gentlemen must excuse me. I only came to leave the food for Captain Sullivan. I shouldn't have interrupted your discussion."

Wilkie stood up too. "No, no, it is I who should be taking my leave. I think I've made the position clear, Sullivan. As a matter of fact this meeting was fortuitous. I only came to New York in person to meet with a man about something entirely different. But having set up the meeting, he's nowhere to be found. Gone without a trace, you might say. And I have no time to stick around and hunt for him. President Roosevelt made it very clear that he wants me back in Washington later today. So I must be on my way back to the railway station if I'm to catch the ten-forty-five train." He held out his hand to Daniel. "I can't thank you enough for your assistance, Sullivan."

"As yet we've nothing to show for it, sir, but we'll keep trying," Daniel said.

"And as for you, lovely lady" — Wilkie took my hand and clasped it between his — "should this bounder not come through with his offer of marriage, then you tell him I'd hire you like a shot."

"You're very kind, sir." I laughed uneasily. "I'll keep your offer in mind." I gave Daniel a cheeky smile. "But I think that Captain Sullivan can be trusted to make good on his offer to me."

"In which case I expect to be on the guest list at one of your dinner parties," Wilkie said. "Until we meet again, Sullivan."

He gave a polite nod to both of us. "I can find my own way out," he said and we heard his footsteps going down the stairs.

"I'm sorry, Daniel," I said, because he was still looking a trifle annoyed. "I had no idea I was going to be barging in on a meeting. I hope I haven't spoiled anything for you."

He smiled then and came over to me, slipping one arm around my shoulder. "You've nothing to blame yourself for, Molly. How could either of us have known that Mr. Wilkie would pay a surprise visit at this hour?"

"Who is this Mr. Wilkie exactly?" I asked.

"You don't recognize him from his pictures in the newspapers?"

I shook my head.

"Well, then remember his face for future reference. He's the head of the United States Secret Service. A very powerful man."

"Secret Service? He's in charge of spies?"

Daniel laughed uneasily. "I don't know about spies, but his jurisdiction is anything that affects our national security."

"He mentioned the counterfeit money that you'd told me about. Is that a matter of national security then?"

"It may well turn out to be," Daniel said. "Enough counterfeit money flooding certain key cities at the same time might be enough to send a financial system crashing and bring a country to its knees."

"But who would do that?"

Daniel shrugged. "There are still plenty of powerful anarchist groups in Europe. Japan and Russia have recently showed their aggressive tendencies, as has Spain."

"But the United States, Daniel. Who would have the might to take on such a powerful country?"

"Nobody has the might, that is clear," he said. "Whoever is doing this is working through subterfuge — agents infiltrating false dollar bills into the system faster than we can detect them. And who knows what other little tricks they may have up their sleeves."

"Speaking of tricks," I said, "I wondered if you'd had any news about Scarpelli and his assistant."

Daniel frowned. "None. I had men looking into it, but so far they've come up empty-handed. The man has gone to ground — or at the very least moved well away from our jurisdiction. He could be in Canada by now, for all I know."

"It's strange that Lily's body has not appeared in a morgue somewhere, isn't it? Surely he can't have gone far with a body. How would he transport it, for one thing?"

"It's my belief that he's buried her somewhere she won't be found — maybe out in the marshes, so that we've no body and thus no chance to charge him with murder."

"You still think he killed her deliberately?"

"I think it's a strong possibility. My men did investigate the rest of the performers and crew at that theater and could find no link or possible motive for wanting the girl dead."

"Or to put Scarpelli out of business?"

He looked at me, then nodded. "As you suggest, to ruin Scarpelli."

"So you're not inclined to believe it was mere equipment failure?"

He shook his head. "I was willing to consider that option until Scarpelli disappeared and the body with him. Why hide a body when her death would almost certainly be ruled accidental? And now we've had to drop the whole thing. With no body and no equipment to prove tampering we've hardly got a case, even if we find him again."

I leaned closer to him. "So how did the illusion work? Did you get him to divulge his secret to you?"

"You can't ask me that. I'm sworn to secrecy," he said, smiling.

"Oh, Daniel, come on. I'm dying to know and I'm not likely to go blabbing it all over New York, am I?" I wrapped my arms around his neck. "Besides, I'm going to be your wife. I'll be able to wheedle these things out of you in your sleep."

"I sincerely hope not," he said. "But if you really must know the whole thing was perfectly simple. It was all a question of levers. The supposed table on which the box rested was hollow. The girl lay flat in the box, and when the lid closed, she depressed a lever and the middle of the box sank down into what appeared to be a flat tabletop. She was also very skinny, of course, and able to suck in her stomach to an amazing degree, so the saw should appear to go almost all the way through the box, but just missed cutting her. Then the saw was removed, the bottom of the box sprang back into place, and out she stepped, unharmed."

"Only this time the lever did not lower the girl where the saw wouldn't reach her."

"Exactly. Scarpelli claimed it must have jammed."

I shuddered. "Horrible. Just horrible. And I'd take it for an accident too, except that I was at the theater again last night and the lock on Houdini's trunk jammed. His wife was nearly suffocated inside. They had to get an ax and —"

"Hold on," Daniel said, moving away from me. "You went to the theater last night? On your own?"

"Well, yes, but —"

"I thought you and I had planned to see Houdini together," he said. "And now you slip away without me?"

"Daniel, don't be sore," I said. "It wasn't like that at all. If you remember I was asked to look after Bess Houdini when she started having hysterics. I took her up to her room and stayed with her until she calmed down. We struck up a nice little friendship and she was so grateful that she invited me to come back and watch the show as her guest." I looked up at him. "Did you want me to refuse a chance to see Houdini perform from the wings?"

"No, of course not," he said quickly. "So how was it?"

"Fascinating, until something went wrong. They were doing their famous Metamorphosis trick, in which Harry is handcuffed and put into a bag, and locked into a trunk and two seconds later he appears, free from all the restraints, and when they open the trunk, Bess is inside the bag. At least that's how it should have gone. But the trunk wouldn't open. They had to send someone upstairs to find the key and in the meantime she ran out of air and they had to break it open with an ax."

"Was she all right?" Daniel aked.

"She regained consciousness, but she was very upset. They were calling for a doctor when I left."

"So two accidents at one theater within the space of a few days," Daniel said thoughtfully. "A little too much coincidence, wouldn't you say?"

"I would," I agreed.

A warning frown appeared on Daniel's face. "And I'll wager you're itching to find out who is behind it."

"I must profess to being a little curious," I said. "In fact I was wondering whether there could possibly be a gang involved. Do gangs charge performers protection money, do

142

you think? Might the equipment going wrong be a warning to pay up? Is that something your men could look into?"

Daniel put his hands firmly on my shoulders. "Stay well away, Molly. Nobody's asked you to poke your nose in and your interference wouldn't be welcome. Especially if you suspect that a protection racket might be involved. Thank heavens you have a case on the books that will keep you occupied. I take it you had a satisfactory meeting with your client last night, before you went to the theater without me?"

"Yes, I did, thank you." I got an odd feeling in the pit of my stomach as I said so. Now that I was actually engaged to Daniel it didn't feel right to be lying to him — not even stretching the truth. Then I reasoned that as a policeman he would have plenty of things he'd have to keep from me. "And I'm sorry about the house you wanted to show me," I added for good measure. "I will come and look at houses with you. It's just that I love my little house. I'm very happy there."

Daniel sighed. "We've been through this before. Don't you see? It's your house, not mine. I'd be the interloper, the intruder. It wouldn't be the right place to start a new life together. I'd never feel quite at home."

"Sure you would," I said. "You'd bring in

all your furniture. We'd make the downstairs back room into your den. We'd buy a new bed." And I smiled up at him as I said this.

"Don't try your feminine wiles with me, Molly Murphy," he said, but he was smiling. "We'll talk about this when we have more time. I am already late for work."

I picked up the food basket from where it had been left on the table. "I'll put this in your kitchen then, shall I? The pork and the salad should go in the ice chest or they'll spoil."

He took it from me. "You're good to me sometimes." He leaned toward me and kissed me gently on the lips. Then he kissed me again, not so gently this time. "September, Molly. My next day off we'll go up to Westchester and set a date."

"Westchester?"

"You'd like to be married from my family home, wouldn't you? It would make a lovely setting in the garden and there's St. Benedict's Church close by."

"You want us to get married in the Catholic Church?"

"Well, I thought — my mother will probably expect it and we were both raised in the faith."

"I'll have to think about it," I said.

We left the house together and parted with

an amicable kiss. But inside my head was whirling. Did I want to get married in church after having rejected it for so long? Did I want a wedding in Daniel's house, where it would be his family, his friends? I had pictured a wedding in the city, with Sid and Gus as my bridesmaids and Ryan looking flamboyant in a long black cape and all my other friends in attendance. But Daniel was picturing the traditional wedding in the country — at his mother's house, no less! As I had said, I'd have to do some thinking about this.

ELEVEN

After I left Daniel I went straight to the theater. I didn't expect to find the Houdinis there, but I hoped that there might be some activity at this hour and someone could tell me where they lived. The Bowery was a regular hive of activity, with women doing their morning shopping, pushcart vendors crying out their wares, and small boys dodging between carts as they played some game. The street itself was clogged with a jam of horse-drawn drays, hansom cabs, the occasional automobile, and trolley cars. The smell of fresh manure and the slops tipped into the gutters were overpowering in the sticky heat, and I was glad when I saw the theater marquee rising above the shops and saloons. The front doors were locked but I went down the alley to the stage door and found Ted, the doorkeeper in attendance.

"You again?" he said. "You keep turning up like a bad penny — and speaking of bad pennies, I'd keep well away from Mr. Irving, the manager, if I were you. He was in some fearful bad temper last night. Not only did he have to stop the show for the second time in a week, and give some people their money back, but it turned out that someone had unloaded quite a few forged banknotes on us. My but he was hopping mad."

"That's terrible," I said. "So what was everyone saying about the accident last night?"

"You know theater folks — superstitious, that's what they are. They were saying that the place is jinxed. First Lily and then Bess."

"And what do you think?" I asked him.

"I'm not paid to have an opinion," he said, "but if you really want to know, I think these illusionists take crazy risks and something's bound to go wrong sometime. Give me a nice song-and-dance act any day." He realized he was chatting with me, stopped, and frowned. "Now what did you want this time?"

"I was upset about what happened to Bess Houdini last night. I wanted to go and see her to make sure she's all right. She quite took to me, you know. So I wondered if you could tell me where they are staying?"

He looked at me appraisingly. "I've been doing this job for a good while and I've learned a thing or two about people and there's something about you I just can't quite fathom out. Something that doesn't quite add up."

"What do you mean?" I asked innocently.

"The first time you showed up, you came back here to collect your lost shawl," he said. "A shawl that had been used to cover a dead girl. What young lady would want her shawl back after that? Any young lady that I know wouldn't want to touch it again, even if it wasn't covered with blood. And then the next time you show up you're supposedly the bosom buddy of Bess Houdini. And you know what else?" His eyes narrowed as he squinted at me. "Every time you've been at this theater, something's gone wrong. So I'm thinking that maybe someone has sent you here — someone who has it in for our theater."

"You think I might be the one who caused the accidents?" I demanded.

He shrugged. "Wouldn't surprise me. Some of these criminal types, they've used pretty young ladies to do their dirty work before now. So perhaps someone's paid you to settle a score with Houdini."

I glared at him. "Settle a score with Houdini. Who might want to do that?"

He touched his nose in a confidential way.

"Remember that affair with Risey on Coney Island? That left bad blood, didn't it?"

"I'm afraid I don't know what you're talking about," I said. "I haven't been in this country for long. Who is Risey?"

"Risey — he's a big noise on Coney Island. He was badmouthing Houdini and calling him a fraud, so Houdini challenged him and locked him in a trunk at Vacca's theater. Risey panicked and they only just got him out in time."

I nodded, digesting this. So Risey, a shady character, had been made to look a fool by Houdini.

"And Risey was heard to say that Houdini better not show his face anywhere near him again," Ted added.

"I see," I said. "Well, I assure you that I am not working for anybody. The first time I came to this theater was with my young man and we witnessed that horrible scene with Scarpelli. My intended went on-stage immediately after the tragedy happened to see if he could help. I went with him. Bess Houdini saw all the blood and had hysterics. I took her away and calmed her down and she became instantly attached to me. She came to my house to thank me and invited me to come and watch the show. That's the whole truth."

Ted stared at me again, then nodded. "Maybe it is, and then again maybe it isn't. I've always found that women make the best liars."

"So you're not going to give me the Houdinis' address?" I asked. He was now beginning to annoy me — partly because he could see through me, I suppose. "I just thought it would be the friendly thing to do to go and check on Bess, seeing that I was there as her guest last night and I was supposed to be meeting her for lunch today, an appointment which she obviously won't be well enough to keep."

This last was a lie, of course, that came to me in a flash of inspiration.

"They've taken a house up in Harlem, from what I hear," he said, "but as to the address, you'd have to ask Mr. Irving, and like I say, he's in no mood to talk nice to anybody today." He turned away, then looked back at me. "Your best bet would be to come back to the theater tonight. Houdini will be doing his act whether his wife is fit to join him or not."

This made sense, but it was Bess I wanted to see and I had seen how protective Houdini was of her. She was now my client, as far as I was concerned. She had hired me to do a job and from what I had seen last night, that job had become all the more urgent.

"Why don't you write her a note and I'll make sure that one of them gets it," Ted said, seeing my frustration.

"That's not going to be any use for my luncheon appointment today, is it?" I said. "Still, I suppose it's better than nothing."

He handed me paper and a pencil and I wrote, "So sorry about what happened last night. If you'd like to talk about it, you know where I live. Yours fondly, Molly." I suspected that Ted would snoop and read it so I left it at that.

As I came out onto the Bowery I passed the front of the theater and saw that a door to the box office was now open. I went inside. A crowd had gathered around the ticket counter and voices were raised. "But we were told we'd be able to see the show for free after it was stopped!" a woman was shouting. "Who is going to give us our money back if the show is sold out?"

I sneaked past them and tried the doors to the theater. They didn't open but there was a passageway down the side, leading to the balcony and the boxes. I went down this, and to my delight found a door that opened into the orchestra stalls. The door closed behind me and I stood, blinking in almost

151

complete darkness. I felt my way forward, row by row, until the orchestra pit opened up in front of me. Then I felt my way around that to the steps at the right and the pass door. It yielded to my touch and I was through to the backstage. Silence and darkness greeted me. The smell of fresh paint mingled with sawdust and stale coffee made me want to sneeze and I put up my hand to my nose to stop myself. I passed through the wings and tiptoed up the little staircase that led to the dressing rooms. There was a glimmer of light coming from somewhere on this hallway and I located the Houdinis' dressing room by the star on the door. It wasn't locked and I went inside. I wasn't quite sure what I hoped to find in there. I closed the door carefully and turned on the electric light switch. Blinding light flooded the room from the bulbs around the mirror and I had to stand with my eyes squeezed shut until I dared to open them again. To be honest I still wasn't used to the glare of electricity, having only gas at my house, which gave a softer and gentler glow.

As I looked around, I was again struck by how Spartan the dressing room was: the counter below the mirror with its jumble of grease paints, cotton wool, and patent medicines; the rack holding Houdini's frock coat and Bess's page-boy outfit; the couch in the corner, a couple of rickety chairs — that was about it. None of their props, I noticed. They were all locked away safely.

I tried the drawer in the dressing table. And then I went through the pockets in the jacket. All they contained was a card: the nine of spades. I smiled to myself. Then I noticed that the waste basket hadn't been emptied. I sorted through cotton wool caked with vanishing cream and makeup, an empty tonic bottle, and then I hit pay dirt. An envelope, addressed to Mr. Harry Houdini, 178 E. 102 Street, New York.

Having had such a stroke of luck, I looked inside to see if perhaps it might have contained something useful like a threatening letter from a gangster — but it was empty. No matter. I had achieved my purpose and gave myself a mental pat on the back. I made my exit from the theater without being detected. There was still a vociferous crowd around the ticket kiosk and I pitied the person inside it.

From the Bowery I took the Third Avenue El, traveling north. It felt as if I were traveling to the ends of the earth, stuck in that hot, crowded compartment with frequent stops and plenty of jostling and shoving. On the way I had time to think about what had happened to Bess and why. I had overheard something that had sounded very much like a threat last night at the theater, when Houdini had told the young man that he was going to hand over something only to his boss. And now today Ted had told me that someone called Risey, who was a big man on Coney Island, had been humiliated by Houdini and had vowed to get even. I knew how New York gangsters bore a grudge and what kind of thing they might do to get even. So Bess had been quite right in her suspicions and had almost paid with her life. If an ax hadn't been nearby, it would have been too late for her.

We crawled northward painfully slowly until finally I alighted at Ninety-ninth Street station. It wasn't a part of the city with which I was familiar and I was interested to see it had the same distinctly Jewish feel to it as the streets of the Lower East Side but without the pushcarts, cacophony of sounds, and ripe smells. I heard Russian and Yiddish spoken and passed a synagogue where old bearded men in black caps stood on the steps in heated conversation with a lot of hand gestures.

The house the Houdinis had rented was nothing fancy — a modest brownstone on a quiet street. Children were playing jump

154

rope on the other side, chanting the same sort of rhymes that we had chanted back in Ireland. This made me wonder whether the Houdinis had any children or, more to the point, whether Bess's nervous condition and collapse might be due to pregnancy. I tapped on the front door and waited.

It was opened by a gaunt-faced old woman. "Ja?" she demanded, eyeing me suspiciously.

"Is this the residence of Mr. Harry Houdini?" I asked.

She stared at me blankly. Then she said in heavily accented English. "Not here."

"Do you know where I might find him?" I asked. "It's Mrs. Houdini I wanted to see. I'm a friend of hers, and I was very upset when I heard what happened to her last night at the theater. I wanted to make sure she was all right."

"Theo?" the old woman turned back and called into the passage, and then rattled off something in a language I couldn't understand.

A young man appeared behind her. At first I thought it was Houdini, then I saw that although the resemblance was striking, this man was younger and bigger.

"Can I help you, miss?" he asked, his hand folded defiantly across a massive chest.

I repeated my request. "I know Bess would want to see me," I added.

He frowned at me. "I never heard her mention your name," he said. "I'm Harry's brother's Theo. They call me Dash, but then you'd know that, wouldn't you — seeing that you're such a good friend of Bess's?"

"Yes, of course," I said. And something I had recently read in a newspaper popped into my head. "You were part of the act, weren't you?"

It was a lucky stab in the dark but he nodded. "Yes, it used to be Harry and I who performed the Metamorphosis, but I was glad to hand it over to Bess. I didn't fit into that trunk so good."

"I can see that." I smiled and so did he.

"Lucky for me, you could say," he said, his smile fading. "That might have been me trapped in there last night and I used to fit in that trunk so tight there was no room to breathe to begin with. I'd have been a goner."

"I was there, watching from the wings. It was frightening," I said.

"I don't know what could have gone wrong." Theo frowned. "That ain't never happened before. Harry's always so careful to double-check the equipment. And of course it would have to be Bess who got

156

stuck in there. She panicked, of course. That makes it worse."

"I hope she's fully recovered," I said. "Is she resting or can she receive a guest?"

"She's not here," Theo said, staring at me, unblinking.

"Can you tell me where she is?"

Theo shook his head. "Some doc's got her under sedation. She was in a bad way last night. Harry was real worried about her."

"Is your brother here or is he with her?"

"He's with her," Theo said, "if he's not at the theater, checking on the props and making sure nothing else goes wrong. I wouldn't be surprised if he didn't want me to join him in the act tonight. There's no way Bess is going to be fit to go onstage."

That, of course, would ruin everything. It seemed I had to see Bess today somehow or I'd be out of a job again.

"Would you tell Bess I called?" I said, biting back my frustration. "My name's Molly. Molly Murphy."

"I'll tell her if I see her," he said. "They might keep her there for a while."

"And where would 'there' be?"

He shrugged. "Some doc's place. That's all I know."

It appeared that all I could do was to go home and wait until Bess Houdini contacted me. And if she was sedated and under a doctor's care, she was hardly likely to be in a mental state to think about her dear friend Molly whom she had hired to protect her husband.

It was now way past midday and my stomach reminded me that I'd had nothing to eat. I told myself that I should probably save the money and try to hold out until I got home, but when I passed a corner delicatessen I gave in and bought myself a pastrami sandwich. Pastrami was another new food for me. I ordered it after asking for ham and getting a funny look from the man behind the counter and the patrons. It wasn't half bad either, served with sour pickles!

The journey back to Greenwich Village seemed to take an eternity. It was stiflingly hot in carriage and the atmosphere grew worse as more and more people crowded in. If I'd been the kind of young lady who swooned, I'd have definitely done so. As it was I sat in my corner and tried to make enough space to fan myself with the empty envelope.

My muslin was a crumpled mess and soaked with sweat by the time I reached my front door. I let myself in and stood in the hallway, relishing the cool darkness. A long drink of water and then a cold wash were in order. Then I noticed that something was stuck in my letter box.

Inside was a note written in a shaky hand.

Molly, I must speak with you immediately. I am at a private clinic at 95th Street and Park Avenue. Could you come right away?

It was signed "Bess."

Twelve

I have to confess that I uttered some words that should never escape from a lady's lips. Actually some swear words that a lady shouldn't even know. But I was alone and I figured they were justified at this point. This day had been one annoyance after another. And now to find that I would have to make that same unpleasant train journey all over again was a last straw. But it had to be done if I wanted this job. And I did want the job. Having witnessed the two accidents with my own eyes, I was itching to sink my teeth into this kind of case. And nobody ever said a detective's work was easy. I took off my crumpled dress, washed it out, splashed cold water over my body, then put on a blouse and skirt before setting out once more.

It was now midafternoon and the heat radiated from the sidewalks and the brick of the buildings. It was like walking through an oven. I passed a horse that had collapsed while pulling a cart loaded with barrels. Small boys stood around staring curiously while the driver cursed and attempted to free it from the harness as it lay dying. I stared at it with pity, wishing there was something I could do, but dead horses were an all too frequent sight in New York in summer. As my train bore me northward again I thought longingly of Central Park and the boating lake and ice cream sodas and I told myself that when I was a married lady, I wouldn't have to venture out on hot afternoons if I didn't want to.

When I alighted, I came down the steps to a lively scene. Small boys had set off a fire hydrant and were running through the jet of water, squealing with glee while a constable tried to drive them off, and grown-ups stood around shouting encouragement and applauding. I stood watching for a while, enjoying the feel of the spray floating toward me, before I dragged myself off. I turned back once, as the scene brought back memories of my childhood in Ireland. I recalled a small skinny girl running through the spray as giant waves crashed onto the beach, daring my brothers to follow me. Then, of course, I remembered the beating I had received afterward for run-

161

ning around in my underclothes and for leading my brothers astray. Life was not all easy, even in those days. I sighed and set off to find the address on Ninety-fifth Street and Park.

I suppose I was expecting a hospital, but the red-and-white brick house wasn't bigger than those surrounding it. In fact I would have walked right past it if a polished brass plate to one side of the front door hadn't caught my eye. It said ASHER CLINIC. Dr. Frederick Asher. I rang the doorbell and it was opened by a nurse in a smart, crisply starched uniform.

"Yes?" she said, appraising me and my somewhat crumpled skirt and cheap straw hat.

"I believe you have a Mrs. Harry Houdini here at the moment?"

"No," she said. "There is nobody of that name here. I'm sorry." She went to close the door.

"Wait." I attempted to put my foot into the closing door. "This is the address she gave me in her note. I was told her doctor wanted her to stay here and rest."

The nurse was staring at me in that impassive way that only nurses can stare. Suddenly it dawned on me. Houdini wasn't their real name. I tried to recall the conversation in the dressing room. Bess had laughed when I suggested that her husband was Italian. She had said that he was Jewish and Houdini was his stage name and his real name was . . .

"Weiss!" I said triumphantly. "Do you have a Mrs. Weiss?"

"We do," she conceded, "but the doctor has ordered complete rest and I am under instruction to admit no visitors."

I fumbled in my purse and produced the note. "She wrote this to me today and asked to see me." As I handed it to her I wondered how Bess had managed to have the note delivered to me past this dragon.

She took the note and examined it. "Please wait here," she said. Clearly I was not to be admitted. There was no shade on the side-walk as I stood and waited, getting more annoyed by the second. Was she going to keep me waiting so long that I gave up and went away? Then I saw someone coming toward me and recognized the well-cut suit, the homburg, and neat blond beard at the same moment that the man recognized me. It was Dr. Birnbaum, an alienist from Germany whom I knew quite well.

"Miss Murphy," he exclaimed, tipping his hat to me. "What an unexpected pleasure."

"Dr. Birnbaum. How good to see you," I replied.

"What brings you to this part of town?" he asked in his clipped German accent. "I hope you are not attempting another dangerous assignment?" He laughed at this, remembering, I presume, the time when he had helped to rescue me from an insane asylum.

"I am attempting to visit a friend who is a patient at this clinic," I said. "My friend sent me a note this morning, asking to see me, but I seem to be unable to get past the dragon of a nurse at the door. She has left me standing in the hot sun for at least ten minutes."

He stroked at that neatly pointed beard in a characteristic gesture. "It so happens that I am here to visit with Dr. Asher. Let us see what we can do, shall we?"

He rapped loudly on the door with his sliver-tipped cane. The same dragon nurse opened the door. When she saw who was standing there, her demeanor changed instantly. She was all smiles, almost coy. "Good morning, Doctor. How very good to see you again. Dr. Asher is expecting you — please do come in."

"There is the small matter of this young lady who is about to expire of heatstroke if

164

she is left in the street much longer." Dr. Birnbaum looked back to me.

"I'm afraid Dr. Asher said no visitors today," she said abruptly. "I'm sorry to have kept you waiting out here. I got waylaid. A difficult patient trying to get out of bed."

"Ah, that would be the young man that Dr. Asher has summoned me to see," Dr. Birnbaum said. "The one who thinks he is a bird? Maybe you should take me straight to him. He sounds like a fascinating case."

"Certainly, Doctor, if you'll come this way," the nurse said, glanced back at me once, then started to walk briskly across the foyer. Dr. Birnbaum motioned quickly for me to follow him into the building. I needed no second urging and slipped into the cool darkness of the marble foyer. The nurse continued up the stairs, her back to me. Dr. Birnbaum followed her. I waited just inside the front door, my heart pounding, not sure what to do next. Find out which room Bess was in, obviously. It wasn't a very large building. It shouldn't be too hard. There would probably be some kind of office or command center in which the patients were listed, but I ran the risk of bumping into another nurse there. It was also possible that the patients' names were on their doors.

I crept up the first flight of stairs and saw

plain wood doors adorned with no name-plates. The landing was pleasingly furnished with bright pictures on the walls, wicker rocking chairs, and a large potted plant — more like a hotel than a clinic.

On the floor above me I heard a door open, and men's voices: Dr. Birnbaum had obviously met Dr. Asher. Then the door closed and I could hear the voices no longer. They were both safely occupied in a patient's room. That left only the dragon woman to be outsmarted. Sure enough, I heard light tapping of feet coming across the floor above me, then starting to come down the stairs. I ducked behind the potted plant. The nurse passed me, her starched skirts almost brushing my bare arm. I held my breath but she continued down to the ground floor, then I heard the sound of a door closing. I was safe for a moment. Cautiously I opened one door after another. Some rooms were empty, some contained sleeping patients. One contained an old lady who sat up excitedly as I came in. "For heaven's sakes!" she exclaimed. "What are you doing on this train, Mabel?"

I gave her an encouraging wave and hastily retreated again. Then I tiptoed up the next flight of stairs to the third floor. There was a broad skylight in the middle of the ceiling, sending rainbow colors onto the polished wood floor below. If Mrs. Houdini was supposed to have quiet, then her room would surely be at the back of the building. The second door I tried revealed a small, dark head curled up amid white sheets. What's more, she was alone. I heaved a sigh of relief, slipped inside, and closed the door behind me. Bess didn't stir. Then, of course, it occurred to me that sedation means sedation. She might remain asleep all day and I was wasting my time.

It was a pleasant room, with a more homey feel than a hospital. The window was open to admit any breeze and looked out onto a small back garden with a big sycamore tree. Birds were chirping and the city seemed far away. I went over and stood beside the bed. Her eyes were closed and I watched the sheet rise and fall with her rhythmic breaths. Now that I was here I didn't like to wake her; in fact I reasoned that trying to wake her from an induced slumber might do more harm than good. But she'd asked to see me as soon as possible, hadn't she? She had taken the trouble to write that note from a hospital bed when she was in a most distressed state. I paced the room uncertainly. If I made it successfully down to the front door without being caught, the chances of my gaining reentry were nil.

At that moment the whole thing was decided for me. Heavy footsteps came up the stairs, tapped across the marble foyer, and straight to the door of the room. I looked around for somewhere to hide, but there was nowhere, no curtain, no closet. I half considered trying to slide under the bed, but there was no time. The door was flung upon and Houdini himself entered. He saw me standing beside Bess, obviously looking guilty, and with a roar of rage he leaped at me.

THIRTEEN

"What are you doing here?" Harry Houdini grabbed my wrist with a grip of such strength that I thought he'd snap my bones. "Who are you? If you are some damned reporter, you'll be sorry you tried this stunt."

"Of course I'm not a reporter," I said. "I came because I got a note from your wife this morning, begging me to come and see her. We are old friends."

"So how come I never met you before?" His grip on my wrist still hadn't lessened. "I know all her friends."

"But we have met before," I said. "The other night at the theater, remember? I had come to see Bess, and I was the one who took her up to her dressing room when she became so upset."

"So how do you know her? How come she has never mentioned you?"

"We met through the theater," I said, trying to think of something plausible while not telling an outright lie.

He eyed me critically. "We've been together for almost ten years in the theater, and I don't recall ever seeing you before."

"Why, we've had a couple of lovely talks this very week," I said. "In fact, she invited me to watch the show from the wings last night. You didn't see me but I was sitting just a few feet from that trunk. I witnessed the whole thing."

"Is that so?" His eyes narrowed. "That kind of thing has never happened to me before, you know. Harry Houdini's equipment doesn't let him down."

Without warning he grabbed me again, this time by the throat. He was only a small man, not quite as tall as I, but he was lifting me off the floor with one hand. "Okay, so who sent you? And you better tell the truth because I can crush your windpipe with no problem, trust me."

"Nobody sent me," I croaked, because he was already putting considerable pressure on my throat. I tried to pry his hand away. It was like trying to remove an iron bar. "Your wife sent me a note to come and see her at the clinic. It's downstairs with the nurse. You can check the handwriting."

"*So Sie haben nichts mit Deutschland zu*

170

tun, gelt?" he asked.

I could feel the blood singing in my head. "Whatever language that is, I don't speak it," I croaked. "Let go of me, before you kill me."

I don't know what might have eventually happened but there was a shriek from the bed behind us. "Harry, what in God's name are you doing? Let go of her this instant!"

He released the hold on my neck. I collapsed onto a nearby chair, coughing and rubbing at my throat.

"I found her in here, poopsie," he said. "She was standing over your bed. I thought maybe she'd come to finish you off."

"Don't be silly, Harry. She was the one I wrote the note to. You know, that note I asked you to deliver for me?" Bess said, "Is that the way you treat my friends?"

"How was I to know she's your friend?" Houdini looked sheepish now. "I never set eyes on her before."

"Sure you have. The other night at the theater." She looked across at me. "I used to know her years ago, before I met you. When I was touring."

"When you were part of the Floral Sisters, Bess?" Harry asked.

"Of course when I was part of the Floral Sisters. Molly was a sweet little kid in those days. Her parents were in the business, isn't that right, Molly?"

Her eyes were pleading with me to agree with her so I had no choice but to nod.

"I'm so glad we chanced to meet up again," Bess went on. "And you know what, Harry, she's trying to get back into the business. I thought we could help her. And now I wake up and find you're trying to kill her."

"How was I to know, baby?" he said sheepishly. "I see a strange woman standing over you. All I can think is that she's come to finish off the job that she started last night. She's come to do harm to me and my wife."

"Well, this is my dear old friend Molly Murphy. And you better apologize to her. Look at her. You scared her half to death," Bess said angrily. If my throat hadn't hurt so much, it would have been funny. Bess, lying frail and tiny in her bed and Harry, whose one hand could have crushed my throat, cowering at her attack on him.

"How was I to know?" he repeated again. "I'm only trying to protect you, babykins. You know that."

"Apologize to her, Harry."

Houdini held out his hand. "I'm sorry, miss, but what was I to think?"

"That's all right. I do understand," I said.

"Especially after what happened last night."

His handshake nearly crushed my hand. This was one extremely strong man. I tried not to grimace.

"I hope I didn't hurt you too much," he said, still looking sheepish. "All I thought was that someone had gotten in here to kill my wife."

"So someone has really been trying to harm you?" I asked.

"Someone sure as hell tampered with that trunk last night," Houdini said. "I got out with no problem, the same way I always do. Those locks on top, they're really just there for show. They should snap open real easy, but one of them wouldn't budge."

"I told you, Harry. Someone jammed that lock," Bess said, propping herself up on one elbow. "And how come the only key was upstairs? What happened to the one you normally carry in your pocket? Someone was trying to kill me, right enough."

"Someone certainly fixed that lock." Harry nodded his head vehemently. "Just like someone tampered with that poor sap Scarpelli's equipment on Tuesday."

"That was awful, wasn't it?" I said. "You haven't heard what happened to her, by any chance, have you? Did she live? I've been looking in the papers but I haven't seen a

173

thing after that one first mention."

He shook his head. "Everyone in the business is talking about it. No one knows what happened or where he went to. Some say he just ran off because of the shame of it, and some say that he ran off because he killed her deliberately and the cops are after him. Some guys even think he stole the body and disposed of it."

"What do you think?" I asked.

Houdini ran his hand through his thick black curls. "What do I think? I think he was rushing to do a trick he hadn't perfected, if you want my opinion. When he heard I was coming back to America and was going to be on the same bill, he knew he had to do something out of the ordinary. As far as I know nobody's tried to saw a lady in half onstage since some guy did it in France years ago. And there are no records of how he did it or whether it was always successful."

"You think it was an accident? A stunt gone wrong?" Bess demanded, her voice rising with hysteria now. "After what happened to me, Harry? Someone is out to get us. Isn't that obvious?"

Houdini nodded thoughtfully. "That certainly was no accident last night," he said. "Bess and me, we've done that stunt every night for the past nine years and never had a problem with it. It's as easy as pie."

"So how did Bess get into the trunk, if the lock was jammed?" I asked.

Bess looked suddenly coy. "We can't give our secrets away. Let's just say it wasn't through the lid."

"And you couldn't get out the same way?"

"Not without revealing to the whole world how it's done. It's our bread-and-butter piece, you know," Bess said.

"So you'd rather die than reveal how it was done?" I looked at her incredulously.

"I thought Harry had the key in his jacket pocket."

"I see." I looked from one of them to the other and a suspicion went through my head. Could this also have been some kind of stunt — some way of heightening the drama? But then Bess's passing out was absolutely genuine. I was close enough to see how horribly pale she was, and how she regained consciousness gasping for breath. And her subsequent hysteria was genuine too.

I eased forward on the chair. "So do you have any idea who might have done this? Has anybody threatened you at all?" Of course I was thinking of the overheard conversation in the theater and the neat young man with blond hair who had pushed past me in the dark hallway. I wondered if he was the same young man who had made what sounded like threats to Bess when he had shown up at their front door and Houdini wasn't home. He'd be back, he had said.

I looked at Houdini, but I didn't detect any reaction as I said the words. Of course I suppose illusionists must have to master their expressions, and if he was being threatened by gangs, he certainly wasn't going to divulge this to a strange woman, or to his wife. So I switched to another tack. "Is there someone in your world you can think of who carries a grudge or is out to get illusionists?"

Harry laughed. "I can name a whole lot of guys who'd love to see the end of me. But none of them was in that theater last night." He perched on the bed beside Bess and took her hand.

"Are you sure? What about the other illusionists on the bill?" I asked.

"Marvo and Robinson? Nah. They're lightweights. They'll never be headliners. And that sword swallower guy they brought in to replace Scarpelli — Abdullah? He was a carnival showman. Nothing to do with us." He paused, and ran his tongue over his lips. "Now Scarpelli — he could have been a threat. We were in Germany together earlier this year and he said some pretty cutting things about me — how my handcuffs were a fraud and how I bribed people from the audience. I had a couple of my guys go over and straighten him out."

"You mean you sent men over to rough him up?" I asked, surprised.

"Something like that. Just to give him a friendly warning."

"Harry, you never told me that!" Bess said.

"I don't tell you a lot of things, sweetie pie. I don't like to worry you. But I'm not having fellow illusionists slandering me. What I usually do is send them a challenge — in public. The same handcuffs, the same stunt — let's see who gets out first. I always win and they're always sore losers. So in answer to your question, yes there are plenty of guys who would like to get even with me."

"Including someone called Risey, from Coney Island?"

Houdini laughed. "That old guy? He was pathetic. I locked him in a box and I had to rescue him when he started hollering for help. He was in a real panic, I can tell you. Talk about egg all over his face."

"But I heard he is a powerful man on Coney Island and he had sworn to get even with you."

"Maybe he had, but that was a while ago. He's all talk."

It suddenly struck me how dense I had been. "The sword swallower they brought in at the last minute. He came from the carnival on Coney Island. You don't think there's any connection, do you? You don't think that Risey sent him to get even with you?"

Harry frowned. Clearly he hadn't considered this before. Then he shook his head. "Couldn't be. The guy just got here and you know what? Whoever did this would have to be familiar with my act. How would an outsider know where the key was kept in my jacket? I've never had to use it until last night. Had to be one of us."

"And yet you don't suspect the other performers?"

"Nah." He shook his head again and patted Bess's hand. "They're both decent guys. I'd trust my old mother with them."

"Speaking of your old mother, I went to your house looking for you. I hadn't realized she lived with you."

"She's just visiting," Bess said quickly. "Usually she lives with Harry's sister, Gladys, or sometimes she stays with his brother Leopold, the doctor."

"You have a brother who is a doctor?"

Harry nodded. "That's right. Lives on the Upper East Side so he's come to visit us a couple of times. And my younger brother came up from Atlantic City, where he was performing to be with us too," Harry said. "Did you meet my brother Dash? We're a real close family, Bess can tell you that."

"They sure are. Harry treats his mother like a queen."

"She deserves it," Harry said proudly. "She had to raise us kids alone in a new country when my father died. I promised him I'd look after her and I have. When I come back from this next tour in Europe, I'm going to buy her a house — a real fancy place, just like this clinic. In a good neighborhood in New York."

"My, you must be doing well," I said.

"Oh, we are," Bess said, gazing at Harry adoringly. "Harry gets paid a fortune over in Europe. He only came home to see his mother, didn't you, Harry? Otherwise he'd have stayed over there."

He sort of half nodded, then turned away. I was watching Harry and there was something in the way he looked away quickly that made me wonder. If he could make so much more money in Europe, why exactly had he left at the height of his success and come

179

home? Was it only just to see his old mother?

Bess propped herself up and leaned against her husband. "Did you know that the Tsar of Russia wanted to make him his right-hand man. He thinks Harry is in touch with the spirits or the supernatural or something." She gazed up at Harry and laughed.

"I should have stayed. Maybe they'd have made me a prince. Given me a palace or two," Houdini said jokingly.

"You know very well there was no way I'd have ever lived in Russia," Bess said angrily. "And to tell you the truth, I've no wish to go back to Germany."

"I told you, poopsie, you can stay in England next time I go over there. All right? Now don't get yourself into another state."

I got to my feet. "Maybe I should be going. I know that Bess is supposed to have absolute quiet."

I looked across at Bess. If she had summoned me so urgently, was she going to let me go again? Was this meeting just designed for me to meet Harry, and nothing more?

"Thank you for coming, Molly," Bess said, holding out her hand to me.

In the manner of old friends I took it and bent to kiss her on the cheek. "My pleasure, Bess. I'll come and visit you again any time you want."

"I look forward to that. I hope to be out of this crummy place by the end of today, don't you think, Harry?"

"Crummy place? Bess, this is costing a fortune. And the doctor thinks your nerves need treating."

"Yes, but it's creepy here. I'd rather be at home. You'll ask the doctor, won't you?"

"Whatever you say, babykins. If you're sure you're well enough to go home."

"I'm feeling much better. So maybe you'll come and see me at the house then, Molly." She was still clinging tightly to my hand. In spite of her frail appearance she also had a grip of steel. And she was staring hard at me, her eyes imploring. "You know the address, don't you?"

I nodded and started to walk toward the door, unsure how to prolong this interview even though it was obvious Bess didn't want me to leave. Was there some kind of hint I should have picked up from Bess upon which I should be acting?

I paused at the doorway, waiting for her to say more. I decided to give her one more chance to say something. "Mr. Houdini, do you think that maybe you should mention what happened last night to the police — if you really believe that someone was trying

181

to interfere with your act, then that's a crime, isn't it? It could even have been murder."

"We don't want the police involved," Harry snapped, dismissing me with a wave of his hand. "I'm only here for a couple of weeks longer. What kind of crowd would we get with police tramping all over the theater? Likely as not they'd shut us down. Don't worry yourself, Miss — Murphy — is it?"

"Just call her Molly," Bess said, "since she's going to be your friend as well."

"So don't worry yourself, Molly. Believe me, I'm going to be taking extra care in future, double-checking everything — until I get back on that liner sailing for Europe."

"You're going to perform tonight at the theater then?" I asked. "Even though Bess is laid up like this?"

"I can't let my American fans down and Mr. Irving has been good to us in the past. And now he's paying us good money. Besides, I can do the act without her," he said. "Of course I can't do the Metamorphosis by myself, nor the mind-reading part, but the public comes to see the handcuffs, don't they, baby?"

"But you always said that the mind reading puts them in the right mood to believe anything, didn't you?" Bess said, looking up at him adoringly.

"Your brother says he used to do the Metamorphosis with you," I suggested. "Maybe he could help you out."

Houdini laughed. "That was when he was a skinny kid. Have you seen him now? There's no way he'd fit into that trunk these days. Besides, he's got his own act now. Know what he calls himself? Hardeen. Don't they say that imitation is the sincerest form of flattery?"

"So he does what you do?"

"Pretty much. Handcuffs, escapes, all the same kind of thing. Doing okay at it too. Of course he's not in my league yet."

The brother who just arrived in town and who called himself Hardeen. I wondered if he now saw Houdini as a rival, maybe.

"Harry, I've just had the cleverest idea," Bess said suddenly. "Molly wants to get back into show business. Why don't you use her in the act, just until I'm on my feet again? I'm sure she's a quick learner and we could teach her the simplest of the mind-reading tricks."

Houdini looked at me critically, then burst out laughing. "You want to use her in the act? Are you crazy? Look at her."

I didn't find this very flattering, I can tell you. I may not be petite but I'm not ugly.

183

"What do you mean? She'd look fine in the right costume and makeup," Bess said.

"But she's too big. She's as big as I am. There's no way she could get into the trunk."

"Of course not," Bess said. "I'm not saying she could do the Metamorphosis. You could do that other stunt by yourself. You know, the one where they put the handcuffs on you and chain up the trunk? The one you did when I didn't come along with you to Russia. The audience loves that one."

"I suppose I could," Harry admitted.

"And she could help you with the mind-reading tricks I do, and act as your assistant."

"I could never teach her the signals in time."

"I'm a fast learner," I said, although I wasn't sure this was true. "I could give it a try."

"You do need an assistant, Harry," Bess said. "You always say that it helps to have a pretty girl onstage for the audience to watch, so that they take their eyes off you."

"She doesn't have a costume, does she?" I could tell he was now fishing for excuses. He really didn't want me but he was scared of crossing Bess. "She'd never fit into anything of yours."

184

"That would be no problem, Mr. Houdini," I said. "I have friends who know a good theatrical dressmaker. I'm sure he could make me something appropriate."

He opened his mouth and tried to think of something else to say, then sighed.

"I know, but — someone who hasn't been in the business? I'm the star performer, Bess. I don't work with amateurs."

"Fine. It was just a suggestion," Bess said angrily. She turned away from him and faced the wall. "But I had a bad scare last night, Harry. The doc says I was lucky to come through the way I did. So I don't know how long it will be before I can trust myself on that stage again and I kind of think that the audience will soon get tired of just watching you standing there with a bunch of handcuffs." She turned back to him. "They like variety, Harry. They like things they can't explain. And they like a pretty girl. You know that."

Harry looked from her face to mine. Bess reached out and took his hand. "For my sake, Harry? Couldn't you at least give it a try? Just a try?"

She was gazing up at him imploringly. For a long moment there was silence. Then he said gruffly, "Okay, babykins. I guess I could at least give her a try."

185

Whether I liked it or not, it appeared I was about to become a magician's assistant.

FOURTEEN

I was already having serious misgivings by the time I presented myself at the house on 102nd Street the next morning. The day had not started particularly well. I had already dragged Ryan out of bed and made him take me to his dressmaker friend who turned out to be a gorgeous young man with eyelashes any woman would kill for. He was introduced as Daniel, which I found amusing as he was about as different as possible from my future groom, and I knew exactly what that future groom would think of him.

"Darling, what am I supposed to do with her?" Daniel asked, looking at Ryan in despair after we had explained what I needed. "She has a waist the size of an elephant."

"I do not," I said angrily. "It's just that I've never seen fit to wear a corset."

"And it shows, darling, it shows. I suppose I could build you something with

187

plenty of whalebones, but you'll have to absolutely pour yourself into it."

"It doesn't have to be like the French Follies," I said hastily. "I don't intend to cancan or striptease. I just have to give an impression of glamour onstage and to distract the audience from what the illusionist is doing."

Daniel shook his head. "But glamour demands an hourglass figure."

"You are the master," Ryan said. "If anyone can create her an outfit, you can."

"Flatterer," Daniel responded. He gave a dramatic sigh. "Oh, well, I suppose I'll see what I can do."

"And I do need it in a hurry," I pointed out.

Daniel rolled his eyes. "You don't need me, you need a miracle-working saint. You Irish know your saints, don't you? Who is the patron of producing instant glamorous outfits?"

I looked at Ryan and we laughed, thus breaking the tension.

"Don't worry, he fusses a lot but he'll do it, and you'll look fabulous," Ryan assured me as we came away. "He really is a genius. I absolutely insist that he makes all the costumes for my productions."

So I had what was probably going to be a horribly expensive costume being made for me with a grudging promise that it would be ready for a fitting in the morning. Now all I had to do was learn how to be an illusionists' assistant in one lesson. How did I get myself into these things? I wondered.

The day was not quite as stiflingly hot as the one before and I was altogether in a better mood when I alighted from the train at Ninety-ninth. That mood seemed to be radiated from the other people on the street. Old men were sitting on stoops, windows were open with bedding draped over sills to air. The girls were still playing jump rope games and women paused from their sweeping and polishing to look up with a smile, remembering the days when they had time for games.

Houdini's brother opened the door to me at their house. "Oh, it's you again," he said. He didn't look too thrilled to see me.

"Has Bess come home from the hospital?"

"Yes, but she's really weak. My mother is making her some Hungarian beef soup."

"And your brother is here?"

"Ehrie? Yes, he's with her."

I hadn't heard him called that name before. "Ehrie?" I asked.

He nodded. "That's his name — Ehrich. I guess that's where he got the name Harry from for his act. Well, I suppose you'd bet-

189

ter come in."

He led me into a dark hallway and then opened the door to a front parlor. It was truly hideous — dark, overstuffed, and Victorian at its worst with velvet sofas, chairs with skirts to them to hide the offending legs, dried flowers and birds under glass domes, in fact not an inch of space that hadn't been decorated with something. Then I remembered that this was a rented house and forgave the Houdinis for the awful taste. It was also clearly a traditional front parlor, the type that is never used, except for weddings and funerals. The pillows looked as if no back had ever leaned against them. I perched uneasily on the edge of the nearest chair and waited.

Soon brother Dash returned. "They want you to go up to the bedroom," he said with a tinge of horror in his voice.

As I started up the stairs the mother's face peered from the kitchen. She shot Dash a sharp question in whatever language they spoke — I wasn't sure if it was Hungarian or Yiddish or a mixture of both. He answered and she gave me a look of pure venom. Clearly I wasn't exactly welcome in the Weiss's household. I wondered if they were Orthodox Jews and I was breaking some kind of taboo. I'd had a brief encounter with Orthodox Judaism early in my time in New York and had learned about all those rules and foods and different sinks. But then Harry and Bess had traveled all over Europe in their profession. They'd have learned to eat and sleep on the road in a variety of circumstances. And I also remembered that Bess wasn't even Jewish. So that couldn't be the reason that Harry's mother resented my presence. I wondered what they'd told her.

Bess was lying propped among pillows. She still looked very pale, but her dark eyes lit up when she saw me. "Here she is, Harry. Here's our girl," she said. "Come on in, Molly."

"Your mother and brother don't seem to think I should be here," I said, coming over to take her hand and nodding to Harry, who stood at the window.

"They don't like the idea of bringing an outsider into the act. Can't say I do either," he said. "I've been thinking about it all night and I am not at all happy about this idea. I can't see how it's going to work. In fact, it's a stupid idea."

"Just give it a try, Harry," Bess said, grasping at his hand. "You promised, Harry. You'd promised you'd give it a try. That's all I'm asking." She gazed up at him. "Let's teach her the basic things and if she can't do it, then fine. You'll have to go on solo."

He nodded. "Right, let's get to work then. The first thing you have to learn is how to move. Have you noticed how the girls move onstage — everything is big and dramatic. They walk like this —" and he crossed the room in long slinky strides. "And always the arm gestures. Light and airy and graceful." He demonstrated those. "And draw the audience's attention to yourself and your shape." He ran his hand gracefully tracing the shape of a supposed female body. It was rather funny to watch this little man pretending to be an alluring female, but I didn't smile.

"Now you do it."

I felt horribly embarrassed as I strutted across the bedroom, gestured to Houdini, drew attention to my own costume. It wasn't until I saw him grinning that I realized how awful I must look.

"Well it's quite obvious you've never done this before, isn't it? You were never a dancer or acrobat, I take it?"

"No, I wasn't."

"That's pretty obvious. Pity. Most illusionists' assistants can do all the acrobatic moves. The odd cartwheel or split never hurts. But there's nothing we can do about that."

"Teach her the signals, Harry," Bess said. "That's the most important thing she needs to know."

"Signals?" I asked.

Harry paced uncertainly. "I'm not sure about this, honeykins. Giving away our secrets to a stranger — to someone we hardly know?"

"I told you, I knew her family when she was a little kid," Bess said. "They were good to me." She certainly lied very smoothly. There was no trace of hesitancy in her voice.

"Yes, but that was a long time ago. You're out of touch for years, then she pops up again, out of the blue, she doesn't have an inkling about how to move onstage, and suddenly she wants to be my assistant." He was staring hard at me. "I don't believe she ever had anything to do with the business, if you want my opinion. So how do we know she's not some kind of plant?"

"What do you mean?" Bess demanded.

"I mean how do we know she's not working for a rival illusionist trying to get his hands on our secrets?"

"She's not working for any rival illusionist, Harry, I promise you."

"How can you promise me? You've been

out of touch with her for years!" Harry was yelling now, his face red with anger. "And if she's not working for a rival, how do we know she's not one of these damned female newspaper reporters. If we show her our stunts you might find them printed all over tomorrow's front page for all the world to see. 'How I out-tricked Houdini into revealing his secrets.' Is that what you want, Bess?"

"I assure you I'm not —" I began, but he cut me off.

"I'm not buying it, Bess. I'm not giving away things we've worked on for years."

"But you promised to give her a try, Harry. You promised." She was sounding close to tears now.

"I said that yesterday because I didn't want you making a scene at the clinic, but it never felt right to me. And you know what? It doesn't feel right now. I don't trust her. I'm not doing it, Bess. I've made up my mind and that's that."

"And if I don't come back into the act for a while?" Bess's voice was yelling too now.

"Then I'd rather go it alone. Or maybe I'll find a new assistant."

"Oh, no!" Bess said, sitting bolt upright. "I'm not having you working with a strange girl, Harry. I know what you're like."

"Honey, babykins, how can you say that?"

She wagged a finger at him. "I've seen those showgirls try to get their claws into you. I've seen them try to lure you to their dressing rooms, and invite you out for a bite to eat when I've been under the weather. Don't think I'm completely blind, Ehrich Weiss, because I know."

"Baby, not in front of your friend . . ."

Bess was now really riled up. "Oh, so she's my friend now, is she? A minute ago she was a complete stranger and someone I couldn't trust because she was here to steal our act!"

I was feeling horribly uncomfortable and decided that something had to be done before their marriage was ruined.

"Stop this, please," I said. "It would be so much simpler if your husband knows the truth, Bess. I can see why he doesn't want to trust me. I wouldn't want to admit a strange person to my act when there have already been two horrible accidents in a week." I turned to Harry and looked him straight in the eye. "I think you should know the truth, Mr. Houdini, and if you tell me to get lost, I'll go."

Bess held up her hand and started to say something but I shook my head. "The truth is, Mr. Houdini, or Mr. Weiss, if you'd rather, that your wife came to me in great distress. She was sure that someone was trying to kill you. As it turned out it appears that someone was trying to kill her, or at the very least wreck your act. So she asked for my help. You see, I'm a private investigator."

"You're what?" Harry said.

"A detective, Harry, she's a lady detective," Bess said. "I was only doing it for you. I wanted her to find out who was out to get you. I wanted to protect you because I love you."

And she broke into sobs.

"Babykins. I'm sorry." Harry sank onto the bed beside her and took her into his arms. Really, were theater folk always this dramatic?

"I did it for you, Harry," she repeated. "Don't be mad at me. I thought you'd nix the idea of having a detective watching out for you, so I invented this crazy scheme. Pretty dumb of me, huh?"

He sat beside her, stroking her hair, gazing into her face. "You're a real sweetie pie, you know that?"

"I knew you'd never tell the police that you were in danger and I had to protect you somehow so I thought a lady detective would work into the act real nice. I was going to pretend I wasn't feeling well but then that awful accident happened, and it just proved what I'd been afraid of all along. So please say, yes, Harry. For my sake."

He stroked her hair and smiled down at her. "I'd do anything for you, babykins, but what good is some dame going to be onstage with me? No offense, ma'am, but if someone has rigged my equipment how the hell are you going to know that?"

"Language, Harry," Bess said.

"I expressed the same concerns to your wife, Mr. Houdini," I said. "Where I think I can help you is more likely to be offstage, keeping my eyes open and asking the right questions. But I needed a valid reason to be with you all the time."

He nodded. "Can't do no harm, I suppose, unless you look so bad up there that you turn my act into a comedy."

"I'll try not to," I said.

"So you'll do it, won't you, Harry?" Bess insisted. "If he's tried something once, he could try again."

Harry shrugged. "If you want a detective onstage with me, watching out for me, then okay, you got it."

Bess gave me a triumphant smile as she hugged him. Harry turned to look up at me.

"I could tell right away you'd never been a performer in your life," he said.

FIFTEEN

There was silence in the bedroom while we all recovered from the excess of emotion. Then Bess lay back among her pillows, looking quite at ease again. "So hadn't you better start teaching her the signals if you want her to go on with you tomorrow night?"

"Tomorrow?" I said as this reality dawned on me. "You think I could be ready to go on by tomorrow?"

"For the mind-reading act," Houdini said. "We have a system of signals. You saw when I went down into the audience and I had someone pick a card? There's no mind reading involved. I told Bess what card it was by the things I did and the movements I made. It's a system as old as the hills and it's really simple. For example, supposing the person in the audience selected the ace of clubs. I would just happen to touch that person's shoulder. That would signify to Bess that it was an ace. And if I was standing with the

199

right foot in front of the left — that means clubs. If I touch my hair it means the next word matters. Nothing to it except for learning the signals and watching carefully. It has to be done ever so casually — the merest brush of a hand. The sort of gesture that people don't even notice."

"Wait a minute," I said. "But part of the time she had a hood over her head. Can she really see through that blind?"

"Of course not," he said. "We have members of the audience test that hood. It has to be the real thing."

"Then how does she know what objects you're holding?"

"Ah." When he smiled he looked like a mischievous imp. "Then we use the verbal clues. We've a whole long list of them. Let me show you. Bess, I'm standing next to a lovely lady here, so pray tell what object she is holding in her hand?"

"A purse," Bess said quickly.

I looked at them, perplexed. "I'm afraid I don't understand."

"Again we have a great long system of code words. If I use the word 'pray' I am referring to 'purse.' If I use 'please' it's 'handkerchief.' 'Say' means 'money,' and so on. We've about twenty items that usually come up at these performances. If it's something unusual — and sometimes they try to trick us — then those same words will be used as letters, to spell out the word or enough of the word for Bess to guess. Supposing someone gave me a child's toy soldier. "I'd say 'Pray be quick,' and I've spelled out 'T O Y.' "

"Then I'd say, 'I'm getting the feeling that it's some kind of toy. . . .' and wait for more clues, and Harry would then spell enough of soldier until I get it." Bess nodded at me encouragingly. "But we rarely get something difficult. It's usually watches, jewelry, handkerchiefs, smelling salts —"

"What is the word for smelling salts?" I asked, intrigued now.

"Speak," Houdini said. "So I'd say, 'Speak up, my dear.' "

"I see." I nodded. "That's really clever."

"I hope you really are a fast learner," he said, "because I've a lot to teach you and not much time."

"I'm ready to start now if you are," I said. I opened my purse and took out my notebook.

Harry shook his head. "Oh, no. You're going to have to keep it all in your head. I'm not having my signals leaving this house. I keep the diagrams for all my illusions under lock and key all the time."

"They live in a suitcase under the bed," Bess chimed in and got a frown from Houdini.

"Do you think that was what someone was trying to steal?" I asked. "Bess said that someone tried to break into your house one night, then ran away when you got up and turned on the light."

He frowned, shot her a quick look of annoyance, then shook his head. "Bess gets nervous at night if she hears the slightest noise. If he was trying to break in, then he was a regular burglar, and obviously I scared him off."

As he said it I picked up a strange undercurrent and got the feeling that there was something that he hadn't told his wife. Again my thoughts went to gangs and protection money. Somehow I would have to persuade Daniel to have his men find out more for me, because for once I agreed with Daniel. This was not something I wanted to investigate myself.

Houdini didn't stop drilling me until it was time for him to leave for the theater. He would have to perform alone tonight, but I was told to watch from backstage.

"Make sure you double-check all your props, Harry!" Bess called after him. "Take care of yourself."

As I sat in the train going home I considered again what a ridiculous task I had undertaken. How could I possibly be expected to protect Houdini? How could I possibly be ready to go onstage as his assistant? I found myself repeating over and over, in time to the rhythm of the train, "right foot forward means spades. Eyebrows raised means . . . mouth open once quickly means . . ." How on earth was I going to master them, as well as moving gracefully like one who is a trained performer, not tripping over my feet and generally looking like a convincing magician's assistant — at the same time as watching out for any potential threat. It seemed like such a daunting task that I was almost ready to go to the theater this evening and tell him that I was quitting.

And I realized another thing, as the train slowed for my station: the subject of money had not come up. I was doing all this without any assurance that Houdini was going to pay me for my efforts.

My intention was to go home, change my clothes, grab a bite to eat, and then go back to the theater to watch again from the wings — and this time to take notes. But as I reached Patchin Place the door opposite opened and Sid's head poked out.

"We've caught you, you elusive creature," she said. "Where have you disappeared to? Are you still working on that case you told us about?"

"I'm afraid so."

"The one involving the theater? Are we to see you as another chorus girl?"

"You know I can't divulge the secrets of my cases," I said.

"How annoying," Sid said. "Does that mean you will not be free this weekend?"

"I'm afraid not."

Sid pouted. "Can't you put your work aside until Monday, because, you see, Gus and I have been invited to a cottage in Newport. Doesn't that sound divine? Away from all this heat and noise and two days at the ocean?"

"It does sound wonderful," I agreed, "but I really can't get away. I'll be thinking of you."

"But Molly — I used the word 'cottage' but you know that it's really a mansion. One of Gus's many cousins has married well. Think of the strawberries and cream and croquet on the lawns."

"I really am sorry, Sid," I said. "I'd really love to come but I've already arranged things with my client to be on hand tomorrow and Sunday."

"You are so annoying sometimes," Sid said. "Why did you have to take up such a demanding profession? I hope you'll have more time for leisure when you are Mrs. Daniel Sullivan. He was looking for you this afternoon, by the way. Pounded on our door and demanded to know where you were."

"He didn't?"

"He most certainly did. When Gus said she didn't know, he almost accused her of hiding you in the hall closet."

"Oh, dear. He is tiresome at times, isn't he?" I said. "Did he say what he wanted?"

"No, but I believe he slipped a note through your front door."

I sighed. "I'd better go and see then, hadn't I? I'm really sorry about your lovely invitation. I wish I could join you, but I can't."

I opened my front door and removed Daniel's note from the letter box.

Dear Molly,

I came to your house in the hope of finding you at home for once. I have managed to wangle myself two days off and thought we might go up to my mother's in Westchester. I have been neglecting her of late. It will be a welcome escape from the heat and we'll be able to formulate our wedding plans in peace. I can introduce you to the church and the priest on Sunday morning. I'll come by to pick you up at nine in the morning so that we can take the nine forty-five to Westchester.

Your future bridegroom,
Daniel Sullivan.

P.S. One of my men tells me that the doorkeeper at Miner's Theatre has reported you as a suspicious character. I do hope [and these words were underlined three times] that you are not poking your nose into the strange goings on at that theater, expressly against my wishes.

"St. Michael and all the angels," I muttered and stood there, staring blankly at Daniel's aggressive black script on the paper. What in heaven's name was I going to do about this? "Daniel is going to be furious" was the first thing that flashed through my mind. Then I asked myself why I was so worried. He had given me very little notice, after all, and I was still leading my own life. Clearly I had to let him know that I wasn't coming so that I didn't have to face an ugly scene on my doorstep at nine o'clock the next morning.

The easiest thing would be for me to write Daniel a note and then pay some street urchin to deliver it for me. I have been called many things in my life but I've never been known as a coward. I would have to tell Daniel to his face. I sighed. I had planned to go straight back to the theater for the start of the performance. But then I reasoned that Houdini's act was not until after nine o'clock. I would have time to go to Daniel's apartment on Twenty-third Street first and then the Broadway trolley would take me straight to the theater.

I changed rapidly into the black-and-white striped two-piece, spread some dripping on bread, and was out of the door again. And to think I could have been spending the weekend at one of the famous Newport "cottages"! Then a wicked thought came to me. I could tell Daniel I had agreed to go away with Sid and Gus this weekend, to Gus's cousin in Newport. It would be so much simpler than trying to explain that I was working, and at least nobody could disapprove of Newport. But as well as not being a coward, I am also not a liar. All those years of getting the strap across my

207

backside for telling fibs certainly left their mark!

I was admitted to Daniel's building by Mrs. O'Shea.

"Well, don't you look a treat." She smiled at me approvingly. "Going out on the town with your young man?"

"No, I'm afraid not. I'm going out with friends, but I hoped to see him. Is he at home?"

"I believe I heard his feet on the stairs a short while ago. The poor dear man works himself to a frazzle," she said. "And he's been looking so worried lately. He's been through a lot, hasn't he, what with being disgraced and losing his poor dear father and all. I'll be so glad when he has a good woman to look after him."

Of course this made me feel even worse about what I was going to do. Daniel needed a weekend in the country, and he needed to see his mother. And we should be planning our future together. It was usually the woman who complained that her man was too busy to pay her the proper amount of attention. In our case I was more guilty than he.

I took a deep breath and knocked on his door. His anticipatory smile when he opened it was like a dagger into my heart.

"Molly! Don't tell me you've come to make me dinner again? Or are you going to use your feminine wiles to persuade me to take you to a restaurant?"

"I'm sorry, Daniel. I can't stay. I just stopped by to tell you that I can't come to Westchester with you this weekend."

"What do you mean? Why not?"

"I" — another deep breath — "this case I told you about. I have already set up appointments with my client for both Saturday and Sunday."

"Can't you rearrange them?"

"I really can't."

He was scowling now. "What could be so important that it has to take place on Saturday and Sunday?"

"I'm sorry, but you know I can't discuss a case with you any more than you'd discuss your cases with me. I have committed to work for my client this weekend and that's that."

"Really, Molly, this is becoming ridiculous," Daniel snapped. "This sort of obsession with work was fine when you were alone in the city and struggling to make ends meet. But you don't have to anymore. Soon we'll be married and I'll be providing for you. Tell your client that something else came up, for God's sake."

I felt myself flushing as I faced him defiantly. "I took the case. I can't back out now. I wouldn't expect you to put aside one of your investigations because I wanted you to come shopping with me, would I?"

"I hardly think you can compare my professional life to yours, or compare a chance to plan our wedding to an afternoon's shopping," he said in clipped voice.

"As to our professional lives, I don't see a difference," I said. "You know how often you are required to work for days without a break, and at weekends too. And anyway, this case will soon be over. Two more weeks at the most. Then you can have my undivided attention, I promise."

"And you have given me your word that this will positively, absolutely be the last assignment you take on, haven't you?"

I was about to nod, but I was beginning to get angry with this bullying treatment. "So you're prepared to look after me from this moment onward, are you?" I demanded in the same aggressive tone that he was using. "Because somehow I have to eat between now and the wedding and I have no other source of income. And I'll need a trousseau, won't I? And a wedding dress. I'd not be expecting my groom to pay for those and I have no family, as you well know."

He swallowed and took a half step back at my sudden attack. "Molly, please. I only want what's best for you and I'm sick of worrying about what might happen to you next. Besides, you'll need time to plan a wedding and have a trousseau made," he continued. "I'm sure you haven't had a chance to find a good dressmaker in New York and I haven't had any indication that you're a keen seamstress."

I laughed. "I can patch and darn when completely necessary. That's about it."

"That's why it's such a pity you can't come with me tomorrow. My mother is a dab hand with a needle. If you stay up with her for a while, she'd be happy to help you with the wedding dress and all the rest. You won't even need to pay a dressmaker."

Oh, Lord — he'd reminded me of my fitting with the other Daniel in the morning. Wouldn't this Daniel be surprised if he knew that I had already hired a top-notch dressmaker to make me something that involved spangles and a lot of whalebone? I suppose I must have grinned.

"What's so funny?" he asked.

"Me, picturing myself making a wedding dress," I said hastily. "I must go, Daniel.

Please give my fondest regards to your mother and tell her I hope to see her soon."

He nodded and gave me a perfunctory peck on the cheek.

"Don't be so grouchy when you can't get your own way," I said. "I would enjoy staying with your mother when the weather is like this and I'd even be prepared to learn how to sew and cook. There, I can't say fairer than that, can I?"

"I suppose not." He managed a smile.

"Now I have to get to work. I don't want to be fired from my last case."

"Oh, and Molly," he said, grabbing my arm as I turned to go. "You read the postscript to my note, didn't you? I don't know what you thought you were doing at that theater against my express wishes, but I don't want you going near it again. It was highly embarrassing to have one of my men report that a theater stage doorkeeper had described a certain Miss Molly Murphy as lurking about suspiciously and up to no good."

He waited for me to say something. Wisely I stayed silent, so he continued. "Just exactly what made him suspicious of you?"

"Daniel, it's a storm in a teacup," I said. "I told you that Bess Houdini invited me to see the show from backstage. What is so strange about that?"

"And then when the second accident happened — to the Houdinis this time, you thought you'd come back and ask a few questions?"

"I may have asked one or two." I gave a nonchalant shrug. "I was worried about poor Bess. So I actually went back to the theater to find out where she was staying so that I could go and see if she was fully recovered."

"Hmmph," Daniel said. "Go and see if she was fully recovered in your case means go and do some snooping, I suspect."

"Not at all. It was an act of mercy."

"There must have been something more than that to make the stage doorkeeper suspicious enough to report you to a policeman."

"All right, if you really want to know, that old man was suspicious because he thought I was a newspaper reporter. He told me so. He thought I was trying to get a scoop on Houdini." I returned the peck on the cheek. "I must run."

Daniel sighed. "Why couldn't I have chosen a young lady who played the piano and practiced embroidery?" he called after me.

"You could have done so, remember?" I

called back. "At least I'm not boring."

"That I don't dispute," he said, laughing as I disappeared down the stairs.

SIXTEEN

I arrived at the theater after the show had started.

"Good evening, Ted," I said to the door-keeper, giving him an innocent smile. "Mr. Houdini is expecting me. I'll go on through, shall I?"

He scowled at me. "Yes, he told me you'd be turning up again like the proverbial bad penny. But let me give you a word of warning, girlie — if all this chumminess is in aid of getting a good story, you'll be sorry. Guys like Harry Houdini — they don't take well to being hoodwinked."

"I can assure you that I'm not here to hoodwink anyone," I said, "least of all Mr. Houdini. Why have you been so suspicious of me? Have other people been coming around, trying to bother the Houdinis? Other, less desirable sort of people, shall we say?"

His eyes narrowed and he squinted at me.

"Less desirable than what? The usual riffraff we get around at the stage door? There's been plenty wanting to get an exclusive interview with him, that's for sure."

"I meant anyone you suspected had come to threaten him — like that young man we saw the other night — the one you said must have come from front of house."

"You know what's wrong with you, don't you," he grunted. "You ask too many questions. It ain't healthy. Curiosity killed the cat, remember that."

"I'll remember," I said.

I walked on into the theater. If that wasn't a direct warning, what was? Old Ted knew something and he wasn't about to tell me. My only reassurance was that he had spoken to the police at some stage, when he had reported me as a suspicious character. I could only hope that he had reported any other suspicious characters at the same time and that the police were now investigating.

Music was playing and the stage was ablaze with light as I entered the backstage area. A burst of applause came from the audience as a dove flew across the stage. Marvo was currently performing.

I jumped as a hand grabbed my forearm.

"Where do you think you're going, miss?" a voice hissed in my ear. It was one of the

216

stagehands I had encountered before — the surly one. Ernest, I believe his name was. "No outsiders permitted during the show."

"I'm here because Houdini asked me to come."

"What for?"

"Not that it's any business of yours, but I'm a friend of the family. Go up to his dressing room and ask him if you don't believe me."

"I'm not allowed up to performers' dressing rooms. You must know that. Besides, I'm working."

"Then you'll have to trust my word, won't you? Now please let go of me."

Renewed applause signaled the end of Marvo's act and the side curtains moved as he swept off past us. Ernest let go of my arm and rushed to remove Marvo's props from the stage. I took the opportunity to get away and position myself where I had been sitting the night before. I could sense Ernest taking another look at me, but he didn't say any more. Clearly I was an object of suspicion for more than one of the workers at this theater. That fact was also confirmed by Marvo the Magnificent. As he came past me to retrieve his props he stared at me in surprise.

"You again?" he said in a low voice.

"I've come to support Houdini because his wife can't be here tonight," I whispered sweetly because the announcer was already introducing the next act.

"I heard he's got an eye for the ladies." He gave me a knowing smirk. "Providing support, are you?" The smirk turned into something close to a leer.

"Don't be ridiculous. I'm actually Bess's friend, not his," I said. "She asked me to come to give him moral support tonight because she can't be here."

"How is she?" He whispered because the announcer had finished and the curtains were opening. "Out of danger? Or was that all just one of her bouts of hysterics?"

There was applause as Billy Robinson came out onstage.

"Recovering, thankfully," I said. "I visited her today."

"Strange thing, that trunk," he said. He put his finger to his lips as the applause died away and the act started.

I watched him go about his business, then turned my attention to Billy Robinson and his card tricks. He seemed like a nice, unassuming man and surely nobody that would see Houdini as a rival. I supposed that he could be jealous of the latter's stardom and large earnings, however. People have done

218

worse things out of spite and it's often the quiet ones who keep their feelings to themselves.

While he was performing to polite applause I turned to see the sword swallower warming up only a few feet from me. He was a big, brawny fellow, naked to the waist, with a fine muscled physique. Definitely handsome in an exotic, Middle Eastern kind of way. He was busy counting and adjusting his own table of props, but he must have sensed me looking at him and glanced up to meet my gaze. He gave me a wink and a roguish smile, then went back to his work. So my presence didn't seem to alarm or worry him, which it might have done if he had been sent from a Coney Island gang boss to do mischief. But then the mischief had been done, hadn't it? The warning had been given. If we were indeed dealing with gangs and protection money, then they wouldn't want Houdini dead — that way he could never pay them what he owed. Unless he had refused to pay, of course.

Billy Robinson finished and the sword swallower went on. Houdini came to stand beside me as fire was swallowed, then blown out, and swords were swallowed.

"When I go on, watch carefully," he said. I thought he meant that I should keep an eye on him in case he was in danger, but he added, "Take note of where everything goes onstage," he whispered. "It will be your job to make sure it's all in place."

"And now, ladies and gentlemen, straight from the royal courts of Europe, I bring you a man — nay, a superhuman — whose feats defy the imagination!" the announcer roared. "Who defies death every time he steps onstage, as we witnessed last night when his lovely wife almost came to a tragic end. I give you the one, the only, the King of Handcuffs, Houdini!"

Houdini stepped out to receive the adulation of the crowd. He held up his hands. "I must apologize that my wife is not with me tonight. As you know, something went horribly wrong the other night and my poor Bess nearly died of suffocation. She is luckily well on her way to recovery but won't be well enough to perform with me for a while. So tonight we'll begin with the handcuff challenge. Who has come to try and win the hundred-dollar prize?"

Three men came up onstage. Harry looked at their handcuffs and nodded. "I tell you what," he said, "to make things a little more interesting, let's put all three pairs on at once."

The three men complied. Houdini turned

220

his back on the audience. We could see his shoulders moving as he worked himself free. A minute went by. Five minutes. I was beginning to feel alarmed. Surely it shouldn't take this long? I could feel the tension in the audience mounting. Then suddenly he spun around, holding up three pairs of handcuffs and laughing delightedly.

Then he called up more men from the audience, had them handcuff him, put leg irons on him, and place him in the bag, inside the trunk. He instructed the men to latch the trunk, then hold up a velvet curtain in front of it. A hush fell on the audience. I have to say that I was holding my own breath. I wondered who might have the key tonight, should he not be able to get it open. But after less than a minute one of the men holding the curtain was tapped on the shoulder, and there was Houdini standing behind him. The curtain was whisked aside to reveal the trunk, still firmly latched. Houdini then opened it with great flourish to reveal it was empty. The crowd went wild. I'd been sitting a few feet away and I hadn't seen how he'd escaped from the trunk. I began to believe that he might be superhuman after all.

"More! More!" The word echoed through the crowd. I could see that the act, though astonishing, was now too short. As the men made their way down from the stage Houdini held up his hand and approached the audience.

"You give me no choice but to perform something I find painful and dangerous," he said, "but will demonstrate the ultimate limits of my power. This time I invite ten men to come up onstage."

There was a buzz through the audience. Those who had seen Houdini before could not think what this illusion was going to be. The men ran eagerly up the steps. Houdini wheeled forward a trolley and whisked the cloth from a small tray.

"On this tray, gentlemen," he said, slowly and deliberately because the audience couldn't actually see, "you will see ten common, ordinary sewing needles. I'd like you to test them to see that there is nothing strange about them and that they are indeed sharp."

Needles were tested.

"Now," Houdini continued, "I would like you each to take one of the needles and pierce my face with it — anywhere but my eyes."

A gasp came from the audience. The men hesitated.

"Go ahead," Houdini said. "Try my cheek first."

One by one the needles pierced his cheeks. It was horrible to watch, but strangely enough, he did not appear to be bleeding.

Then he removed the needles and, one by one, he put them into his mouth and ate them. I could actually hear them being crunched. Then he had the men examine his mouth to make sure he had swallowed them all.

"Needles are no use without thread," he said and promptly swallowed a length of sewing thread. A hush fell over the audience. Houdini nodded to the orchestra pit. A drumroll began. He put his hand to his mouth, gagged and acted as if he was about to vomit. The men stepped hastily away from him. Then he reached into his mouth and started to pull out a piece of thread. Out it came, longer and longer, and the audience gasped as all ten of the needles were threaded on it. At last he held up the thread triumphantly, the needles glistening in the stage lights.

The applause was thunderous. Even the men onstage applauded. The curtain came down, then Houdini went through the center opening to take several more bows.

He came back, looking flushed and triumphant.

"You see what the job of the illusionist is, don't you, Molly?" he said. "Always keep them surprised and guessing. The audience never has to know what is coming next."

"Those needles," I said, staring at his face, because it showed no signs of having been pierced, "don't they hurt? How do you make sure they don't get stuck in your throat?"

He laughed. "My dear, you should know by now: an illusionist never gives away his secrets. But I'll tell you one thing — that's a trick I wouldn't want on the bill every night. I had to do it tonight because I guessed they'd want more than I had to offer. Tomorrow let's hope that we can soften them up with the mind reading first."

And so I went home, having agreed to meet him at the theater at eleven o'clock the next morning.

I woke early, my stomach in a knot about what I had ahead of me. I was ready and raring to go by eight, and I wanted to pay a call on Daniel the dressmaker, but I knew better than to disturb theater folk before ten. I made myself walk slowly in his direction and on the stroke of ten I knocked on his door.

"Just call me a miracle worker, but I think I've come up with a solution to our problems," he said, opening the door to admit me into his cluttered room. "Rather stylish, if I say so myself."

He handed me the garment that had been lying beside his sewing machine. I looked for somewhere to retire when he asked me to try on the garment but he laughed. "I can tell you haven't been in the theater, my darling. We don't worry about such things. Besides, I've seen it all before and you are in no danger from me."

So feeling rather foolish, I removed my dress and allowed him to help me into the costume. It really was rather lovely: white satin bloomers, a frilly white jabot at the neck, and over it a bright green cape, lined with sparkling gold.

"We show off your legs, which are your only good feature, apart from the hair, which is rather striking, I have to admit," he said. "And we draw attention away from the waist, or lack thereof, by the frills at the neck and the flowing cape."

"It's lovely," I said, because I could tell this was expected and the reflection in his mirror was quite pleasing. "Could it possibly be ready for tonight?"

He rolled his eyes again and gave a dramatic sigh. "I told you I was a miracle worker, didn't I? I suppose if I work slavishly all day . . ."

So I left him with at least one thing in place. Now all I had to do was become the person who was to wear that costume. I arrived at the theater to find Houdini pacing impatiently.

"There you are at last," he said. "Right, let's get down to it. Lots to learn and no room for error. You think you can do this?"

"We'll know by the end of the day, won't we?" I said. "But I'll give it a good try. If not, I can always watch you from the wings, if that's what Bess wants."

He paused, considering this. "The act goes better with a second person," he said. "You saw last night. They weren't satisfied with just the escapes." He clapped his hands and started barking orders.

My goodness, how we worked that day. I've never been afraid of hard work in my life. After all, I had to run a household and look after my father and three brothers after my mother died and that was no easy task. I worked in a sweatshop for twelve hours a day once when I was on a case. But I don't think I've ever had to work as hard as that day with Houdini. He was a perfectionist himself and demanded perfection.

"Again," he would say, clapping his hands as if I were a performing animal. "No, never turn your back on the audience. Wrong hand. This way. Now, cross the stage. No, not like that. And don't stick out your behind when you wheel in the cabinet."

Over and over it we went until I was so tired that I felt close to tears. He only released me just before six o'clock to take a cab to pick up my costume.

"What about makeup?" I asked.

"You can use Bess's tonight."

So there I was, dressed in my new costume, my face made up, my hair piled up with an egret's feather ornament in it, and feeling absolutely terrified. I was about to go out there, in front of all those people, with one of the most famous entertainers in the world.

"Don't let me down," he said, as we made our way down to the stage.

It was interesting to watch the reaction of the other theater folk. Old Ted had only frowned when I had arrived in the morning to rehearse. But when I came back for the performance he said, "So that was what this was all about — trying to wangle yourself into a job? At least I suppose it's better than what some young ladies will do to be cast in the theater."

"I'm only helping out because Bess Houdini isn't well enough to go on," I said. "Let's just say I was in the right place at the right time."

"If that's what you say," he said, clearly not quite believing me.

The stagehands had reacted with astonishment and amusement when they saw me rehearsing. And after they had gotten over their surprise at seeing an intruder turned into part of the show, I provided good entertainment for them as I stumbled my way through learning the physical positioning of the act. And Mr. Irving, the theater manager, had come stomping onto the stage as we were in midrehearsal.

"What's this I hear about some new girl?" he demanded. "What is this?"

He frowned as he stared at me. "You've been hanging around for a few days."

"That's because I'm Bess Houdini's friend," I said. "She invited me to the show, and then she begged me to take her place when she wasn't well enough to go on and she knew that Houdini needed an assistant."

"So you've done this before?" Mr. Irving snapped. "I run a top-class house here. I've no time for amateurs."

"Do you think I'd permit an amateur to

work with me?" Houdini stepped between us with the kind of flourish only he could produce. "If she hadn't been up to par, there is no way I would have considered having her onstage with me. You'll see. She'll be all right on the night."

"She better be," Irving muttered, "or you might find that you've just broken the terms of your contract."

So now I had the added worry of not disgracing Houdini so that he actually got paid for the performance. I didn't have a chance to see the other performers before I went onstage as I was up in the dressing room, thinking that I was about to be sick. Why did I put myself through these things? Then I remembered that I had promised Daniel this would be my last case. At that particular moment I thought this was the best idea in the world.

We made our way downstairs to the backstage area. A thought struck me.

"Where is the key to the trunk?"

"In my jacket pocket," he said.

"A lot of good it will be in there, if you're trapped inside," I said.

"In case you haven't been watching properly, I hang up my jacket before they truss me up and put me in the bag," he said. "So the key will be hanging from the coatrack.

But it won't be necessary. I have yet to find anything that can hold me."

At that moment I heard the announcer's voice, booming out in dramatic tones, "And let's put our hands together in a rousing welcome for the lovely Molly, who has graciously agreed to take the place of Bess Houdini until she is well again."

"You're on." Houdini gave me a shove. And I stepped out onstage, my heart racing and my eyes blinking in the strong lights. I hadn't realized how bright they would be. Out in the darkened auditorium I could just make out that sea of faces watching me and tried to make my body act like a glamorous magician's assistant as the announcer whipped up the crowd into a frenzy for the appearance of Houdini.

I was vaguely aware of Houdini speaking to the audience, saying that the Irish were noted for their second sight, and how he was lucky enough to have stumbled across a true Irish medium with remarkable powers of mind reading. I managed to walk across the stage and to sit in the chair that had been placed in the center. With that he made his way down into the audience and asked someone to pick a card, study it, and then place it in a box.

"All right, Molly," he said. "You are going

to tell this nice lady what card she has put into this little black box."

Oh, Holy Mother. Did I really see him wiggle his eyebrows up and down? And he touched the woman's right shoulder, didn't he?

"Molly?" he repeated. "What card comes to your mind?"

I opened my mouth but no sound would come out. "The five of hearts?" It was scarcely bigger than a whisper.

"Louder!" he boomed. "Let those in the back row of the balcony hear it too."

"The five of hearts!" I exclaimed.

He handed the box to another audience member. "Would you see what card is in this box?" he asked.

"The box is empty," the man replied.

"That's strange," Houdini said. "Where can the card have gone?"

He ran back onstage and made me stand up. I was sitting on the five of hearts. Vaguely I was aware of the applause.

Then we went into the part with the hood over my head. He made it easy for me, with the most obvious of clues that we had practiced. I guessed successfully a fan and a pocket watch. The rest of the act went without a hitch, although I'm sure I didn't move across the stage with the glamorous grace of Lily. But Houdini successfully escaped from the handcuffs and from the trunk and there I was, standing in front of the curtains, taking a bow.

"Well done," Houdini said, putting his hand around my waist as we came offstage. Such a gesture would have resulted in a slapped face in the outside world, but this was the theater, after all. But I did recall Bess's jealous outburst and moved aside with agility.

"We got through it, didn't we?" I agreed.

"In one piece," he added. He was half joking but I moved closer to him again.

"Tell me, Harry, do you really suspect that someone is trying to kill you, as Bess thinks?"

He thought for a moment, then shook his head. "Until yesterday I would have said no. Bess does tend to — well, you've seen what she can be like. But I'd like to know what happened to the key to that trunk. The key was in the inside pocket to my coat. Who would have known about that?"

"Bess said that strange men have been coming to your house," I ventured, taking this further. "Making what sounded like threats. And at the theater one night I overheard you talking to a young man — well dressed, light hair. Clearly didn't belong in the theater and the doorman had no idea how he got in."

"Oh, that." He stopped abruptly, then he shook his head. "That was something quite different altogether."

I decided to take the risk. "It sounded to me as if he might have been delivering a threat from his boss."

"On the contrary," he said. "I want to meet with his boss. I had hoped to do so by now but there has been no time. I can't think why —" Then he gave me an exaggerated smile, took my hand, and patted it.

"So let's assume that all will be well. Only one more night here, then new theater, new show, new people."

SEVENTEEN

I woke on Sunday to a lovely morning —
not too hot, blue sky, exactly the right sort
of day to spend in the country or on the
seashore. That thought prompted another
one. Coney Island. As a detective, did it
behoove me to take a trip to Coney Island
and ask questions about the infamous Risey
and his threat to get even with Houdini?
Much as I hated to go back to that place
because it was connected with such horrific
memories, I decided that today would be
the day to do this. It would be crowded with
city workers escaping from the heat and toil
of the city. So I put on an inconspicuous
shirtwaist such as a factory worker would
wear and off I went to catch the trolley
across the Brooklyn Bridge.

The trolley and then the train to Coney
Island were packed and I regretted that I
had ever had such a foolish idea. Memories
came back to me of the time I'd had to find

a killer lurking in the funfair and had had a nightmare experience in a freak show. I found that I was sweating and not just from the heat. Did I really want to go through with this? However, when we descended at the terminus the crowd streamed toward the amusement parks and the beach and I felt my spirits lifting a little. The sea was sparkling, everyone was having a good time, and what's more, a new amusement park had sprung up since I was there last. I could hear screams and laughter as fairgoers were swung around on the new rides.

I tried to remember where the Cairo Pavilion had been, then did remember — along a street called the Bowery, after the well-known thoroughfare in the city. It was a shady kind of place with legitimate amusements side by side with girlie shows, bars, and dance halls. I was propelled along with the crowd, my hand firmly on my purse because the place was notorious for pickpockets, and came to the Arabian arch that led to the Cairo Pavilion. I recalled that the fire-eater had stood outside it, luring in the crowds, and to my surprise, there he was.

"Step right up, ladies and gentlemen!" a voice was shouting through a bull horn. "All the wonders of the mystic East — ride a real camel, take a forbidden peek inside a harem . . ."

The man who had been introduced in the theater as Abdullah ran a firebrand along his bare arm, making a passing girl scream and grab on to the young man she was with. The fire-eater glanced in her direction, then he spotted me and his dark eyes flashed recognition.

"Hello," he said. "Didn't expect to find you here. You with somebody?"

I was surprised to find he spoke with a New York accent. I didn't like to admit that I was there alone. "I'm supposed to be meeting some friends," I said, "but I don't know how I'm going to find them in this crowd."

"I get a break in a few minutes," he said. "Stay around and I'll buy you a soda."

"All right."

This was working wonderfully — maybe too well to be true. Daniel had told me over and over that a good detective never goes anywhere alone and never without telling someone where he is going. I, with a detective agency of one, had to work alone all the time and consequently had gotten myself into too many difficult situations — including one in this very place. But I couldn't pass up a chance to interview someone who had appeared on the scene right before

Houdini's act went wrong, and a soda fountain, in the middle of a crowd could hardly be classed as dangerous, could it?

I waited out of the sun beside a shooting gallery, watching young men trying their hardest to impress their lady friends by shooting down a row of ducks. The crowd surged past me — working girls from the factories, courting couples, families with excited children — all making the most of a day out of the heat and oppression of the city. But the waiting also gave me time to think. My own memories of this place were so tinged with horror and regret that I began to wish I had never come here. In fact I was just deciding that I was acting stupidly and should go home when Abdullah appeared from the Cairo Pavilion and came to join me.

"So your name is Molly, is it?" he said as we walked down the Bowery together. "I heard the announcer say it."

"That's right. And is yours really Abdullah?"

He laughed. "That's just for this act. It's really Mike. I'm Irish like you. My parents came over in the great famine."

"Irish?" I looked at his bronzed torso, then I noticed that his eyes were that alarming blue of the so-called Black Irish, just like

Daniel's, in fact.

He laughed again. "You'd be surprised what a little walnut juice will do and I usually spend my spare time sunning myself on the beach, to keep up appearances."

"So what are you doing still working here?" I asked. "I thought you'd have left this place when you were hired by a real vaudeville house. Surely that was a lucky break for you, wasn't it?"

"I'm not stupid enough to give up my job here, especially Saturdays and Sundays when we get the crowds. I do quite well for myself. I'm not just paid to perform, you know. I'm also supposed to keep an eye out for the wrong types. The boss don't want no one who might cause trouble, you understand. And sometimes I'm needed as a bodyguard."

"A bodyguard for whom?"

"Ah, that would be telling, wouldn't it?" He grinned and gave me a wink. "Let's just say that not all the things that go on around here are as wholesome as watching a belly dancer or petting a camel."

"Criminal activities, you mean?" I asked.

"Oh, no," he said with exaggerated innocence. "All the bosses around here are as pure as the driven snow." Then he laughed again. "So tell me about yourself. How long

238

have you been in the business?"

"Not long," I said. "In fact I'm not really a performer at all. I'm a friend of Bess Houdini. She asked me to take her place until she's well enough to come back."

"So what do you do the rest of the time, when you're not performing?"

"Whatever I can get," I said. "It's not that easy for someone arriving from Ireland, as you know yourself. I was a chorus girl a few months ago. I worked in a sweatshop once."

"So this is a big break for you too," he said.

We reached the soda fountain and went inside. He ordered me an iced sarsaparilla and assisted me onto the high stool at the counter. I noticed that his hands lingered a little too long on my waist.

"So tell me about the fire-eating and sword swallowing," I said. "Aren't they terribly dangerous?"

"Only if someone gives me a push at the wrong moment," he said. "On the whole it's no more dangerous than the things those illusionists do."

"That's right if this week is anything to go by," I said. "You heard about what happened to Lily, then."

"Lily? The girl who got cut up with the saw? Of course I did. It's because of her that I'm here."

"You knew her?"

"No, I mean they needed an act to fill in at the last minute, didn't they?"

"And how did they come to hire you?"

"Let's just say I'm a friend of a friend. Somebody owed somebody a favor."

"Lucky for you," I said. "So will you just be filling in for this week and then going back to your old job?"

He shrugged. "Depends," he said.

"On what?"

"You ask a lot of questions, you know that?" He leaned toward me and touched the tip of my nose in a rather too intimate gesture. "Aren't young ladies supposed to be coy and demure?"

"If you're also Irish you'll know that we're seldom coy and demure," I said and he laughed.

"I like a girl with fire and spirit; in fact I like you, Molly. So how about going out for a little late supper with me after the show tonight?"

Now I really was in a dilemma. Obviously Daniel would be furious if I went out to supper with another man, and it might not be prudent to go out alone with someone who had been regarding me with something close to a lecherous leer — and might also work for a boss with criminal connections. On the other hand it would be a great opportunity to encourage my fire-eating companion to let an indiscretion or two slip from his lips.

"I'll think about it," I said, giving him a coy smile. And I decided to take another risk. "Tell me, do you know a man they call Risey?"

"Risey? Everyone knows him. He's an institution around here. How did you hear the name?"

"Someone at the theater told me that he'd challenged Houdini once, several years ago, and he'd been a sore loser. I just remembered it when I realized it had taken place on Coney Island. He's an important man around here, is that right?"

"Used to be. I'd say his glory days are over. He owns a theater farther down the Bowery."

"So did you ever perform in his theater?"

He laughed. "Hardly. It's a girlie show. I don't dance the cancan."

I laughed with him.

"Oh, I get it," he said.

I froze, then he continued. "You're looking for someone to hire you when Houdini goes back to Europe, aren't you? You're not the type who'd work for Risey. You're too —

nice. His girls do more than dance the cancan, if you get my meaning."

"I only asked because I heard someone at the theater say that Risey was one to carry a grudge and the accident with the Houdinis' trunk might be Risey's way of getting even."

Mike shrugged. "Risey's way of getting even would be to send a couple of his guys to wait for you in a dark alley with brass knuckles on," he said. "He ain't known for his subtlety."

He drained his glass and got up. "I gotta go. There would be hell to pay if I show up late. See you at the show tonight then, and afterward, who knows?"

He rested his hand on mine briefly, then hurried out, leaving me not much the wiser but definitely in a predicament. From the easy way he reacted to my suggestion, I was fairly sure that he hadn't been sent by Risey, but he'd admitted he got the job because someone owed somebody a favor, and he admitted to being a bodyguard to his boss who might or might not be involved in criminal activities. Which brought me back to my former theory that the whole thing somehow involved a gang of whom Houdini had fallen foul.

I arrived back home looking rather the

worse for wear, having been squashed into a train and then a trolley with a sticky, dirty mass of humanity. I'd have loved a cool drink, a bath, and a rest, but I had only time for a quick wash and a snack before I headed back to the theater. It was the last night at Miner's. On Tuesday Houdini opened in a new theater in Brooklyn with new acts on the bill. And then a few days later he sailed back to Europe — out of reach of any kind of gang protection racket. Out of reach of rival illusionists. So far I had picked up no clue as to who might want to do him harm. I certainly got the feeling that he knew more than he was willing to tell either Bess or me and if he was not going to divulge any details, then I didn't see how I could help him.

I arrived at the theater and went up to change my clothes in the dressing area they had let me use. It was usually intended for chorus girls when the normal vaudeville acts performed. At the moment I was the only occupant. It was cold and cheerless, with a long counter at which the girls sat to put on their makeup. As I sat alone at that counter, dabbing circles of rouge onto my cheeks, an uneasy feeling crept over me. I was alone in this bleak and bare room and I felt what Bess had described — a feeling of wanting to look over my shoulder. A feeling of danger nearby. I told myself I was being stupid, but I got up and went down the hall to tap on Houdini's door.

"It's the lovely Molly," he said.

"I hope you don't mind," I said, "but I'd like to finish my makeup in here. The light is terrible in that room."

"Of course, come on in. I must say that the transformation is not at all bad." He eyed me appraisingly and I thought of Bess's remark about not trusting him with other women. Maybe I was asking for trouble being alone in a dressing room with him.

"No, the dressmaker worked wonders, didn't he?" I pulled up the stool to the dressing table and started to apply the stick of Carmine 2 to my lips before this conversation could continue. But he confirmed my thoughts by saying, "Bess is coming to watch the show tonight. She wants to see how her replacement is doing."

"Is she well enough to be out at night like this?"

"My brother Dash is bringing her in a cab. They'll be in the stage box."

"That will make me extra nervous," I said. "Bess will notice every little thing that I do wrong."

"Don't be silly. She'll be delighted that you were able to take her place. After all, you're doing this for Bess, aren't you?" Then he added, "We're both doing this for her. She's the one who believed I was in danger."

"And you don't? After what happened?"

"I suppose I have to, don't I? But it wasn't I who was almost killed, it was my wife."

"A warning to you, do you think?" I asked.

"A warning?" I could see from his face that he was considering this. Then he shook his head. "Oh, but that's ridiculous."

I turned from the mirror to face him. "Look, Mr. Houdini — Harry — you've hired me to find out who wishes you harm and yet I have the feeling there are things you are not willing to share with me. How can I help you?"

"I don't believe you can," he said. "You must realize that I'm only doing this to pacify my wife. What could a young girl like you do to protect me from the sort of man who might wish me harm?"

"I can't answer that until you tell me what sort of man that might be," I said. There was a silence so I turned to him again. "I think you suspect who it is, don't you?"

"Not really," he said.

I waited. There was a long silence as he stared at his hands, then he looked up and gave me an easy smile. "After tomorrow this should all be behind us," he said with an airy wave of his hand.

"Tomorrow? What is happening tomorrow?

"I'm taking a little trip. Then at least I will have done my part. The rest isn't up to me."

"Your part in what?"

"A little extra job, shall we say."

He paused in front of the mirror and smoothed a wayward dark strand of hair into place.

"What kind of extra job?"

"I really can't tell you anymore. But just be assured that by the time we open on Tuesday your only task will be to assist with my illusions, until Bess feels confident enough to come back."

I wrestled with smoothing my own wayward hair into a sleek chignon then stuck a dozen hairpins in savagely. I couldn't think how I was going to get any more information out of him and it annoyed me to know he had only agreed to my presence to pacify a hysterical wife. But if he knew who was out to harm him, why wasn't he doing anything about it?

"You really can trust me, you know," I said.

"Maybe I can, but as I said, I think tomorrow will put all this behind us. And I am still not convinced that I am actually in any danger."

"I don't believe that. Bess has been really worried about you. She says you've been unusually tense and worried, getting up in the middle of the night to scribble things down on paper."

"Bess reads too much into things," he said. "An illusionist's head is always full of the ultimate illusion, the one that can't be done."

"And have you come up with that?"

"Maybe."

"And would anybody kill to steal it from you?"

He paused in his pacing. "The problem is that the adversary may have many faces," he said. I thought it was an odd thing to say.

Makeup was completed. We went over signals once more in the dressing room while the other illusionists performed, then the callboy summoned us down to the stage. Houdini squatted in the shadows backstage and examined the trunk, checking and double-checking the locks. He flexed his fingers, he went through his deck of cards, he rotated his shoulders in a sickening display of double-jointedness, as the announcer began to present us.

The band struck up our music. I stepped out onstage, conscious that critical eyes would be watching me from the stage box. I tried not to look in that direction. I thought I heard a gasp. Maybe Bess wasn't expecting my costume to be so alluring. Houdini was announced and swept out onto the stage. He went through the same patter as the night before about the Irish and their sixth sense and how lucky he was to have me filling in for Bess. Then he acknowledged her in the box and she stood to a nice round of applause. The card tricks went well, but maybe that Irish sixth sense was working — I was so tense I could hardly breathe. And it was not just stage fright either. Then two men were selected from the audience and the hood was placed over my head. I identified a comb, a train ticket, and a locket with a lock of hair inside it. I was feeling rather pleased with myself.

"I'm holding up an object belonging to a good-looking young man," Houdini said. "At least it belongs to him at this moment. So quickly, Molly. Can you picture it?"

"It's round," I said, picking up his signals. "Is it a ring?"

There was applause and I removed the hood.

"Here's the ring back, sir," Houdini said. "I suspect you don't intend to wear it yourself. It's a little small for your fingers."

"No, it was intended for someone else," the man said. I took a step forward to peer into the darkness. Because I recognized that voice. It was Daniel.

I don't know how I managed to get through the rest of the act. I'm sure I didn't drift across the stage with grace as we went through the handcuff challenges. All I could think of was what I was going to say when I had to face Daniel. That, and the fact that he had a ring in his pocket, which he might or might not give me after what he had witnessed tonight.

Then at last came the trunk illusion. I went to retrieve it from the wings. A stage-hand helped me carry it into position. Houdini removed his jacket and hung it up. Men were invited up onto the stage to inspect the trunk, try the locks, and then to bind Houdini hand and foot. When he was trussed up like a chicken, the bag was pulled up over him and drawn closed. Then he was placed in the trunk and the locks were snapped shut. I wheeled out the cabinet from the wings, displayed that it consisted of nothing more than a three-sided frame, covered with fabric, then turned it to conceal the trunk from the audience. The drumroll started. I crossed the stage to take up my position near the watching men on the opposite side of the stage, to divert eyes from the trunk until the right moment.

The previous night Houdini had popped out of the trunk almost before I had time to cross the stage. Tonight I turned, gestured toward the trunk, stood, and waited. I was conscious of the drumroll increasing in volume and intensity. He's stringing it out to heighten the suspense, I thought, remembering how I had held my breath during the moments of drama when I had been in the audience. Always keep them surprised, he had told me.

I heard the announcer reminding the audience that there was only enough air in that trunk for someone to survive for a few minutes, and someone struggling to free himself from bonds within the thick fabric of that bag would use up the air all that faster. A minute had to have passed. Two minutes. Three. I could sense the restlessness in the crowd. I glanced across at Mr. Irving, standing to the side of the stage. He too was looking worried. But this was Houdini. It was reputed he could hold his breath longer than any other human being. He had supernatural powers. He was in league with the devil.

"I really think this has gone on long enough," one of the men onstage said. "The poor fellow obviously can't get out. We tied the bonds too tight. Open the trunk."

I sensed the agony of indecision in the face of Mr. Irving.

"Open it up! For God's sake open it up!" Voices were coming from the audience.

"Who has a key?" Mr. Irving demanded.

"I know where the key is." I ran to Houdini's frock coat and reached for the inside pocket. My fingers touched what felt like two keys. Clearly he hadn't been taking any chances at one getting mislaid this time. I was so tense by now that my fingers refused to obey me, fumbled, and got caught up in the jacket lining. I forced my hand to obey me, grabbed both keys, and rushed across the stage to the waiting men. They had already wheeled aside the cabinet. The trunk lay there, still locked and untouched.

"Here." I handed Mr. Irving the key and he knelt beside the trunk. At any second I expected to hear a laugh and to see Harry Houdini appear from somewhere else in the theater.

"I fooled you good and proper that time,

didn't I?" he'd say.

Mr. Irving tried the key. "It doesn't fit," he said.

"There's a second key. Try this." I thrust it into his hand. He put it into the lock and jiggled it. Then he tried the second lock. "This one doesn't work either," he said, throwing them down. "Someone get the ax again. We'll have to break it open."

I watched in fascination, still half expecting this to be a stunt. Someone ran backstage, found the ax, and handed it to Mr. Irving. "Hold it steady, Ernest," he commanded, and swung at the first lock. After several attacks the locks swung open and he lifted the lid. The dark velvet bag lay in the trunk, not moving.

"For God's sake get him out of there!" someone shouted.

Stagehands rushed forward to help the volunteers and the manager to lift the bag from the trunk and place it on the stage. One of the men was fumbling to undo the knot that held the bag tightly shut. "It won't open. Get a knife!" he shouted.

"Is there a doctor in the house?" the manager had to ask for the third time in a week.

Someone came running back with a knife and slit the string that held the mouth of the bag shut. At last he had it free and wrenched open the bag. Then I heard a gasp from those around me and stared down in disbelief and horror.

A complete stranger lay in the bag, tied up with rope, eyes wide open in surprise, not moving.

EIGHTEEN

At first the audience thought this was a good stunt. Some of them started to applaud, but the applause petered out as the manager stood up again.

"He's dead," he said in a stunned voice. "Somebody go for the police."

There was a shriek from the stage box. "Where's my husband? What's happened to him?"

"Yes, where is he?" other voices echoed. "Where's Houdini then?"

"Find Houdini. Don't let him leave the theater!" the manager shouted. "Lock all the exits. Bring up the houselights."

There was an eerie silence as the lights came on in the auditorium and then chaos broke out. I had been standing by the body so I hadn't noticed that Daniel had come onto the stage.

"Ladies and gentlemen, please." He held up his hands for silence. "Take your seats.

Nobody move. I'm Captain Sullivan of the New York police, and this is now a police matter. Nobody is going anywhere until my men arrive. I ask for your complete co-operation. Ushers, would you please man the doors." He turned to the manager. "Is there a telephone available?"

"In my office."

"Then go and call police headquarters and tell them that Captain Sullivan wants the detective on duty here immediately with a team of men. Tell them there has been a murder."

"Are you sure it's murder?" the theater manager asked. "Not just a stunt gone wrong?"

Daniel gave me a brief glance as he knelt to examine the body. "Help me get him out of this thing," he ordered the men standing around him. "Gently." Willing hands pulled away the bag from the body. It was a young man wearing a brown suit — a very ordinary, respectable-looking young man with light brown hair and the beginnings of a mustache. Daniel opened the jacket. There was an ugly red stain across the front of the shirt.

"Hardly a stunt gone wrong," Daniel said dryly, undoing the shirt buttons. "Stabbed through the heart. Very efficient. Very professional." He examined the body more thoroughly. "And it doesn't look as if he's been dead very long. Rigor mortis hasn't set in yet." He looked up at those around him. "Anybody know who he is?"

Blank faces stared at him.

"Never seen him before in my life," one of the stagehands muttered.

"So he doesn't work here at the theater?"

The men shook their heads.

Daniel now looked up at me. "You were apparently part of this act. So none of this was prearranged?"

"A murder? Prearranged?"

"I meant that it might have been part of the act for Houdini to change places with someone."

"Absolutely not," I said. "Usually his wife performs the Metamorphosis act with him, in which they do change places. But tonight's trick was a simple escape. Houdini was just supposed to free himself from the ropes and emerge from the trunk. Yesterday it took him less than a minute to do so."

"I see." Daniel's eyes held mine, as if he wanted to ask more, then he turned his attention back to the body and started going through the young man's pockets. "Interesting," he said. "He seems to be carrying no form of identification. No keys, no wallet, no money. Nothing. But if someone didn't want him to be identified, why place him here, where everyone can see him? Why not just dump him into the river?"

The words were said more to himself than to anyone else.

"And if he is here, then where the devil is Houdini?" Daniel looked up at me again. "Presumably you have some idea how this trick was supposed to work. How could the body have been placed here?"

"Houdini didn't share his secrets with me," I said. "I was merely the assistant."

"There were other acts on the bill," Daniel said. "Where are they?"

"Probably still in their dressing rooms," someone suggested.

"Then go and bring them down here. I'll want to question them."

The manager looked at his stage crew, then shrugged and went himself. At that moment there was the sound of raised voices, a woman screaming just offstage behind the curtains to our left.

"What now?" Daniel demanded, getting to his feet. "I thought I instructed everyone to remain in their seats."

Bess came running onto the stage. Her eyes were wild and her mouth was open in pure terror. "Where is he?" she screamed.

"What have they done with Harry?"

"Who is this?" Daniel demanded. "How did she get up here?"

"This is Mrs. Houdini," I said, over the loud, gasping sobs coming from Bess. "She usually performs with her husband, but I was taking her place after the accident that happened the other night."

"I see." Daniel put his hands on Bess's shoulders. "Just calm down, Mrs. Houdini. This isn't going to help us find your husband." He turned to the stagehands who had now gathered around the body and were staring as if dazed.

"You men, go and search the backstage area," he said. "Every inch, every closet where someone could be hiding."

"Hiding?" Bess screamed. "You don't think my husband did this, do you? Harry would never hurt a fly."

Daniel held up his hand again. "And if you come across a body," he said in a low voice, "stay well away. Don't disturb anything but come and get me."

"He's dead. I know he is." The words came in great gasps. I went over to Bess and put my arm around her. "We don't know anything yet. Maybe he's quite safe. Why don't you sit down?" I pulled up a chair for her. She collapsed onto it, her face in her hands, her body convulsed with sobs.

Daniel again went toward the audience, who had been sitting and standing in horrified fascination. "Does anybody out there recognize this man? Did he come with anyone here? If you know him, please come up to the stage now. And ushers, I'd like you to take a look at him and see if anyone remembers admitting him."

The requests brought no response, except for one of the ushers, who commented, "He's not exactly the sort of man who would stand out in a crowd, is he? I don't know if I'd remember if I'd shown him to his seat."

This was true enough. He was the sort of man you'd pass in a crowd and not notice. The first police constables arrived, presumably those patrolling the street outside the theater. They hurried up the center aisle and began to mount the steps to the stage.

"What do you want us to do, sir?" one of them asked.

"Control the exits for now," Daniel said.

"When can we leave?" a man shouted from the audience. "My wife is feeling faint. I should get her into the fresh air immediately."

"Your patience for a little while longer, sir," Daniel said. "I want only one exit opened and my men stationed there. Then the audience will be allowed to leave, row by row. I need you to give my constables your names and addresses as you file out in orderly fashion. If there's pushing and shoving, we may sit here all night."

I had to admire Daniel's great presence. In his own way he was as commanding as Houdini had been. This was a man who was used to being obeyed, I realized. No wonder he had such a hard time with me. I could hear the shuffling of feet and clattering of seats as the audience began to leave. Daniel turned back to us as there was the sound of footsteps from backstage, and Billy Robinson and Abdullah the sword swallower appeared, both now in street clothing. Robinson was fully dressed, but Abdullah was in shirtsleeves and still held a cotton ball in his hand with which he had been removing makeup.

"What's all this about?" Robinson demanded. "I was about to go home and I was told I couldn't."

Then he saw the body. "Who the devil is that?"

"I was hoping one of you could shed light on that," Daniel said. "But there were three acts. Where is the man with the birds?"

"Marvo? He's already gone. He had an

assignation with a young lady, so I believe," Billy Robinson said.

"I see." Daniel turned to the manager. "I'll need his name and address. And when my men get here we'll want a statement from everybody who —" he broke off because Houdini's brother Dash had come back onto the stage and was whispering something in Bess's ear. Daniel reacted with such obvious surprise that I realized he had mistaken the brother for Houdini himself.

"This is Houdini's brother," I said. "He is also an illusionist."

"Rather an escape artist," Dash said. "I do the handcuffs and that sort of thing."

"Then you can tell me how the devil this body got into that trunk," Daniel said.

"I have no idea," Dash said. "The way that illusion is performed, I can't see how a body could be substituted."

"You usually perform this, Bess," I said. "Can you think how it was done?"

Bess looked up and shook her head.

"You'll find that illusionists are very tight with their secrets," I said.

"And they might find that jail is an uncomfortable place to spend a night if they don't cooperate with the police," Daniel replied.

"I just want my husband found," Bess said.

"They are searching for him now," I answered gently.

"And neither of you recognizes the young man?" Daniel asked. "Take a good look at him."

Dash shook his head. "I've never seen him before."

But Bess got to her feet and went over to the body. She shuddered, then suddenly she put her hand to her mouth. "I think I have seen him," she said. "He was the young man who came to our house that time when Harry was out. Remember I told you about him, Molly."

"He came to your house? For what reason?" Daniel asked.

"He asked for my husband. I said he wasn't there and he said to tell Harry that he'd be back. When I asked his name he said Harry would know who he was. It sounded like a threat to me."

"Interesting." Daniel stared down at the corpse. "So has your husband been getting threats, Mrs. Houdini?"

"I think he has," she said.

"From whom?"

"I don't know. When I asked him he said I was imagining things."

Daniel stared at her for a moment, then looked back at the young man. "He doesn't look to me the type who would be employed by the criminal classes. So what kind of threats could he have been making? Was your husband in any kind of trouble?"

"If he was, he didn't tell me," Bess said. "He knows I get upset."

"But you said he was worried about something," I reminded her. "You said he paced up and down at night and he got up to scribble things down on paper."

"Yes, but that could have just been working out a new stunt," she said. "He's always in his own world when he's working something out. Absolutely obsessed. Didn't want to be disturbed." She let out a great shuddering sigh. "I just want him found."

Stagehands were returning to the stage. "He's not anywhere," one of them said. "We've searched the whole place, top to bottom. And Ted at the door says no one's been in or out that way, except for Marvo, and he went some time ago."

"Are there any other ways out?"

"There's a service door leading to the back alley, when they need to bring in big pieces of scenery, but that was bolted from the inside," another of the stagehands said. "It's hardly ever used."

"We'll wait until my men get here then we'll go over the whole place again."

"I should take Bess home," Dash said. "My mother will be worried about where we've got to. And Bess was supposed to be resting. She's only just out of the clinic. She shouldn't have come tonight at all."

"I'm not leaving until they find my husband," Bess said, her voice rising hysterically again. "He's got to be somewhere. He can't just have vanished."

Daniel put a calming hand on her shoulder. "As you say, Mrs. Houdini, he can't just have vanished. Don't worry, we'll find him. Now why don't you go home, as your brother-in-law suggested. We'll need to talk to you in the morning."

Bess reached out imploring hands to me. "Molly — come with me. I'm scared."

I looked up at Daniel, not sure whether to comply with this request.

"I'll need to question this young lady before she can go anywhere," he said. "Go home to your family now. I'll send a constable with you and we'll put a guard on the house tonight. We'll let you know as soon as we have any news."

"I'll come in the morning to be with you," I said. "You'll be quite safe."

"I won't." She started to sob again. "I'll

never be safe again."

As she was led away sobbing, Daniel looked at me and rolled his eyes for a moment.

"And I thought I was going out for a pleasant evening at the theater," he said.

NINETEEN

The theater was emptying out in remarkably orderly fashion. Most people, I'd imagine, were just glad to be able to escape from a scene of such horror. I wished I could escape myself. Three such shocks in one week were a little much for even the strongest of constitutions. And in this case I couldn't shake off the feeling of guilt that kept nagging at me. I was hired to protect him, a voice kept whispering in my head. I should have been able to do something. Of course this was nonsense, since he had been unwilling to divulge his own suspicions to me, but the thought kept haunting me. Also I was now cold and shivering in my flimsy costume.

"Would it be all right if I went to change my clothes?" I asked. "I'm really cold."

"That might be a good idea." Daniel eyed me up and down. "But I don't want you wandering around back there. Not until my men have had a chance to search the whole place."

"I'd be happy to escort this lady to her dressing room if you fear for her safety," Abdullah said.

"Thank you, but I prefer that everyone remain here right now."

"Here, miss, put this around you." One of the stagehands took down Houdini's frock coat and put it around my shoulders. Suddenly, I remembered the keys in the pocket. Two keys that wouldn't fit the trunk. I glanced down at the ground, noticed them still lying where they had been dropped, and bent to pick them up. I glanced back to see whether Daniel was looking, but he was interviewing the other illusionists. I tucked the keys into the waistband of my costume where there was a little pocket.

"Would it be all right if we went now?" I heard one of the volunteers from the audience ask as I straightened up again. "After all, we were nothing to do with the show. We only volunteered to come up here. My wife will be waiting for me. She was still in the audience."

"I understand, sir. It's inconvenient for all of us," Daniel said. He looked up with relief as a voice called out, "Captain Sullivan?"

"Up here, MacAffrey!" Daniel called and

a fresh-faced young policeman came up to the stage, followed by a retinue of constables.

"Take a look at this," Daniel said, and explained what had happened. "Examine the body and tell me what you think." He stood up to address the men who had accompanied MacAffrey. "I want this place searched. Every inch of it. I want to know where this man was killed, so look for traces of blood. He was obviously caught by surprise and finished off efficiently, so I don't expect to find any sign of a scuffle. And you're looking for any place that someone could hide." He indicated two of the men. "You two. Outside the theater. Ask anyone working nearby — flower sellers, vendors, whether they saw Houdini come out. His picture is all over the posters so I'm sure they'd have recognized him. He can't just have vanished. If he's not here, he left the theater somehow."

The men went about their duty and Daniel knelt beside the young detective. "Have you brought a photographer?"

"Yes, sir. Jackson has the photographic equipment."

"Then let's set it up and get a photograph of the body right away."

A policeman began setting up equipment

and suddenly there was a blinding flash and the air smelled of sulfur.

"So what do you think, MacAffrey?"

"Definitely killed here, I'd say, sir," the young detective said. "And not too long ago."

"That's what I thought too. And a nice neat job, wouldn't you say?"

The shirt was now fully open and they were examining the wound on the chest. Actually there was a surprisingly small amount of blood, compared to the horrors of what had happened to Lily the other night.

"A stiletto, from the size of the wound," the younger man said. "And he knew exactly where to put it to cause instant death."

"So we're dealing with a professional," Daniel muttered. "A professional assassin comes into the theater, kills a man, and substitutes his body for Houdini in a trunk that doesn't ever leave the stage. A pretty puzzle, wouldn't you say." He glanced up at the other illusionists. "Any suggestions, gentlemen?"

"Don't ask me. I'm just a carnival man. I know nothing about this kind of thing," Abdullah said. "I'm not one of their fraternity at all."

"He certainly is not," Billy Robinson said

disdainfully. "And I stick to cards. But I have to admire the skill involved in this. Whoever pulled it off knows his stuff."

"So would you say we were dealing with a professional magician?" MacAffrey asked.

"Illusionist," Robinson said. "Magicians are for children's parties. But in answer to your question, I think you have to be dealing with a damned good illusionist."

"Like Houdini, would you say?" Daniel asked.

"As good as Houdini, yes."

"And there aren't many of them around." Robinson nodded.

"Jackson. I want you to telephone HQ and put out a general alert. I want men at the train stations and ferry docks and the newspapers informed. I want the whole city searching for Houdini and I want him found right away.

"Now let's get on with it," Daniel said. "MacAffrey, I'd like you to start interviewing these people. Begin with Mr. Robinson and the sword swallower fellow. We need everyone's movements from the moment they entered the theater tonight and what they observed backstage. I'm going to go to the manager's office to interview this young woman."

I saw MacAffrey eyeing me with interest.

270

"What exactly was her part in this?"

"That's what I'm about to find out," Daniel said dryly. "But it seems that she was acting as Houdini's assistant. I noticed she was the one who brought the trunk onto the stage." He gestured to me. "Please come with me, miss."

I followed him. He said nothing as he stalked ahead of me. I started feeling sick, like a small child who knows it has done wrong and is about to feel the wrath of a parent. Down a dark hallway Daniel led me, and into a small office that smelled of stale cigar smoke. The moment he shut the door he grabbed me by the arms and spun me to face him. His eyes were blazing with anger. "Now, do you mind telling me what the devil is going on here? I come home early from the country because I think my poor fiancée is working hard and I'd like to surprise her with the two tickets I have managed to obtain to tonight's show. Only she isn't home. So I go alone and what do I find but this same future wife parading around in a costume that leaves little to the imagination and apparently taking part in a murder."

I had been feeling guilty but suddenly I'd had enough. "Don't be ridiculous. Taking part in a murder, indeed." I glared at him, eye to eye. "Look, I'm sorry if you're offended, Daniel," I said. "I couldn't tell you what I was doing because I was on an assignment. I can now let you know that I was supposed to be guarding Houdini."

"You, a bodyguard? You've now expanded your detective services, have you? A strange choice, wouldn't you say?"

We were inches away from each other, still glaring.

"Bess Houdini hired me because she believed someone was trying to kill her husband and she wanted me to find out who it was."

"That's hardly a matter for a private investigator, is it?" Daniel said coldly.

"Look, I told her that they should go to the police, but Houdini wouldn't hear of it. In fact he kept denying that there was anything to worry about, even after Bess was trapped in that same trunk and nearly suffocated."

"And did the job really require you to parade around making a spectacle of yourself?" He was still glaring at me. "Do you realize what an embarrassing position this puts me in? At some stage I'll have to admit to those men out there that the young woman showing her legs to the world is none other than my future wife."

"Don't be such a stuffed shirt, Daniel," I said. "Plenty of eminent men have married chorus girls before now. Even English dukes, so you're in good company."

I was trying to lighten the mood with flippancy. When he didn't smile I touched his arm. "You can also let them know that I was working undercover, as a detective," I said. "They'll admire my enterprise, I expect. And if it makes you feel any better, I would have been quite happy to have observed from the wings. But I was persuaded to take Bess's part after she was almost killed. Believe me, I haven't exactly relished the role, although I do believe I mastered the mind reading rather quickly." I couldn't resist a grin. "Including what was in your pocket."

"Yes, that was quite impressive," he agreed.

I saw his expression soften, then change. "My God, you look so alluring I could almost ravish you right here on this desk," he said.

"As tempting as that might be, I think you'd find it hard to explain your methods of interrogation to your junior officers if we were surprised," I said.

He laughed and let his arms slide down around my waist. "Damn it, Molly, how do you get yourself into these things?"

"The same way you do. It's my profession."

He sighed. "So what has the great private investigator managed to find out so far?" he asked. "Have you solved the case and can I send all my men home?"

"I have to confess I am completely at a loss," I said. "I tried questioning Houdini but he revealed almost nothing to me, except that whatever was bothering him would be settled after tomorrow. He told me he was planning to take a trip and then he would have done his part. That's what he said."

"And do you have any idea what that meant?"

"No idea at all. My hunch was maybe he had run afoul of somebody — some gang maybe, and that the episode in the trunk the other night had been a warning, but I don't see how a gang would have the expertise to pull off a trick like tonight's. And I don't see what that young man would have to do with it. I've seen gang members. They don't dress like that."

Daniel nodded. "After tomorrow," he said. "Somebody knew that something was going to be settled tomorrow so they had to act swiftly. But if they wanted to stop Houdini from doing something, why kill somebody else?"

"Houdini's missing," I said. "It's possible he's also dead. Or kidnapped."

"Or he has just committed a murder and fled the scene. That is the obvious conclusion, isn't it? It was his act, his trunk. He was inside it and somehow switched places with a dead man. I was watching. Nobody else came onstage."

"I know," I said.

"And that trunk was not big enough to hold two men, was it?"

"I saw it before they put Houdini inside. It was empty. And I helped carry it onto the stage, remember?"

"Damn these illusionists," he said. "They can make you believe anything they want to. It has to be one of their fraternity, doesn't it? Those other men on the bill, if you've been guarding Houdini, what do you know about them?"

"Marvo and Robinson didn't seem to pose any threat to me. They seemed like pleasant enough men and Marvo had gone home tonight before Harry started his act. Abdullah the sword swallower comes from Coney Island. I thought he might have been sent to settle an old score for a man called Risey."

"Risey? That's right. Houdini made a fool of him — but that was years ago and Risey no longer holds the power he once did."

"I went to Coney Island today and talked to Abdullah — whose real name is Mike, by the way and he's Irish like us. I didn't sense that he had anything to hide. In fact the only indication I got was that he was interested in me. He wanted to take me to supper after the show — don't scowl, Daniel."

"It all comes down to what the motive was behind this," Daniel said.

"Until now I was wondering whether it was to discredit famous illusionists and wreck their acts. First Scarpelli's act goes horribly wrong, then Bess is trapped in a trunk and has to be rescued. So I would have said at that time that we might be looking for a disgruntled magician who felt he had been denied the limelight."

"If you feel you've been denied the limelight, do you go around killing people?" Daniel said quietly. "I suppose these entertainers are more highly strung than most, but it would have to be some kind of personal grudge or affront wouldn't it? Was Houdini not well liked and respected?"

"Bess Houdini told me that other illusionists were jealous of Harry, also that he dealt his own brand of justice to anyone who challenged him or copied him or called him a fraud."

"Meaning what?"

"Usually a challenge — Houdini would set up some kind of public escape stunt and see who could escape more quickly. But I gather that he had sent men to pay a call and rough someone up before now. Bess said he did that to Scarpelli when they were in Germany."

"I see. That puts a whole different complexion on things, doesn't it? Someone else could have sent his own men to repay the compliment. Maybe one of those men was the guy who now lies dead on the stage. Houdini surprised him and dealt him a fatal blow, then realized he'd committed murder and pulled off this stunt."

"That does seem possible, I suppose," I said. "But that young man — he wouldn't be the sort you'd send to rough somebody up, would he? Houdini could have made mincemeat of him if he'd wanted —" I broke off as I realized what I had just said.

He glanced at the door. "We should go back to the others. So the next step would be to check out the men on tonight's bill and then see which other illusionists might be in the vicinity of New York."

"That would include Scarpelli," I said. "I

take it he still hasn't been found."

"You're right," he said.

"Maybe Scarpelli thought that Houdini was somehow responsible for what went wrong that night," I suggested. "And we know that he had an old score to settle."

"And maybe he got rid of his assistant in what he hoped would be taken as an accident. But then realized he had witnesses who had seen him tampering with his equipment so that it would not operate as planned, so he realized they had to go too. Perhaps this young man was one who spotted him. But then nobody in the whole theater seemed to recognize him, which is strange. We won't know any more until we find out who he is."

"How will we do that?"

"We'll try to get his photograph to the newspapers in time for them to insert it into tomorrow's edition," he said. "And it's possible that someone will come forward to say that a husband or son is missing. Other than that . . ." He shrugged expressively.

"Come on, let's go and rejoin the party." He bent to give me a quick kiss as he passed me.

"Don't do that. You really will make them suspicious if you come back with lipstick on you," I said, wiping away the telltale red mark from his lips. He managed a smile as he went to escort me out of the office.

"That ring in your pocket," I couldn't resist saying. "I take it that it was meant for me."

"Now what gave you that idea?" He looked back at me, then nodded. "It was."

"Was? You've changed your mind?"

He must have seen my face. What woman can know that her fiancé has a ring in his pocket meant for her and not want to see it?

"Later, Molly," he said. "This is neither time nor place to give it to you. As you said, we're both working. Now march." And he slapped my behind.

Just before we came back onto the stage he took my arm. "Oh, and Molly, I've been thinking." He said in a low voice, "You promised you would visit Mrs. Houdini in the morning. That might be most fortuitous. See if you can get any more out of her, or out of Houdini's brother. They may know more than they've been telling you. And it's possible he'll have tried to contact them by morning if he is on the run."

"So I see you now want my help after all," I said. "That's nice to know."

"It's just that she already trusts you and I presume she doesn't know of your connection to me?"

"I don't believe so."

"So she may be willing to reveal more to a dear friend in a moment of distress than she would to one of my men."

"You see, women do have their advantages," I said triumphantly.

"I've never doubted that you have many advantages," he said, eyeing me in a completely unprofessional manner.

MacAffrey looked up expectantly as we came back onto the stage. "Nothing so far, sir," he said. "The men have gone over the whole place. It's like a warren back there. Underground tunnels and walkways up above. But I can guarantee he's not still hiding here."

"And what about these men?" Daniel's gaze swept from the illusionists to the stagehands. "Did none of them see anything unusual? Presumably that large bag containing the body must have lain somewhere before it was placed in the trunk. And whoever placed it there would have had to have carried or dragged it. That would take a strong man or men. Didn't anyone hear sounds of dragging or bumping down steps?"

Blank faces met him.

"Someone's always on duty backstage

during a performance," the theater manager said, "especially when there are illusionists on the bill. They like someone to keep an eye on their equipment at all times."

"And which of you men did that?"

"Reg and I were working that side of the stage," Ernest said, "and Mr. Irving himself stands there between announcements."

"And the trunk was exactly where before it was brought onto the stage?"

"I'll show you," I said. "I saw Houdini himself double-check it right before the act."

"And did you happen to see if it was empty then?"

"It was," I said. "I saw him open it."

"And how long have you been his assistant, miss?" Detective MacAffrey asked.

"I'm just taking the place of his wife, since she suffered that accident earlier this week," I said.

"I see." MacAffrey glanced at Daniel. "So you're new to this theater? Have you worked with Houdini before? Does Captain Sullivan have all the details of where you've worked before tonight?"

"I have a complete statement from her, MacAffrey," Daniel said, holding up a hand to stop the question. "I'll fill you in on all the details on the cab ride back to Mulberry Street."

"Can we go yet?" one of the audience volunteers demanded angrily. "I've given my statement. I don't know if my wife has gone home or if she's still waiting for me outside and I certainly don't want her on the street alone at this time of night."

Daniel glanced at MacAffrey. "I think we can let them go, don't you? If you have names and addresses and statements from everyone here."

"I think so, sir."

"Very well then. Off you go." He looked up at the theater manager. "I presume you'll want to stay around to make sure the place is secured for the night. We may be a while yet."

Mr. Irving shrugged resignedly. "And my stage doorkeeper? Can he go home?"

"We've already questioned him, sir," one of the constables said to Daniel. "He claims Houdini could not have come past him, and he confirms that the man called Marvo left before Houdini's act started."

"I think I'd like a brief word with him myself before he goes," Daniel said. "I'll escort this young woman out that way and find her a cab. It's time she went home too." He ushered me from the stage.

Once we stepped into the gloom beyond the side curtains he moved closer to me.

"How well do you know this place?"

"Not that well. I know where the dressing rooms are and I've poked around a bit backstage."

"You know which dressing room was Houdini's?"

"Of course."

He sighed. "I don't suppose there is any point in taking another look in it. My men will have done a thorough job."

"And there's nowhere to hide. It's quite Spartan in there."

"All the same, I think I will take a look. He may have left some kind of clue that has been overlooked. Where is it?"

"Up those stairs and along the hall. He has his name and a star on his door. You can't miss it."

"And the other dressing rooms are also up there?"

"They are, including mine. Can I get changed now? I'm freezing and I can't go home looking like this."

"Of course you can't. Come on, then. Show me your room first."

I took him up the stairs and he took a brief look around the long, bleak room. "Not very inviting, is it?" he said. "I'll leave you to get changed while I take a look down the hall."

"All right." He left and I found I was so

tired and upset that it was hard to undo the hooks. I fumbled my way into my street clothes. I only then realized that I hadn't taken off my theater makeup and was about to do so when there was a tap at the door and Daniel's face appeared around it. "Ready to go then? I'll see you to your cab. You look worn out."

"It's the shock," I said. "I'm not used to bodies turning up on a regular basis."

"After this, let us hope that you will have no future contact with such unpleasant matters," he said firmly and ushered me down the hallway, grasping my elbow. "Is this the way out?"

"Yes, this leads to the stage door," I said.

Old Ted's head stuck out of his cubicle as we approached. "How long am I expected to hang around here?" he demanded. "I'm not as young as I used to be."

"Just a few questions and you can go home," Daniel said. "And I'd like you to take a look at the body that has turned up in Houdini's trunk. I'm just going to find this young woman a cab and then I'll be right back."

"If you ask me," Ted said, eyeing me steadily, "all the trouble started when that one showed up for the first time. If she's not involved then she's a Jonah — bringing

284

us bad luck. I hope you've questioned her thoroughly and you're not just letting her go."

"Don't worry, I've found out everything there is to know about her," Daniel said, "and you're right. Trust me, I'm keeping my eye on her from now on."

"Thank you for ruining my reputation," I said as we emerged into the alleyway.

Daniel grinned. "At this moment it's more useful if they think you're a suspect not hand in hand with the police."

We came out to the Bowery. Even at this late hour there was still some traffic — a trolley going past, the odd cab or carriage clip-clopping on the cobbles, and some establishments were still open, but it was quiet compared to the daytime bustle.

"Just be careful," Daniel muttered as he hailed a hansom cab for me. "One illusionist's assistant has already come to a tragic end this week."

Then he helped me up into the cab, gave some money to the driver, and hurried back into the theater.

TWENTY

Early the next morning I was leaving Patchin Place, on my way to Bess Houdini's house, when I bumped into Gus coming home with a bag of fresh rolls and the morning paper.

"You're up bright and early," she said. "Come and have breakfast and hear about our ordeal at the cottage."

"Ordeal?"

"My dear, you were so right not to have accompanied us. If we'd known what a boring and bigoted bunch they would be, we'd never have gone. Nothing but tittle-tattle and gossip of the most idle sort, and worse still, my cousin's wife's mother spent the whole weekend trying to get me together with her unmarried son — who had pimples and a stutter — and kept lecturing me on how life was passing me by and I'd be doomed to be a hopeless spinster. She was quite put out when I told her that I didn't mind that prospect at all."

"I'd love to come and hear all about it," I said, "but I'm afraid I'm working. I take it you haven't read that paper you are carrying yet."

"I haven't, but the newsboy was yelling something about a murder in the theater and Houdini having vanished," she said.

"That's right. I was at the theater last night. I saw the whole thing firsthand. And Houdini's wife is expecting me."

"My dear Molly, what an exciting life you lead," Gus said, eyeing me with envy. Most women would have been reaching for their smelling salts by this time. "I do wish we could come with you. I don't suppose you could take us along — as your assistants, maybe?"

I smiled. "No, I couldn't take you with me."

She sighed. "You will keep us *au fait,* won't you? I can't wait to tell Sid. She'll be positively agog."

So we parted and I caught my train northward. As we made our slow progress, I had time to think. My head was clear after a night's sleep and I found myself full of energy and ready for anything. I went through the whole performance of the night before, wondering if I had overlooked

287

anything. Was there anything I had observed while I was waiting in the wings to go onstage? Anyone who had been near the trunk? Anything lying there that shouldn't have been? I could think of nothing. Of course I had been wound up and nervous about going onstage so I may have overlooked a good deal, but the point was that Houdini wouldn't have overlooked anything. He was meticulous in his preparation.

So it all came down to whether he was victim or murder suspect. If he had cleverly planned this whole thing, then did Bess know about it? If so, she was a brilliant actress. But then she was a stage performer — it was her job. I found myself wondering if I had been deliberately hired as the stool pigeon — someone who knew nothing of the theater, little about the Houdinis' act, to be an alibi of sorts for them. I had found myself used by my clients before and I didn't like to think of myself as gullible enough to have been made a fool of again. But I did see how the whole thing could have been part of a well-orchestrated plan — Bess locked in the trunk, me persuaded to take her place so that there was no suggestion that Houdini had accomplished the switch with an accomplice.

I didn't know whether to wish that he was a murderer or that he was the victim, because I rather liked him. I was still deep in these thoughts as I disembarked from the train and made my way along 102nd Street, so I was startled when a large figure in blue uniform stepped out to intercept me as I went to mount the steps to the Houdinis' front door. I had forgotten that Daniel had promised Bess Houdini protection when he sent her home the night before.

"Just a moment, miss," the constable said.

"St. Michael and all the angels spare me," I muttered. Now I'd have to go through another round of explanations before I was admitted and frankly I could no longer remember if I was supposed to be Bess's dear friend or the detective come to keep an eye on her. This whole thing was becoming tiring. But to my relief the constable said, "It's Miss Murphy, isn't it? The captain said to expect you. He'll be by later himself."

"Thank you," I said. "I promised Mrs. Houdini last night that I'd stay with her today so I'll definitely be here."

"I don't suppose you've heard any word about him yet, have you?" the constable asked hopefully. "Houdini, I mean. They haven't found him yet?"

"Not that I've heard," I said.

"Well, good luck to you then." He resumed his position beside the front door and I gave a good rap on the knocker.

The door was opened by Houdini's mother. "You?" she said, pointing at me accusingly. "Where is my boy?"

"I wish I knew," I said. "Everyone is looking for him."

"They say he kills a man. My son never kill nobody!" She spat the words at me in her strongly accented English. "Where is he? Something bad has happened. I know it." She clutched her bosom in dramatic fashion.

"How is Bess?" I asked. "She asked me to come and be with her."

"How do you think she should be?" she demanded. "Her husband is gone, maybe dead. She won't leave her bed. She won't eat. She won't sleep. She will make herself sick. She will die of grief."

"I'll go straight up to her then," I said, trying to give her a friendly smile. It was like smiling at a gargoyle. "I expect she'll be glad to see me," I added.

She gave the sort of shrug that indicated that might or might not be the case. Houdini's brother Dash did not put in an appearance as I went up the stairs to Bess's bedroom. I tapped on the door and went in. She was awake, lying in bed, and staring at the ceiling. When she saw me she sat up, her face alight with hope. "They've found him?"

"I've heard nothing," I said. "I came straight from my house."

She sighed and lay down again. "He's dead, isn't he?" she said. "He has to be dead or he'd have contacted me by now. He'd know how much I would worry and he'd have found a way to let me know he was all right."

I didn't like to suggest that he may have been kidnapped if he was still alive, and if he was guilty of the murder, then he couldn't risk contacting his wife.

"Is there anywhere else he might have gone if he was in trouble?" I asked. "Any friends with whom he might be hiding out?"

"His brother Leopold lives in the city," she said. "You know, the doctor. But Dash went round there last night and Leopold hadn't seen him. He has friends in New York, I'm sure. Other performers he's worked with over the years. But I couldn't tell you who they are or where they live. And why would he go to one of them, knowing that his poor wife was sick with worry?"

One only had to look at her to see that

she was not a player in this charade — if charade it was. She looked terrible with dark circles around her eyes and hollow cheeks, as if she hadn't slept a wink.

"Bess," I said, carefully measuring my words, "I have to ask you this — but did you have any suspicion at all that your husband might have planned this?"

"Planned it? What do you mean — planned to get kidnapped?" Her voice rose dangerously.

"I meant that this was an illusion planned to get rid of someone who was bothering him. You said that the victim was the young man who came to the door and made what sounded like threats."

"That is crazy," she said. "My husband wouldn't do that. Never."

"You said he'd taught fellow illusionists a lesson by having them roughed up."

"That's different," she said. "Illusionists are always rivals, but that doesn't mean they go around killing each other. Besides, the dead guy wasn't one of us."

"But if it wasn't Harry who did this? It had to be another illusionist," I went on. "Someone out to pay back your husband? It's logical that it was the same person who trapped you in the trunk."

I saw her expression change for a second.

"Not necessarily," she said. Then she shook her head. "I don't know what I'm saying. I'm crazy with worry. Find my Harry and I'll be in your debt for the rest of my life."

"I rather hope you'll pay me a good fee," I said with a smile.

She managed a watery smile back.

"Have you had some breakfast?" I said, trying to sound cheerful. "You're looking horribly pale."

"I'm not hungry. And besides, his mother doesn't like walking up the stairs."

"What about his brother?"

"Gone," she said.

"Gone? Where?"

"Back to Atlantic City. Caught the train early this morning."

She must have seen my expression become guarded. "He has a show to do tonight," she said. "He has to perform when he's booked into a good house like that. It doesn't do to get into the bad books of the theater managers, or they won't hire him again."

This made sense but my mind was still jumping to other conclusions. The younger brother, banished from the act when Houdini married, now imitating his more famous brother but without his celebrity — would that make him bitter enough to take revenge and maybe take over the limelight? Who better would know how to exchange bodies in a trunk? And he was big and strong enough to make that exchange.

"What's the name of the theater in Atlantic City?" I asked.

"It's the Majestic on the pier," she said. "It's a good house. Of course I expect my husband helped to get him hired at a good house like that. That family, they're so close, they'd do anything for each other." I saw her staring at a photograph in a silver frame of Mrs. Weiss, surrounded by her offspring — Houdini, a sister, the taller, sturdier Dash, and a distinguished-looking man with a beard I decided must be Leopold.

I kept my suspicions to myself and glanced around the room. It wasn't exactly tidy, with half-unpacked trunks and piles of magazines on top of dressers. "Would you mind if I took a look to see if there is anything here that might give us a clue as to what kind of trouble your husband was in?"

"Anything," she said. "Anything that can help find him, although I don't know what that could be."

I felt awkward as I started rummaging around, feeling her eyes on me. I wouldn't have wanted anyone poking around in my bedroom. And I had no idea what I might be looking for anyway. "Where did he write his letters?" I asked, hesitating before I opened drawers. "Did he keep his correspondence and business papers in a desk downstairs or up here?"

"Anything important would have been up here with us," she said. "Harry is very close about his business dealings." I read into her look that his mother would well snoop if correspondence was left around in a desk downstairs. Then she added, "All the details for his illusions are in that suitcase under the bed. But he keeps it locked and I don't know where the key is."

"I'm not interested in his illusions," I said, then I reconsidered this. "On second thought, maybe I am, and maybe you can help me. I need to know how he substituted that body during the act. I was onstage, only a few feet away."

"He didn't substitute the body," she said angrily. "Harry would never kill anybody."

"Somebody substituted that body," I said. "I'm not saying that your husband did it. Let's assume he was also a victim here. But somebody else knew his stuff well enough to pull off this switch. Tell me how you do the Metamorphosis."

She frowned, then shook her head.

I put my hand on her frail white shoulder.

"Bess, how can I help you if you can't trust me?" I said. "The police are going to ask you anyway, so you might as well tell me. I was part of your act, after all."

She turned away from me, staring out of the window, where a spindly tree was swaying in the wind. "It's quite simple really," she said. "The back of the trunk is only held on with two screws that pull right out. As soon as Harry goes into the bag he takes off the handcuffs and the leg irons so that by the time they have it tied up and have lifted him into the trunk he is free. The bag also has an overlapped opening down the back, so Harry can get out of it without undoing it. Then he pulls out the screws and the back panel swings outward and he's out of the trunk. There's a drumroll to mask any noise. Then there's a flash and he appears. Big applause. He comes forward to bow, taking the audience's eyes away from me. I slip into the trunk and the bag the same way and I've got little wrists. It's easy to put on the handcuffs. By the time they unlock it, I'm all trussed up the way he was."

"Fascinating," I said. "And do you think he could have substituted a dead body in the same way?" I saw her frown and corrected myself. "Do you think that someone could have substituted a body that way?"

She frowned. "Where would the body have come from? The trunk's in the middle of the stage, isn't it? And you were there yourself."

"True enough," I said.

"It's one thing for a person like me to crawl into the trunk. I'm small and I'm agile and I've practiced for it. But it would take a lot of effort and time to get a deadweight into that bag."

I nodded. "And I heard or saw nothing."

"Then I don't know how it was done."

All the time we were talking I was busily examining anything that could have hidden a threatening letter. There were the piles of magazines, all to do with magic, so it seemed. Then there were several scrapbooks. I leafed through them. There were playbills and newspaper cuttings, some of them in a foreign type that I didn't understand — presumably German. But I noted some headings: "Houdini Exposes Rival as Fraud," and "Battle of the Handcuff Kings Ends in Disgrace for Cunning." So it would be worth taking a closer look at them later. These were the men publicly humiliated by Houdini. Men with the expertise to pull off such a stunt and bearing a grudge against him. And it was interesting to note that he had carefully mounted all his victories in a nice leather-bound scrapbook. I put the scrapbooks on a chair and continued my search. But I came across nothing incriminating. No threats or demands for money. Only a couple of letters from friends asking how long he'd be in New York, some admirers asking for autographs, some scribbled notes for an article he was apparently writing for a magazine, and then, in the drawer beside the bed, his passport.

"At least he hasn't fled the country," I said, holding it up. I glanced at it, then stared more intently. "I thought you said he was born in Hungary," I said.

"He was."

"But this is an American passport and it says he was born in Appleton, Wisconsin, on April sixth, 1873."

"That's not right," Bess said, sitting up now. "He was born in Budapest. And his birthday is March twenty-fourth. Why would he have given false information for his passport?"

"I've no idea," I said.

Bess took the paper from me and examined it, still shaking her head. "And he applied for this in 1900. He already had a passport long before that. I don't understand. Unless —"

"Unless?"

"Unless it might have been difficult for a person who was a Hungarian Jew to get into Russia and to some parts of Germany," she said, "so he decided to claim to be American born."

"He was taking a risk then, wasn't he?" I said. "Lying on a passport application, especially someone as well known as he. It's a wonder he didn't wind up in jail."

"I don't understand," she said at last. "I don't understand anything anymore. I just want my husband back safely. Find him for me, Molly. Promise me you'll find him."

"I'll do my best, I promise," I said, hoping that this was a promise I could keep.

TWENTY-ONE

I had just put the passport back in its drawer when I heard voices downstairs — a woman's voice raised in anger and a man's deep, calm tones. I opened the door and picked up the pronounced accent of Houdini's mother. "No, I vill not allow —" she was shouting.

Then, "Calm yourself, madam, please."

Then heavy steps coming up the stairs and Daniel's face appeared from the darkness of the hall.

"Ye gods, she's a harridan, isn't she?" he demanded. "Wasn't going to let me in even when I told her I was a policeman." He nodded politely to Bess, who now sat with her bedclothes drawn up in a display of maidenly effrontery, which I found amusing, considering she spent most of her time appearing in front of strangers in a scanty costume.

"I'm Captain Sullivan. We met briefly last

night," he said.

"You have news for me? You've found him?" Her voice quavered.

"Not a trace so far. That's why we need your help," Daniel said. "Do you think you'd feel strong enough to accompany us back to the theater? We haven't touched anything since last night. I'd like you to take a look for yourself and see if you notice anything unusual that might give us a clue as to what happened."

"If you think it will help, I'll come," she said.

He smiled at her. "Good girl," he said. "Hurry up and get dressed, then. I'll be waiting in the automobile outside."

"An automobile. Fancy that." She looked rather impressed. "Harry was talking about buying one in Germany this year. We were even shown around the factory where they make them."

"Were you?" Daniel looked equally impressed. "Mercedes-Benz, you mean?"

"Oh, yes. They adore Harry over there. He's always so interested in the latest machines they're making. He says they are so much more advanced than we are and of course they love showing off their superiority. They think a lot of themselves in Germany, you know."

"We shouldn't waste Captain Sullivan's time," I said, as she appeared rather taken with him and willing to go on chatting. "Do you need me to help you get dressed or should I wait in the automobile with Captain Sullivan?"

"You can help me if you like," she said. "I don't know how steady I'm going to be on my pins after what I've been through."

"We'll see you downstairs then," I said. Daniel nodded and closed the door behind him.

"He's awfully charming for a policeman, isn't he?" she said as she stood up. "Good looking too."

"Not bad, I suppose," I agreed. "Now what will you be wearing, do you think? It's a hot day out there again."

"That's one of the things I liked about England," she said. "It was never too hot. I liked England a lot better than Germany but there's no place like home, is there?"

I wondered if she'd also seen that new play *The Wizard of Oz* where that line featured prominently, and smiled to myself.

It took a while to lace her into her corsets, given that I wasn't used to the process myself, and then to fix her hair to her satisfaction, but Daniel greeted us with no sign of impatience as he assisted Bess into the front seat of the automobile beside him and then me into the back.

"Hold on to your hats, ladies," he said and we set off at a great rate.

"I'd like to get some details straight before we reach the theater," he said over the pop-popping of the motor. "You've been away from America for a while, I gather."

"Three years," she said. "Most of it in England and Germany, but we were also in Hungary and Harry went to Russia too. I stayed behind that time. Harry thought that Russia might be a dangerous place for me."

"Why so long away?"

"The money," she said. "They treat Harry like a king over there. He gets paid enormous sums to appear in the theaters and sometimes he is invited to perform for royalty and nobility too. The Tsar of Russia was so taken with him he wanted him to stay on as his adviser. And the Kaiser gave him a gold watch. We only came home this summer because Harry worries about his mother, and I hadn't been well and was homesick. But we're booked to sail back to Europe in a couple of weeks from now."

We paused to let a horse-drawn jitney cross in front of us. The driver glared as if we were a menace. Little boys ran over to examine our contraption.

"What makes it go, mister?" one of them asked.

"Magic!" Daniel called as the coast cleared and we moved off.

"And I understand that last night wasn't the first occasion that something unpleasant has happened to you during this visit?" Daniel continued.

"It wasn't. In fact I've felt uneasy from the moment we landed here. That's why" — she glanced back at me — "I should probably tell you that this lady in the backseat is not an entertainer at all. She's a detective, hired by me."

"Is she really?" Daniel said. "I suspected something of the kind."

"You did? Why?" Bess asked.

"You only had to watch the way she walked across the stage to know she wasn't a professional," Daniel said.

I thought I saw a smirk. I wanted to hit him but kept my self-control.

"And why did you hire her, Mrs. Houdini?"

"Because I thought my husband's life was in danger."

"And you didn't come to the police?"

"You don't know Harry," she said. "He's a proud man. He thinks he's invincible. Besides, he wouldn't admit there was anything wrong."

"But then I gather you yourself almost suffered a similar fate in that trunk a few nights ago," Daniel continued. "Something went wrong and you were trapped in there?"

"That's right." Bess put a handkerchief up to her mouth. "I thought I was going to suffocate."

"Did you have any suspicion at all about who might have done this?" Daniel asked. "You say your husband's life was in danger, but this was you who nearly died, not your husband that time."

"I know. I thought it was maybe to give Harry a warning."

So she was a good liar when she needed to be. I resolved to have a private word about it later with Daniel, but I kept quiet for the moment.

"Who?" Daniel asked, more sharply now. "Who wanted to give your husband such a strong warning?"

"I've no idea. Honestly." She shook her head so violently I thought her hat might come flying off in the breeze.

"Yet you said that you recognized the dead man last night. He came to your house, you said, and made threats?"

"They sounded like threats to me. He asked for Harry and when I said he wasn't home he said that Harry would know who he was and to tell him that he'd be back."

"And what did your husband say when you related this to him?"

"He said it was nothing to worry about. Just a spot of business."

"And he gave you no indication of the man's name or where he came from?"

"Nothing. As I told Miss Murphy, Harry was very close about business matters. He didn't like to bother me with details."

"I overheard a similar conversation at the theater," I said, leaning forward between them as we skirted the park. "Tell me, Mrs. Houdini, did you ever meet a well-dressed young man with light blond hair and light eyes and a sort of haughty air to him?"

"I can't say that anyone comes to mind," she said.

"Well, I overheard your husband speaking with such a man. They said something about it being 'serious stuff' and the other man said, 'You can't be too careful' and that your husband should 'hurry up and hand it over.'"

"Interesting," Daniel said. "Did you pick up any ideas about what 'it' was?"

"Not at all," I said. "And when I asked Mr. Houdini about it he said that everything would be taken care of the next day — that would have been today. So it seems that he had something that someone else wanted, and what happened last night prevented him from delivering it."

"Or he didn't want to hand it over, killed the messenger who came to collect it, and quietly disappeared," Daniel said.

"No!" Bess said vehemently. "I keep telling everyone that Harry would never kill. Well, maybe to protect his mother or me, but not for any other reason."

There. She had admitted that he was capable of killing. I really didn't know what to believe. I knew how strong he was and thought how easily he could overpower another man, especially a man like the one in the trunk who was slight of build. Houdini had said everything would be taken care of by tomorrow. So had he been planning this all along — rigging the trunk so that the accident happened to Bess and thus making himself a more likely victim in a second accident? I thought about the first accident. Why hadn't the key been in his pocket as usual that first night? Why had someone had to run to his dressing room for it, and . . . most damning of all, why did the King of Handcuffs, the man who could open any lock in the world, have to wait for an ax to release his imprisoned wife?

"When you feel strong enough, Mrs. Houdini," Daniel continued in the front seat, "I'd like you to jot down a complete list of the people you know in New York and your recollections of what you have done since you arrived back in the States. We have to find out how your husband was linked to the dead man."

"You still don't know who the man was?" I asked.

Daniel shook his head. "Maybe someone will come forward after his picture appears in today's newspapers. He must have family and friends. He looked like such a normal, everyday sort of fellow, certainly not like any criminal I've come across."

"And not like anybody in the entertainment business either," Bess said. "They usually dress with more pizzazz than that."

While we had been talking we had passed fashionable shopping districts and Macy's spanking new department store that took up a whole block along Broadway. Then at last Midtown gave way to the crowded streets of the Lower East Side and we made slow progress, inching between delivery drays, trolleys, and pushcarts. Ragged children darted across the street with no apparent concern for their safety and the air rang with the cries of vendors, the clang of construction from a new building, the shrill squeals of children, and the clip-clop of horses' hooves. A veritable cacophony, but one that I had come to love. It was the sound of a city full of life.

We pulled up at last outside the theater, where a constable standing in attendance made a vendor of Italian ice cream move his cart so that we could place the automobile there. The Italian went, grudgingly. It was obviously a good pitch for him. Outside the theater new bills had been posted, advertising this week's acts. ALL-NEW SPECTACULAR! was splashed across the bill along with vignettes of pretty girls posing in an acrobatic pyramid and another illusionist with a white dove in his hand.

"Anything I should know about, O'Malley?" Daniel asked as the constable held open the door for us. "Is Detective MacAffrey back yet?"

"No, sir. He's over at the morgue for the autopsy."

Daniel nodded. "Make sure we're not disturbed. No newspaper reporters."

"I've kept them out all morning, sir, and that doorkeeper has fended them off at the stage door."

"Anyone else here?"

"No, sir. They canceled tonight's performance, so we've got the place to ourselves," he said bitterly.

"Lucky for us. Or we'd have them clamoring to be able to use the stage."

"We did have a couple of new acts turn up, wanting to put their props in place, but I told them they wouldn't be allowed in until the captain said so."

"What acts were they?" Daniel asked.

"A troop of girl acrobats — the Flying Foxes, they called themselves, and another magician with his assistant."

The interior of the theater felt dark and cold after the overpowering heat of the street and I shivered. It was like stepping into a crypt as we picked our way down the center aisle toward the stage. Another constable was standing by the stage steps and stood aside to let us mount them. Daniel took Mrs. Houdini's hand and escorted her up, thus ignoring me. But I wasn't annoyed this time. I saw what he was doing. She responded well to male attention. He was softening her up.

"So here we are, Mrs. Houdini," he said. "Everything exactly as it was last night, except that the body has been removed. I want you to take a good look around and see if there is anything different from the usual way you perform your act — any little thing."

She nodded. "Of course Molly was the assistant last night, not me, but I was watching from the box and it all looked just fine to me."

She moved around as if on tiptoe, gently touching the frame of what they called the cabinet, then the table on which the hood and the playing cards still lay. Then she stopped, her head to one side, like a bird's.

"That's a bit off," she said.

"What is?"

"The trunk. We usually perform that trick over to stage left. Why did you put the trunk so close to center stage, Molly?"

"I don't know. Someone helped me carry it onstage and we just put it down. I didn't think it mattered that much where it was."

"It doesn't, but . . ." she stopped, then knelt beside the trunk. "Can I touch it?" she asked.

"Go ahead. We've already extracted fingerprints from it."

She examined it briefly. "I thought something was wrong," she said. "This isn't our trunk."

TWENTY-TWO

Daniel squatted beside her.

"Are you sure?"

She looked up and nodded. "Quite sure. I already explained to Molly how we manage to pull off the switch so quickly. The back of the trunk is only held together with two screws that come out real easy, and then it swings open. This one is solid, see?" She banged on it. "Apart from that it's an excellent copy, from what I can see."

Daniel continued to stare at the trunk. "So someone knew exactly what your trunk looked like and had a copy made. How easy would it have been to get a good, close-up look at the trunk?"

"Well, you'd only have to come to the show for a couple of nights to get a good look, wouldn't you?" she said. "And during our act it's right there, in the wings, until it's needed, so anybody backstage could get a good look at it then."

"So that's why the keys didn't work!" I exclaimed.

They looked up at me. "When the trunk wouldn't open I found the keys in Houdini's pocket, but neither of them worked. Because it was a different trunk."

"Someone has gone to a lot of trouble to pull this off," Daniel said, staring down at the empty trunk. There was no sign of bloodstains and it was hard to imagine that a body had lain in it not too long ago. "In New York there are plenty of dark alleys and hired killers if you just want to get rid of someone. And the body turns up floating down the Hudson a few days later. This person wanted to do more than kill someone. But what?"

"I can think of several answers to that," I said. "Either he wanted to publicly humiliate Houdini, at the same time as paying him back, or he wanted to send a strong message to the entire band of illusionists. Or —" I paused, collecting my thoughts. "He just wanted to show how clever he was."

"Or none of the above," Daniel said. "There is a fourth scenario. Houdini himself finding a clever way to get rid of an annoyance."

"No!" Bess said again. "You've seen how Harry deals with his rivals. He challenges

313

them. And he always wins. He's an honor- able man, Captain Sullivan, not a dirty trickster who stabs in the dark."

"Let's hope you're right, Mrs. Houdini, for your sake as well as mine," Daniel said. "Now, I'd like you to show us your dressing room, where your props were kept — any- thing that might help us uncover where and how the trunks might have been switched. Are you up to that?"

"I'll try," she said, "but Molly could show you those things."

"I want your perspective on this. You were the only one who could tell us that the trunks had been switched, after all. So let's start right before your act. You stand in the wings where?"

Bess led him through the curtains and indicated the spot.

"And who else would be standing nearby?"

"Stagehands. The theater manager."

"We're having our men check into their backgrounds," Daniel said, "but I don't see that any of them could have the skill to pull this off."

"Besides," I said, "we'd have noticed a second trunk. I was in Bess's place last night, remember? I helped carry the trunk onto the stage."

"How heavy was it?"

"Not too heavy. Certainly not heavy enough to have a body in it."

Daniel poked around a bit. "There's not much room back here. Nowhere to hide that second trunk, apart from among these curtains. Then the passage to the manager's office goes off and the stairs to all the dressing rooms, is that correct?"

"That's right," Bess said. "And over to your left is the way to the stage door, and around on the left side of the stage is the stage manager's office and the props room."

"But you didn't keep your props in that room?"

"None of the illusionists do. They all have their own crate or some way of keeping their props locked up. Illusionists are always worried that a rival will see something and steal their act."

"But we know your husband was a whiz at opening locks. Presumably there are other illusionists who are equally skilled?"

"Not as good as Harry, but sure, there are men who have tried to call themselves the handcuff king. Cheek, if you ask me. But none of them was working here."

Daniel sighed. "That's just it. Any outsider would have been noticed. There's just not that much room backstage and nowhere to hide, and stagehands all over the place. Now you'd better show me the way up to your dressing room. I went over it last night, but again you might notice something that we haven't."

Bess led the way up the stairs, looked around her dressing room, and shook her head. "It's all just the way it was. There's my costume and there are Harry's street clothes, waiting for him to change back into . . ." She burst into tears again.

Daniel glanced over her head at me. "I'll have one of my constables escort you home, Mrs. Houdini. You're clearly not up to anything more here today. But I would ask you to do one thing for me when you feel a little better. Remember I asked you to write down everything you have done since you came back to America — every person you've seen, every person who has spoken to your husband. I'd also like a list of any illusionist you can think of who was at odds with your husband. Those famous challenges. Anybody who might have considered himself your husband's rival."

"He has scrapbooks," I said. "From what I could see, he has all of these challenges pretty well documented."

"Then we'll compare the scrapbooks to Mrs. Houdini's own recollections," Daniel

316

said. "Maybe something will emerge. Maybe there's one name that he left out."

Bess nodded. "All right. I'll try and remember everything."

Daniel helped her back down the stairs and gave instructions to one of the constables.

"Are you coming with me, Molly?" she asked.

I looked at Daniel.

"I'd like to keep this young woman a little longer," he said. "I have some more questions for her. Your husband's mother is with you, is she not? And his brother?"

"His brother has gone back to Atlantic City. He left early this morning," I said, and a quick look passed between us.

"He has another brother who is a doctor, doesn't he?" Daniel said. "Maybe he can be summoned to attend to you."

That's odd, I thought. When Bess almost died, why did Houdini take her to a private clinic instead of summoning his brother, who was a doctor?

As she made her way down the theater aisle she turned back to us. "You will let me know the minute you have any news, won't you?"

"I will, and the same goes for you, Mrs. Houdini. If your husband tries to contact you, please let us know."

With that she pushed open the doors and was for a moment a black silhouette against the fierce sunlight outside.

"So what do you think?" Daniel asked me as soon as we were alone. "Did he do it?"

"I don't know what to think," I said.

"But I saw your reaction when you told me that the brother had left for Atlantic City."

I nodded. "Yes, it just struck me as being too convenient that he had to go out of town before the police could talk to him. Maybe this is family business, Daniel. They're a very close-knit family. Houdini worships his mother. He pampers a neurotic wife, calls her 'babykins' and 'poopsie' and other such ridiculous nicknames."

"I gather you won't want to be called such things when we're married," Daniel said.

I gave him a withering stare.

"Go on," he said. "So what are you suggesting?"

"The brother who just did a bunk — he was Houdini's younger brother. He'd been part of the act until Bess came along. Some resentment there at his brother's success, maybe? He seems a nice enough fellow. They look very similar, although Dash is bigger."

"Dash?"

"That's his nickname. His real name is Theodore, I believe, but the family calls him Dash and he's known professionally as Hardeen."

Daniel gave me a knowing look. "Somewhat similar to Houdini, wouldn't you say? Cashing in on big brother."

"Or wanting to be like big brother."

"And he's another illusionist. Does the same kind of tricks," Daniel said thoughtfully.

"And he's close enough to his brother in appearance that nobody would look twice if he were prowling around backstage," I went on. "And he was in the theater last night, wasn't he? In the stage box. It would have been easy enough to slip out and back again without Bess even noticing that he'd gone."

"Do you think he planned this to kill or harm his brother, or do you think he planned this whole thing with his brother, to get rid of a person they found to be a nuisance?"

"I hadn't considered that before," I said "but who would the dead man be? Someon who was somehow disrupting the family?"

Daniel put a hand on my shoulder, hi eyes alight. "What if he was bothering Bes Houdini — an old suitor maybe? Someon

Harry didn't want hanging around her."

I shook my head. "She didn't recognize him immediately."

"Maybe she didn't look at him too closely. Women are squeamish about looking at dead bodies — apart from you, of course, who seem to possess no delicate sensibilities of your sex."

"You're right. I've never had the vapors in my life." I laughed, then grew serious again as I considered his hypothesis. "I'd imagine Houdini could be horribly jealous. You should have seen the way he fussed over her."

"Now we're getting somewhere. So he enlists his brother to do the deed, then somehow they manage to switch trunks, and Houdini is spirited away." Daniel nodded in satisfaction.

"But you've seen how upset Bess gets at the least little thing. Wouldn't she have been more upset when she saw it was an old flame?" I asked.

"She was upset, remember. She was quite hysterical. The brother had to take her home."

"So she was. You know what, Daniel? I think I might take a little trip to Atlantic City."

"Oh, no." Daniel shook his head. "I'm not

letting you go chatting to a potential murderer."

"But don't you see, I'm the ideal person. He thinks of me as Bess's dear friend from childhood. I could find out more easily than the police could. I could even say that she sent me up there because she had some things she wanted to ask him."

"What things?"

"I'd think those out on the train," I said confidently.

When he didn't answer I said, "Well, I'm going whether you approve or not. I've been hired by Bess and I have to do all I can for her. At the very least Dash can give me a hint where his brother might be hiding out, and I can let Bess know he's alive and safe."

"And if he actually killed his older brother? What then?"

"I'm no threat to him, I told you. He would have no idea I'm working with the police. I'll tread very carefully, Daniel. If I get any hint of danger, I'll back off, I promise."

"This is criminal business, Molly. It is absolutely out of the question for you to go to see this man. If I'm to go along with your intuition, then I'll contact my colleagues in the police department at Atlantic City. If you want to be of help to us, then your place is at Bess's side. It's just possible she may be in on this and Houdini will send her a message." He gave me an appeasing smile. "So you see, you will be providing valuable assistance."

"Oh, yes," I said. " 'Valuable assistance.' "

We stood in the darkness of the backstage area while I fought to contain my temper. I suppose part of me didn't want to travel to confront Houdini's brother, but I was still driven by that stupid desire to prove myself as a detective. I didn't want to be the one who provided "valuable assistance."

Strange, cold drafts wafted up from below us. Daniel shivered. "At least this is a good place to come on a hot day," he said. He looked around. "This theater is more extensive than I thought. Plenty of opportunities to hide a body. Look at those walkways up there."

"They're called the flies, Daniel. They use them when they're rigging backdrops. But you'd have to be a mighty strong person to carry a body up and down those ladders. I've been up one, so I know."

"Why doesn't that surprise me." Daniel rolled his eyes. "But look. That ladder carries on down, below the stage."

And indeed there was a hole cut in the floor with the ladder descending on down into darkness.

"I didn't notice that last night," he added.

"It must lead to a storage area under the stage." I went over and peered down. The cold draft came up to meet me. Below was complete darkness.

"I wonder if there are any electric lights down below," Daniel said. "There is little point in going down to no light. I wonder if my men actually discovered this last night. I'd better take a look."

"I'll come with you," I said.

"I'll go down first and see if I can find a light switch." He started down the ladder. I watched his head disappear into darkness, feeling a knot in the pit of my stomach. Surely everyone at the theater knew about this basement area? Surely it had been searched last night? I heard Daniel give a muttered curse.

"What?" I called.

"Hit my shin on some kind of box," he said. "And I can feel no kind of light switch on the wall."

"They are bound to have a lamp or at least candles in the props room," I said. "I'll be right back. Don't go anywhere."

Sure enough I found an impressive candelabra among the props, rooted out some candles and then matches to light them.

"Holy Mother of God, you look like the Ghost of Christmas Past, standing there like that!" Daniel exclaimed as he spotted me standing above him. I handed down the candelabra, then climbed down myself. It was indeed pitch-black down there and smelled damp and musty, as if it flooded during rainstorms. We picked our way forward, searching the various piles of wood, boxes, and old scenery that had been dumped there. At least, I let Daniel do the searching. I had no wish to touch a spider, or worse. But we found nothing.

"They must have searched this last night," Daniel said. "See all these footprints in the dust on the floor?"

Suddenly there came a strong draft. The candles flickered, danced, and went out.

"Damn it," Daniel muttered.

I wanted to grab on to Daniel's arm but forced myself not to. I had my reputation of being a fearless detective to live up to. But instead of being in total darkness we found the floor painted with thin stripes of light from above. Light was shining through the cracks in the floorboards and ahead of us was a larger square of light.

"We must be under the stage," Daniel said, looking up. And indeed this part of the basement was cleaner and tidier, as if more frequently used.

"That square of light would be where the prompter stands," I said. "You can get down here from the front of the stage — at least you could in the last theater I worked in."

"Ah, yes. Steps up to your left," Daniel said. "And what have we here?"

He paused by a square wood-and-metal platform, raised just above floor level, then he looked up, looked around, and nodded. "I've an idea," he said. "Hawkins!" he yelled.

"Yes, Captain? Where are you?" came the voice from above.

"Under the stage. I want you to listen carefully. Draw a chalk line on the floor around the trunk and then move it carefully to one side."

"Right you are, Captain."

"What is it, Daniel?"

"Just a hunch."

We waited, then heard the trunk being dragged aside. Once the trunk was gone, a thin rectangle of light shone down.

"Stand back, Hawkins!" Daniel shouted. He went over to the wall and pulled a lever. A trapdoor opened up on the stage, sending light flooding down to us.

"Aha, so that was how it was done." Daniel sounded jubilant. "Now watch this." He raised a second lever and the platform beside us ascended at great speed.

"You see that!" He was almost like a small boy who has found a new toy that works as well as he hoped. "That's how they did it, Molly. The trapdoor opened — this platform was waiting below to whisk the first trunk down. The trunk was hauled off and the second trunk substituted. Then up it went, shoved into place, trapdoor closed again."

"How did you work that out?" I was rather jealous of his detective skills.

He grinned. "I saw a production of *Faust* not too long ago. The devil appeared miraculously from a trapdoor in the middle of the stage."

"So someone had to make sure that the trunk was placed in the right position to fall through the hole when it was opened," I said.

He nodded. "Who helped you carry the trunk onto the stage?"

"I really didn't notice. You're told never to turn your back to the audience and the lights are quite blinding. I was just conscious that somebody helped me. I thought it was a stagehand, but it could have been anyone."

"Someone who knew exactly what he was doing," Daniel said. "Come on, let's get out of here. I'll have my boys come back and dust that platform for fingerprints."

"Do you think this fingerprinting idea actually works?" I asked as Daniel made his way to the steps on our left.

"I think it's a brilliant idea," Daniel said. "No two fingerprints are alike, you know. A fingerprint can provide absolute proof. The hard part is trying to persuade judges to make them admissible evidence in a court of law. No one's ever succeeded yet."

He opened the little door at the top of the steps, pushed aside a curtain, and we were up in the wings again.

TWENTY-THREE

It was close to lunch hour by the time I arrived home. Washington Square was deserted in the midday heat. Even the customary little boys who made the constable's life a misery by trying to climb into the fountain had given up and gone home. I felt my dress sticking to my back as I hurried up Patchin Place. It was no weather for hurrying, but on the train ride home I had come to a decision. I was going to go to Atlantic City today. So what if Daniel had forbidden me to go? He didn't yet have authority over me, and I suppose part of my decision was simply to prove this fact to myself. And the more I thought about it, the more convinced I became that Houdini's brother Dash had to have participated in switching the trunks. I also had reluctantly come to think that Houdini himself had to have been involved. Would he not have noticed and done something if the trunk had been placed differently from usual? I sighed. Poor Bess. Either her husband was a wanted criminal or a kidnap victim.

This last thought made me reconsider my rash decision. I was leaving Bess alone when she needed me and I was going to visit someone who may have just killed a man most brutally — who may have even killed two men. Then I told myself I had been hired to find out the truth not be a nursemaid. I was just doing the job for which she had hired me.

I was approaching my house when I saw Gus waving from her front window. She opened the window and beckoned me over. "Ah, there you are," she said. "There was a man at your door not too long ago."

"What kind of man?"

"Ordinary looking. Respectable. Young."

"Do you know what he wanted?"

She shrugged. "I was painting up in my studio. I heard the knocking, looked down, and spotted him, but by the time I had come down two flights of stairs, he was gone."

"I wonder if he left a note," I said. I opened the front door. The letter box was empty.

"No note," I said. "Ah, well, if it's important no doubt he'll call back. If you see him again would you tell him that I've had to go to Atlantic City, but should be back tomorrow."

"Atlantic City, how delightful," she said with great enthusiasm. "A breath of sea air is what we all need in heat like this. Maybe Sid and I should come with you. I've a great desire to dip my toes into the Atlantic again, haven't you?"

"I'm afraid I'm going there on business," I said. "I'll have no time to dip my toes into the Atlantic."

"Nonsense. Anyone can make time for a lovely dip in the ocean. So refreshing," she said. "And come to think of it, I have a cousin who spends her summers there. Why don't we come and keep you company, then we can all stay with my cousin."

"I think I'd better go alone," I said. "I have to interview a suspect there. I'd rather be as unobtrusive as possible."

"Interview a suspect. My, doesn't that sound impressive." Her eyes lit up. "If you wait a minute, I'll write a letter of introduction to my cousin. At least you'll have good company for dinner and a comfortable bed for the night."

"Thank you, but I'll probably just stay the night at a boardinghouse near the station," I said.

"But Molly, it's Atlantic City. You have to stay near the boardwalk and enjoy the ocean breezes and take a stroll down the pier," she said. "And my cousin is utterly charming. One of the few members of my family who would still welcome me into her home, in fact."

I was anxious to be off but trying not to offend Gus in the process. Lord knows, she and Sid had been good enough to me.

"You're very kind, but no thank you. I make it my policy not to mix business with pleasure. And I may be out and about until late evening, which would be very rude to any hostess."

"As you wish," she said. "You do have our new telephone number, don't you? I'm sure there is a line all the way from Atlantic City these days and you could put through a call to us if you find yourself in any kind of jam."

"Thank you again. I must be off."

"You never seem to have time for civilized chats these days. You are working yourself too hard," she said.

"I know, but just think, soon I'll be married and have all the time in the world for civilized chats," I said.

"I can't see that happening." Gus laughed. "Besides, your lord and master will forbid you to mix with people like us, just you see."

"I will never have a lord and master. I can tell you that right now. And I'll mix with whom I please." I pushed open my front door and went inside. It felt delightfully cool and I had visions of soaking in a cool tub, then eating lunch. But I had no time. I rushed around, packing essentials into an overnight bag, made myself a cheese sandwich and grabbed a couple of plums for the train journey, and I was out again, heading for the ferry across the Hudson to Exchange Place on the Jersey shore, the terminus where the trains left for Atlantic City — there being no way to bring a railway line across the mighty Hudson. On the way I wondered who the mystery man at my front door had been. Another client, maybe? That would be useful, as this case might not be continuing if my suspicions proved to be true. I'd probably not be paid, either.

I enjoyed the hint of cool breeze as the ferry chugged across the Hudson. Then as I entered the train station, I felt the excitement one always senses at a place where great journeys begin and end. I bought my ticket and was on my way to the platform when a man came up beside me.

"Here, miss. Let me help you with your bag," he said, tipping his hat to me before he tried to take the bag from me.

"You're most kind, but I don't need any kind of help," I said. I gave him a long look. He seemed respectable enough — young, clean shaven, straw boater, light-flannel trousers. I wondered if he made a habit of making advances to young women on railway stations.

"Where are you heading?" he asked.

"Atlantic City. And yourself?"

"As luck would have it, we're going the same way," he said, giving me a friendly smile. "Why don't you let me carry your bag? You seem encumbered and as you notice, I have no luggage of my own."

"I'm really just fine, thank you. I'm a strong, healthy woman and I don't need any help."

"But at the very least you'll let me escort you to your carriage," he said. "I find train journeys so tedious and the thought of sitting beside a pretty girl has cheered me no end."

He was beginning to annoy me. There was something about his overfriendliness that made me wary. "I have to warn you that this pretty girl is about to be married to someone else," I said. "I would go and do your fishing elsewhere if I were you."

He laughed. "And witty too. How delightful."

I tried to walk ahead of him. He took my arm and steered me across the station toward one of the platforms. I really didn't want to make a fuss amid all these people but I was going to clobber his straw boater if he kept this up.

Smoke swirled upward, then parted, revealing the destination board.

"Wait a second," I said. "This isn't the platform for the train to Atlantic City."

"No more it is," the man said, his grip on my arm tightening.

"Let go of me. What are you playing at?" I demanded. "Do you want me to scream for help?"

That's when I noticed that a man had come up on the other side of me. I felt something dig into my side.

"I wouldn't scream if I were you," the second man said in a low voice. "There is a knife in my hand. I can slip it in between your ribs and you'll be dead before you know it. Much less noisy than a gun. Now be a sensible girl and you'll not get hurt."

"Where are you taking me?" I asked.

"You'll soon find out." A train was already standing at the platform, puffing out steam as if impatient to be on its way. Down the platform they bore me, past families waving good-bye, porters wheeling trolleys of luggage. I couldn't believe what was happening. A small voice in my head was saying, "You're being kidnapped," but it seemed too absurd to be true. My brain started racing, trying to think how I could escape from them. If I gave the one with the stiletto a hefty push and started screaming, would I have a chance to run before he could stab me? I could feel the prick of sharp steel against my skin so I knew his threat was not idle.

Before I had time to contemplate any longer the first man opened a carriage door. "In you get," he said.

"Where are you taking me?"

"You'll soon find out. Now sit down and shut up."

He pushed me into the seat and sat on one side of me. The man with the knife had slid into place on the other side. I noticed that the compartment said RESERVED and that there was no corridor. The first man immediately pulled down the blinds. I glanced up at the emergency cord. If I caught them off guard, I could leap up and pull on it, but then they'd have killed me before the train came to a halt and the conductor found my carriage. I looked from one to the other, trying to decide who they were and what they wanted of me. They

335

certainly didn't look like the criminal classes. Nor did they look like entertainers. More like — more like the young man who had lain dead in the trunk. Bank clerks, shop assistants, respectable wage earners.

On the platform outside there was a piercing whistle and a shout of "All aboard!" Then the sound of doors slamming up and down the platform. The engine gave a mighty huff, and we lurched forward. At the last moment our carriage door opened and a man got in. My two captors nodded and jumped out. The train picked up speed. I looked at the man who had replaced my abductors. He was older than they, avuncular-looking actually, with a gray beard and horn-rimmed spectacles. He gave a sigh and promptly removed the beard and glasses. I stared at him again and gasped as I realized with a jolt of surprise that I recognized him.

TWENTY-FOUR

"Mr. Wilkie, isn't it?" I demanded.

He smiled benignly and removed his homburg. "It is indeed. A pleasure to meet you again, Miss Murphy."

I didn't return the smile. I fact I was furious, as one often is after a big fright. "So those unmannered louts work for you?"

"I'm afraid so. I hope they didn't alarm you too much?"

"Only kidnap me, stick a knife into my side, and threaten to kill me," I said. "I was on my way to Atlantic City."

"I know. That's why we had to act quickly. I apologize for their behavior but I did tell them to make sure you reached this carriage before the train pulled out."

"They could have tried saying that Mr. Wilkie, head of the Secret Service, wanted to speak with me urgently. Maybe I'd have come along of my own accord."

"Ah, but I couldn't let them use my name

337

or let anybody know that we were meeting. Actually I didn't want anybody to even know I was anywhere near New York City. I slipped through the station, hopefully incognito." He leaned closer to me. "And I had to speak to you in a place where I could guarantee that we were not followed or overheard."

"Good heavens. Why all the secrecy? Or does the Secret Service always operate this way?"

The train was chugging along merrily across the Jersey marshes and the outer sprawl of civilization. "Where are we going, anyway?"

"The journey is what matters, not the destination," he said. "You can get out when the train stops in Philadelphia if we've concluded our business by then, but I find it expedient to conduct strictly confidential cases on a train. It's like a private world, isn't it?"

"I'm surprised you didn't set up a hot air balloon," I said and he laughed.

"I like you, Miss Murphy. You've been through a scare and you're feisty and witty as ever."

"So why do you need to speak to me so privately?" I asked.

"Houdini, of course," he said.

"Houdini? What is that to do with you?" I was taken completely off guard.

"A lot, as it happens," he said. "And I understand that you are also somehow intimately involved."

"I was hired to assist Mr. and Mrs. Houdini with a problem, yes."

"Can you share the nature of that problem with me?"

"If you can share the reason for your involvement with me," I said.

He smiled again. He had a charming, avuncular smile and I found that I was bristling slightly less than before.

"Quite right, Miss Murphy. Actually I have set up this little assignation so that we can pool our knowledge. You see, I came to New York to meet with him, only to find that he had vanished."

"You were the one he was planning to meet with?"

"He told you about it?"

"He said that something would be sorted out the next day and then he'd be off the hook."

"Ah," Wilkie said.

"So why would Houdini need to sort something out with you?"

"He was working for me, Miss Murphy," Mr. Wilkie said in his soft, calm voice.

"Don't look so surprised. The Secret Service has found it most useful to employ entertainers, particularly magicians, as spies. They can move freely in foreign countries. They are invited to places like royal courts that normal foreigners never enter. They have perfect opportunities to overhear and to observe when those in power are at ease and speaking freely. And Houdini was one of the best."

"Really?" I paused as my brain processed the implications of this. "So you do think that the incident at the theater last night had something to do with you?"

"I'm sure of it," he said. "The man who was killed. He worked for me. I had placed him to keep an eye on Houdini because we had word that German agents were after him." He leaned closer to me again. "Houdini had discovered something important, Miss Murphy. Something so vital that he couldn't communicate in the normal manner."

"Which was?"

"I wish I knew. There could be no direct communication between us, ever. He wrote articles for various magicians' magazines, seemingly harmless reports on illusionists and performances, but with coded messages in them. Or he placed information in classified advertisements."

"And you think he had discovered something important?"

"I'm sure of it. The future of our country may even be at stake."

"Holy Mother of God!" I exclaimed. "You really mean that?"

"I believe so. What he discovered was too risky or too complicated to put in a magazine. Or perhaps he knew that the other side was onto him. Either way, he refused to hand over the information to anybody but me. That's why I had come to New York last week, only he couldn't be located and the president summoned me back to Washington before I could get in touch with Houdini. I sent a couple of my men in my stead, but he insisted on meeting only with me. He was supposed to have caught this train today. He should have been sitting opposite me and all would have been well. Now he may well be dead."

"Do you have any idea who might have done it?" I asked.

"I only know what I read in the morning papers," he said. "A clever illusionist. One who is working for the other side."

"Is Germany the other side now? Are they our enemy?"

"At this moment, no. But the Kaiser has

grand ambitions, Miss Murphy. They are seeking to expand their empire and they are building up their armaments at an alarming rate. That's one of the reasons Houdini was so useful. He was fascinated with gadgets so the Germans were happy to show him around their factories. They're proud of their mechanical superiority, you know."

"So you believe they have sent an illusionist over here with instructions to kill Houdini?"

"Before he could make a report to me, I must assume," Mr. Wilkie said.

"How many German illusionists can there be in New York at this time? Surely it will be easy to flush him out?"

"Not necessarily a German, I'm afraid. If I can persuade magicians to work for me, then presumably some can be persuaded to work for alien powers, if the money is enticing enough."

"Oh, I see. So who else knew that Houdini was working for you?"

"Nobody should have known, except for a couple of my own men — and the president, of course. He takes a keen interest in what we are doing."

The carriage was warm and smelled of stale cigar smoke but I knew better than to open the window and have the smoke from the locomotive blow in on us. I fought to stay alert, trying to digest everything I had been told.

"I wonder if Bess knew?" I said.

"I'm sure she didn't. Houdini once told me, on a train journey similar to this one, that he would never confide matters of importance to his wife. He said she had too fragile a nature to bear the strain of worry."

"He babied her," I said. "She's in an awful state at this moment. I really shouldn't have left her side, but I felt I had to speak with Houdini's brother, who has left New York to perform at a theater in Atlantic City."

"Hardeen, you mean?"

"Yes. Was he working for you too?"

"Absolutely not."

"Then could it be possible that he is working for the other side? He was also performing in Germany, wasn't he?"

"You think he'd murder his own brother?" He shook his head. "I very much doubt that, Miss Murphy. They are a devoted family from what I've heard. Very close. No, I don't think that Hardeen is our man. In fact I rather suspect that our man is working for both sides."

"What makes you think that?"

"This," he said, and handed me a cutting

from a magazine. I started to read. It seemed innocuous enough, reporting on the various acts currently performing in Berlin.

"Illusionists are always popular with the crowd and there seems to be a crop of good ones at the moment, including the amazing Mr. Harry Houdini —" I looked up and Mr. Wilkie smiled.

"He was never particularly modest about himself when reporting as a supposed third person. Read on."

The article went on to describe Harry's act, and then that of other magicians. Then came the words, "The interesting thing about illusionists is that they can make you believe anything. You think they are working on one side of the stage, when really they are on the other. It's all done with mirrors — that's what they say, don't they?"

I looked up and handed him back the piece of paper. "Do you think that's what those last words mean — that someone in Germany was working for both sides?"

"I'm sure of it," he said.

The train lurched as it went around a bend, throwing me off balance. Mr. Wilkie put out a hand to steady me.

"Why have you told me all this?" I asked.

"Because you struck me as a particularly intelligent young woman and because you're

344

a detective, and you were already working with Houdini," he said. "A most useful combination for our purposes."

"Your purposes? You want to hire me to work for you?"

"I want you to work for your country, Miss Murphy."

I had to smile at the irony of this. "I'm not even a citizen here, and an outcast from my own country."

He returned the smile. "All the more reason to repay the debt to the country that has taken you in, wouldn't you say?"

I was about to say that the country hadn't exactly done much for me yet. There had been times when I had been close to starvation and had only survived through my own wits, but Wilkie went on. "It is essential that we find out what Harry Houdini had discovered and was about to hand over to me. I want you to go back to New York and see what you can find."

I considered this. "Why me? Don't you have a host of men you could send to search Houdini's residence?"

"I do, but at this moment I'd rather work with the element of surprise. I don't want the enemy to know what we're doing. I gather you're well in with Houdini's wife. He may have let slip something to her —

something she'd confide to you but not to me. I want you to go through his things and bring anything suspicious to me."

"Harry Houdini was trying to bring something to you and he wound up missing or dead," I said. "I'd rather like to stay alive, thank you."

A brief smile crossed his otherwise expressionless face. "Then shall we say 'bring it to my attention?' If you find anything you think I should know about, you will send me a wire saying 'Thank you for birthday present,' and sign it 'Your niece.' I will arrange to meet with you directly."

"I see," I said.

"I'll post one of my men to keep an eye on you."

"Not the one with the stiletto," I said quickly.

He actually laughed this time. "Those two are on this train with us returning to Washington. No, it will be a new man, one you've never seen before. It doesn't do to leave operatives in one place for too long. The opposition is too darned clever." He paused, looking at me long and hard. "I won't say there isn't some degree of danger involved. But we hope that you are only seen as a friend of Bess Houdini, keeping her company. And the house will be guarded, as it is possible that someone may try to break in if they think there is something vital to be found there."

"They did try to break in once," I said. "Bess told me that Houdini scared a burglar off."

"I rather wish the brother hadn't gone back to Atlantic City," Wilkie said. "He was a male presence in the house. An extra defense."

"You will check into him, won't you?" I said. "Just to put my mind at rest that he wasn't the one working for the other side?"

"You're saying that I should pay attention to your feminine intuition?"

"Nothing of the sort," I replied hotly. "Just that you should pursue all suspects."

"Spoken like a true detective. I can see that Sullivan has trained you well."

"Indeed he hasn't trained me at all," I retorted. "In fact he's desperately against my being a detective. Everything I know I've learned the hard way, and I still have a lot more to learn."

"I think you'll do splendidly," he said.

"So does Captain Sullivan know about our meeting?" I asked. "Does he know that Houdini was working for you as a spy? Is that why you really came to New York when I met you at his apartment the other day?"

"He knows nothing of it," Wilkie said. "And I would appreciate it if you didn't mention your meeting with me to him. Not that I don't trust him, of course. Splendid fellow. Sound as an oak. But in these cases, the fewer people who know the facts, the better. He is searching for Houdini, which is good, but I rather fear that he'll not find him, or that his body will turn up weeks from now, probably quite unidentifiable."

"Oh, dear," I said. "Poor Bess."

He nodded. "It will be hard for her, I agree. And it's always harder not knowing, isn't it? I'm glad you're returning to her today. You can provide comfort as well help-ing us."

I plucked up courage to mention some-thing that had been going through my head, but that I hadn't dared to ask before. "I don't want to sound crass, but am I to be paid a fee for my services or am I supposed to be doing this for the good of the coun-try?"

Wilkie threw back his head and laughed. "I do like you, Miss Murphy. You have none of the usual female sensibilities. Find us what we're looking for and there will be a handsome fee."

"Do you have any idea at all what you're looking for?"

He shook his head. "None whatsoever. All we know from Houdini was that he'd discovered something important in Germany and that he wouldn't share his news with anyone but me. I'm sorry I can't be more helpful, but I don't know whether this was information or something of substance like papers or drawings that he wanted to hand over."

"You're not giving me much to go on," I said.

"All I can say is that some of the information may be contained in a magazine article he was writing. It may, of course, have been all in his head, in which case it is lost to us, but I suspect he'll have wanted to show us some kind of proof. Now, these are the magazines I want you to look for." And he opened his briefcase.

"Magazines?" I took them with interest. *Conjurers' Monthly. Mahatma* magazine. *The Dramatic Mirror.* "I've seen these before. There were piles of them in their bedroom."

"You have searched their bedroom?" He looked impressed, or was he amazed at my cheek?

"This morning. I wanted to see if there was any clue as to where Houdini might have gone. The police suspect that he was part of the murder plot, you see. And I rather thought that he and his brother might have planned it between them. I suspected it was a way to get rid of someone who was bothering them — threatening or demanding money, maybe. As you can see, we were all barking up the wrong tree."

"So there are magazines in his bedroom," Wilkie said. "But it's not an old magazine I want. Those I have. Those we have been through with a fine-toothed comb. I need a new article he might have been writing. One that has not yet been published. Or his notes."

"If he had such vital information for you, why didn't he just telephone you?"

Wilkie laughed. "Telephone me? My dear Miss Murphy, do you know how many exchanges a telephone call has to go through between New York and Washington? A telephone message is about as private as shouting from the rooftops. For all I know any telephone call from my headquarters could be monitored by unfriendly ears. In the same way that letters could be steamed open and wires read by unfriendly eyes. In my business you can't trust anybody."

"And yet you seem to think you can trust me."

He gave me a long, hard look. "My dear Miss Murphy. I pride myself on being a good judge of character. I'm certain I can trust you."

The train chugged on across flat New Jersey countryside, occasionally crossing rivers with boats bobbing in blue water. There were farms and leafy glades and everything looked very peaceful and rural. I watched a young woman taking in a line of dry laundry while a child and dog romped at her feet. In a nearby field men were harvesting corn with great baskets on their backs. I bet these people never have to worry about crimes, I thought. They wake with the sun. They work in the fields and they fall asleep tired and content. Maybe that was the kind of life to have, not always having to be alert, on guard, in danger.

"You will soon have a more peaceful life if you want it," an inner voice whispered in my ear. At this moment it came as a relief to think it.

Chief Wilkie took out his pocket watch and checked it. "Ah, we will be coming into Philadelphia soon. I suggest you disembark and catch the next train back to New York. You'll need money for the return ticket." He reached into an inside pocket and drew out an envelope. "Advance against fees," he said.

I nodded politely as if men handing me

money in railway compartments was a usual business for me, and put the envelope into my purse.

"And everything is clear?"

"One more thing," I said. "You have told me how to contact you if I find anything important. How do I contact your man if I find myself in danger?"

"My man should be within hailing distance at all times," he said.

"You sent a man to watch over Houdini and he didn't prove to be much assistance, did he?"

"Good point. But frankly I don't expect this to take long. You'll search the house. Either you'll find something or you won't. By tomorrow we should know. And there are constables on duty, guarding Mrs. Houdini, are there not?"

"There are."

"Then go to the house and stay there until your assignment is complete," he said. "But I really don't think you are putting yourself in danger. You are staying with a dear friend at a time of distress. What could be more natural. And they'll never be expecting us to use a woman."

"I see," I said. I wasn't sure whether to be flattered or annoyed.

We were passing through the outskirts of

a city — ragged wooden houses, then more orderly rows, then solid brick buildings as we neared the center. Then the train pulling up beside a platform.

"Good-bye then, and good luck, Miss Murphy." Mr. Wilkie stood and held out his hand to me. I shook it. He took down my overnight bag and opened the door for me.

"If you hurry, I believe there is a train to New York in a few minutes. No need to purchase a ticket. If you choose a regular carriage you can pay the conductor on board. Tell him there was a family emergency and you had to return unexpectedly."

"Thank you," I said, before I paused to wonder why I was thanking him for anything. Does a kidnap victim usually thank her abductors for taking her out of her way, then laying a difficult task before her? As I stepped out of the carriage and accepted my bag from him I looked down platform to see where I should cross and saw someone I recognized shoving his way through the crowd. It was none other than the fair-haired and arrogant young man whom I had overheard talking with Houdini in the passageway at the theater.

"That man." I hissed out the words, leaning close to Mr. Wilkie. "The fair one, coming toward us. He was talking with Houdini at the theater a few nights ago."

"Was he? Interesting," Wilkie replied and to my astonishment he waved.

The young man quickened his stride, passed me as if I didn't exist, then went to haul himself into the carriage beside Wilkie.

"Sorry, sir. I was held up. All in order?" he said in polished tones of one educated at a good school.

"All in order," Wilkie said. "I was just saying good-bye to this young lady. Miss Murphy, this is one of my associates, Mr. Anthony Smith."

Mr. Smith tipped his hat to me politely.

"Aren't all your associates called Mr. Smith?" I asked.

Wilkie laughed. "Valid point. But this one really is. This young lady has a rapier wit, Smith."

The young man seemed to really notice me for the first time. He stared at me, obviously trying to recollect where he had seen me before. Then he said, "Should I close the door, sir? We're about to be off."

"I think so, Smith. The young lady will be leaving us here. Such a delightful journey, my dear. Enjoy yourself in Philadelphia."

"Thank you, I will."

I smiled at them politely, then turned to walk down the platform. So Mr. Smith was not to be told of my mission. Or maybe Wilkie was waiting until the train left the station, just in case the wrong person was listening. I decided, as I went to find out the platform for the returning train, that I should make a terrible spy. I'd surely spill the beans to the wrong person.

As I came to the end of the platform newsboys were waving early editions of the evening newspaper. "Philly Flooded with False Money," the headline read. So Daniel's case had spread from New York. Or maybe the forger had found the police too hot on his heels and had moved on. That's probably what the obnoxious Mr. Smith had been doing in Philadelphia, I decided.

And as the train pulled out of Philadelphia Station, I noticed a poster on the wall advertising Signor Scarpelli — Prince of Magicians. I tried to see what date was on it — whether it was an old poster or not, but the train had already gathered speed and whisked me past it.

TWENTY-FIVE

During the long journey back I studied the magazines I had been given. *Mahatma* magazine was the official organ of the American Association of Magicians, with reports from all over the world. Wilkie had placed a pencil mark next to "Our Berlin Correspondent," whom I presumed was Houdini. And I saw that in several issues he had written articles under his own name, including, interestingly enough, how to use chemicals to create an ink that vanishes after a few seconds as well as various invisible inks. Useful for a spy as well as a magician, I decided.

In *The Dramatic Mirror* he wrote under his own name. I read through everything he had written. All his reports sounded innocuous enough, and even looking for a double meaning, I couldn't find a single one. I wondered if I'd have better luck back at the Houdinis' house. What sort of thing would

356

he have seen in Germany? Surely nothing that might threaten the might of the United States of America? Whatever it was, it was enough to have him kidnapped and probably killed.

The magazines made fascinating reading for an outsider like myself. I learned how to use mirrors to make a box appear empty. I even amused myself by reading the classified advertisements. It seemed that one could buy almost any kind of unlikely contraption. I was intrigued by something called a "deception cabinet." Fine, light wood on top, ebony below. Opens two ways. And the afterthought, "suitable for the most dangerous tricks, so watch out." I was about to move on when something about it caught my attention. "Made in Germany." But then I presumed that many clever devices were manufactured in that country.

I wondered how one operated a deception cabinet. Maybe I'll give up being a detective and start a new career as a magician with my deception cabinet, I thought with a chuckle. Then I remembered that an illusionist's life was no safer than a detective's — less safe, in fact.

It was with heavy heart that I made my way from the ferry to the Houdinis' house. I wasn't looking forward to dealing with a possibly hysterical Bess. Another constable stood guard outside and I was admitted again by Houdini's mother. She looked at me with the same hostile glare with which she had greeted me on previous occasions, but she didn't ask, "Where's my boy?" this time, making me wonder whether they had received bad news.

"How is Bess?" I asked.

"She wait for you," the old woman said, now apparently accusing me because I hadn't been there. "All day she ask me why you not come?"

"I'm sorry. I know, I should have been here, but I had important business. I'll go up to her now, shall I?"

She shrugged as if it was no business of hers, but I felt her eyes following me all the way up the stairs. Bess seemed to be asleep, so I tiptoed into the room and went over to the magazines and papers on top of the dresser. I searched diligently but didn't come across anything that I thought would be of significance. But then I decided that Houdini was hardly likely to leave something so vital that it could only be imparted to one man out in full view, especially when someone had already tried to break into the house once. My gaze fell to the suitcase under the bed, where Houdini kept the details of his illusions. I dropped to my knees and was pulling it out when Bess stirred.

"Molly. You came back! I was so worried that something bad had happened to you," she said, staring at me with those big, helpless eyes. Of course then I felt terrible. It had never occurred to me that my absence would have given her something else to worry about.

"I'm so sorry, I should have been here with you. Something came up and I had to leave in a hurry, but it was thoughtless of me not to let you know that I was all right." This of course was partially a lie. I'd been kidnapped and bundled into a train. Not exactly all right, then. But I smiled at her brightly. "I've been working on your behalf, trying to find out what might have happened to your husband," I said.

"Is there any news yet?"

"I have none, I'm afraid. I don't know how the police are getting on," I said. "Let's just hope for the best, shall we? Have you eaten anything?"

"I didn't feel like food."

"You should eat. I'll ask your mother-in-law to make you something nourishing. I'm sure she'd like to be busy at a worrying time like this."

"Okay." She nodded, then seemed to realize that I was kneeling beside the bed with the suitcase in front of me. "What are you doing?"

"I was wondering if we might find any clue to Harry's disappearance inside this suitcase," I said. "Are you sure you have no idea where we might find the key?"

"But Harry wouldn't want anyone going through that suitcase," she said in a shocked voice. "He'd never let anyone see the diagrams for his illusions."

"Look, Bess, do you want your husband found or not?" I demanded. "I'm not interested in his illusions. I'll make sure nobody sees his diagrams. But it's just possible he kept other personal things in there while he was traveling. So where do you think we'd find the key?"

"I really have no idea," she said. "Honestly."

I rummaged through the drawer where I'd found the passport. So that was why his passport showed him as a natural-born citizen, rather than as a European Jew. I thought — so that he could pass more easily into countries like Germany and Russia. Very useful for Mr. Wilkie. Then I looked in his stud box, and all the places where one keeps keys.

"Of course he could have carried it on his person all the time," Bess said. "The police parceled up his suit and delivered it to me this afternoon. It's hanging up."

"And you didn't go through the pockets?" I asked, marveling at this lack of curiosity.

"The police said they were keeping the contents of his pockets as evidence for now," she said. "You'd better ask them if they've got the key."

Then suddenly it came to me. Of course. How thick could I be? There had been two keys in the inside pocket of his tailed coat. One was presumably for the trunk, but the other . . . the other could well be the key to this suitcase. It was small enough. And what's more, I still had them in my possession. I remembered now that I had kept them clutched in my hand after I had picked them up onstage, and then I had — I tried to recall. Everything had been so chaotic. Bess had been screaming. Police everywhere. I had tucked them into the waistband of my costume — and promptly forgotten about them. There they would still be, unless they had fallen out.

"Bess, I'm going down to see if your mother-in-law will make us supper," I said. "Then I have to collect an overnight bag from my house and I'll spend the night here with you."

Of course I already had the overnight bag sitting in the hall downstairs, but it was a good excuse to go home. She accepted it, at any rate.

"Thank you, Molly. I really appreciate all you're doing for me."

Houdini's mother agreed to make a good chicken soup with dumplings for Bess. "About time that one ate something," she said. "She's so thin, you'd think the wind would blow her away. A girl should have meat on her bones — like you."

I wasn't sure if this was a compliment but at least she wasn't scowling at me. I told her I'd be back within the hour and caught the El down to Greenwich Village. I let myself into my house and stood for a moment, relishing the quiet security of my front hall. My own little haven away from the craziness of the world outside. Then I noticed a letter caught in my mail slot. I took it out and saw Daniel's forceful black scrawl.

Molly — where are you? I went to question Bess Houdini, expecting to find you there, but she didn't know where you were. I hope you have not disobeyed my orders and tried to go to interview

Hardeen! Please get in touch with me the minute you read this! Can you find a telephone and call me at Mulberry Street or at home (depending on the hour). I need to know you are safe.

I decided that Daniel could wait until I had carried out my primary mission. I went upstairs. My costume was lying across the back of a chair, where I had left it when I came home exhausted last night. With trembling fingers I felt inside the waistband and there they were — two small keys. Triumphant, I went across the street to find Sid and Gus getting ready to go out to an early supper before the theater. I never failed to be struck by the differences in other peoples' lives. Their biggest concern was whether the feather in their headdress matched the green of their gown, whereas it always seemed that I carried an enormous weight of worry on my shoulders — either for myself or for one of my clients.

"Molly, I thought you were off to Atlantic City," Gus said as she opened the door to me. "That was a flying visit."

"I never went, after all," I said, deciding to leave out the part about being kidnapped. "It proved to be unnecessary."

"Molly dear, you're looking pale and worn

out." Sid came to join her at the front door, looking dramatic in black silk trousers and a black cape lined with red. "Come to supper with us, and then we're going to see a most amusing show at the Empire. We plan to chuckle merrily all evening. It would be good for you."

"I'm sure it would," I said, "but I have a client I can't leave at the moment and work that has to be done."

"I find that the whole concept of work is overrated," Sid said. "I'm sure God never intended people to work all day — why else would he have put Adam and Eve in a delightful garden with everything they needed around them?"

"They were cast out because of sin, remember?" I pointed out. "That's why we have to work. Because of Eve and that stupid apple."

"We refuse to accept responsibility for Eve and the apple," Sid said. "Don't we, Gus? Our creed is that life is made to be enjoyed every single moment."

"It's all right if you have money to live like that," I said.

"You'll be married to Daniel soon and be a pampered wife," Gus said, with an amused glance at Sid. "Then you'll find out what you've been missing."

"Maybe," I said, "but in the meantime, I have a job to do and I have come to ask if I might use your new telephone to call Daniel."

"By all means. Any time. Our telephone is your telephone. . . ." Gus waved me toward the contraption on the wall.

I asked to be connected to police headquarters, only to be told that Captain Sullivan wasn't there. I left a message that Miss Murphy was home but planning to spend the night with Bess Houdini, then I called his apartment. Nobody answered there, so I decided I had done all I could, and set off back up to Harlem. I had just turned onto Sixth Avenue when a furious honking of an automobile horn made me look around. The auto came to an abrupt halt beside me and I saw that the person behind the motoring goggles was Daniel.

"There you are at last," he snapped, opening the passenger door for me to get in beside him. "Where the devil have you been?"

Passersby stopped to observe with interest.

"I had some things that needed to be done," I replied with dignity.

"I've been looking for you all day," he said. "Come on. Climb in. We are holding up traffic!"

Oh, I was so tempted to say that I didn't need a ride, thank you, and I'd prefer to take the train, but my curiosity won out over my pride. If he'd been looking for me, he might have important news he wished me to know.

I hitched up my skirts, showing an improper amount of ankle, and negotiated the high step into the automobile.

"There's no need to shout," I said as we drove off, swerving around a parked carriage.

"I have every reason to shout," he said. "You were going to Atlantic City, weren't you? Against my express wishes."

"I hardly went to Atlantic City, conducted my business, and then returned, unless I've developed wings," I replied.

"Then you must have seen sense at the last moment," he snapped, "because you were observed getting on the ferry to the rail terminus."

"You are having me followed these days?" I demanded angrily. "Am I a suspected criminal? Or do you plan to have a man on my tail every day after we are married, just to make sure I behave myself?"

"I had men observing the ferry in case Houdini was spotted trying to sneak out of town," he said. "One of my men recognized you."

I gave him a frosty stare as we came to a halt behind a jitney that had stopped to let off passengers. "Then let me just reiterate that I did not go to Atlantic City, as you must have now realized, given that I am already back in the city."

"But you were going to go, weren't you? And common sense won out at the last moment?"

I gave him a long stare. "I can truthfully say that common sense did not win out at the last moment."

"Then where did you go?"

"Daniel, you know very well that I can't discuss my cases with you, any more than you discuss yours with me," I said. "Suffice it to say that my business is concluded. I didn't meet with any murderers, and I will not have to leave town again."

"You realize that this is not your case any longer, Molly. Your client is either kidnapped, dead, or on the run from police. Either way this is now a criminal case and you are to have nothing more to do with it, do you understand?"

"Keep your hair on, Daniel. I might have other cases on the books, you know. Other perfectly simple, normal divorce cases that involve my gadding around town at odd moments, and about which I can't tell you."

"You are infuriating, do you know that?" he stormed. "I was worried sick about you, Molly. Don't you realize that I worry about you all the time?"

I reached up and touched his cheek. "You don't have to, Daniel. I can take care of myself."

"I do have to," he said. "This ridiculous profession of yours constantly puts you in harm's way. You should never have accepted an assignment like this in the first place. If you really thought Houdini's life was in danger, you should have come straight to me."

"I would have, in fact, that was what I suggested. But my client wouldn't hear of it."

Daniel shook his head in disbelief. "Thank God this is all coming to an end," he said. "I can't wait to have you safely under my protection. Do you realize how many lucky escapes you have had?"

"More than my fair share, I agree," I said. "And you're right. I should never have taken this case in the first place."

"Molly Murphy admitting she was in the wrong! Well, I never thought I was going to hear those words." Then he ducked. "Don't hit me while I'm driving. It's dangerous."

We glanced at each other and a smile passed between us.

"So what did you want to see me for?" I asked as the traffic moved on again. "Presumably you must have had a reason to hunt me down all over the city."

"Actually I came to tell you that the trunk, or one resembling it, was found floating in the East River."

"Oh, dear. But no body in it?"

"It was empty. So we can come to one of two conclusions: that whoever murdered that unidentified man also killed Houdini and dumped his body into the East River, where no doubt it will surface in a day or so, or that Houdini was part of the plot and threw the trunk into the river to make us think he was the victim."

I tried not to let my expression betray that I now knew the truth, and that Houdini wasn't part of the plot. I also thought of those keys in my purse. Should I mention that I had in my possession proof as to whether the trunk really was Houdini's or not? This presented a tricky problem. Daniel had already ordered me off the case, so he'd want me to hand over the keys. I wasn't ready to do that yet.

"So were there any bloodstains in the trunk?" I asked.

"Young ladies don't normally ask questions like that." Daniel chuckled. "The trunk had been underwater and had collected floating debris, so it's hard to tell at the moment. But our lab boys are working on it to see if they can extract any trace evidence that it belongs to Houdini."

"So did the back come off easily and swing outward the way Bess had described?"

"The back had broken off, but yes, it appears that it was designed to swing outward."

"So you can pretty much conclude that it was Houdini's trunk." I sighed. "You haven't mentioned any of this to Bess yet, have you?"

"Absolutely not, and I don't think you should either. No sense in upsetting her unnecessarily, although I'm afraid either option does not bode well for her, does it?"

"Poor Bess. She'll be lost without him," I said. "I'm planning to stay with her for a while."

"And we have a man on his way to Atlantic City to interview the brother, you'll be pleased to know," Daniel said.

"You do?"

He nodded. "I thought over what you said and I decided you might be onto something. At the very least we have to check the brother out. The fact that he made such a hasty departure from New York is suspicious in itself. And even if he's not involved personally, Houdini may have confided in him."

"I'm glad you're finally listening to me," I said, not able to admit that going to Atlantic City was now a waste of time and money. But then was it? Harry Houdini's brother had also been in Germany. Whatever Mr. Wilkie thought, it was just possible that he was the spy we were looking for.

Twenty-Six

Bess was sitting up in bed sipping soup when I returned to her house. The windows were open and a refreshing breeze wafted through the room, sending the aroma of the food in my direction. My stomach reminded me that it was my dinnertime too and I had just turned down a delightful invitation to dine with friends. I wondered how Mama Houdini would feel about feeding the intruder. But I had more pressing things to do first.

I knelt on the floor and pulled out the suitcase.

"I think I may have found the key," I said.

"Where? Where did you find it?"

"In Harry's top pocket at the theater. Remember when we tried to open the second trunk, only neither key would work? I must have stuck the keys in my belt and forgotten about them. Lucky, wasn't it?"

I took out the keys and knelt in front of

the suitcase.

"I don't know, Molly. Harry's going to be awful mad if he finds out."

"Bess," I said, my patience and good nature wearing thin after a very trying day, "if your husband has been kidnapped and is waiting to be rescued, don't you think we should do everything we can to find him?"

"Of course, but I don't see what —"

"Look," I said, trying to measure my words so that I didn't give too much away. "The police think he may have something in this trunk that someone is willing to kill for. I have no idea what that might be, but we have to look. Either I can look here and I promise not to study how he does his illusions, or I can hand the whole suitcase over to the police, which is probably what I should be doing now."

She chewed on her lip, looking ridiculously like a helpless child, then nodded. "Yes, I see. Thank you, Molly. I do understand that you're trying to help. You're trying to do what's best for us. Okay, go ahead then."

I put the first key in the lock. It was too big. So that must be the key to Houdini's trunk. I replaced it in my purse. I tried the second key and heard a satisfying click as the suitcase opened. I don't know what I expected to see — an envelope marked TOP SECRET or something, but all I saw was a lot of incomprehensible diagrams with words scribbled across them, sometimes in English and sometimes in what must have been Hungarian. If I'd wanted to steal Houdini's secrets, I'd have been none the wiser. The diagrams meant nothing to me. I read their titles: "Making Orange Tree Grow — after Robert-Houdin." And scrawled underneath, triumphant: "I finally figured out how he did it!" Various boxes, coffins, handcuff designs, and then, "Possible new stunt. The amazing underwater illusion." What followed were some complicated diagrams, a device shaped like a large bullet with what looked like flower petals at one end, with arrows around it, and tiny words scribbled in another language.

"Underwater illusion," I said. "That sounds ambitious. Does he do an underwater stunt?"

"No. He's talked about doing one for some time — using a milk churn, I believe. I didn't want him to think about it because it's so dangerous. But he got this bee in his bonnet on the way home from Germany. He was sitting in the cabin for hours, working away at it. I asked him about it but he didn't want to talk. He's like that sometimes

374

when he's concentrating. Wouldn't even come to the dining saloon for meals. I told him I didn't want him doing any trick that involved being underwater. Too dangerous. Other magicians have talked about doing it, but nobody's had the courage yet to pull it off."

"I don't see how this would work anyway," I said, putting it aside and moving on to the next thing. "It looks more like some kind of machine. How would he use a machine underwater? Maybe he plans to escape from ―"

I broke off, picking up the sketch again and examining it more carefully. There was a hatch on top of it that opened. The amazing underwater trick. Had Houdini fooled us all and planned his escape from the East River using such a contraption, leaving his trunk floating to make us think he was dead? Was this in fact a design for an underwater machine? Did such things exist? I wondered if this was something that Mr. Wilkie would want to know about. And it didn't make sense that Houdini had planned his own escape, seeing that one of Mr. Wilkie's men was dead and Houdini was working with him. Unless he was the one working for both sides. I remembered the passage he had written about illusionists working on both sides of the stage and deceiving everyone. I glanced up at Bess. Everything I was discovering seemed to be worse and worse news for her.

I resolved to sleep on it and decide whether to tell Mr. Wilkie in the morning. I went through the rest of the suitcase then closed it again, making sure I locked it.

"That's that, then," I said. "Nothing more of interest in here."

"Other illusionists wouldn't say that," Bess said. "They'd kill for the contents of that suitcase." She realized what she had said and put her hand up to her mouth. "Do you think that's what happened, Molly? Then we're not safe here if that's what they want."

"There is a police constable on guard outside and a good sturdy front door," I said. "I'm going to make sure you get a good night's sleep."

I took her tray from her, carried it downstairs, and found Houdini's mother in the kitchen, now making what looked like some kind of bread.

"You see, Bess finished every drop," I said. "You must make good soup."

"Try for yourself," she said, nodding at the stove. I needed no second invitation but filled a big bowl and wolfed it down. Mrs. Weiss obviously approved of a good appetite as she then produced some plum dumplings and some honey cake.

"You're a wonderful cook, Mrs. Weiss," I said. "You must miss your son when he's away."

"I stay with other son — Leopold, and with daughter, Gladys," she said. "They like when I cook food from old country for them."

"You're lucky to have such a nice big family," I told her.

"You have no family?"

"I had a father and three brothers. My mother died when I was a child. Now my father and one of my brothers are dead, and I don't know when I'll ever see the other two brothers again."

"Life is hard," she said. "But you are healthy young girl. You get married, no?"

"Yes, I'm getting married soon," I said.

"Your young man. He has good steady work?"

"Yes, he's —" I broke off. Of course I couldn't let her know he was a policeman. "He's got a good job," I finished. "He'll take good care of me."

"That is as should be. Show business. Pah! My son make lots of money, but what kind of life, huh? Never know where you will be tomorrow. And always danger. And now —

who knows if he is still alive." Her voice broke as she said these last words.

I surprised myself by going over and putting an arm around her. "We can only hope for the best," I said. "I know how hard this must be for you."

She put her hand up to her mouth and nodded. Then she turned away. "I make us coffee," she said gruffly.

We were sitting at the kitchen table finishing our coffee when there came a loud knock on the front door. We looked at each other.

"I'll go if you like," I said, expecting it to be Daniel.

"It may be my son Leopold. He may come to see his mother."

I went to the front door and opened it. A strange man and woman stood there. She was dressed in a rather old-fashioned dark costume and a bonnet that hid her face, and he in a somber black-tailed coat and top hat. He also had a remarkably bushy gray beard. I glanced past them to see the constable standing beside the steps.

"Can I help you?" I asked.

"We've come to see Mrs. Houdini," the man said.

"You're friends of hers?"

"We are acquainted, yes." He handed me

his card. It read, "Harold and Bertha Symmes, Mediums. Your gateway to the spirit world."

"You're a spiritualist? A medium?" I asked. The man nodded.

"We came as soon as we could," the woman said. "To offer our services to poor Mrs. Houdini."

"We heard she was out of her mind with worry," Mr. Symmes said. "We are volunteering to try and contact her husband's spirit for her."

"What makes you think he's dead?" I asked.

"We don't know, do we?" the woman said. "But if he is dead, then I'm sure we'll be able to contact his spirit and at least we'll be able to put her mind at rest if she receives a message from him."

"I understood that Houdini did his best to expose spiritualists like yourselves," I said.

"Fake mediums, yes. There are, unfortunately, a lot of them around," the man said in his grave voice. "It tarnishes the wonderful work of those who really do have the gift of contact with the spirit world, like ourselves."

"We've come to show that we bear no ill will for Mr. Houdini's harsh words. We have come to make amends, to welcome Mrs. Houdini into our bosom," the woman said. She was a skinny person, and the irreverent thought flashed through my mind that she didn't have much bosom.

It was almost dark outside. The gas lamps had been lit, throwing small pools of light at intervals along the street, and the children had vanished from the sidewalk. From an upstairs window came the sound of a pianola playing "Just a Song at Twilight," and farther down the street a baby crying. All so peaceful and normal but my mind was racing. I didn't want to let any strangers into the house, and yet it wasn't up to me to make decisions.

I made one anyway. "Look, I'm sure you mean well, but I think that Mrs. Houdini still hopes her husband is alive," I said. "I think that what you intend to do would distress her greatly."

"If he's still alive, we shall not be able to contact his spirit," the man said. "May we not at least speak with her — to offer our support?"

I glanced into the house and then back to the street to make sure I could spot the constable. Was it up to me to play guard dog for Bess? Unfortunately I had had dealings with spiritualists before and they had evoked the same feelings of mistrust that I was now experiencing.

"Why don't we wait to find out what has happened to Houdini," I said. "And if he has died, then I'm sure Bess will want to contact his spirit. Until then —"

"Exactly who are you, miss? A relative?"

"I am her best friend," I said, "and frankly she's in a bad way at the moment. She's taken to her bed and the doctor has given her a strong sedative. So you see she is simply not in any state to receive visitors."

"A great pity," the man said. "But you will let her know that we called to offer our services, won't you? And our best wishes to the rest of Houdini's family. I take it his family is still in residence?"

I was about to say that his brother had now gone, but I could feel a warning voice in my head. "That's right. So you can see that Bess is well looked after. Now if you'll please excuse me, I must go back to her bedside. It was good of you to call. Good night." And I shut the front door. They didn't try to stop me. But when I went and looked from an upstairs window, I saw them still lingering in the street.

Had I sensed danger? Were they really who they claimed to be or were they trying to find a way to gain entry to the house? I made sure the big bolt and chain were on the front door and then checked that the lower windows at the front of the house were all locked. As I went back to Bess I felt quite shaky. I just wished this whole wretched business were over.

TWENTY-SEVEN

I said nothing to Bess about the visitors. I made her some hot milk and she took the sedative powder her doctor had prescribed for her, then I found a bed for myself in a room across the hall from her. As soon as she dozed off I went in there and took with me the magazines and scrapbooks. The house had not yet been converted to electricity and I read in the softer, hissing light of the gas bracket. The most recent scrapbooks documented Houdini's time on the Continent and most of the articles he had clipped from newspapers were in German. Sometimes there were pictures accompanying them and I stared at them, looking for faces that I recognized. But in the half darkness it was hard to distinguish features, other than large mustaches or beards. Underneath the articles Houdini had often written his own comment, most of these in German or Hungarian. Finally I closed the books in frustration. I would need to find someone to translate for me.

What was I looking for? I really didn't know. All I could surmise was that a skilled illusionist had pulled off the remarkable stunt so smoothly that I, standing a few feet away, had not been aware of it. A skilled illusionist who had recently been in Germany and who was now in the pay of the German secret service. And who was also a skilled killer. I scanned through the German text for names I might recognize, but the Gothic type was so different that I didn't know what I was reading. Eventually my eyes started watering from the poor light and the exhaustion of the day caught up with me. I turned out the gas and looked out of the window before I went to sleep. I couldn't see the constable from my window, but I thought I saw the shadow of a man standing across the street. I hoped he was Mr. Wilkie's agent, sent to keep watch over me. I tried to reassure myself as I fell asleep.

In the morning I woke to the sun streaming in through my window and the sound of horses' hooves as the milk wagon made its way down the street. I felt surprisingly refreshed and ready to take on the world. Bess was still blissfully asleep but Houdini's mother was up and bustling around the kitchen. She had made little pancakes that she served to me with sour cream and nodded again with approval as I ate heartily.

"What we do now?" she asked as she sat opposite me with a cup of coffee. "What happens to us?"

"We have to wait, I suppose," I said. "Wait until there's any news of your son."

"He is dead. This is what you think, no?" she asked.

"I really don't know," I said. "I am still hoping for the best." But I wasn't quite sure what the best could be. One man was dead and Houdini had been spirited away in a trunk. The trunk had been found floating in the East River. So the chances of his still being alive were slim, but I didn't want to give up hope.

"I'm going to keep looking for him," I said. "Maybe you can help find out what happened to him."

I went upstairs and brought down the scrapbooks. "I can't understand German," I said. "Can you help me translate?"

She glanced at the newspaper cuttings then shook her head. "I speak some German, but I don't read it. Yiddish I can speak. Hungarian I can speak. But in my town they did not educate girls to read German. My son Leopold — the doctor. He could maybe help you. He is an educated man."

"Thank you," I said. "Can you give me his address?"

She gave it to me, but then asked, "How can these old newspapers help you find my son? He is not in Germany. He is in New York."

"I don't know, but at the moment we can't leave any stone unturned."

"Please?" She frowned at the image I had used.

"I mean that we just have to try everything. I'll go and see your son Leopold this morning."

"Please say his mother sends love and asks why he does not come to see us? We need him. He is our comfort."

"I'll tell him."

I took Bess some breakfast and woke her gently. Her big eyes shot open at my touch. "Any news?" she asked, attempting to sit up.

"None yet, but let us hope that today will bring some. See — your mother-in-law has made these pancakes. They're awfully good."

I left her picking at them halfheartedly and went to retrieve the scrapbooks. My first task for the morning would be to find brother Leopold and see if he could read the latest articles to me. Then I had another idea. *The Dramatic Mirror,* one of the publications Houdini wrote for, appeared to have its editorial offices in New York City. It was just possible that he had submitted an article to them that had not yet been published. Worth a try, anyway. And while I was walking around I'd come to a decision as to whether I should inform Mr. Wilkie about the amazing underwater trick, or whether I was being too fanciful with what was probably just another flight of an illusionist's fancy.

I put the scrapbooks into my overnight bag and peeked in at Bess's door.

"I'll be back soon," I said. "I'm going to your brother-in-law to see if he can read these German articles to me."

"What do you hope to achieve with this?" Bess asked.

"I'm really not sure," I said. "It's possible that something that happened in Germany is responsible for your husband's disappearance."

"What kind of thing?" She looked puzzled.

"I don't know. We're grasping at straws here, Bess, but somebody pulled off a really clever trick and killed a man in a full theater. Somebody had to have a really good motive for doing that."

I came into the room and sat on the bed beside her. "Think back to your time in Germany. Was there any ugly incident? Any time that your husband felt threatened? Anything that just felt strange to you?"

She shrugged. "Everything felt strange to me in Germany — the food, the people. And there were several incidents —"

"What kind of incidents?"

"Men claiming Harry was a fraud. Cheating him with handcuffs that couldn't be opened. But you know, he gets that kind of thing all the time."

"Can you give me the names of any of these men?"

She frowned with concentration. "One was called Graff, I believe. And then there was Ciroc or Cirnoc. Harry outsmarted him."

"Any fellow Americans who were touring Germany at the same time?"

"Harry's brother, of course. And a guy called Wyatt. He and Harry never saw eye to eye. And Cunning and Stevie Summer. But none of them was as successful as Harry. He is adored over there. He's invited everywhere — the police love him, and the nobility. He's treated like a king." She gave a big sigh. "You're trying to tell me that something happened in Germany to make someone want to kill Harry? If it did, I don't know what it could be. Illusionists are always rivals. They're always suspicious of each other. But they don't go around killing each other."

"Someone killed twice in the same theater, here in New York," I reminded her. "First they ruined Scarpelli's reputation by killing his assistant in a failed trick and then the man in the trunk. And presumably the same man trapped you in the trunk. Is there someone who is angry with his whole profession, do you think?"

She shrugged, then looked away from me. "One thing I should probably tell you," she said, still looking away and twisting her bedsheet uneasily. "I meant to tell you before, but I couldn't bring myself to do so."

"What?"

She was still staring out of the window. "That incident when I was trapped in the trunk — I did that myself. I hid the key."

I stared at her in disbelief. "You rigged up your own death?"

She turned back to me. "Oh, I didn't intend to die. It's just that — well, I knew that Harry would never go for you taking over as his assistant and I just wanted him protected, that's all. So I had to come up with a good reason why I couldn't be part of the act for a while."

"So you were just pretending? You hadn't really passed out?" I was trying to control my anger.

"Oh, no, I really did pass out. I really did nearly die. You see, I didn't expect it to take so long, and then I started to panic and next thing I knew I was lying there."

"So why didn't you say something before?"

"Because I felt like a fool, that's why," she said. "And because I knew it had nothing to do with the other things that happened."

"Well, I suppose at least it's one piece of the puzzle that's now in place," I said.

"Are you going to tell Captain Sullivan?"

"I'll have to," I said. "But I have so many other things to do this morning that I probably won't get a chance to speak to him for a while."

"How long will you be gone?" She looked like a small child, worrying about its mother.

"I'll try to be back as quickly as possible," I said. "The house is well guarded. You have nothing to fear."

"But I do fear," she said. "I'm terrified. I want my husband back."

"I hope to have some news for you when I return," I said.

■ ■ ■ ■

It did cross my mind that Mr. Wilkie had told me to go to Houdini's house and stay there. Instead I would be gadding around New York. But then if nobody knew my connection to Wilkie apart from a man supposedly guarding me and two men back in Washington, I would be safe, wouldn't I?

So I made sure that Bess was comfortable, gave Mrs. Weiss instructions not to open the door to anybody except the police until I returned, and I set off, lugging my heavy bag of scrapbooks. As I stepped outside I found that the day, even at this early hour, was already a sultry one, as humid as walking though a hothouse. Not a day for scouring the length and breadth of New York City — from Dr. Leopold Weiss to the magazine offices. Even as I was making my list, the wheels in my brain started turning over something I had just said to Bess. Scarpelli — who had so conveniently vanished. Was he the one? Had he killed his assistant because she found out he was a German spy and was about to report him? Maybe she had even found out that his mission was to kill Harry Houdini and had stood in his way. I should have done more to check into Signor Scarpelli, rather than leaving it to the police. Then I reminded myself that he had supposedly disappeared from the face of the earth after the accident onstage. Every policeman in New York had been looking for him, which made it highly unlikely that he had been able to gain access to the theater on the night that Houdini was kidnapped. But I remembered his obvious dislike of Houdini, not to mention his jealousy and the fact that he had also toured Germany recently. I decided it might just be worth checking out where he had stayed while he was in New York. So I should visit the theater while I was downtown. I would be able to find out his address in New York from their records.

I found Dr. Leopold Weiss's residence in the East Eighties and knocked at the door. It was opened by Dr. Weiss himself. I saw the resemblance to Houdini instantly, although he wore a neatly trimmed little beard and round spectacles, and looked altogether older and more somber.

"Miss — uh. Good day. Can I help you, miss?" He seemed surprised to see me, although a patient turning up at a doctor's door couldn't have been that unusual. I thought I saw a flash of recognition cross his face, but we hadn't ever met before, unless he'd been in the audience and seen me onstage with his brother.

"I'm Molly Murphy, a friend of your brother's wife," I said. "I'm helping to try and find out what has happened to Houdini."

"A terrible business," he said. "Hard for us all to endure. How is my mother holding up? How is Bess?"

"Bess is taking it very hard," I said. "And so is your mother, although she is made of sterner stuff and doesn't show it."

"I must try to pay them a call later today, if I can," he said. "I am so sorry they have to go through this. Are they well protected?"

"Yes, there is a policeman standing guard outside at all times."

"That's good to know," he said. "I hope one policeman is enough against these fiends."

"Your brother hasn't tried to contact you, has he?" I asked. "We're still not sure if he's dead or alive."

"I feel it in my heart that he is still alive," he said. "One must always have hope and patience. You will tell that to my mother and to Bess, won't you? Tell her to continue to have hope."

"I have a favor to ask, Dr. Weiss," I said. "These scrapbooks document Harry's time in Germany. Unfortunately I don't read German and I wondered if you could translate the articles for me."

He came out and stood beside me as I showed him one of the scrapbooks, then he shook his head and retreated.

"Much as I would want to help you, I'm afraid that I was on my way to a very sick patient and I shall be operating at the hospital for most of the day. Perhaps later this evening I shall find time to visit my mother and Bess and then I can look at your scrapbooks for you — although I have to tell you that my German is not very good. I was a small child when I came here and essentially I speak English with some knowledge of Hungarian and Yiddish. But I will do what I can if you can't find anyone else."

"Thank you," I said. "I look forward to seeing you later today then, and I know Bess will be glad to see you."

"As I shall be very glad to see her," he said warmly. Then he bowed in that stiff European manner that reminded of another doctor I knew — Dr. Birnbaum, my alienist friend from Vienna. Splendid, I thought. Why hadn't I considered him before? He was a native German speaker and I remembered that he also spoke Hungarian. He could translate for me and I wouldn't have to wait for Leopold's bumbling attempts. Thus I quickened my step to the nearest Second Avenue El station and was soon heading south. As usual it was sweltering and uncomfortable in the carriage and I was glad when I could disembark at Eighth Street and then faced the long walk across town back to Washington Square.

Dr. Birnbaum kept a suite at the Hotel Lafayette, just off the square and across from the university. I asked for him and was met with a blank response. "I'm sorry, there is no gentleman here of that name," the clerk said.

"But I saw him a few days ago," I said. "Could you find out where he might have gone?"

The clerk shrugged but went through into a back office, bringing with him another young man whom I recognized. "I'm afraid Dr. Birnbaum has given up his rooms here," he said.

"Oh, I see. Did he leave a forwarding address?"

"I'm afraid not."

I was beginning to feel that I might explode. "Surely he left an address for forwarding his mail?"

"I understand he made arrangements with the post office."

"Thank you," I said through my teeth, then remembered that someone in the hotel might know. Instead of returning to the street I made for the staircase, much to the surprise of the two clerks, I expect. I knocked on Ryan O'Hare's door and it was finally opened by a bleary-eyed Ryan, still in his emerald-green and peacock-blue robe.

"Molly," he muttered. "Why do you always have to come to visit me so confoundedly early?"

"It's ten o'clock, Ryan," I said.

"As I said, confoundedly early. You know I am not at my best before luncheon." He sighed. "Well, I suppose you had better come in. What can I do for you, or have you come to cheer me up?"

"I've come for information," I said.

"You only come to see me when you need something. How callous of you," he said. "Very well. What is it?"

"Dr. Birnbaum," I said. "Do you know where he's gone?"

"Never mention that man's name to me again," Ryan said bitterly. "We are no longer on speaking terms. I hope he's gone to the ends of the earth. In fact I hope he falls off the end of the Earth."

I tried not to smile, in spite of everything. "So you and he had a falling-out?"

"You knew that. He decided that I was not helpful to his reputation and his career."

I could see that. "I'm sorry," I said.

"I'm not. He was horribly boring, if you want to know."

"So you've no idea where he lives now?"

"None at all."

"Thank you anyway." I started for the door.

"Stay and have breakfast with me," he said. "I may force myself to eat."

"I'd love to but I'm in the middle of a case."

"Always rushing around. It's not healthy."

"Sid and Gus said the same thing."

"Dear Sid and Gus. I must go to visit. They'll cheer me up if nobody else can. I haven't been out for days."

"Then you won't have heard any gossip about what happened to Houdini?" I asked cautiously.

He shook his head. "I haven't spoken to a soul," he said.

"If you do speak to a soul in the near future, do try to find out what the theater people think has happened to him," I said,

Ryan shrugged. "As I told you before. He is vaudeville, I am legit. Never the twain shall meet, my dear. Now I'm feeling weak again and must take to my bed, if you don't mind." He lay down with great drama and I made my exit.

I tried to control my frustration as I came out and went to sit in Washington Square for a few minutes to calm down. Nothing seemed to be working out today. I turned the pages of the scrapbook, staring at the pictures and willing the words to make sense. Here and there I picked out a name, but it seemed that in German half the words in a sentence started with a capital letter. Houdini shaking hands with the Kaiser. That much I could understand, and some kind of picture of a courtroom, under which he had written, "Houdini triumphs again."

The branches of the tree above me moved in a sudden breeze and the sun shone full on the page of my book, bringing the characters in the sketch on the page into harsh focus for me. It was a group standing onstage and a face at the back of that group stirred something in my memory. I had seen that face recently, or a face that resembled it. Somewhere else in the scrapbooks, perhaps? I flicked through page after page, but the face didn't appear again. I scanned the article, trying to pick out a name I recognized but in the end I had to give up, frustrated. So I'd have to wait for Leopold

to translate for me this evening after all.
And I never was good at being patient.

TWENTY-EIGHT

So what to do next? Go to the theater and find out about Signor Scarpelli's residence or visit the press that published *The Dramatic Mirror* magazine? It was not the sort of weather to go rushing around any more than necessary. The humidity today made it feel like wading through a Turkish bath. Actually I had never been in a Turkish bath since they are strictly reserved for gentlemen, but I had read about them. Every step seemed an effort. Clothing stuck to me in an unbecoming manner. I could feel the sweat trickling down the back of my neck and my hat felt like a deadweight on my head. Patchin Place was so close by. I could go home, have a cool splash of water, and a cold drink. I stood up, tempted, then turned resolutely to my task. Theater and magazine were not too far from each other — one on the Bowery, the other on Pearl Street.

I decided on the magazine first. Theater

folk are notoriously late risers and I'd probably find the place deserted until at least eleven. So I caught the trolley south down Broadway. Although it was crowded, its sides were open and it was more pleasant traveling than in the closed carriages of the El. As we neared the southern tip of Manhattan we picked up a hint of cooler breeze coming in from the ocean. As I alighted I stood, breathing in the air with a hint of sea tang and picturing myself standing on the cliffs at home, feeling that cool, salty wind in my face. How long ago that all seemed now, as if it was a distant dream.

As I went into the office of *The Dramatic Mirror* a loud clatter of machinery was coming up from the basement, so that I had to shout my request to the young woman who came to greet me.

"An article by Houdini?" she shouted back. "Yes, he often writes for us."

"Do you have his latest articles here for me to look at?"

"May I ask what this is about?" she asked.

I decided this was a time for straight talk. "You've heard that he has disappeared and has probably been kidnapped," I said.

"Yes, I read it in the papers. Shocking, isn't it? Whatever next?"

"I am a detective, working with Houdini's

401

family and the police on trying to trace him. We'd appreciate any help you can give us." I produced my card that read, "P. Riley Detective Agency. M. Murphy Co-Owner." I had taken the liberty of having the cards printed after Paddy Riley died and I was left holding the baby, so to speak. So I wasn't really co-owner, just owner by default.

She looked at the card, then at me. "Wait here please," she said. "I'll get Mr. Goldblum."

She went into a back office while the machinery downstairs clattered on. I wondered how anyone could get work done with that sort of noise nearby, but then the whole city was full of workshops and small factories. It was hard to find a quiet backwater like Patchin Place.

Mr. Goldblum looked tired and stooped. "You're asking about Houdini, miss?"

"I am. I know he wrote regular articles for your magazine. I have the latest edition but I wondered if there were any articles you've received from him that are not yet published."

"We have an edition going to press, even as we speak. You can hear the noise, no doubt." He gave a tired smile. "And, yes, he has an article that will appear in that edition."

My hopes rose. "May I see it?"

"It would still be down with the typesetters, but I expect I could retrieve it. But may I ask on whose authority you are here and what you hope to achieve?"

"I'm here with the full backing of the Houdini family and the police," I said, although this wasn't quite true. In fact, Daniel had said in no uncertain terms that this wasn't my case any longer, but Chief Wilkie and the Secret Service counted as police, didn't they? "And as to what I hope to achieve — we can leave no stone unturned to find Mr. Houdini. It's just possible that something he saw or did in Germany has put him into this current danger. Some kind of feud with another magician, maybe."

"I see." He frowned. "I remember reading the article and it seemed perfectly harmless to me. But I'll go and see if I can retrieve it for you. Anything to help Houdini's family — and the police, of course."

He was gone quite a while. Nobody offered me a seat, and indeed there didn't seem to be an extra chair in that outer office. The girl had gone back to her filing duties and nobody else appeared. At last

Mr. Goldblum came up the stairs, huffing and puffing a bit.

"Not as young as I used to be," he said. "Here you are. Here is Houdini's article, literally hot off the press."

I read it, my disappointment growing. It was little more than a list of which performers were touring the Continent from America and where Houdini himself would be playing when he returned. "And I expect to have some new tricks up my sleeve when I return," he concluded. "There are some kinks to be worked out but I think you'll all be suitably surprised and impressed."

The amazing underwater trick, I thought. He was going to perfect it. Was it unique enough to make someone kill him to get their hands on it? I handed the paper back to Mr. Goldblum.

"I'm afraid there's nothing there that could help me," I said. "I'll have to try the other magazines he wrote for. Do you happen to know where *Mahatma* is headquartered?"

"Up in Boston, I believe," he said.

That was a long way to go just for a magazine. I thanked him and was about to leave when a young man, his face and hands smudged with ink, came up the stairs.

"Here you are, sir," he said, and handed

some papers to Goldblum. Goldblum smiled, then handed the booklet to me. "Here's the entire new edition, with my compliments," he said.

I came out into the deep shadow of Pearl Street where tall buildings blotted out the sun and made my way though to the water-front at the South Street Pier. I put down my bag, and stood for a while, watching the commerce on the East River, listening to the sounds of a busy dockland — the toot of tugboats and sirens of bigger ships coming in from a long ocean voyage mingled with the shouts of stevedores as they unloaded sacks of coffee, crates of bananas. Above these sounds came the squeals of small boys jumping off the docks into the cool water. At which of these docks had Houdini's trunk washed up? I wondered. I should have asked Daniel, but then he'd only have reminded me that it wasn't my case.

I stared at the river, at the Brooklyn Bridge, and the almost completed East River Bridge and wondered exactly where his captors had dumped him into the river. It was always so busy, even at night when ships were unloaded by the glow of lamps as ships' companies employed their own police forces to keep the merchandise safe.

Why had nobody seen or heard the splash of something heavy being thrown in? Perhaps they had, but surely the police would have pursued this line of inquiry.

I sat on a packing case, enjoying the rich, rank smell of the river and the cry of the gulls overhead, and looked through the magazine I had been given. I knew that sometimes Houdini wrote anonymously and even placed advertisements. And to my growing excitement I saw there was an article from "Our Berlin Correspondent, Herr N. Osey."

After a few lines of gossip about life in Berlin, I read a passage that caught my attention. "Expect an invasion of German talent on the New York scene in the near future. German magicians plan to take America by storm — just as Houdini and his like have become the darlings of Europe. Look out and prepare to be surprised by the amazing underwater escape trick."

I stood there, my heart beating very fast. There. Absolute proof that Houdini had written the article. But what did it mean? Could it possibly mean what I thought it might — that Germany was planning to invade New York soon? Not our enemies yet, Mr. Wilkie had said, but the Kaiser was ambitious and sought to expand his empire.

That's rubbish, I thought. They wouldn't dare test the might of the United States. The sound of some kind of machinery across the river set my teeth on edge — the whine of metal cutting metal. I looked across at the Brooklyn shoreline. A large ship was out of the water in a dry dock and men were working on its hull. And at the back of the ship was something similar to the flower shape that Harry Houdini had drawn on his underwater device. I stood and stared, trying to understand the implication of this. The strange bullet-shaped device, the motor, the hatch, the flower-shaped addition at the rear that obviously must propel it . . . It wasn't an illusion at all. What this had to be saying was that Germany planned to attack using a new submarine that Houdini had witnessed when he toured German factories.

Twenty-Nine

I had to let Mr. Wilkie know immediately. I could hardly breathe with excitement as I asked for directions to the nearest telegraph office. I expect the man behind the counter wondered why I was so agitated and spending all that money to send a message that said, "Thank you for birthday present. Your niece."

"I take it you won't need to wait for a reply, miss," he said in a bored sort of voice.

"No, I don't think so." Mr. Wilkie had already instructed me that he would come to me and I didn't think he'd risk naming a meeting place or time.

"It must have been a very nice birthday present," the clerk said, "when someone spends two dollars just to thank him for it. A nice uncle you've got there."

"Very generous," I said frostily, because I could tell what he was hinting — that he was not my uncle but a very different sort of relation who had been showering me with gifts. Since I didn't look like the kind of girl who had rich admirers, he was probably bemused by this. "The wire will be sent immediately, I take it?" I asked.

"It has to wait its turn. If the line's in use it may take a few minutes. It's not that urgent, is it?"

"Very urgent," I said. "It has to reach my uncle before he sails to South America."

"Don't you worry, miss. We'll get it out to him," he said in a patronizing way now. Maybe I was just overwrought but I had a desire to slap him. Instead I gave him a curt nod and stepped back out into the street. Why were men so insufferable when dealing with women?

I found a church clock and checked the hour. Eleven thirty. That meant that even if Mr. Wilkie received my message instantly, he could not be in New York before five o'clock at the earliest. So I had some time to follow up on my other plan for the day, namely to find out what might have happened to the elusive Mr. Scarpelli and if he had really met a bad end, as the police believed. I wasn't too keen about lugging that bag of books around for the rest of the day, but I didn't have much choice. It was lucky that I'd grown up used to carrying sacks of potatoes and peat from the fields, wasn't it?

As I stood outside Miner's Theatre I found that my stomach was clenched in fear. There was danger inside those doors. People had died there. I hesitated on the sidewalk while the stream of pedestrians flowed around me, and it occurred to me that someone connected to the theater had to be involved. Of course it would have taken an illusionist to pull off the switching trunks trick so smoothly, but someone had to know exactly where the trapdoor was on the stage. Someone had to be able to help move a body without being noticed. And a thought crossed my mind. Mr. Irving the theater manager. He was there all the time, standing on the stage right in front of that little door behind the curtains that led to the area below the stage. And the passage that led to his office was on that side of the stage as well. Wilkie's man could have been lured into the office, stabbed, and then taken down below in a trunk.

So did I really want to go back in there? I certainly wasn't going to face Old Ted at the stage door again. He already thought I had ulterior motives and was up to no good. And to be honest, I didn't want to find myself in the dark passages of backstage.

"Come on. Don't be such a ninny," I said to myself. They only knew of me as Bess's friend and Houdini's fill-in assistant. What did I have to fear?

I shook my head and stepped into the cool shade of the theater foyer. The box office was doing a lively trade for the matinee. People were pressing around the kiosk and I could hear excited whispers: "They're not sold out already, are they?" "Do you think anything terrible's going to happen this week?" "Did you hear there was a curse on this theater? Some are saying there's a monster lurking in the basement."

I wondered if the new illusionist was as famous as Houdini, or if the reason all these people were here was merely that morbid human fascination with death. Did they want to see another girl sliced in half or another dead body roll from a trunk? Apparently they did. I hesitated, not sure whether to push past the throng and into the theater or not. As I waited I studied this week's playbill. The new illusionist was called Stevie Summer and he too sported an impressive handlebar mustache. Was this a requirement of illusionists, I wondered? In which case why was Houdini clean shaven? I stared at the face again. There was something about the deep-set eyes that

411

caught my attention. It was as if the face was set in a perpetual worried frown.

"Wait a minute," I muttered, and stepped into the far corner of the foyer where there was a gilt-and-velvet bench. I sat down and brought out the scrapbooks. I had seen those eyes, that worried scowl, I was sure of it. I thumbed hastily through the pages and, yes, there he was. It was a group photo taken onstage in Berlin. Houdini was standing front and center, looking rather pleased with himself, but right behind him, much taller and thinner, his face half obscured in shadow, was a man who looked remarkably like this Mr. Summer, only he was clean shaven. The article below was in German, of course, but I scanned through the words, hoping to find something familiar, and came across the word "Fommer." Was that character an "F," as I had previously decided, or an "S" in the German script? In which case was "Sommer" the German equivalent of "Summer"?

I hurried to rejoin the throng around the ticket booth. I had to come to the matinee this afternoon and see this Mr. Summer for myself. As I was jostled forward toward the booth I wondered why I was so excited to find that Mr. Summer might also be Herr Sommer from the Berlin newspaper. Even if he was the same person, he hadn't been at this theater last week. I supposed I could dare to pay a visit to the suspicious stage doorkeeper and ask if Mr. Summer had shown up in advance, but that would probably mean admitting that I was working for the Houdini family and that message could be passed along to unfriendly ears.

The important thing, as far as I was concerned, was that I now had one tangible link between Houdini and Germany. The two men had stood close together on a stage not three months ago. And his name, in the German newspaper, was not Summer, but Sommer, which might suggest that he was of German origin. I calculated that I would have time to attend the matinee before Mr. Wilkie could possibly arrive in New York and make his way up to Houdini's residence to find me. I reached the ticket booth only to hear the young man inside it saying to the person ahead of me. "All sold out now, I'm afraid. I can sell you a ticket for tomorrow, if you'd like."

"Forget it," the woman snapped, and pushed past me angrily.

I stepped up to the ticket booth. "So there is nothing at all left for this afternoon?" I asked.

"Only a stage box with partially obscured

413

vision," he said, then translated in case I was particularly dense. "That means you might not see everything that's going on all the time. Especially the acrobats."

"But it's close to the stage, right?"

"Almost on top of the orchestra," he said. "You have to lean out a bit."

"I'll take it," I said.

"It will cost you a dollar."

"A dollar? For a seat I have to lean out of to see anything?"

"It's a box, isn't it? And box seats go for more."

I had no alternative. I paid the dollar, wondering as I did so whether I'd ever see any money from the Houdini family. But I did have the advance from Mr. Wilkie. And promise of more.

"By the way," I said. "That illusionist who was at the theater last week — Signor Scarpelli. Any idea where he was staying before he vanished? I need to get in touch with him."

The man laughed. "Doesn't everybody? It seems he owes half of New York money. But if the police can't find him, then you're not likely to either."

"So who would know his address?"

"The manager, I suppose."

"So this manager — is he likely to be in

his office at the moment?"

The clerk shrugged. "I couldn't tell you, miss. I just sit out front here and do my job. And a right busy job it's been these last couple of weeks too. Sold out every performance since that first accident happened with Scarpelli."

"I'll go and see if I can find the manager in his office then," I said, sounding a lot braver than I felt. I pushed open the frosted glass swing doors and stood in the darkness and silence of the theater. Every step forward I took, I felt more reluctant. Did I really need to know where Scarpelli had taken rooms in New York? Was it at all relevant to Houdini's disappearance? And surely the police must have searched his rooms most thoroughly. So was I putting myself in danger for nothing?

I had to come up with a good, convincing lie. Why would I need Scarpelli's address? Think, I commanded myself. Use your brain. But my brain refused to work. I went along the side aisle, up the steps, and pushed open the pass door. The backstage area was eerily quiet and shrouded props loomed like ghosts ahead of me. Mercifully, there was a small light on in the narrow hallway leading to the manager's office and light shone from a half-open door. I tapped on the door nervously, then pushed it farther open and went in. The office was empty. I couldn't believe my luck. Now all I had to do was to find some kind of file or card system that he kept on the performers. Of course it was possible that there was nothing of the kind in this little back office and that the circuit that owned this theater took care of all the booking arrangements, but surely a theater manager must be able to get in touch with his performers?

The desktop was messy in the extreme, but seemed to be all random papers, plus a couple of ashtrays that needed emptying. I went to the filing cabinet on the wall and pulled out the top drawer. It contained financial statements and I didn't feel comfortable going through them. I closed it again and tried the drawers below. The bottom drawer contained contracts. I found one for Scarpelli (alias Alfred Rosen), and noted that the address stated, "represented by Morgan Highfield management, 294 Broadway."

I heaved a sigh of relief. It would be easier to face his manager and I might even learn something from him. Just as I was closing the drawer I heard the sound of heavy footsteps coming toward me. I spun around guiltily as Mr. Irving came into his office.

He started in surprise when he saw me, frowned, and tried to place me.

"Miss — uh?"

"I'm Bess Houdini's friend, remember? I was the one who filled in as Houdini's assistant when Bess was taken ill," I said.

"Ah, of course." I detected no flicker of interest.

"I'm sorry to trouble you, sir, but I was very upset when I left the theater that night, and I rather fear that I left behind a small cameo brooch that I always wear for good luck. It was given to me by my departed mother, you see. So I just wondered if it had been turned in to you?"

He frowned even harder. "A cameo brooch? I haven't seen one. Nobody's mentioned it."

"Oh, dear. That's a pity," I said. "Then it might have fallen on my way into the cab and somebody's nabbed it."

"Too bad," he said. His expression was unreadable. Had he glimpsed me at his file cabinet? Did he suspect me of being anything more than a friend of the Houdinis?

"You can come and check the lost property closet if you like," he said. "Someone may have just put it there without telling me."

Again I hesitated. Was my gut telling me

not to go with him?

"That's all right," I said. "I really shouldn't trouble you anymore. I'll give it up for lost."

"The closet's right here," he said, literally steering me back down the passage. "I'd hate for you to lose your beloved trinket." And he opened a door in the passage.

I was truly expecting to be shoved inside, or to find it led to a flight of dark stairs, but it was a perfectly normal closet. I looked through it for what seemed the required amount of time and was about to close it when I noticed a bag on the bottom shelf. It was a canvas bag and across it was painted in bold letters SCARPELLI.

"That's Signor Scarpelli's bag," I said. "So I see he never came back to collect it."

"Nobody's heard a squeak from him after he took Lily off in an ambulance," Mr. Irving said. "If you want to know what I think, I think he's scared he'll be charged with a crime. The police didn't think it was an accident, you see. So he's lying low for a while."

"I could take it to his manager, if you like," I said. "I'm on my way there right now."

"Are you? What for?"

I attempted to look coy. "He also represents a friend of mine who's away on tour. I need his address on the West Coast. He promised to write but he hasn't. I expect he's been too busy."

"Yes, I expect so." He gave me an understanding smile. "Well, I suppose you could take the bag to his manager. It's only cluttering up the place here."

And he handed me the canvas bag. I went off triumphantly. I had done something risky and I had succeeded. I always love it when things go right.

THIRTY

As soon as I was out of sight of the theater I opened the bag and went through it. To my disappointment it contained only things that were clearly professional props — some scarves, a wand, and several pieces of false hair, including a variety of mustaches, a box of matches, a packet of cigarettes, and a new jar of makeup-removing cream. But nothing incriminating or threatening. No letters. No addresses.

It didn't take long to find Morgan Highfield's office on Lower Broadway for which I was glad, as I was now carrying two bags. Scarpelli's was remarkably heavy, given the contents, and it seemed to get heavier by the minute. The office was in a seedy area and up on the third floor so that I was panting and sweaty by the time I made it up all those steep stairs. A balding, paunchy man was sitting with his feet up on his desk, wearing no tie and his shirt collar open, and smoking a cigar.

"And what can I do for you, little lady?" he asked, not bothering to remove his feet.

I held out the bag and said that I'd come from Miner's Theatre, where I'd also been working and thought that he might want to forward the bag to Scarpelli.

"Thank you, my dear. Most obliged. Very kind of you," he said. "I can certainly do that."

"You know where he is?"

"I haven't heard a peep from him since he took off that night," he said. It came out smoothly enough, but I got a feeling that he did know but wasn't going to say.

"So how will you know where to forward his things?" I asked.

"It's my belief that he was shocked beyond belief about what happened," he said. "So what do you do when you've had a shock? You go home to recover. I expect he's gone home to Boston. And when he's ready to pick himself up again, who's the first one he's going to contact? His agent, of course."

"Boston?"

"That's where he's from. Poor man. I bet he just can't face talking to anybody at the moment. I know how he feels. What a terrible tragedy."

I nodded agreement. "I was in the theater.

I witnessed it. It was horrible."

He leaned closer to me so that his paunch draped over his desk. "I really can't understand how it happened. He swore to me that the trick was foolproof. It's my belief that someone tinkered with his equipment. Jammed it, you know."

"Why would someone do that?"

He shrugged so that his impressive sagging jowls quivered. "Who knows? Out of spite, maybe. These illusionists — they're a high-strung bunch. Always want to be the best and the first. And if one of 'em feels he's been slighted, well, he'd find a way to get back at the person who had slighted him, wouldn't he?"

"I don't know. That seems excessive to me," I said.

He nodded. "Like I said, a highly strung bunch. They'd have to be, cheating death every day. Of course it could have been one of Lily's spurned lovers. She liked to keep a trail of men behind her. I don't suppose we'll ever know now. But the show must go on — that's what we say, don't we? I expect I'll hear from him any day now that he's ready to go back on."

"Performing that same trick again?"

"Nah, I don't think he'll be trying that one again for a while. I can't see any girl volunteering to take Lily's place, can you?"

"I wouldn't," I said.

"You in the business, my dear?"

"I have been," I said.

"As it happens I'm looking for a girl at the moment — rest of the summer in Atlantic City. What can you do?"

"I've been a magician's assistant," I said.

"Have you? Who have you worked with?"

"Houdini," I said. "I help out when Bess isn't feeling well."

"Then you've been on the Continent with him?"

"No, only over here."

"So you know more than me about what happened the other night. Some say he's on the run and he killed that guy. Others say he's feeding the fishes at the bottom of the river. What do you think?"

"I have no idea," I said. "About Atlantic City. How soon do you need to know?"

"As soon as possible. I need a girl to take over on Tuesday."

"I'll get back to you," I said. "But in the meantime, do you have the address where Scarpelli was staying while he was in New York? He told me that his landlady might have an extra room and I'm looking for one for a friend."

"I expect she would. These theatrical

boardinghouses — people are always coming and going, aren't they?"

"So what's the address?"

"Ma Becker's. If you're in the business, you'll know Ma Becker, won't you?"

"Oh, yes, Ma Becker." I tried to look confident as I said this. "I've had friends that stayed there. What street was it on again — Canal, was it?"

"Delancey," he said.

"That's right. I know I've been there. Thanks for your time and I'm glad that Signor Scarpelli will be getting his props back when he asks for them."

"When he does, I'll let him know that you did him the favor. What was your name again, miss?"

"I didn't say," I said, "But it's Kathleen. Kathleen McCarthy. He probably won't remember me."

Then off I went toward Delancey Street. I hadn't had the nerve to ask him the number and Delancey is a long street, so I had to stop and grab a bite to eat and drink at a Jewish delicatessen to fortify myself before I finally met people who had heard of Ma Becker's and I trudged up the steps to her front door. Machinery was clattering away loudly from a workshop in the basement and I wondered how theatrical folk could

424

stand such a noise, seeing that they liked to sleep late in the morning. But perhaps beggars couldn't be choosers.

Ma Becker was the archetypal landlady — hatchet-faced and clearly allowing no hanky-panky within her walls. Keen on money too, as I saw her eyes light up when I asked about vacant rooms.

"Your friend, what does she do in the business?" she asked.

"She's a dancer."

"Chorus girl?"

"Acrobatic dancer," I said, feeling stupid that I was allowing this farce to continue.

"Solo act then." She was positively beaming at me now. "I'll take you up and show you the room. When will she be in town?"

"In a couple of weeks, I hope," I said.

Along the dreary, dark-brown hall and up the dark-brown worn linoleum of the stairs we went. The room was truly dreadful — dark, looking onto the tenement behind, and smelling of bad drains. "It will do just fine," I lied. "I'll write and tell her."

As we came down the stairs I turned and said breezily, "So which room did Mr. Scarpelli have here? He always spoke so fondly of you."

"Did he now? Well, I'm not about to speak fondly of him. Up and leaving me without paying the rent."

"So he never came back here after the tragedy?"

"I ain't seen hide nor hair of him since," she said. "I kept expecting him to get in touch because he's left all his stuff, but I haven't heard from him. Typical of these men. Never think of anybody except themselves. So now I don't even know if I am supposed to re-let the room or if he wants it kept on."

"Could I see it?" I asked. "Just in case he doesn't want to keep it. I may be needing a room myself as well."

"I don't think I should be showing Alfred's room," she said. "It's not right, is it?"

"But if he owes you money then you've no obligation to keep it for him, have you? Why, he might be away for months. He might never come back. And I can pay."

I saw the struggle between money and a loyalty to Scarpelli going on in her head until she finally said, "Well, I suppose there's no harm in showing it to you, just in case he won't be needing it again. It's this one here." She opened a door on the first floor. This room was much nicer altogether — it had a big bay window that overlooked the street, a gaily patterned carpet, and an impressive wardrobe.

"This is lovely," I said.

"Well, Scarpelli, he's one of my best returning customers," she said. "Or at least, he was. Who knows now?"

"Nobody seems to know where he is even," I said.

"That's right. Disappeared into the blue, hasn't he?" she said. I thought I detected a twitch of smile as she said this and it occurred to me that perhaps she did know. In which case had she written to him, asking for the money she owed him? And why was she smiling?

I was looking around the room as she talked. She went across to the window and opened it, letting in the fresh air. "Stuffy in here," she said.

The clatter of machinery rose up from the basement, a deep, rhythmic thump. I was dying to open that wardrobe and the drawers in the dresser, but I couldn't think of a reason to do so. Besides, at least now I knew he lived in Boston and I could pass that information along to the police, if they didn't already have it. If they still wanted it.

"His agent thinks he might have gone home to Boston," I said.

"Boston? Fancy that. The scoundrel," she said, and again it came out a little as if she were delivering lines onstage.

"So why don't you pack up his stuff and then you could re-let the room until he comes back? I'm sure my friend would rather have this room than the one upstairs."

"The police were round here several times and they told me not to touch anything," she said. "But if he's gone to Boston — well, that's a different matter, isn't it?" Again I could see the struggle between doing what the police had told her and recouping her losses. "They can't expect me to keep this room untouched forever, can they?" She said, as if thinking out loud, "I mean, what if he never comes back. I expect —" She broke off as she heard her name being called.

"Ma — where are you? There's a man at the front door for you!" a male voice was shouting.

"I'm coming, I'm coming!" she called back, and left the room.

I didn't wait a second longer. I dashed over to the wardrobe and opened it. The loud clattering of the machinery in the basement hid any noise that the opening door made. I had no idea what I was looking for and I found myself looking at a black suit and a cape. Hardly a revelation but it did show that he hadn't taken his costume with him, so he had never returned here after that night. On the floor, half hidden under the cape, was an canvas bag identical to the one I had carried to the manager's office. I lifted it out and opened it. It was empty. I was about to stuff it back when it occurred to me that it was heavy, just as the one I had carried to the office was heavy, given the number of items in it.

I opened it again and fished around at the bottom. The canvas was only loosely sewn. It came loose, I snapped the remaining threads, and beneath it I pulled out a wad of twenty-dollar bills. I could hardly believe my eyes. Hastily I stuffed them back and put the bag back where I had found it.

What could this mean? Scarpelli had left town owing people money. He hadn't paid his rent and yet he had all this money. Was it possible he was also a crook — a robber? And Lily had found out and was about to go to the police so he killed her?

The noise of the machinery was overpowering. Why had he stayed here when he had enough money in that bag alone to stay at a good hotel? Unless. . . . Slowly things pieced themselves together in my mind. The sound of that machine was identical to the sound I had heard before that morning — the sound of the printing press at the magazine. What if that money was forged? Scarpelli had been in Philadelphia and now Secret Service men were in that city investigating the flood of forged banknotes there. I couldn't wait to share my suspicion with Daniel. Then I remembered that I couldn't let Daniel know what I'd been doing. He had forbidden me to investigate anything to do with Scarpelli. So I'd have to tell Mr. Wilkie instead. Another coup when I saw him later this afternoon.

I heard slow steps coming up the stairs. I closed the wardrobe again and was looking out of the window when Ma Becker reappeared.

"Ah, still here?" she asked. "Ain't no use setting your heart on this room because I'll have to wait until I get word from Alfred. And who knows when that will be."

"Thank you for your time," I said. "I'll let my friend know about the other room."

She followed me down the stairs. I bet she's part of it too, I found myself thinking as I peered down the basement steps before I went on my way. Ma Becker was still standing at the door, hands on hips, watching me go. She must be in on it. Someone who was as keen on money as she wouldn't leave the best room empty when she had a chance to rent it again, especially if she was owed money for it by someone who had disappeared into the blue, as she put it. That little smirk had given her away.

The chime of a clock reminded me that I had better make my way back to the theater for the matinee. I threaded my way between pushcarts and women with shopping baskets until I reached the Bowery and joined the line waiting to go into the theater. I noticed some men of the press watching with interest. Were they anticipating yet another disaster?

Gradually the line moved forward until I was in the blissful cool of the theater. I made my way around to the stage box. It was exactly where Bess and Houdini's brother had sat on that fateful night. What was I doing here? I wondered. Even if this Mr. Summer had been in Germany with Houdini, he hadn't been in the theater when Houdini disappeared. So what did I hope to gain from watching his performance? Then I reasoned there was nowhere else I should be, apart from back with Bess, and frankly, I was glad to sit and rest after a day of rushing around in the heat.

The orchestra struck up a lively tune and the show began. It started with a pair of comedians in blackface who exchanged a string of corny jokes and then did a soft-shoe dance. Then followed a female singer who probably broke the heart of every male in the audience by singing, "The Boy I Love Is up in the Gallery."

Finally the announcer boomed, "Ladies and gentlemen, it's Summer time! Back from a triumphant tour of Europe, where he played to kings and nobles, it's that master of magic, that prince of prestidigitators, Stevie Summer, with the lovely, the exotic, that dangerous feline, Kitty."

And Stevie Summer swept onto the stage, accompanied by a gorgeous dark-skinned beauty. She was dressed in a startling red satin costume that left little to the imagination, and her magnificent black hair was worn loose, cascading over her shoulders. Over her eyes was a provocative black cat mask. I heard a collective intake of breath from the men in the audience.

The act began. First the usual sort of magic tricks to warm up the audience. Summer took off his top hat and poured a pitcher of water into it. Then he replaced it on his head. Collective gasp from the audience, then applause. I suppose a week or so ago I would have gasped, but I had become used to magic tricks. After a few such stunts the exotic Kitty wheeled an upright cabinet onto the stage. Summer extended his hand to her and she stepped into it from behind. Her face could be seen through a hole in the top section, her hand waved through the middle, and her foot protruded from a hole at the bottom.

"And now, ladies and gentlemen," Summer announced in his deep, booming voice, "we shall see whether the lovely Kitty enjoys being divided into three pieces." He started to push the middle section of the cabinet to his left until it was barely in contact with the top and bottom sections. I knew a little about illusions now, but I couldn't even begin to imagine how this was done. The hand still waved from that middle section, the head and foot still appeared at the top and bottom.

I found I was holding my breath, waiting for something to go wrong. But Summer reassembled her to great applause and she stepped unharmed from the cabinet. I suppose that has to be the deception cabinet I saw advertised in the magazine, I thought. Suitable for the most dangerous stunts?

The cabinet was whisked away by a stage-hand and in its place a glass table was carried out. Summer then invited Kitty to lie on the table. He announced that he would put her into a trance and then float her across the stage. As she lay on the table he bent over her. "Look into my eyes," he commanded. "You are getting sleepy. Your limbs are becoming heavier and heavier. When I snap my fingers you will awake and be completely in my power."

I was staring at the stage, hypnotized almost as completely as Kitty. I couldn't believe what I was seeing, because I had witnessed this same scene before, on this very stage. Only one of the players had then been an aged doctor and one a dying girl. You can disguise your face with false hair and makeup, but you can never completely disguise your voice or your manner of movement. This man had been the doctor who appeared from the audience to whisk Lily away to a hospital, and — I blinked a couple of times, wondering if my eyes were deceiving me — the brown-skinned beauty who lay on the glass table was in shape and movement exactly like Lily. The hand that draped languidly from the side of the table resembled that long white hand I had held as I put my wrap over her. I almost laughed out loud. The whole thing had been an incredible illusion.

THIRTY-ONE

I couldn't wait to get out of there and pass along this astounding information to Daniel. He'd be amazed that what we had witnessed was not a crime at all but a brilliantly executed illusion. The question, however, was why? Why make it seem that someone had been killed onstage — unless it was to get rid of Scarpelli, to make him flee from New York. What did they want to do — take over his successful forgery business? I shouldn't forget that Sommer was possibly German and had been with Houdini in Germany, so Mr. Wilkie might well be interested in hearing about him, although how this tied in with the disappearance of Houdini, I couldn't fathom.

I shifted uneasily in my seat, longing to make my escape. However I thought it wise not to move while they were still performing, in case they noticed me. In fact I leaned back from the front of the box so that my face was in shadow. I sat perfectly still while Summer apparently hypnotized Kitty/Lily and then removed the table that supported her so that she lay unmoving in midair. It was a wonderfully convincing illusion but I didn't really appreciate it because my head was trying to make sense of what I had deduced.

If the "accident" during the sawing-the-lady-in-half trick was an illusion, what had they hoped to accomplish with it? What if Scarpelli was in on it? Maybe the forged money was all part of the same plot. Maybe all three were German agents. But he had seemed so genuinely upset and stunned by what had happened. He was a performer after all, so perhaps he was simply a good actor.

So what had the accident achieved? Well, to begin with it had taken Lily out of the picture so she could no longer be a suspect in any subsequent crime. But if she was supposedly dead, she couldn't have risked coming back to the theater to kidnap Houdini. She would surely have been spotted by one of the stagehands —

As the word "stagehands" went through my mind I leaned forward again, digesting what I had just seen. The man who whisked away the cabinet and brought out the table was one of the stagehands called Ernest. And now I remembered that he was the one who helped me bring out the trunk and who placed it for me on the stage, exactly over the trapdoor, as it turned out. So Ernest was in on the plot too. He was the one who had gone for the ambulance to whisk Lily away. All beautifully orchestrated to fool us.

A stirring round of applause announced the end of the act onstage. They came forward to take a bow and I ducked down, just in case they looked in my direction. The moment the curtains closed I slipped from my seat, down the side corridor, and out of the theater. It is always a shock to come out of a theater and find it is broad daylight outside, but it's also a shock to emerge to find the weather completely changed. Whereas I had entered the theater to sultry, merciless sunlight, I came out to find heavy clouds had gathered overhead and odd breezes swirled to herald the arrival of a thunderstorm. I glanced nervously at the heavens. I hadn't brought a brolly with me and quickened my pace toward the closest El station.

Now all I had to do was make my way back to Harlem and wait for Mr. Wilkie to come to me. But as I threaded my way through the busy crowd on the Bowery I realized that I was about to expound a preposterous theory and wondered if he'd believe me. What proof did I have, apart from a strong hunch? Surely many magicians' assistants were willowy with long elegant fingers and I couldn't really see her face because of the mask that covered her eyes.

Then suddenly I changed direction and darted across the street between a trolley car and a delivery cart. I did have proof. At my house, carefully wrapped in tissue paper, was a bloody cloth I had retrieved from the rubbish bin at the theater. I made up my mind to go home and to take the cloth to Daniel. He would probably be angry with me but I couldn't afford to waste another minute before having that cloth tested. If it revealed that the substance wasn't human blood at all but some kind of theatrical paint, then they'd take me seriously.

Patchin Place seemed so delightfully normal and safe as I left the bustle of Jefferson Market and made my way over the cobbles. Flowers were blooming in window boxes. A window was open and someone was playing the violin. How I longed to shut myself in my own house and stay there, not be involved any longer in this dangerous business, but I couldn't back out now. And in truth I was feeling rather pleased with myself at my great discovery that had eluded everyone else. A triumph for Molly Murphy, I said to myself in the way that Houdini had penned similar sayings under his newspaper clippings. I took the cloth from the drawer in the scullery where I had kept it. It looked remarkably unappealing and extremely like blood, not paint. It smelled like old blood too, I thought, and I wondered if I had made a terrible blunder after all. But I was determined to go through with it. I put the tissue parcel into my bag and off I went again.

I was just locking my front door behind me when I heard my name being called and saw Gus was waving from the bedroom window.

"Molly, you will never guess — I've just sold a painting," she said excitedly. "To one of the members of our suffragists' group. Isn't it thrilling? I'm a true professional artist at last. Sid is arranging for me to have a show in the fall so I'm painting up a storm. Come and see my latest effort — I think it's my best work yet."

"Gus, I'd love to but I have to go to police headquarters this minute," I said, "and a man is arriving by train from Washington to see me."

"Mercy me," she said. "Well, I won't keep

you then." She sounded disappointed and I felt terrible. They had been such good friends to me and she was so anxious to show me her painting. But she and Sid would never understand that life for me was not all play, that when you work for a living and run your own business, you can't take a break anytime you feel like it.

"I'm sorry," I said. "I'll come and see it tomorrow, I promise. And if Daniel shows up, please tell him to meet me at police headquarters right away. It's very urgent."

"All right." She nodded, then called after me. "Molly, take care, won't you? Don't do anything reckless."

"Don't worry about me," I called back as I turned the corner.

Given the importance of the situation, I hailed a cab and we were soon clattering toward Mulberry Street.

"I'm here to see Captain Sullivan," I said. "Is he in his office?"

"He is, miss, but —" the young constable at the desk said, as I pushed past him. "You can't go up there!" he shouted after me as I started up the stairs. I didn't slow down and got surprised looks from a couple of detectives as I pushed past them down the hallway to Daniel's office. Through the frosted glass front wall I could see that he had someone with him, but even that didn't deter me. I knocked and burst straight in. Daniel's surprised face, plus that of Detective MacAffrey, stared up at me.

Both men rose to their feet.

"Molly, what on earth is the meaning of this?" Daniel asked. "I'm in the middle of an important meeting. Didn't they tell you downstairs that I wasn't to be disturbed?"

"I'll only take a minute of your time," I said, "but I have something I want you to do for me right away." I looked from one face to the other. "It's extremely important or I'd never have barged in on you this way."

"I'm sorry about this, MacAffrey," Daniel said.

The other man gave him an understanding smile that said that women were an infernal nuisance but had to be humored occasionally. "I'll come back in a few minutes," he said, and tactfully stepped outside, closing the door behind him.

"Molly, this is inexcusable," Daniel said. "You simply can't burst in on me like this. You'll make me the laughingstock of the police force."

"Daniel, before you go on anymore, just shut up and listen to me," I said. He was so surprised that he opened his mouth, then closed it again.

441

I rummaged in my bag and brought out the tissue-wrapped parcel. "I take it you never did locate Lily's body?"

"Lily?"

"The illusionist's assistant who was supposedly killed last week."

"Supposedly? You mean you think she recovered from that wound?"

"I mean that the wound was an illusion, that I've seen her, alive and well, in the theater this afternoon."

"That's — preposterous. Are you sure?"

"Not one hundred percent sure," I said, "but I have proof here." I put the parcel in his hands.

"What's this?"

"It's a blood-soaked cloth that I took from the rubbish bin at the theater after Lily was killed," I said.

He opened the parcel gingerly, staring in disbelief at what lay in his hands.

"What the devil possessed you to take it in the first place?"

"I thought it might be useful as evidence later," I said. "And as it turns out, I was right."

"What exactly do you want me to do with it?" he asked.

"I want it tested to see if it really is human blood or just another theatrical illusion. If it's not Lily's blood then I know that I'm right and she didn't really get hurt."

"But why would anyone pull off such a gruesome stunt?" he said in a more normal voice now.

"I'm not quite sure yet, but it has something to do with the body in the trunk and the disappearance of Houdini," I said.

"Molly!" He wagged a finger at me. "Are you still pursuing this when I made it very clear that you were to have no part in a criminal case?"

"I'm still employed by Houdini's family," I said cautiously. "They want him found and I'm trying to find him." I felt bad as I said it, but then I reasoned that I wasn't lying to my future husband. I was just leaving out the whole truth about Mr. Wilkie. "You can't stop me from doing that," I added to make myself feel better.

"Actually I can. I could have you arrested for interfering with police business," he said.

"So have the police discovered what happened to Houdini yet? Has his body been discovered? Have they come up with any suspects or a motive for the crime?"

"Not as yet," he said cautiously.

"Then maybe the police could use a little help," I said.

He looked at me, head tilted sideways,

then he laughed. "You're impossible, do you know that?"

"So you've said before."

"And you think that this Lily person is somehow responsible for Houdini's disappearance? What motive would she have?"

"I'm not sure of that yet," I said cautiously. "I will probably be able to tell you by tomorrow. How long do you think it will take to have the blood tested on this cloth?"

"I'll have it sent round to the laboratory that does this kind of testing for us," he said. "I don't believe it should take them long."

"Then let me know immediately," I said. "I'll be at Houdini's house, keeping Bess company."

"Thank heavens for small mercies," he said. "At least you can't get yourself into more trouble if you stay there with Mrs. Houdini and one of our men outside the door." He put down the parcel and opened his door for me. "You're really going directly there?"

"I really am," I said.

"At least I'll know where to find you for once."

I paused in the doorway and looked back at him. "By the way, have you found Scarpelli yet?"

"No. We've pretty much given up looking

for him," he said. "We decided we'd never be able to prove that the unfortunate incident wasn't accidental. And if it really turns out to be another illusion, then I'll be glad we haven't wasted the manpower."

"His agent thinks he might be in Boston if you want him," I said. And I gave him a big triumphant smile as I swept from the room.

THIRTY-TWO

I was feeling pleased and excited as the train took me slowly northward to Harlem. I had proved that I was a real detective. Oh, I had solved cases before, but sometimes more by luck than by observation and deduction. Paddy Riley, my former mentor, would have been proud of me. I thought Mr. Wilkie would be equally impressed. I had the drawings of the underwater escape to give him and the piece from the magazine that hinted at possible invasion. And I had an illusionist who had recently been in Germany and had pretended to be a doctor when a girl pretended to die. Not to mention a bag full of counterfeit money and a house with a printing press in the basement. All in all a most satisfying day.

I peered out of the train window, hoping to spot a clock somewhere. Really, I would have to save up enough money to buy myself a watch soon. I thought it couldn't be later than four, so I'd arrive at Houdini's residence in good time to meet Mr. Wilkie. I left the train at Ninety-ninth Street and felt a spatter of raindrops. I had been in such a hurry that I had forgotten to pick up my brolly when I had been at Patchin Place. How shortsighted of me, as the clouds overhead loomed black and menacing and from the east came the growl of thunder. I quickened my step. Houdini's house was several blocks away and the first spatter of raindrops sizzled onto the hot sidewalks. Thunder clapped nearby now and a horse neighed and reared in alarm as it stood waiting in the shafts. I looked for an awning to shelter under, but I had already left the commerce of Third Avenue behind and the street ahead of me was purely residential, so I had no choice but to push on. The rain began in earnest, hard and cold on my skin. I would clearly be meeting Mr. Wilkie looking like a drowned rat and I worried about the scrapbooks I still carried in my bag getting ruined. I clutched the bag to my person in a vain hope of keeping it dry and looked around desperately for a passing cab. But cabs do not patrol streets where there is little likelihood of picking up fares. In fact the street was deserted, save for one smart black carriage coming swiftly toward me. I stepped back from the curb so that I didn't get even more drenched with the spray from the wheels, but to my surprise it came to a halt beside me and the door was thrown open.

"Miss Murphy?" a horrified voice exclaimed from the interior. "Get in quickly, before you are soaked to the skin. Here, take my hand."

A hand came toward me and I saw that the man leaning out of the carriage was Anthony Smith, the young Secret Service agent. He took my arm and assisted me into the carriage, then leaned across to close the door behind me. "What a stroke of luck. I've just been to Houdini's residence to find that you weren't there and I wasn't sure what to do next."

"A stroke of luck for both of us," I said as the heavens opened and the rain came down in a solid sheet, bouncing from the carriage roof and the sidewalks.

"What beastly weather," he said. "I must say I didn't come prepared for a deluge, and neither did you by the look of it. Here, I have a handkerchief if that will help." He produced one, white and neatly folded with his initials embroidered in one corner. "You'll probably want to dry off before we meet Mr. Wilkie."

"Mr. Wilkie sent you to fetch me?" I asked as the carriage took off again.

"Of course. He thought it wise that you should meet where there is no possibility of being overheard."

"Another train ride?"

"I really can't tell you. I was sent to find you and then I imagine my task will be complete. He doesn't confide in anyone, you know. More cautious than he needs to be, but a solid fellow, nonetheless."

I had removed my damp straw hat and attempted to dry off my face and neck with the handkerchief. My dress was already clinging to me in a way that would have horrified Daniel and it did cross my mind that I was most inappropriately attired to be alone in a carriage with a strange man. But he didn't seem to have noticed. I stole a glance at him and he was leaning forward, apparently focused on the straw boater and silver-tipped cane he held across his knees.

"So you were actually staying at Houdini's house?" he said. "I envy you that opportunity. I'm a great admirer, you know. He's the best there is. I'm a keen amateur magician myself, as is Mr. Wilkie, of course. He likes to engage fellow magicians to work for him."

"I presume he finds sleight of hand a useful skill in your profession."

"Quite." He gave something between a laugh and a dry cough.

Thunder rumbled again nearby and what sounded like hail was bouncing off the carriage roof with a clatter like loud applause.

"Did you come with Mr. Wilkie from Washington?" I asked because the silence was making me uneasy.

"No, I was already here," he said. "I met him at the station."

Ah, so it was later than I thought. I stole another glance at him. It was dark in the carriage and his hair and face looked like one of those floating heads that spiritualists can conjure up. The carriage slowed, and the rain abated for a moment so that I could hear the clip-clopping of other horses' hooves and the chime of a large clock. One, two, three, four. I counted the strokes. Then I sat up, suddenly alert. I hadn't misjudged the time. It was four o'clock. Mr. Wilkie couldn't possibly have arrived in New York yet. And at the same time several unconnected thoughts raced through my mind. The passage that Mr. Wilkie had circled in the magazine: something about the problem with illusionists is that you think they are working on one side of the stage when really they are on the other. "I'm a keen amateur magician," Smith had just said.

And that advertisement for the deception cabinet. Light wood on top, ebony underneath. Works both sides. Used for the most dangerous tricks. And made in Germany. Houdini had been describing Anthony Smith. He even had a Germanic look to him. There were faces like his in those photographs of the German royal court — proud, haughty young officers with light hair. And I knew why I had been uneasy ever since I stepped into the carriage. Anthony Smith was a double agent. That was why Houdini insisted on meeting Mr. Wilkie in person, why he could send nothing by mail. He knew that among Mr. Wilkie's team of men there was one that couldn't be trusted.

And now I was alone in a carriage with him. I stole a quick glance in his direction and noticed that the blind on his window was down. Also that he had locked my door behind me. I had no idea where he intended to take me but it certainly wasn't to meet Mr. Wilkie. My one chance was to show no alarm, to act naturally, and wait for an opportunity to jump out. It was, after all, still daylight and the streets would still be full of people. There would be constables on every corner. I put my bag on my knee, pretending to brush it down with the now-sodden handkerchief, but in reality to hide the door latch. I then leaned across, waited for the noise of the rain to pick up again, and flipped the lock open. Now one swift turn and I could jump out.

It did go through my mind that I would have no proof of my suspicions if I left the carriage now, but I wouldn't be much use trying to testify as a corpse either, and I had seen what Smith and his kind had done to those who stood in their way. I looked out of the window, trying to see where we might be going but it was still raining too hard to recognize in which direction we were heading. The carriage was not rattling too much so we were not going over cobbles. That meant a major thoroughfare — probably one of the avenues. It would be helpful to know where to run if I made it safely to the street. Surely he wouldn't have the nerve to chase me in broad daylight, especially if I screamed for help?

I would like to have hitched up my skirt as it would be a long jump down from the carriage, but I couldn't do that without his noticing and I worried about taking the bag of scrapbooks with me. I didn't want to leave it behind. It might even show a snapshot of Anthony Smith in Germany, but it was definitely going to be an encumbrance when I tried to jump out.

We clipped on for a good while at a steady pace. My brain raced desperately for something to say.

"So what kind of tricks do you like to perform, Mr. Smith?" I asked.

"Me? Only the small stuff — cards, linking rings, that kind of thing."

"So none of the more impressive tricks that illusionists are doing these days?" I said gaily. At least I was attempting to sound gay and girlish. "Of course they are terribly dangerous, aren't they? Do you know I was actually in the theater when that poor girl was sliced open with the saw. It was all I could do not to faint."

"Yes, I heard about that," he said. "No, I don't think I'd ever attempt to saw someone in half."

"And what kind of tricks does Mr. Wilkie like to perform?" I prattled on.

"I really couldn't say." He snapped the words out and I realized that he too was feeling the tension now.

"Then I'll have to insist that he give me a demonstration when we're together," I said. "Are we nearly there?"

"Who knows, in this infernal downpour," he said.

The carriage came abruptly to a halt and I thought I heard the driver shouting a curse. I didn't wait for a second. My hand turned the door handle and pushed it open. Rain came flying into my face. I grabbed the bag, stood up, and — was just conscious of a swift movement behind me.

THIRTY-THREE

I opened my eyes to pitch darkness. By the way my head was throbbing, I surmised that I had been struck on the back of the head as I . . . as I what? I tried to remember. Rain in face. Jumping . . . and then it came back to me. I lay still, hardly daring to breathe. At least I'm still alive, I thought. They must be keeping me alive for a reason. I tried to find that reassuring. Where was I? The floor beneath me was rough and cold and the place smelled damp and musty with a hint of sawdust and turpentine that made me want to sneeze. Then I remembered where I had been recently with a similar sort of smell. I was in the basement of the theater.

I moved my hands and feet experimentally. I didn't appear to be tied up and I wondered if I was alone and had just been dumped here while the German agents made their escape. But why then had they bothered to take the time to capture me? I had obviously been brought here for a purpose, and given their past behavior, the outcome was not likely to be good. I attempted to sit up and the whole world swung around as nausea overcame me. My head was throbbing violently. I would have to wait a while before making a dash for freedom then.

As I lay back down again I heard voices coming toward me in the darkness.

"Why didn't you get rid of her immediately?" It was a woman's voice with a trace of foreign accent, possibly German. "What on earth made you bring her here of all places?"

"We have to find out what she knows and what she has already told Wilkie. She was living with Houdini, after all. He may have confided in her." This voice sounded like Anthony Smith — clipped, well-bred, and arrogant. They came toward me, bearing a small lamp. I lay back and closed my eyes.

"You must have given her a good whack for her to be out this long," the woman said. "Are you sure you haven't killed her?"

I felt my arm being lifted, then roughly dropped. "The pulse is steady."

"Thank you, Doctor," the woman said, and she laughed. So Lily and Summer were present.

I wondered if I played dead any longer,

they would leave me again and I'd have a chance to escape or at least hide. If I could hide for long enough the theater would come to life for the evening performance and any noise I made would attract attention. Then I remembered that the man in the trunk had presumably been killed and Houdini spirited away while a full theater watched the show go on.

"Wake her up," the woman said. "We haven't got all day."

Then suddenly I was hit in the face with cold water. I sat up, spluttering.

"What's happening?" I asked, looking around me in bewildered fashion. "Did I faint?" Then I looked around, pretended to study each of their faces in turn, and asked, "Where am I? Is this where Mr. Wilkie is going to meet me?"

"I think that's hardly likely," Anthony Smith said with something like a smirk.

"Then who are these people?"

"That is irrelevant," Lily said. She held the lamp up to my face. Close-up I could see that she had light eyes that didn't go with her dark complexion. That was why she wore the cat mask on stage. "What we need to know is how much you told Wilkie."

"I don't know what you're talking about," I said.

She slapped me hard across the face. "Don't be foolish. Of course you know. Wilkie is coming to New York to meet with you. You and he had a long, private conversation on a train and let's just say that Mr. Wilkie doesn't waste his time in idle chat. You have information he wants and obviously you haven't given it to him yet or he wouldn't be coming here."

"So what exactly have you discovered?" Summer asked in a gentler tone. "We have no quarrel with you. If you tell us what you know then you can go free."

"I hardly think that's likely," I said, "since you've already killed one, possibly two men who were on your trail."

He laughed. "The young lady has a keen wit. I like that."

I was trying desperately to come up with something to tell them. If I mentioned the design for the submarine device, there was nothing to stop them from going to Houdini's house to retrieve it. As that thought crossed my mind I realized something else. They were the two so-called spiritualists who had come to Houdini's house. No wonder my instincts had prevented them from entering. But what could I give them that might satisfy them yet not aid their cause?

"All right," I said slowly. "For one thing, I discovered that Scarpelli has probably gone up to Boston, and that he's somehow involved in forged money."

This made all three of them laugh. "I'm sure that is important news," Lily said, "but nothing to do with us."

"He is not working with you?" I asked, my mind going to the forged banknotes.

"Not on this particular assignment."

"He really believed he had killed you?" I asked.

"Of course not. Lily needed to cease to exist and Scarpelli — well, it was wise for him to vanish too at this moment. He's on a boat bound for Germany right now, having sailed out of Boston as you so cleverly deduced. He has been most useful to us. His career will get a boost as a reward for services rendered."

"A boost?" I blurted out.

Summer looked at Lily and laughed. "He's guaranteed packed houses for the rest of his career, isn't he? The illusionist who accidentally sliced a woman in half. They'll all want to see if it's going to happen again."

"Enough of Scarpelli," Lily snapped. "You found out that Smith was working with us, didn't you?"

"No, I —"

459

"Why else would you have tried to escape from the carriage?"

"I — didn't think that Mr. Wilkie would have sent someone to pick me up," I said cautiously. "I was uneasy."

I thought Lily was going to press me on that one but Smith cut me off. "More to the point, what exactly did Houdini tell you?"

"Houdini told me nothing," I said firmly. Lily raised her hand again, and I put up my arm to shield myself. "I swear I'm telling the truth. He told me nothing."

"So you're bringing Wilkie up here just to tell him that Smith is working for both sides?"

"Isn't that rather important?" I asked. "I'd like to know which of my staff I could trust."

There was a pause.

"See, I told you she was a waste of time," Lily said. "You should have dispatched her while you could, in the carriage. Now we'll have the bother of getting rid of the body."

"Nonsense. Plenty of places to leave a body down here," Smith said, "and your little helpmate Ernest can put her in a sack and get rid of her like the other one."

"Hello?" A voice echoed through the theater above us. An electric light must have been turned on because I could see chinks

460

of brightness shining through the cracks in the floorboards above us. "Hello down there," the voice repeated. "Can you help me? I'm looking for something."

Then a door opened above us and someone started coming down the steps from the side of the stage. I stared at him in wonder — the last person I expected to see here. He was dressed, as I had seen him this morning, in an immaculate frock coat with a neatly trimmed beard and round wire-framed eyeglasses.

"Who the hell are you?" Summer asked, getting to his feet.

"I am Dr. Leopold Weiss," he said. "I am the brother of the man you call Houdini. I have been sent by his family to retrieve his possessions. I understand he left his props and other personal items at the theater. The family would not wish them to fall into unfriendly hands, so I have been sent to collect them. If one of you would be good enough to show me where they can be found —"

"We're busy at the moment," Summer said. "You'll have to come back at another time."

"But I have a carriage waiting outside for this purpose, and a man to assist me," Dr. Weiss said. "And the theater manager received my telephone call earlier today. But it seems there is nobody in the theater but you at the moment."

He started to walk forward and an absurd thought crossed my mind as I watched him. I was probably quite wrong, but at the very least it was worth a try. "Dr. Weiss," I said. "I worked with Houdini. I know where the props are. Maybe I can help you find them."

As I tried to stand up I felt a warning prick of steel at my back.

"We need the young lady to help us down here at the moment," Smith said. "If you go to the manager's office, he should be back within the hour. And the stagehands will be arriving. They can be of assistance."

"Dr. Weiss," I said clearly, trying to keep my voice steady. "Will you not be needing the key? Will the key not be found at Houdini's own house?" I brushed back my hair that was falling across my face.

His dark eyes flashed as they held mine. "Very well," he said. "You may be right. These magicians. They keep everything locked up, don't they?" He bowed to us. "I shall return later as you suggest, with the key."

He turned and went. Nobody spoke as his footsteps died away.

"That was close," Summer said with a

sigh. "Of all the bad timing. And such good manners. If he only knew what we'd done with his brother." And he chuckled.

"Kill her and let's get out of here," Lily said. "We must be away from the city before Wilkie can discover the girl is missing."

I looked around for anything to use as a weapon. All I could focus on was the glint of that blade in Smith's hand. There was an open paint pot with a brush in it, but I could hardly defend myself with that.

"Wait," Smith said. "She may be more use to us alive. Just in case we need a hostage."

"It's too risky to have her with us," Lily said impatiently. "Give me the damned knife. I'll do it if you're squeamish."

As they discussed what to do with me I had been inching closer to the wall. I picked up the paint pot and flung it into her face as she reached for the knife. At the same time I pulled down the lever on the wall. The trapdoor opened and the little platform descended onto them. Not quickly enough to harm them, unfortunately, but at least they had to jump out of the way. Lily was screaming and as I looked at her it seemed as if blood was pouring from her face. Then I realized, of course, that it was red paint.

She let out a string of German curses at me as I fled up the steps to the wings. Smith and Summer were right behind me and I didn't think I'd get far, but at least I'd not give up without a fight. As I crossed the stage there was a click and all the stage lights came on. We froze, blinking in the brilliant glare.

"Hold it right there, gentlemen," a voice said, and to my utter relief I watched policemen coming up the steps onto the stage.

"Stand back," Smith said. He grabbed me and held the knife at my throat. "One step nearer and this woman dies."

An eerie silence fell as the constables stopped moving.

"Don't do anything stupid, sir," one of them said. "Let the young lady go and nobody will get hurt."

"She's coming with me and nobody will try to stop us," Smith said.

He started to drag me backward. Then something strange happened. I heard a whooshing noise and was vaguely conscious of someone standing behind us. The knife tightened on my throat for a second and I felt it nick my skin. I heard Smith give something between a grunt and a gurgle. Then another hand came around Smith's.

"Drop it," a voice said, and slowly Smith's hand was pulled away from my throat and his arm was twisted around until he whimpered in pain.

"I said, drop it."

"Stop it, you're breaking my arm!" Smith screamed.

"With pleasure," the voice said.

I took the opportunity to struggle free. Smith's arm was now up behind his back and his assailant had forced him to his knees. That assailant was Dr. Leopold Weiss.

"Here you are, gentlemen. He's all yours," Weiss said. "Please take good care of him until Chief Wilkie of the Secret Service gets here. He's a dangerous German agent. And I suggest you stop the illusionist Summer and his assistant from leaving the theater by the back door."

Men rushed past us. Anthony Smith was put into handcuffs and taken down from the stage.

"And the stagehand called Ernest," I called out. "He is also one of them."

"German spies, you mean?" a young policeman asked in surprise.

"Exactly."

Two constables exchanged glances. "Who would have thought it — here in New York?" one of them said.

I must have swayed a little.

"Are you unharmed?" Dr. Weiss asked me.

"I think so. I was hit on the back of the

head and it's certainly throbbing like billy-o, but other than that, I think I'll survive. Do you really have a carriage waiting? Mr. Wilkie will be arriving at Houdini's house any moment."

"Then let us go," he said. He took my arm and steered me down the steps and through the theater.

"I'm taking this young lady to be examined," he said. "She had received a blow to the head. Please tell your superiors that we may be found at Houdini's residence, on 102nd Street in Harlem."

Then he steered me outside. The thunderstorm had passed, the sidewalks were steaming, and the evening sunlight hurt my eyes. He hailed a cab and helped me up. I sat back with a sigh of relief. Then, as we set off, I remembered something. "Your scrapbooks. That fiend Anthony Smith must have them, or they are still in the carriage in which he transported me."

"My scrapbooks?" He looked at me with interest.

"It is Mr. Houdini, I presume?" I asked with a smile.

Thirty-Four

The cab set off with a clatter of hooves. We sat side by side in the semidarkness.

"How did you know?" he asked me.

I turned to look at him. "I saw a photograph of your family. Leopold was quite a bit taller than you, although you have his beard and hair perfectly. What's more, you recognized me this morning and I knew that Leopold had never seen me. Also, Harry Houdini and I were about the same height so Leopold would have been taller than me. I didn't realize it right away, but you have a certain way of thrusting out your jaw when you speak. So when you appeared in the theater, I thought I'd take a chance that it was you and not your brother. I gave you the signals you'd drilled into me, and you understood them."

He smiled. "Very clever, Miss Murphy — you even remembered to touch your hair when you said the words 'will' and 'key,' so that the message read 'Wilkie at Houdini's house.' You were a good pupil."

"How did you know I'd be at the theater?"

"I saw you in the stage box earlier this afternoon. I wanted to get a good look at Summer and Lily for myself. To tell you the truth, I had suspected him all along. I wasn't sure about her. And of course I have had to be extra cautious. They nearly killed me once. I didn't want to give them a second chance."

"Did they really throw you into the East River in the trunk?"

"They did," he said. "I was stunned when the trunk dropped from the stage, so I couldn't move as fast as I usually do. I couldn't get the cuffs off in time. Then when I tried to get out of the trunk I suppose someone whacked me over the head, because I don't remember any more. I came to my senses as I hit cold water and went under. The trunk was sinking fast. I knew I had to make the fastest escape of my life — and I did it. Luckily I had trained myself to hold my breath longer than any other living person and this helped me. I must have been underwater for several minutes. Long enough for my enemies to decide that they'd finished me off, anyway. I made my escape from the side panel of the trunk and came to the surface."

He looked at me for affirmation.

"How incredible," I said. "That was indeed your best escape ever."

"I may try to incorporate it into my act," he said, with that swagger returning.

"So what did you do then?"

"I made my way to my brother's house and have stayed hidden there until I knew it was safe to venture forth. I thought it safer all around if I was presumed to be dead. Among other things, I sure didn't want to put Bess at risk by letting her know I was alive."

He turned to me. "I hoped I could rely on Mr. Wilkie to realize the truth from the articles I had written. But you were the angel who appeared to work on my behalf. When you showed up at Leopold's house this morning and then at the theater, I knew you were on the right track and in great danger. I alerted the police and tried to keep an eye on you. I hadn't banked on Smith whisking you off in a carriage. That scared the pants off me. I just prayed we weren't too late."

"You saved my life," I said.

"As you did mine," he said. "If you hadn't arrived at the truth, I should never have been safe again."

The cab came to a halt outside Houdini's house. The street appeared quiet and undisturbed. The constable outside saluted to us.

"Has Mr. Wilkie arrived here or left a message?" I asked.

"No, miss. Nobody's been here," he said. "It's been quiet as the grave."

I thought that was a poor turn of phrase, considering.

We knocked and were admitted by Houdini's mother. "Leopold!" she exclaimed. She went to hug him, then drew back as if burned. *"Du bist nicht Leopold."* She held him at arm's length, then she let out a stream of words out of which I could only make out, *"Mein Ehrich."* But the way she hugged him and cried made it clear that she'd worked out who he really was.

With that he stripped off the beard. "Bess!" he yelled. "Bess, come down here. Your husband has returned from the grave."

There was a scream from up above and Bess came flying down the stairs. We were in the midst of a touching reunion when there was a bang at the front door. We froze. Houdini's mother went to answer it and I heard Mr. Wilkie's calm, deep voice. In he came, and in his wake was Daniel.

Daniel pushed past him and swept me into his arms. "Thank God," he whispered.

"Thank God." He held me close, his heart thumping against mine. Then he released me, holding me at arm's length and frowning at me. "I've only heard the sketchiest account of what you might have been doing, but it's never going to happen again, do you hear that? I utterly forbid it."

"Don't worry," I said. "I have no aspirations to become a spy."

"I can't believe that you kept it from me," he said, his eyes flashing angrily now. "You deliberately lied to me."

"I was sworn to secrecy," I said. "I had no choice. I'm sorry."

"Miss Murphy has just endured a most harrowing experience," Houdini said, and he recounted it.

Wilkie sighed. "I am sorry to have put you in such danger," he said. "We have long suspected that one of my own men was a double agent, but I had no way to make him show his hand."

"So you used me as bait," I said angrily.

"I rather fear the answer to that is yes," he said. "But it never occurred to me that he'd reach New York before me. Or that he'd realize you had discovered his true identity."

"I did more than that," I said. "I found out why the German agents were so eager to keep Houdini from meeting you." I looked across at him.

"I was taken around a factory," Houdini explained. "They were proud to show off their engineering superiority. I glimpsed a design for an underwater craft that could transport many men undetected. And then, on another occasion, when I overheard a plan to launch a surprise attack on the East Coast of the United States, I realized how dangerous this craft could be."

Wilkie nodded. "We were half expecting something like this."

"Why would the Germans want to attack the United States?" Daniel asked. "Do they want to wage war against us? Do they have the might to do so?"

"Not yet," Wilkie said. "They merely mean to alarm us. They wish to expand their presence in the Americas — to establish colonies in Central and South America — and they think such surprise attacks would make a good bargaining tool with the country that dominates the Americas."

"How foolhardy of them," I said. "Smaller incidents have led to out-and-out wars, haven't they?"

He nodded.

"So what will happen now?"

"We will let them know that we know. They will mumble apologies, claim that they meant no harm, that they were merely formulating possible strategies, that their agents overreacted, and the cat-and-mouse game will begin all over again."

My head suddenly started throbbing again and weariness and pain swept over me. I clutched at Daniel. "I'm not feeling very well," I said. "Would you please take me home?"

Soon we were sitting side by side in a hansom as it clip-clopped southward through the park. It was a glorious evening. Children played and couples strolled in the balmy air. The trees glowed in late sunlight. It felt as if the whole world had suddenly been put right.

Daniel slipped his arm around my shoulder. "Molly —" he began.

"I know. It can never happen again. Don't worry. I agree with you. I have no wish to go through that again ever. Let's pick a date and get married soon."

"September?" he suggested. "It's a lovely month, isn't it? Cooler, fall colors beginning. A perfect time in Westchester."

As he spoke I pictured it: tables on the lawn, an open carriage from the church with my veil blowing in the breeze. It did seem rather inviting. "All right," I said. "We'll get married from your mother's house if it means a lot to you, only I'm inviting all my friends and I don't want to hear any complaints from you."

He looked at me and laughed. "I wouldn't dream of crossing someone who has just taken on the cream of German espionage and won," he said. "I want you to know that I'm very impressed. Mr. Wilkie said it was too bad you were a woman."

"And what did you say?"

"I said it was absolutely perfect that you were a woman because I was madly in love with you."

I laughed and turned my face toward him to be kissed. A long time of silence then ensued.

"So you will agree to give up this detective business, as promised?" he asked.

"I suppose I'll have to if I'm to be a married lady," I said, "but I'm willing to offer my superior detecting skills to my husband, should he need them."

"I'll remember that," he said.

"By the way, did you analyze that bloody rag I gave you?"

"We did," he said. "It was pig's blood. Your instincts were quite right."

I allowed myself a little smirk, which then broadened as I remembered something else.

"Tell me," I began, "have any forged banknotes turned up in Boston yet?"

He looked astonished. "How the deuce did you —"

I grinned. "You can tell Mr. Wilkie that you have solved the problem of the fake money," I said. "Or at least part of it. I suspect they are being printed in New York, below a theatrical boardinghouse, and are being distributed by the vanishing Signor Scarpelli, alias Alfred Rosen. Maybe other entertainers are in on it, and I suspect that we'll discover that German agents are behind this as well."

"Why didn't you tell this to Mr. Wilkie when we were with him just now?"

I hesitated. In truth I was still too much in shock to be able to think straight about anything and in the heat of the moment I had forgotten the banknotes. So I permitted myself one small last lie. "I thought it might look good for my future husband's career if he solved the case," I said at last.

"Well I'm —" Daniel started. I put my finger on his lips.

"No bad language from now on. It won't be good for the children."

He laughed and swept me into his arms, hugging me fiercely.

"I love you, Molly Murphy," he said.

"And so you should," I replied.

Suddenly a strange expression came over his face. He sat up and reached into his pocket.

"It wasn't the right time to give you this before," he said. "But I can't carry it around forever." He drew out a small embossed leather box and opened it. In the shadows of the cab I saw the sparkle of diamonds.

HISTORICAL NOTE

Do not read until you have finished the
book! This is an order.

This is, of course, a work of fiction but not
such an outlandish story as you might
imagine. It is an established fact that John
Wilkie, head of the Secret Service at the
time, used entertainers to spy for him in
Europe. A good case has been put forward
that Houdini was indeed one of those spies
and he corresponded with Wilkie through
articles he wrote for magicians' magazines.
He really had worked on things like vanishing ink and shoes with hollow heels, which
might have been useful for more than stage
tricks.

Many countries were working to perfect
the submarine at that time. Germany was
gaining superiority in the building of machines of many kinds, and also eager to
expand its colonies to include footholds in

South and Central America. It has been suggested that they were planning surprise raids on cities on America's East Coast. Whether one of these would have led to a war, who can surmise?

And as for Houdini and Bess, I have tried to make them as true to life as possible, as described by their biographers and in their letters. And their illusions are portrayed exactly as they have been described in newspapers of the time.

We hope you have enjoyed this Large Print book. Other Thorndike, Wheeler, Kennebec, and Chivers Press Large Print books are available at your library or directly from the publishers.

For information about current and upcoming titles, please call or write, without obligation, to:

Publisher
Thorndike Press
295 Kennedy Memorial Drive
Waterville, ME 04901
Tel. (800) 223-1244

or visit our Web site at:

http://gale.cengage.com/thorndike

OR

Chivers Large Print
published by AudioGO Ltd
St James House, The Square
Lower Bristol Road
Bath BA2 3BH
England
Tel. +44(0) 800 136919
email: info@audiogo.co.uk
www.audiogo.co.uk

All our Large Print titles are designed for easy reading, and all our books are made to last.